A MID-LIFE CRISIS THRILLER

TIES THAT KILL

DEVEN GREENE

CASTLE BRIDGE MEDIA

CASTLE BRIDGE MEDIA
Denver, Colorado

Cover photo by Double Brain/Shutterstock.
This image has been modified.

ISBN: 979-8-9872083-9-7

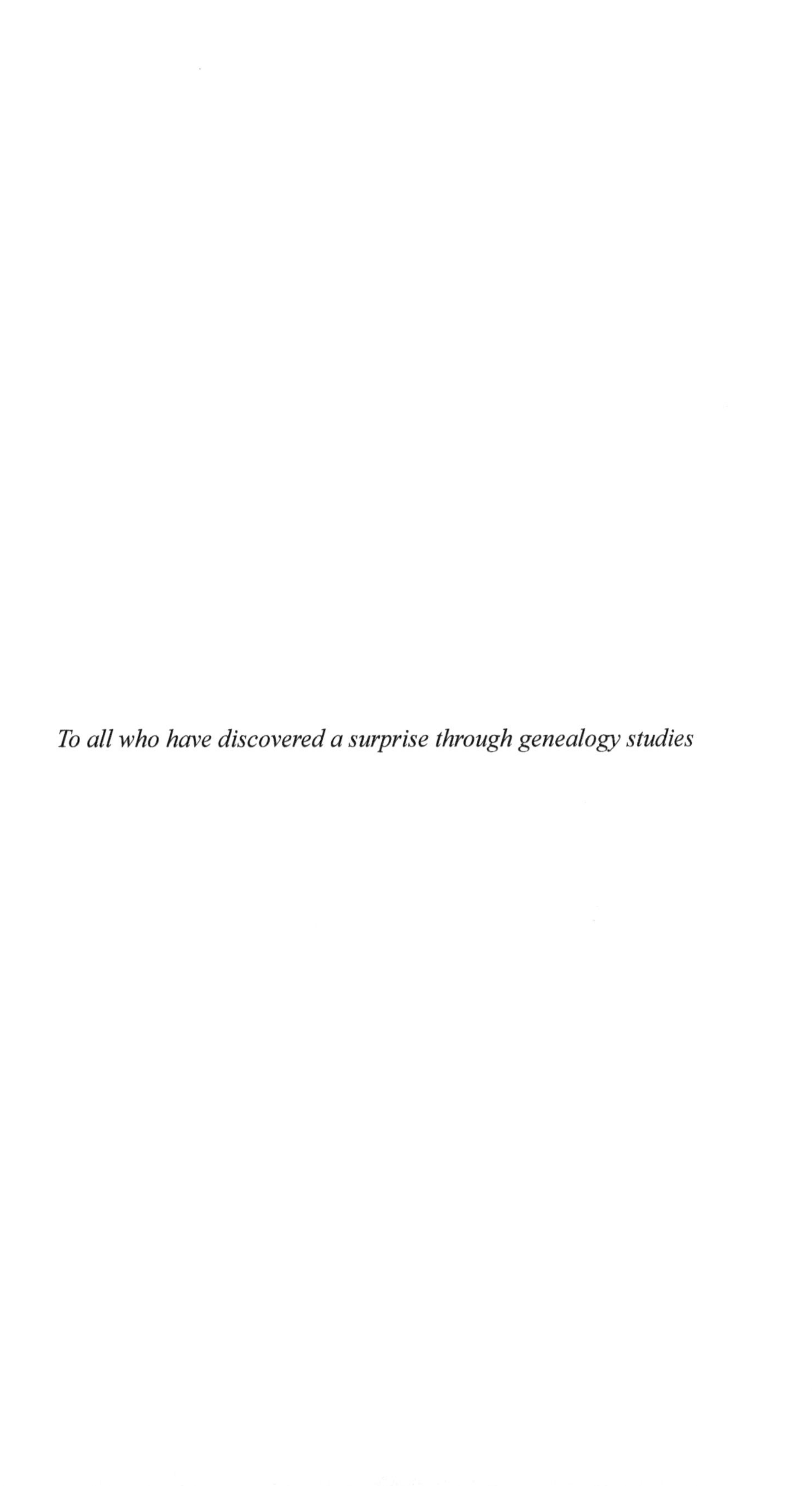

To all who have discovered a surprise through genealogy studies

Chapter 1

ABOUT HALF THE TWO-HUNDRED and fifty seats in the lecture hall were occupied. Even on this first day of class, many students slept in, planning to watch a video of the presentation later. As a few frenzied-looking stragglers slipped into seats in the rear, a hush swept through the audience.

Professor Martin Starling, a pleasant-looking man forty-four years of age, was dressed in his usual khakis and a short-sleeved button-down shirt as he walked behind the counter at the front of the auditorium. "Welcome to Chem 307. For most of you, this will be your first organic chemistry course. Some of you may be worried. Organic Chemistry is difficult. Everyone who studies it has alkynes of trouble. If you didn't understand that brilliant pun, you will soon. We'll be starting with the nomenclature and structure of organic molecules, so you'll soon know what an alkyne is. Don't worry—although I often make bad chemistry puns, I only do it periodically."

Martin paused for a moment, pleased with the groans from the audience, most members of which appreciated the reference to the periodic table of the elements. "After you have all mastered nomenclature and structure, we'll go . . . ." Dr. Starling stopped speaking as he looked momentarily confused and gazed at the students before him. After a few awkward seconds, he shook his head and continued. "We'll go into stereochemistry and . . . ." The professor again stopped speaking, but not before his last words were noticeably slurred. He appeared disoriented as he reached for the counter with his left hand, then collapsed to the floor, hitting his head on the edge of the counter on the way down.

A murmur arose from the students as a few started to walk towards the professor. It was clear that this group of mostly nineteen-year-olds was unsure what to do. The man who had been operating the audio-visual equipment sprinted past them to the front of the room and bent over the professor.

"Dr. Starling, are you okay?" he asked in a loud voice, gently shaking the professor's shoulders. As two students approached, the man turned his head towards them and shouted, "He's still breathing. Call 911."

#   #   #

Gradually becoming aware of rhythmic electronic beeps, the sounds of distant hurried footsteps, and unintelligible chatter, Martin wondered if he'd been dreaming. If so, he had no recollection of what his dream was about. Was he dreaming now? He slowly opened his eyes, squinting against the bright light. He scanned the small room. *Where am I?*

A woman screamed, "You're awake! Thank god you're awake."

Startled at first, Martin recognized the voice of his wife, Georgia. He was immediately comforted when he turned his head and saw her. Holding onto his arm, she was smiling as a lone tear trickled down her face.

"What's going on?" Martin asked, his speech slurred. Noting the wires affixed to his chest, the device attached to his right index finger, the beeping monitor by his bed, and the IV tube inserted into his left arm, he tried to make sense of the situation. Futilely searching for the words he needed to ask the next question, he settled on simply "Hospital?"

"Yes, this is the ICU in Saint Joseph's. You've been unconscious for over twenty-four hours."

"Accident?"

"I'm afraid you had a stroke. I've been so worried. Of course you don't remember what happened. You were starting your first organic chemistry lecture of the semester when you collapsed. Paramedics brought you here after someone called 911."

Martin's head was spinning. He was confused and had so many questions. He was alive, but what had he lost? Could he walk? Think? He was thinking now, wasn't he, but could he figure out something complicated? He was having difficulty finding words.

As he tried to formulate his next question despite the fog in his brain, Georgia kissed him on the cheek. "Don't wear yourself out trying to speak. The doctor will explain everything to you. Don't worry, you're getting the best care. Now let me tell your nurse you're awake. She'll be so excited, she'll notify your team right away."

Martin watched as Georgia left and headed to the nurse's station, visible through the glass windows of his ICU room. Moments later, a team of doctors and medical students, all wearing white coats over their street clothes, entered. The senior-most doctor, a trim, balding man of approximately sixty years, introduced himself and added that he was the chief of neurology. He conferred with the others as they began a thorough neurological assessment.

Finally, at the end of all the poking, prodding, and questioning, the group huddled briefly, and all but the neurology chief gathered near the door. The chief took a seat next to Martin as Georgia made her way to stand on the other side of the bed.

"The good news, Dr. Starling, is that you're doing much better than expected," the chief began. "I don't know how much of what I'm going to say you'll understand, but I'll go ahead and explain a few things anyway. You had a stroke in your left cerebral hemisphere. We don't know why you had a stroke. It appears that a blood clot formed in one of your arteries and traveled to your brain. We found no evidence of significant atherosclerotic disease or atrial fibrillation, conditions that can lead to strokes. We tested you for abnormalities in your blood clotting system that can lead to what we call thrombophilia, which is a fancy word for a tendency to form blood clots too easily. None of your tests for thrombophilia were positive. We often never find out the reason someone has an abnormal clot, so your case isn't unusual. Because there was no clear precipitating event, you will need to be on a blood thinner for the rest of your life. This shouldn't affect your day-to-day living, although you'll bleed a little more than usual. For instance, if you cut yourself shaving, it will take a bit longer for the bleeding to stop. Without the treatment, you are at risk of developing more abnormal clots. Another clot in your brain would cause another stroke. A clot in your lung, called a pulmonary embolism, could be deadly. A clot in the artery of an arm or leg might result in an amputation.

"Unfortunately, the stroke has made your right leg quite weak, so it's important that you don't attempt to stand on your own for a while. You also have speech deficits, which you are probably noticing right now. You may be trying to say things but can't find the words. I know it can be quite frustrating, but I expect your speech and strength will improve with intensive therapy. I can't predict how much function you'll recover, but you'll have to work hard to get the most benefit from your rehabilitation exercises. I expect a man as accomplished as you is not afraid of a little hard work. Are you understanding me?"

"Serious."

"Yes, this is a serious situation, but as long as you're willing to put in the work with your therapists, you'll improve."

"Did you hear that, Martin?" Georgia said, grabbing Martin's hand. "You'll have to work with therapists, but I'll be at your side the whole time. We're going to get over this. Together."

Martin's face looked blank as the doctor rose and walked towards the door. He stopped to speak to Georgia in a hushed voice, then left with the rest of his entourage, leaving the nurse to check on Martin's IV, empty his urine bag, and adjust his pillows.

Returning to her husband's side, Georgia took his hand. "I don't want you to worry. You're going to get all the help you need. A speech pathologist will be here soon to do in-depth testing, and you'll start physical therapy following that. After they have a chance to observe you for a day, they'll move you out of the ICU to make room for someone who really needs it." Georgia smiled as she squeezed her husband's hand. "The doctor thinks you'll be ready to go to a rehab hospital soon."

Martin struggled to think of a pun. While thoughts swirled in his brain, he couldn't come up with the words. Moments later, a woman with gray hair and a friendly smile came into the room and introduced herself as the speech pathologist. Time passed slowly for Martin as the kindly woman ran a series of tests, which included an assessment of his ability to swallow.

"Well done," she said. "Looks like you're able to swallow. We'll start you off with something easy to eat."

Feeling hungry for the first time since waking, Martin was happy when an aide brought in a serving of applesauce and peeled away the foil top of the plastic container. Finding his right extremity difficult to control, he was nonetheless able to consume the hospital staple unaided and without incident under the observing eye of the speech pathologist. He didn't remember ever enjoying applesauce so much.

In the late afternoon, a physical therapist came by for a short session, in which Martin was asked to use his various muscles to push against resistance.

A half hour after the therapist left, Martin was asleep.

Chapter 2

OPENING THE DOOR OF HER Tesla Model 3, Brooke was looking forward to the thirty-minute commute home to her white colonial-style house in Madison, Alabama. She'd have time to call her parents who still lived in a suburb of Boise, Idaho, then listen to her podcast of choice without interruption. Her job as a managing director in the Huntsville NASA Space Flight Center was demanding, but less so than if she'd worked in a place like Lockheed-Martin. The security checks going in and out were bothersome, but she'd gotten used to that. By now, it was just background noise.

A quick call to her childhood home reassured her that her dad was recovering well from his lithotripsy for kidney stones. She then began to stream a Fresh Air interview. As was often the case, her mind drifted from the podcast to the new project she was involved with. As usual, she wasn't permitted to discuss it with anyone on the outside, not even her husband, an electrical engineering professor at Alabama A&M University. He had served as a consultant on some of the space center's projects, but his clearance wasn't as high as hers.

The nature of the new undertaking brought with it increased security risks, and she worried about being kidnapped by agents from a government such as China, Russia, Iran, or North Korea. They would benefit greatly from the knowledge she held, and she'd recently made a practice of being more vigilant than usual.

It was dark when she reached her home, but the streetlights allowed her to look up and down the street. Several houses down from hers, she noticed a car she'd never seen before. Her heart rate increased as she turned into her driveway. The tension in her chest and shoulders intensified as she waited impatiently for the garage door to open. Looking in the rearview mirror, she noticed someone dressed in black emerge from the car. She planned to floor the accelerator once the door had risen enough. Hopefully, she would have enough time to close the garage door behind her before the person could reach her, if that was their intent. Focusing on the door before her as it neared the clearance she would need, she moved her foot to the accelerator. A moment later, Brooke slumped in her car, the result of a bullet that traveled through the car driver's window and ripped off the back of her skull.

Three more similarly-executed murders took place in the Atlanta area over the next four days. There were no suspects.

Chapter 3

"HOW ARE YOU THIS BEAUTIFUL morning?" Georgia asked Martin as she put the breakfast tray of coffee, toast, and scrambled egg whites on the bedspread covering her husband's legs, then flung open the curtains in the sage and dusty peach-colored bedroom. Despite the gloominess outside, a ray of sunlight broke through a gap in the grey clouds and shone a spotlight on Georgia.

"If I didn't know better, I'd say you have a halo around your head," came the reply. "And to answer your question, I'm feeling better every day. I think it's time I started eating breakfast at the kitchen table like a normal person. You don't need to keep bringing me breakfast while I'm still in bed."

"I don't want you pushing yourself too hard. If you must know the truth, I enjoy bringing you breakfast. I value the alone time we have. Not that I didn't appreciate our hectic mornings having breakfast with the boys before your stroke."

"I'm thankful for everything you do for me, but it's been five months already—six weeks since they let me out of rehab—and you're still treating me like an invalid."

"Are you forgetting that you still need to use a cane when you walk? And you need additional speech therapy and more testing before you can return to work?"

"I know all that, but I'm getting close to feeling like my old self."

"Granted, you've recovered better and faster than anyone expected, but

I still worry."

"You worry about everything."

"Goes along with being a mom. Speaking of being a mom, I have to get Greg out of bed. He gets mad when I wake him up on weekends, but he promised to give the Harrison boy a batting lesson this morning. He has to be at the batting cages in less than an hour."

"I wish he put half as much effort into his studies as he puts into baseball. I need to talk to him again about the importance of going to a good college."

"Okay, but remember, he's still dreaming of being a professional baseball player, and he's been guaranteed the shortstop position at the community college. He's young and has plenty of time to apply himself to his studies if he doesn't get picked up by a four-year college or the pros later."

"That's nothing more than a . . ." Martin stopped speaking mid-sentence, a look of desperation on his face.

"What are you trying to say?"

"It's nothing more than a . . . some kind of dream."

"I think you mean pipedream, dear," Georgia said.

"That's it. Pipedream. Damn, I still can't find my words. I guess I do still need you." Martin smiled at his wife of almost twenty-two years. He still had issues with his speech and motor abilities following his stroke, but his memory was fully intact.

He thought about the first time he saw Georgia when they were both undergraduates at the University of Idaho. He was a junior chemistry major and she a freshman, looking confused as she searched for the building where her English class would be starting soon. It was the beginning of the fall semester, and many of the new students were having difficulty finding their classes.

Not normally outgoing, Martin was instantly struck by his future wife. She wasn't the most beautiful woman he'd ever seen, nor was she the shapeliest. But she had a quality that immediately snagged him. Some combination of her long, wavy hair and large, dark eyes held an air of mystery. He impulsively asked her if she needed help before weighing the pros and cons in his mind. Had he done that, as was his usual practice, he would have ultimately talked himself out of it. Once he heard her voice and saw her smile, he was hooked.

"What's your name?" he asked.

"Georgia. And no, I'm not from Georgia, so don't even ask. My dad's a distant descendent of King George of England, and he wanted a son to name George. Instead, he was stuck with me, a girl, so he named me Georgia."

"I think you have more in common with a Georgia peach than King George." From that moment on, Martin called her Peaches.

Martin soon discovered that Georgia was kind and intelligent. She majored in political science and although she had hated her high school chemistry class and had no intention of taking any more classes in that subject, there was plenty of chemistry between them.

At first, Martin had a great deal of competition for her affection, Georgia being naturally outgoing and adventurous, but he ultimately won her over with his rendition of Careless Whisper on the saxophone, an instrument he'd played since grade school. The couple was married the summer after Martin received his undergraduate degree. Georgia followed him when he left Idaho to get his doctorate at an Ivy League college, transferring and getting her bachelor's degree two years later. Following graduation, she volunteered to work in local elections until they had their first child, Gregory, two years later.

After five years of marriage, Martin earned his Ph.D. in chemistry. Although he had many academic and industry offers of employment, Martin and Georgia decided to return to the Boise area where both were from, so they could be close to both of their families. He'd dreamed of teaching since he was a youngster, so Martin took a job in the chemistry department of the local university. Nicholas, their second son, was born a year later.

Martin enjoyed teaching undergraduates and was one of the students' favorite chemistry professors. He also succeeded academically, publishing numerous papers in his areas of interest, green energy, and carbon capture. Lately, the chair of the department had been pressuring him to work with a local oil company to increase yields from their fracking sites by developing more efficient procedures using chemical by-products generated during the synthesis of alternative energy sources Martin had developed. The department would share the resulting patents with the oil company, projected to bring in a great influx of funds. Martin didn't want to participate in the project, given the environmental damage caused by fracking, preferring to devote his time to earth-friendly projects. The not-so-subtle coercion of the chair was troubling, but the positives of his job still outweighed the negatives. When he was away from work, Martin enjoyed playing his saxophone, sometimes joining jam sessions with a local jazz group, The Potato Heads. Although occassionally frustrating, he found watching his sons develop as they approached manhood most rewarding. *Yes, it had been a good life.*

"One more thing," Georgia said, interrupting Martin's train of thought, "Dean keeps calling me—he wants to discuss the results of that genealogy test he did on you. He's very excited about his new company, so can I tell him to come by later today?"

"It's fine, as if it would matter if I objected."

"Wonderful. I told him to come around three p.m., after your speech pathology appointment. Please try to act interested."

Georgia kissed Martin on the forehead and exited the room, leaving Martin smiling as he sipped his coffee and challenged the speech center of his left brain with a crossword puzzle. He hadn't seen his old friend since being discharged from rehab. He and Dean, a biochemistry professor at the same university where Martin worked, had been friends for years, both joining the faculty the same year. Dean had been the only friend he'd allowed to visit during his stay at the rehab hospital, but he hadn't yet visited Martin since he'd been discharged.

Language was still a struggle for Martin, but he was able to finish the eighth-grade-level crossword puzzle in a half hour. After putting the breakfast tray aside, he grabbed his nearby sturdy metal cane. With four prongs at the base, it could stand without being propped up. Martin slowly brought himself to his feet and waddled his way to the dresser where Georgia had laid out his clothes for the day. He'd worked out a system with his occupational therapist for dressing himself using a nearby chair, his cane, and a grabber. Although Georgia could have dressed him in less than half the time, Martin had insisted on dressing himself for the past two weeks.

Leaning heavily on his cane, Martin went to his study. A room originally designed to be a den, this was the place Martin went for relaxation and contemplation. Before his stroke, he often took short breaks from his work to play his saxophone, but it now sat idle in its stand behind his desk.

In better times, Martin did his best work in that room, seated at the sizeable heavy oak desk facing the door, a large computer screen in front of him. With walls bedecked in manly dark wood wainscoting, and built-in shelving crammed with books, he felt surrounded by warmth and contentment. He swiveled around in his chair to look out the large picture window behind the desk and gazed at the clouds overhanging the green grass and trees in his backyard. He often achieved what could best be described as a meditative trance in that room.

He now planned to surprise Georgia by playing the saxophone for the first time since his stroke. He scooted over to the instrument and dragged it into his lap. That was as far as he got—not even his good hand could find the right keys, and blowing into the mouthpiece proved to be too much for him. Defeated, it took maximal effort on his part to return the saxophone to its stand. He refused to ask anyone for help, lest they know he had attempted to play it but failed.

Nick, the couple's younger son, age fifteen, was at the kitchen table eating a bowl of cereal when Martin tottered in.

"How're you doing, Dad?" Nick asked. "Can I get you anything?"

"No thanks, Son, I'm fine. I'd just like to sit here and talk to you for a few minutes until the occupational therapist shows up. Got anything special planned for today?"

"I'm going to Kenny's house. He's going to show me the new microscope his parents bought him for his birthday. It came with slides of different things like insects and plants and all sorts of cool stuff."

Martin smiled. *At least this one is curious about the world. Definitely more academically oriented than his brother.* "Don't you have homework?"

"Not much. I can do it all tomorrow. Don't worry. I'm doing well in all my classes."

"I know, I know. I like to remind you of things because I can't do much else until I'm better."

"Don't worry. Mom can take care of everything."

Those words cut deeply, but Martin did his best to hide his shame and frustration at being unable to do more for his family while depending so much on Georgia. Still unable to analyze the articles in chemistry journals the way he used to, he wondered if he'd ever be able to function as a chemistry professor again. "Be patient. These things take time," his speech pathologist kept telling him.

His thoughts were interrupted by the chime of the doorbell. The sound of Georgia's footsteps approaching the front door was followed by the squeak made when the door opened. Martin recognized the voice of his occupational therapist and headed to the living room for his session.

The day proceeded like many others, with occupational therapy, physical therapy, and speech pathology sessions. Between appointments, Martin practiced exercises given to him previously.

He looked forward to Dean's visit after his last session was over. The fact that Georgia knew his friend wanted to talk about his new company, something that would require Martin to understand some technical details, indicated she thought her husband was ready to start slipping back into his old life. With some trepidation, Martin prepared to test the waters.

Chapter 4

DORIAN REMOVED HIS GOGGLES AND shook his head vigorously, sending a spray of water into the warm air. He never tired of snorkeling in the waters of Tunnels Beach on the north shore of Kauai, the Hawaiian island known as the Garden Island. Later that day, after reading through two movie scripts his assistant thought worthy of his attention, he planned to go scuba diving, expecting to see larger sea creatures. The last time Dorian had done that, he'd seen a giant manta ray.

He picked up his towel and dabbed water from his hair. He looked up at the cliff above the beach, where the roof of his home peaked out behind a group of coconut palms. He smiled, thinking of his wife and sixteen-year-old daughter still asleep, having stayed up late the previous night entertaining company.

He barely made out the top half of a figure dressed in black near the edge of the cliff. Strange, he thought. He started walking towards the path leading up to his home when he was felled by a bullet striking him on the crown of his head.

The following evening, another man was cut down by a bullet while walking on his estate in a remote area near Lahaina on the island of Maui.

The local police had no leads.

Chapter 5

MARTIN WAS SITTING AT THE kitchen table reading a freshman college chemistry textbook. It all made sense to him. He felt buoyed, knowing he was on his way to becoming his former self. Maybe he'd never be able to walk unaided or play the saxophone again, but he could live with that. Throughout his path to recovery, Martin had been more concerned about his brain. He didn't think he could adjust to a life in which his intelligence was permanently compromised. His thoughts were interrupted by the familiar chime of the doorbell.

"You can get that, Martin," Georgia yelled from the bedroom. "I'm sure it's Dean."

Martin hadn't greeted anyone at the front door since his stroke, other than opening the door for Georgia during staged occupational therapy exercises. This would be the perfect time to answer the doorbell for real.

Martin grabbed his cane which was standing near the edge of the table. He scooted his chair out and grabbed the metal shaft, inadvertently sweeping the chemistry textbook onto the floor.

"Shit," Martin yelled. As he reached for the book, he toppled over, making a racket. Georgia ran into the room and crouched beside him.

Her husband didn't need words to express his exasperation. It was written on his face.

"It's okay, honey," Georgia said. "I'm sure you were excited at the prospect of seeing Dean, but you have to remember to take things slowly.

Here, let me help you. You remember the drill—push up with your left leg."

"I know, I know."

Georgia pulled on both of Martin's arms, and he pushed hard with his strong leg until he was standing and supporting himself on one limb. Georgia grabbed his cane and handed it to him.

"You're still adjusting," she said. "In time, you won't have these accidents. Now go greet Dean."

Paralyzed by thought, Martin stood, immobile.

"I mean it," Georgia said. "Get going and have a good visit."

The professor sprung to life. "Thanks, Peaches. I needed that."

Martin ambled to the door and let his friend in. Dean, a tall man with thinning brown hair and a nose too big for his face, was holding an olive-green backpack. The two friends sat in the living room, a modern yet welcoming space decorated in shades of brown, black, and white. Martin sat in one of the brown armchairs, his cane standing nearby, while Dean slumped on the matching couch, his backpack at his feet.

The men shared pleasantries, in which Dean marveled at how well Martin seemed to be doing. Neither being big fans of chit-chat, Martin's guest wasted little time before reaching into his backpack and pulling out papers which he spread out on the glass coffee table.

"I'll hand these over to you so you can have a closer look," Dean said. "Before your stroke, I told you about DNA Discoveries, the small company I started to develop algorithms for analyzing people's DNA so we can determine their ancestry, that is, where their ancestors lived around five hundred years ago."

"I remember."

"Several large companies are doing that already. As you know, tracing ancestral genealogy has become a popular pastime for many people. I'm not sure if that's what's driving the success of these companies, or if these companies are driving people's interest in genealogy. Whatever the reason, my ultimate goal is to trace the migration patterns of the most ancient humans. For that, I need to compare the DNA from people who lived in certain places hundreds of years ago to DNA from around the world preserved in ancient human bones, millions of years old. Only then will we know where these populations truly originated from.”

“I remember you telling me that. You intend to use the income you generate from providing ancestry information in your commercial company to fund your studies regarding theories of ancient migrations.”

“Correct. You seem to remember everything so well, I’m wondering if you really had a stroke,” Dean said, chuckling.

“What I had was a stroke of bad luck,” Martin responded, laughing at his own pun and feeling satisfied that he had just put into words the pun he had wanted to come up with while he was in the hospital.

Dean smiled and looked at his friend. “I’m no doctor, but I think that if you can still make those stupid puns of yours, that brain inside your head must be pretty indestructible. It probably won’t take much time for us to start complaining about those remarks of yours again, serial punster that you are.”

“I was going to stop making puns, but I remembered that no one likes a quitter.”

“Before you get a chance to attack me with another pun, let me continue.”

“Of course. I’d say, ‘be my guest,’ but that could be considered to be another pun.”

“The first step towards my goal,” Dean said, shaking his head, “is to compare my company’s genealogy results with those of commercial companies, so we can be sure we’re doing that part accurately. I’m happy to say we’ve completed several hundred studies successfully. We had some glitches at first, but we corrected them, and it’s been smooth sailing ever since. Right now, we’re working on increasing the speed of our analyses. The commercial labs have throughput magnitudes greater than ours. When we have a large enough database, we plan to match people with potential relatives, but it will take some time to collect enough samples. I estimate it will be over a year before we can do that, although our data can be uploaded to the established companies that can do the matching now.”

Dean picked up two papers from the coffee table and handed them to Martin. “Here’s a table showing our results on two hundred of our specimens, compared to those of the three largest commercial companies.”

“Pretty impressive,” Martin said after paging through the data for a few minutes. “Your results fall in line with these others quite well.”

Dean smiled. "Now, would you like to see your results?"

"I almost forgot. As you know, I've never been interested in where I came from. I care more about where I am now."

"I hear you. But since I have the data, I thought I'd share it with you." Dean picked up another sheet of paper from the coffee table, glanced at it, and handed it to his friend.

Martin looked at the results, at first appearing mildly interested. Then he held the paper closer to his face and stared intently. "I was expecting the British and German. But Scandinavian? Are you sure?"

"As sure as I can be. The three companies I sent your sample to are sure too."

"I wonder if my mom has any Scandinavian blood."

"She doesn't."

Martin looked up. "How do you know?"

"I tested her as well. Georgia asked me to. Since you don't know anything about your biological father, she wanted me to test your mom so I could figure out what came from your mom and what came from the anonymous sperm donor who is your biological dad. Turns out your mom is British and German. The sperm donor is British and Scandinavian."

"So I have a bit of Norse code in me."

Dean groaned before continuing. "I know you were close with your dad and never expressed any desire to learn about your biological dad, but you might want to think about looking for half-siblings. It's quite possible the donor's sperm was used in a few other pregnancies, and he might even have a family of his own. You've never had siblings, but using the genealogy sites, you could perhaps find some matches. Even though sperm banks keep the identity of sperm donors a secret, lots of people have located relatives this way."

"I've never thought about that before."

"You should consider it. You might not have any matches, in which case nothing will change. On the other hand, you could discover a few half-siblings out there. Maybe they're wonderful people, and if they live around here, they might be a positive addition to your life. I'd caution you, though. They could be people you don't want to associate with. You wouldn't want to divulge too much about yourself until you got to know them."

"Let me mull that over."

"If you decide to do it, I'll send you your DNA data in a form you can upload to genealogy companies, and I'll give you a list of the biggest ones. Some people have their data with only one company, while others send theirs around to many. Each company searches their databases only, so you have a better chance of finding a match if you submit your DNA information to multiple companies."

"I'll see what Georgia thinks. After all, if I do identify some half-siblings out there, it could affect her too."

"True. There's one other thing I wanted to talk to you about. Remember Arthur, that old college roommate of mine I've mentioned before?"

"Yes. He's doing some sort of medical research in San Francisco."

"Correct. I recently spoke to him about your stroke, and how there was no obvious reason for you to have had a blood clot. Turns out he's working on mechanisms of thrombophilia and is very interested in your case. He wanted me to ask if you'd be willing to talk to him about the specialized testing he does in his lab. He might be able to figure out why you had that blood clot."

"From everything you've told me in the past, he's a very smart guy. Sure, I'd be happy to talk to him. It would be nice to know why I had this damn stroke."

"Also, as he explained to me, if there is a genetic component, it could be helpful to your boys."

"Damn. I hadn't thought about that. Have him call me."

"Call you what?" Dean asked, laughing. "See? You bring out the worst in me."

"Orange you glad we're friends?"

Chapter 6

AS USUAL, HILLARY WAS THE last to leave the office that night. She followed her normal routine, making sure her notes were complete, and she had answered all phone calls. Lastly, she checked her patient schedule for the next day. Her Oak Park pediatric practice near Chicago was busy, downright hectic at times, but she enjoyed it. Except for the overly demanding parents wanting medical excuses so their children could miss school for a vacation, get extra time on tests for an invented medical condition, or be approved to return to sports practice with an injury that hadn't healed yet.

She turned off the light, ensured the door was locked, and headed to her car, bracing herself against the cold wind. Thankfully, it wasn't snowing at the moment, and Hillary looked forward to dinner with her sister, Hazel. She had already prepared the lasagna, which was waiting in her refrigerator to be heated up. Now that her husband had left the house after their recent divorce, Hillary sometimes felt lonely and lately had found she enjoyed visits with her sister even more than she had in the past.

Checking her watch, she realized she was late and hoped her sister remembered to look for the key under the flowerpot by the front door. Not a good hiding place, she knew—an amateur burglar would probably look there first after trying the doorknob—but break-ins in her upscale neighborhood were rare. To be sure her sister could access the house, she dialed Hazel's cell, but it went to voicemail. She left a message before getting in her car for the drive home.

By the time she arrived, twilight had turned to darkness. As Hillary drove up her long driveway towards the garage, she noticed Hazel's car parked to the side, but no lights were on in the house. She slammed on the brakes as she almost ran over something next to the driver's door of her sister's vehicle, visible only when her headlights shone on it. Was that a pile of clothes? A body? She swung her car door open and stepped out to investigate. Before taking her first step, she was cut down by a bullet to the back of her skull.

Two additional murders resulting from gunshots to the head took place in the Chicago area over the next two days. The killer remained at large.

Chapter 7

THE CALL FROM ARTHUR CAME two days later. He explained to Martin his interest in blood clotting, especially his research into what can go wrong. "Most people take normal blood clotting for granted, although they're familiar with hemophilia, the decreased ability to form blood clots which can be life-threatening. From what Dean told me, your problem is thrombophilia, which is at the other end of the spectrum."

"Precisely. I have to confess," Martin said, "I never gave clotting much thought before I had my stroke. As I understand it, the normal mechanism of clot formation is quite complicated, and probably not completely understood."

"That's right. A lot of people think clotting starts when a cut or abrasion exposes blood to the oxygen present in the air, but that's completely false. When the body is wounded, the tissue around the injury site releases chemicals that start the clotting process. That's what normally happens. In your case, for some reason, a clot formed without an inciting incident. Only about half the people with thrombophilia have a positive test with the panels routinely run in medical labs. We do a more in-depth search in my lab."

"Interesting. It sounds like you are more on the cutting edge." After he said it, Martin realized he had inadvertently made a pun.

"I like to think so," Arthur said, chuckling slightly. "Let me tell you about my research. In my lab, we look for new, currently unknown genetic changes leading to thrombophilia. The clotting system encompasses many factors, mainly proteins, which interact in a series of reactions that end with formation of a stable blood clot. These factors themselves must be tightly regulated to ensure just the right amount of clotting takes place—not too much, and not too little. The Goldilocks zone."

"In my case, something was off."

"Exactly. There are a few known genetic disorders linked to thrombophilia. In those disorders, specific proteins involved in the clotting system are mutated and either don't work properly or aren't made in sufficient quantity to be effective. Obviously, since many people with unexplained thrombophilia do not have mutations in any of these well-characterized proteins, other mutations or acquired disorders play a role. Sometimes many members of a family are recognized to have thrombophilia, but when they are checked, none of the known abnormalities test positive, despite the clear indications they have an inherited disorder."

"I suppose that's where your research comes in."

"Exactly. We're looking for patients who have experienced a significant blood clot where no explanation has been found. Sometimes people acquire clotting disorders from cancer, autoimmune diseases, or malformations, but you have none of those."

"Precisely."

"From what Dean told me, I think you would be a perfect candidate to study. Would you agree to participate?"

"Absolutely. I'd like to find out if I have an identifiable mutation and, if you find one, screen my kids for it."

"I'd like to test your mother too."

"She's never had a clotting issue."

"As I understand it, you don't know who your biological father is. It would be nice to study both of your parents, but just having only your mom participate will be helpful. I'll send a questionnaire to you and another to your mom. Once I have those back, I'll confirm that you meet all the parameters for our studies. The next step will be to get your medical record and your mom's if possible. All the information will, of course, be held in the strictest confidence. That will require permission from you and your mom. Are you okay with that?"

"Sure."

"Once all the paperwork is done, we'll arrange for some of your blood, and some of your mother's blood, to be sent to the lab. Assuming all goes smoothly, we should be good to go in less than two weeks."

After they concluded their conversation, Martin phoned his mother, who was happy to cooperate with the study. She lived in a nearby town and had been closely involved in Martin's rehabilitation program, often volunteering to help Georgia as needed.

Within days, Martin and his mother had filled out the questionnaire and requested their medical information be sent to Arthur. A week later, a woman from the lab visited Martin, then his mother. At each stop, she collected several tubes of blood with different colored stoppers.

The following day, Arthur called Martin to inform him his lab was ready to begin testing the blood. If they found an abnormality, he would call Martin immediately. It would take approximately four months to complete all their tests.

At first eagerly awaiting notification, Martin checked his phone frequently for messages from Arthur. With time, his expectation of finding out the cause of his stroke faded. One month after his blood was sent to Arthur's lab, the professor was deemed physically and mentally ready to return to his job. To celebrate the milestone, he picked up his saxophone which had rested in its stand untouched since he'd attempted to play it shortly after returning from the hospital. This time, he had enough strength to play with both hands. Not able to move his fingers as deftly as before, he was pleased with his recognizable rendition of "Summertime," one of the first tunes he'd learned to play. When Georgia rushed in to congratulate him, she was greeted by Martin wearing the biggest grin possible to make while playing a wind instrument.

On his first day back, walking slowly with the help of his cane, Martin was met with smiling faces, well wishes, and cake in the department lunchroom. Ruth, the secretary he shared with several other members of the department, was especially happy to see him return. A woman nearly twenty years Martin's senior, she was particularly fond of Martin as he always remembered her birthday and never lost his temper, something that couldn't be said of many of his colleagues.

Martin didn't have any teaching responsibilities until the following semester and was happy he'd be able to spend most of his time directing the research in his lab. He appreciated finally getting his life in order again.

A week after his return to work, Martin got a call.

"I have the answer. "

Chapter 8

LIFE IN GREENWOOD VILLAGE, COLORADO, agreed with Kurt, where he had a dream house, a beautiful wife, and two wonderful kids. He hadn't regretted moving there after transferring to his job at Newmont Mining, where he was a liaison with the company's South American gold mining operations. The job called for him to travel to mining sites in Latin America every year, something he enjoyed. He often brought his family along with him for an extended vacation during which they explored exotic places.

Leaving the Newmont Mining building, he shivered in the cold night air. Heading for his car, Kurt thought he might tire of all the travel his job required in a few years, but for the time being, all was good. During the drive home, his attention turned to the present he needed to buy for his wife's birthday the following week. Jewelry was always a good bet—he could pick something out quickly, and Esther would appreciate it. Her birthstone was aquamarine, but she seemed to prefer diamonds. He arrived at his house and pulled into the driveway. As the garage door opened, his inner debate of necklace vs. bracelet vs. earrings was interrupted by the bullet through the windshield that pierced his head, ending his life.

Two murders, similarly carried out, took place over the next three days near Topeka, Kansas, leaving the police stymied.

Chapter 9

MARTIN WAS IN THE HALLWAY walking from a small conference room back to his office. The ambient noise made it difficult to hear, or even recognize the voice on the other end of the call.

"You said you have the answer?"

"I went over the data this morning to make sure the evidence was tight."

As he listened, Martin recognized the voice of Arthur. He was surprised, yet delighted, to hear from him, having resigned himself to never finding the explanation as to why he had a stroke.

"You have a mutation in your fibrinogen gene. Fibrinogen is a protein that is cleaved to make fibrin, a smaller protein that forms blood clots. Some fibrinogen mutations result in bleeding disorders, while others result in thrombophilia. Your particular mutation has never been described before, so it appears to be unique to your family line."

"No wonder it wasn't found with the routine testing they did in the hospital."

"Exactly. As you probably know, you have two copies of every gene. We found that you have one copy of the abnormal fibrinogen gene, and one normal fibrinogen gene, so your mutation is what is known as dominant, meaning if you inherit just one copy of it, you will have the disorder. That usually means the defective molecule produced by the abnormal gene interferes with the function of the normal molecule. We tested your mother, and she doesn't have it, so you must have inherited it from your biological father. Unless, of course, it was a spontaneous mutation that developed when you were being formed. "

"What now? What's the next step?"

"This doesn't change your need to remain on an anticoagulant, or blood thinner, for the rest of your life. Each of your sons has a fifty percent chance of inheriting your abnormal gene, so I would suggest you let us get some of their blood to test."

"Damn! I could have given this to my boys."

"Don't blame yourself. We all have some genetic imperfections that we pass on, we just usually don't know what they are. Your kids are lucky you were tested, so they can be started on medication at a young age if they are positive for the mutation. Meanwhile, my lab will be working on a way to suppress the mutated gene, so the abnormal fibrinogen won't be made. Success with that will likely take years, though. I'll have someone out to your house next week to draw your sons' blood."

"Thanks."

"One more thing I'd like to suggest. You can appreciate how important it is for someone to know they carry this gene. If the sperm donor had kids of his own, or donated additional specimens to a sperm bank, those offspring could have inherited this gene. It is unlikely they would know about it as the testing we do in our lab isn't offered anyplace else. Your biological father and some of his other children, if they exist, may already have had abnormal clots, and are hopefully being treated. But some may be completely unaware they are in danger. It would be very helpful to them if they were informed. It could save their lives."

"I understand, but I have no way of knowing who they are." Martin paused a few moments. "Are you suggesting I upload the data Dean generated from my DNA to commercial genealogy sites?"

"Exactly. You might find some half-siblings, people with the same biological father as you. Maybe even your biological father. You'd be surprised how many people find relatives this way."

"Interesting idea. If I do that, though, I might get matches who are distant relatives, or related on my mom's side."

"You can have your mother's DNA tested, too, and eliminate all those who match with her. The closeness of the relationship is always reported with the match information. Half-siblings share about twenty-five percent of your DNA. Same with grandparents, aunts, uncles, nieces, and nephews. I would expect half-sibs to be within twenty years of your age, but we might as well test all the twenty-five percent paternal-side matches that show up."

"That could wind up being quite a few people."

"Probably not more than ten, unless there are some big families on that side. Our budget will allow us to test up to fifteen."

"I'll ask Georgia about it. She'll probably go along with it, but I want her okay before I start looking for long-lost relatives. They could be trouble."

"I suggest you talk to Dean about where to send your data. He knows a lot more about it than I do."

"Okay, I'll contact Dean. But first, I want to try something else."

Martin had heard of the Donor Sibling Registry, an organization that helps find half-siblings of people conceived through artificial insemination. All they need is the name of the agency that supplied the sperm and the donor number.

Martin called his mother who gave him permission to share her DNA data with genealogy companies. Then he asked her if she had the name of the sperm bank and the number of the sperm donor she used.

"My doctor never told me any of that information," she said. "I wonder if he was supposed to. I never thought about it before."

"From what I know, he was required to give it to you. Maybe you could get it now," Martin said. "You remember the doctor's name? He must have records."

"That would be Dr. Kirby Sanborn, but he's been dead over twenty years."

Martin spent an hour searching for someone who might have the doctor's old files but learned that the physician who took over Dr. Sanborn's practice destroyed all his old records years ago when they went digital.

\#   \#   \#

Dean sat in Martin's living room, across from Martin. Martin took notes as his friend explained the process of DNA testing to find relatives. As Dean stopped to sip coffee from the mug Georgia had brought minutes earlier, Martin took the opportunity to ask a question. "23andMe, Ancestry DNA, Family Tree DNA, MyHeritage, and GEDMatch. These are the most popular sites to use for finding matches, and you say there are literally millions of people who have submitted their DNA to at least one of these?"

"Correct. So you have a pretty decent chance of coming up with at least one match. Start with one of those websites and see what turns up. These companies are pretty quick. If there's a match, you'll probably be notified within a day or so. More may come in later, as additional people send in their DNA or upload their information."

"Can these companies test any possible matches for the fibrinogen mutation I have?"

"From talking to Arthur, it appears that your fibrinogen mutation does not fall into one of the segments usually analyzed by commercial companies. At this time, they don't sequence most of the DNA from their customers, just certain selected spots, so any matches you come up with will have to be tested for the fibrinogen mutation elsewhere. It makes sense to do that in Arthur's lab, as he's all set up for it."

"Sounds simple."

"It is. Go to the website of the company you choose and fill out their form." Dean reached over and handed Martin a small object. "Here's the data for you and your mom. Upload it, sit back, and wait." As Martin turned the thumb drive over in his left hand, Dean leaned forward and said, "Good luck."

#   #   #

Late that night, Martin sat in front of the computer in his study, holding the USB drive. *Amazing. On this little device is an incredible amount of information about DNA from my mom and me.*

Still slow to type with his right hand due to the stroke, he did a Google search for a smaller genealogy company, read the instructions, filled out the form for himself, uploaded his data, and paid the fee with his credit card. Then he did the same for his mom. He opted to keep his and his mother's information private, so others couldn't discover him, although he could discover matches of people who chose to make their information public. It was late, and Martin was tired, so he headed off to bed. As he lay next to Georgia, he wondered if anything would show up when he checked the website in the morning.

Chapter 10

"I'M GOING HOME NOW, DR. Angela."

Angela, a professor of economics, looked up from her desk and smiled. "Have a good weekend. I'll see you Monday."

"Going to Fairview?"

"It's Friday, isn't it?"

"I'll take that as a 'yes.' I sure do admire you for all you do. Have a safe trip."

Angela finished proofreading the first half of the article she was writing and locked her office door before leaving the building. The sun was still low in the sky, and she enjoyed walking past backpack-toting students engrossed in lively conversation on her way to the parking garage. Once on the road, she was en route to the modest house she'd bought in rural Utah, near the town of Fairview. There, she provided room and board for six lost boys—young men who had been expelled from their Mormon compound, a practice still followed by some Mormon communities to ensure there were plenty of women to marry so the relatively small number of remaining males could have multiple wives.

The lost boys had little education and few skills, often becoming impoverished, turning to alcohol, drugs, and petty crimes. Once a week, Angela checked on the boys and the elderly woman who ran the house. She'd found them work on nearby farms and small businesses and so far had been responsible for eight of them "graduating" so they could live productive lives on their own.

Angela turned on an audiobook and enjoyed the peaceful, uninterrupted, ninety-minute drive. Upon reaching her destination, she pulled to the curb and took a moment to regard the house. It was dark, with no moonlight, but Angela could see the young men watching a TV show and horsing around, things young men their age should be doing. As she prepared to exit the car, a bullet traveled through the driver's window and penetrated the professor's temple. She slumped against the door, her hand still on the car door handle.

Two people were similarly executed within a hundred miles of Salt Lake City over the next three days. No arrests were made.

Chapter 11

MARTIN WOKE AT SIX-FIFTY A.M., ten minutes before the alarm was set to go off. Georgia was still sleeping soundly when he went to the kitchen to brew coffee. A hot mug of French roast in his hand, he headed to his study and booted up the computer. Seconds later, he was on the website for the genealogy company he'd submitted the DNA information to from his mother and himself. His heart raced as he logged in. He surprised himself with the degree of tension he felt. This seemed like the beginning of a new, exhilarating adventure.

First, he checked his mother's matches, wanting to save the most exciting, his own, for last. He knew his name would not appear on her match list, as he had opted to keep his data confidential. Already his mom had six matches, listed in order of match percent, starting with the highest. Four matches were with relatives he knew. He hadn't been aware those people were interested in genealogy. Each was correctly identified as having a DNA match consistent with their known relationship—one cousin, two nieces, and three nephews. The remaining two names were unfamiliar to Martin, and were consistent with distant relatives of his mother, on the order of third cousins, according to the percent of shared DNA.

The professor steeled himself and clicked on the matches for himself. There were twenty-five names, including the six that matched with his mother. That left nineteen related on his biological father's side. Two of the matches shared a minuscule amount of DNA with Martin and may have been distant relatives or people completely unrelated. One shared eleven percent of her DNA. Just seventeen years of age, she could have been the child of a half-sibling. The remaining sixteen people shared approximately twenty-five percent of their DNA with Martin, consistent with a half-sibling, aunt, uncle, full niece, or full nephew. Since he knew he had no full siblings, it followed that he had no full nieces or nephews. That left the possibility these sixteen were half-siblings, aunts, or uncles. One was a year older than him, while the rest were younger, up to fifteen years his junior. The young ages made it unlikely any were his aunt or uncle. Martin stared at the names. He now had an entrée into the lives of sixteen half-siblings he didn't know existed a moment before. The large number of them was shocking.

Never interested in hunting down relatives on his father's side before, Martin was now excited at the prospect of having half-siblings. He shared his feelings with Georgia, who encouraged him to contact them soon. For the rest of the day, he went over in his mind who he would contact first, and what he would say.

After dinner, Martin went to his study as usual. Instead of preparing for a lecture, proofreading a paper for publication, or reading journals as was his custom, he stared at the names of his twenty-five percent matches. The was Brandon Bradberry, forty-one years of age, followed by Colleen Leopold, twenty-seven, Zoe Clyburn, thirty-six, Oliver Feinberg, forty-four, and Daryl Slocum, thirty-two.

He went from one name to the next. Did he want to start with a brother? A sister? When he was younger, he would have wanted a brother—someone to throw the ball in the backyard with, get advice about girls from. Now he saw the perks of a sister—more caring and nurturing. He emailed twenty-seven-year-old Colleen Leopold. It was after eleven p.m. by the time he pressed the send button.

Dear Ms. Leopold,

I recently submitted my DNA profile to GeneLife and found that you are probably a half-sister of mine (you are too young to be my grandmother). I am forty-three years old, live near Boise, Idaho, and teach chemistry at the university. I am an only child and was raised by wonderful parents, but my biological father was a sperm donor. I am now interested in connecting with my half-siblings, and believe you are one!

I am new to exploring genealogy and would love to chat with you. You are the first person I am contacting, although it looks like I have fifteen other half-sibling matches. Please email me back so we can set up a time to talk, if you're interested. I look forward to learning more about you.

Sincerely,

Martin Starling

Feeling tired, Martin stopped by the door to Greg's bedroom and noted his son's light was still on. He knocked lightly and spoke through the door. "Time to go to bed, Son."

Hearing "Sure, Dad. I'm just doing a few things. Be in bed soon," he started to walk towards the door of the master bedroom. For a moment, he thought he heard the giggle of a girl, but figured it was just Greg laughing at something on Twitter or whatever. Passing by Nick's room, he saw no band of light under his door. As usual, Nick had followed the lights off at eleven-o-clock rule. Martin chuckled to himself. *If I didn't know better, I'd swear there's no way those two boys could be related, even though they look alike.*

Georgia was getting ready for bed when Martin entered the room. "I wrote to one of my half-sisters," he told her.

"I was wondering how long it would take you."

"I'm a bit nervous. Hope I'm not opening up a whole can of worms."

"What's there to worry about?"

"I worry about all these relatives I don't know asking me for money."

"They're related to you—most of them are probably fine, upstanding citizens."

"What about those who aren't?"

"You'll just have to get better at saying 'no' when you don't want to do something."

"I hope I'm not making a big mistake."

"It's the right thing to do. Your siblings need to know about the mutation."

#   #   #

A response from Colleen Leopold was waiting for Martin the following morning. Looking at the time stamp, the message was sent at three a.m. *Curious. Colleen must be a night owl. Perhaps she works the night shift at a hotel.* He raced through the message.

Dear Mr. Starling,

I'm so happy you wrote to me. Although I have been on the GeneLife site for almost a year, you are the first person to actually contact me! Really! I am too shy to write to someone first, and maybe others are, too. When I was six years old, my dad died. My mom and I were very sad. That's when she told me he wasn't my real dad— my real dad was a sperm doner. I guess she thought it would make me less upset, but it didn't. I don't understand too much about DNA, but we probably have the same sperm donor dad! And you're my half big brother! That makes me very happy because I don't have any other brothers or sisters. I'm so proud that you teach chemistry at the university. You must be very smart. You can call me anytime, but I work from nine p.m. to two a.m. most nights except Wednesdays, and I usually sleep until close to noon. I live in Caldwell, which isn't too far from Boise. My number is 555 217-3945.

Sincerely,
Colleen Leopold (nickname Cat)

Martin read the message three times. He wasn't sure what to make of it. Colleen, or "Cat," seemed friendly, although her writing style was somewhat juvenile, even for a twenty-six-year-old. His mind started drifting to worries about Cat being after his money. Not that he had a lot, but probably more than her. He called Georgia into the study and showed her the letter.

"Well, what do you think?"

"Give me a minute. I haven't finished reading it yet." Georgia had just sat in front of Martin's computer.

Martin was silent until Georgia pushed the chair back and looked up at him.

"She sounds like a very nice young lady, probably working in a low-wage job because she lacks a good education. Could even be a dangerous job, like a bodega. I believe she's truly happy to make a connection with you, and you owe it to her to offer testing for your mutation. You don't have to give her your ATM PIN or even your address, but I think you should talk to her. Remember, about twenty-five percent of her DNA is as honorable as yours. Don't be so suspicious."

"Ok, I'll try to get her after work in the next day or two."

"Why don't you go ahead and email another match, now that you've dipped your toe in the water? You want to get these people notified about their genetic condition soon, don't you?"

"You're right. I'll email the other matches tonight."

"You'd better start getting ready for work. I'll have breakfast ready when you're dressed."

Coffee, an orange, and a bowl of raisin bran were waiting for Martin when he entered the kitchen. Nick was finishing his breakfast as Martin sat.

"Wish me luck on my geometry test today, Dad," he said.

"Geometry test? I'm sure you're angling to do well. You always do." His comment was overheard by Georgia who was pouring herself some coffee. She groaned and gave her husband a look of disapproval, as he had broken the rule of no puns in the house.

"Thanks, Dad," Nick said, getting up from the table. He kissed his dad on the forehead and exited the kitchen, almost bumping into his older brother.

"Outta my way," Greg mumbled as he shuffled in, still wearing his pajamas. He rubbed the sleep from his eyes and asked his mother if he could have eggs for breakfast. "They're going to time us in the fifty-yard dash today, and I want to do my best."

"Maybe you should have thought about that last night and gone to sleep at a reasonable hour. Your father told me you were still awake after eleven. And be nicer to your little brother."

"Aw, Mom . . ."

"Think about that next time you have something important in the morning," Martin said. "Someday you'll learn that the universe isn't going to take care of you."

Once finished with breakfast, Martin headed to the hallway where Nick was adjusting the books in his backpack before leaving for school. Martin tousled his hair and wished him luck on the test, not that he needed it. As usual, Martin spent ten minutes after breakfast in his study reading the morning newspaper online. Once done, his thoughts turned again to his half-siblings. The sound of the front door squeaking, then slamming shut, jerked him back to the present, and he sighed as he rose from the chair to take on the day. He kissed Georgia on the cheek before exiting through the garage where he kept his car, his cane in his left hand, his briefcase strap slung over his right shoulder.

The professor had a busy day ahead of him, and he tried to fight the urge to think about connecting with his half-siblings rather than go over the important points he wanted to make in his new grant proposal. There was also the continued pressure from the department chairman to work with the local oil company, which loomed large in his mind. He had to come up with a good reason to turn down the collaboration.

As the day wore on, Martin couldn't shake his interest in finding and warning his relatives. He decided to let his work slide for a while. He'd use his recent stroke as an excuse. Surely, the Chemistry chairman wouldn't expect him to hit the ground with his feet running as quickly as he might have in the past. He'd allocate parts of his workdays to contacting his newly-discovered family members before devoting himself to his departmental responsibilities.

Recently, he'd considered doubling up on his exercises so he might walk without his cane, but his physical therapist had cautioned him against having unrealistic expectations. Now he thought the better of it. To keep the department chair off his back until he got the half-sibling project to completion, he needed to appear as infirm as possible.

Fortunately, the workday he had planned wouldn't be too stressful, other than the mandatory conference with the oil company. They had smart lawyers who were able to counter every legal roadblock environmentalists could think of. He'd hoped others would have found a reason to stop the project, but it looked like he was going to have to be the one to put an end to it. If he withdrew, no one else in his department had the proven ability to take his place. His chairman wouldn't be happy, and Martin wanted to put off that unpleasant discussion as long as possible. He remained silent during most of the meeting, never fully committing to offering his time or expertise.

The professor spent the rest of the afternoon going over data with his graduate students, most of whom were working on innovative ways to trap atmospheric carbon into solid organic compounds which could be stored safely. The hope was that some of these compounds could be used to create substances capable of being molded into furniture and building materials. Most such products available were flawed, and he hoped to synthesize more robust materials. He loved his research, but for now, his main focus was on making contact with his recently discovered family members and making sure they were properly screened for the abnormal fibrinogen he had inherited.

After dinner, Martin retired to his office and stared at his cell phone as he rehearsed what he would say to Cat. Finally, he dialed her number.

After three rings, he heard a young-sounding female voice. "Hello?"

In that instant, Martin forgot what he had rehearsed, and instead started speaking naturally.

"Cat?"

"Yes."

"This is Martin. Your half-brother."

"Oh, Martin! I'm so glad you called."

"I've been very eager to talk to you. Have you done any work building a family tree? I want to learn about all the half-siblings I have out there. I also want to be sure you're my half-sister. With the amount of DNA we share, you could be my grandmother or aunt. Since you have no siblings, you can't be my aunt. From your age, I'm almost positive you're not my grandmother."

Cat giggled.

Continuing, Martin said, "Since you didn't match with my mother at all and your father was a sperm donor, we must be related through our biological father."

"I don't understand any of that stuff you were just talking about, but I'm glad you wrote to me. My mom died several years ago. I have an uncle, my mom's brother, but we never had anything to do with him. As far as I know, he and my mom were my only relatives. That's not counting you and the other matches I have, of course."

Martin relaxed more. Cat seemed so young and naïve, she put him at ease. "Maybe you could tell me a little about yourself, Cat."

"There's not much to tell. I was seven when my dad, the man who raised me at first, died. After that, my mom had a lot of problems. She went through four husbands. We never lived anyplace for too long, and she never had a lot of money. A few years ago, she died from liver failure."

"I'm sorry to hear that."

"She didn't take care of herself. I'd already left home by then and was living on my own. I would have liked to go to college, but never went because I needed to work."

Here it comes. She's going to ask me for money so she can go to college. "What kind of work do you do?"

"I'm a dancer."

That wasn't the answer he expected. For a moment, Martin pictured his half-sibling dancing for the Boise Ballet Company, possibly having the lead in productions such as *Swan Lake* or *Sleeping Beauty*. He'd seen those a few years back and had been impressed by the talent of the dancers and the artistic director. Before his imagination got too carried away, Martin remembered that Cat worked nights until two a.m., not the usual hours of a prima ballerina.

"Where do you work?"

After an uncomfortable silence, Cat answered, "The Exotic Bunny Club." After another pause, she added, "I'm an exotic dancer."

"Oh." *This was a big mistake. Next, in addition to asking for money, she's probably going to try to sell me drugs.*

"Look, I know what you're thinking. Me and my daughter are just trash. But Emerald is only three years old and the sweetest little girl in the world."

"You're a mother?"

"Yes, I'm a single mom. I may have made some mistakes, but Emerald's done nothing wrong. She's going to go to college and make something of herself. Meanwhile, I make good money at The Exotic Bunny, they treat me fairly and don't make me do lap dances or anything like that. The tips are great, and I have an apartment that's plenty big for the two of us. I don't do drugs, and I don't steal."

Martin listened intently as Cat revealed her circumstances. He'd never met anyone like her before, and now there she was, his long-lost half-sister. Should he make an excuse and get off the phone, never to speak to her again? Or should he try to develop a brotherly relationship with her? It wouldn't be unreasonable to suspect that someone in her profession might require some protection, or at least guidance, now and then. Could an association with her lead to endangerment of his own family? At the very least he felt obligated to warn her about her risk of having abnormal fibrinogen. If she had inherited it, her daughter could have, too.

"Do you have health insurance?" Martin asked, not knowing what else to say.

"I have Obama Care, so Emerald has gotten all her vaccinations. We're both healthy, so we haven't needed to see doctors."

I have to get off this call and consider all my options. Cat seems like a sweet girl, but I don't know what kind of scumbags she's connected to. "It's been a pleasure talking to you this evening, Cat, but it's getting late, and I have some things to do. There's a few more people I matched with but haven't spoken to yet, so let me do that before we speak again."

"Okay, brother Martin. You have my number."

After they disconnected, Martin thought about their conversation. The way she'd said "brother Martin" pulled at his heartstrings in a way he never expected. She may have had a rough life, but she was a relative and seemed to be doing as well as possible under the circumstances.

He saw no need to waste more time before letting all his half-siblings know about their fifty percent chance of being at risk for a life-threatening blood clot. He spent the next hour emailing the remaining half-siblings identified on the website. In an attempt to capture all the half-sibs he could, Martin filled out forms for the three largest genealogy websites, uploading his DNA information as well as his mother's.

As he lay in bed, he anticipated finding a few more matches, as he had now widened his search. The thought of having sixteen or more half-siblings excited him. He hoped he could develop a good rapport with at least some of them. In the past, he'd often looked at large family gatherings with envy. To be part of such an ensemble would bring him much joy. Sure, he had his mother, but she wouldn't be around forever. His cousins and an uncle lived several states away, and he hadn't seen them in years. Georgia's parents were both deceased, and her estranged sister lived in Australia. The idea of a large, supportive family comforted him. Even if he hit it off with only three of them, that would be a gain of three half-siblings and their families. He looked forward to what was ahead.

Chapter 12

THE CALIFORNIA SUN WAS LOW in the sky as Quentin sped down the country road in his new silver Porsche Carrera. The vehicle held the road as he turned into a sharp bend. Sure, his neighbors had complained about his driving and warned him to drive slower, but he knew better. He'd taken the car to a racetrack in Monterey and had confidence in his ability to handle the four-hundred-and-forty-horsepower engine around curves and stop on a dime, or the head of a pin if needed.

This was the life. Work during the week at his Santa Barbara law office, then enjoy the three-hour drive home to his rural estate near Cambria, where he would spend the weekend with his wife, three children, horses, chickens, and pet sheep.

As he waited in the driveway for the garage door to open, he thought about the wine tasting he and Sally would be hosting the following evening for a few of the couples in the area—the area being within a radius of twenty miles. Thoughts of the lively conversation they would have once everyone had loosened up from the alcohol were his last thoughts, just before a bullet pierced the back windshield, then his skull.

The following day a man in Monterey was murdered with a single bullet to the brain. The people with motives were quickly dismissed by police once their alibis were proved to be solid.

Chapter 13

MARTIN AWOKE BEFORE THE ALARM sounded, and headed straight for his study to check for responses to the emails he'd sent his half-sibs the previous night. The first message he opened was from Zoe Clyburn. She taught high school math in a suburb of Boise. Zoe had been told at an early age that her father was a sperm donor and had hoped to find out more about her family through the genealogy website.

Next, Martin read the message from Brandon Bradberry, an accountant who lived in Boise. He, too, had been curious about relatives on the side of his sperm-donor father.

Daryl Slocum was a software engineer who lived in rural eastern Oregon and worked remotely. He was an outdoor enthusiast who discovered he was the product of artificial insemination when he learned in his high school biology class that it was impossible for him to have brown eyes if both his parents' eyes were blue.

Oliver Feinberg owned a shoe store in another suburb of Boise. He had never suspected the man who raised him was not his biological father until he'd searched for his ancestry. The father he knew was an Ashkenazi Jew, and Oliver had always been proud of that heritage. He'd suffered a sense of deep betrayal upon learning he had no Jewish ancestry whatsoever at the age of forty-two. When confronted, his parents admitted that his father wasn't able to have children, and they'd conceived Oliver using the sperm of a donor. After not speaking to his parents for several weeks, they'd made amends, but Oliver was now determined to find out as much as he could about his paternal side.

Next, Martin decided to check the genealogy sites he'd contacted the previous night. Going in alphabetical order, he clicked on the first company's website. He started by checking his mother's matches. There were about twenty more than had appeared on the smaller site. No surprise, as they would have access to more customers, and therefore more potential matches. He perused the list of names and recognized those he'd seen on the first website. The new names that had popped up were in the second or third-cousin category.

Lastly, Martin looked at his own matches. As the data loaded, he closed his eyes, aware his heart was racing. He opened his right eye, then his left. *This must be a mistake. There's way too many names listed here.* There, before him, was a list of names so long it reached the bottom of the page. He scrolled to the next page, then the one after that, still not reaching the end of the list. He sat for a moment before deciding what to do. Again, the names were organized such that the closest matches were at the top. The closest match was twenty-eight percent. This was followed by a long list of matches gradually dropping to a low of twenty-two percent. There were eighty-seven names in all. Most, if not all of these, would be half-siblings. *This is impossible. There must be something wrong with their algorithm.* On closer inspection, Martin noted that none of the matches were old enough to be a grandparent. Ages ranged from eighteen years younger than him to one year older, consistent with being half-siblings with the same donor father.

Below this long list were the people related to his mother, as well as six people not related to her. These, all under twenty years of age, shared approximately twelve and a half percent of their DNA with Martin. These were likely half-nieces or nephews on his paternal side. Countless distant cousins, sharing less than two percent of his DNA, were at the bottom of the list. Before dwelling on the large number of close matches, Martin decided to check the other popular sites. If they showed only a few matches, as he expected, he would ignore the large number identified by this company.

Martin went to the website of the second largest company and clicked on his mother's information. The results were similar to those of the first website he'd checked that morning. Next, he clicked on his own information and again closed his eyes, opening one eye, then the other after a few seconds. The data was still loading. By the time all the data had been filled in, there were pages of names, a few more than on the first website. Before him was a list of ninety-one people who were approximately a twenty-five percent match, with an age range similar to that on the previous site. If that didn't convince him something strange and unexpected was going on, the third website did. That site showed ninety people with a twenty-five percent match.

Martin needed to make sense of this. He wondered if there were glitches in the software of these companies that gave rise to false matches. This idea was far-fetched. It would be next to impossible for all these companies to have the same bugs—they all used their own proprietary software. It would be unlikely for such a problem to result in so many matches near twenty-five percent, with no gradual increase or decrease away from that number. The one person he had contacted also had a sperm donor for a father. He'd check with Dean later to see if he had an explanation—an explanation other than that Martin's sperm donor father had fathered countless children.

Who would do such a thing? Weren't there laws about how many donations a single donor could make? Weren't there age restrictions? There was almost a twenty-year difference in the ages of the half-sibs. Contacting all these people would be an onerous task. A form letter seemed too impersonal, yet he couldn't imagine doing it any other way.

At breakfast, Nick asked his dad for help in coming up with ideas for a biology project he had to start soon. "Mom didn't have any good ideas, but she said you would."

"How about growing plants, like peas, under different conditions of light and temperature?"

"That's pretty lame, Dad. At least three kids do the same thing every year."

"You could spend time in the local blood bank to learn about blood typing and testing."

"That sounds boring," Nick said. "Besides, who's going to drive me?"

"Good point," Martin said. "How about correlating the standardized test performance of Greg and some of his friends with the hours spent playing video games and watching TV?"

"As if Greg and his idiot friends would cooperate. All your ideas so far are lame. I want to do something really important."

"He wants something with more of a wow factor," Georgia said. "But it has to be something he can accomplish."

"I promise to think about it some more today," Martin answered. An idea for a science project was forming in his head, but he needed to mull it over.

On campus, Martin tried his best to immerse himself in his work. At eleven a.m., he was finally able to break away for a short call to Dean. Fortunately, Dean was free and able to hear why Martin thought the information from the three large genealogy companies was flawed.

"Sorry, Martin," Dean said. "I think you're all wet."

"You mean my idea doesn't hold water?"

Dean moaned. "No pun will change the fact that I trust the data. It looks like you are the proud owner of a lot of half-siblings. Same with them. It looks like someone back in the day didn't follow the accepted practices to prevent this sort of thing from happening. Probably some egomaniac who thought his genes were a gift to the world. Or was hard up for cash since donors usually get paid. I'm sure he never thought there'd be a way through genetic testing that he'd be found out. Of course, the donor is probably up there in years by now, possibly dead. Meanwhile, you've got to decide what to do with this information. Given the flawed fibrinogen gene you have, and knowing that half of these people probably harbor that gene without their knowledge, it makes it tough to ignore."

Martin let out a long breath. "I guess it's about time I had a meeting with Georgia and my kids. I need everyone to be on the same page."

Before leaving work, Martin called his mom and told her about the large number of matches. She remembered Dr. Sanborn assuring her the donors he used only gave one or two samples at the most. Too many offspring from one donor risked future marriages between half-siblings, unaware they had the same father.

#   #   #

Georgia made meatloaf for dinner that night, a family favorite. The table talk was lively, centering around the boys' school activities, especially Greg's baseball practice and Nick's recent acing of his trigonometry exam. As they were finishing the main course, Nick brought up his mandatory biology project.

"Don't worry, Son," Martin said. "I have something in mind that you might find interesting, a project unlike anything kids at your school have done before."

Nick's expression perked up. "What's that, Dad?"

"You'll have to wait until after dinner to find out. We'll have a family meeting after dessert."

"Family meeting?" Nick asked, his brows knitted. "We've never had one before. Are you and Mom getting a divorce?"

Martin felt sorry for his choice of words, noting the worried expression on Nick's face. "Of course not, son. Your mother and I love each other now just as much as we did when we were first married. I seem to be incapable of even getting mad at her when she runs into things with her car. Isn't that right, dear?"

"It was just a small dent." Georgia smiled at Martin as she continued. "If your father can keep his promise not to use puns around me, I see us being happily married for years to come."

"Are you filing for bankruptcy?" Greg asked. "Olivia said her parents might have to do that because they lost a lot of money in that Rainbow Fund scandal."

"Nothing like that. We never invest in crazy get-rich-quick schemes like that, by the way. No more guesses. There's nothing to worry about, but I've discovered some things about our family—relatives we never knew existed before—that your mother and I think you should know about."

"I hope we're distant relatives of Bill Gates and stand to inherit a shitload of money when he croaks," Greg said.

"No such luck," Martin responded. "FYI he said a few years ago that he's going to give all his money away. Won't be leaving it to his kids."

"I'll bet a Nigerian prince has reached out to Dad and all he has to do is send him ten thousand dollars to get a few billion," Nick said. Both boys giggled.

"You'll just have to wait. Now, Peaches, what's for dessert?"

After oatmeal cookies and milk for the boys, cookies and decaf coffee for the adults, they all retired to the living room.

Martin sat in one of the armchairs, while Georgia sat in the other, and the boys took positions on the sofa. The professor looked at his feet for a few seconds to collect his thoughts.

"It's hard to know where to begin, really, so I'll begin with a fact that you're all aware of. My dad, Grandpa Joe, was not my biological father. My mom and dad never hid the fact from me that dad was unable to father children after a nasty case of mumps when he was in his twenties. My parents were left with the option to have no children, adopt, or use a sperm donor."

Greg demonstrated his boredom by snoring as his dad explained how he discovered he had a fibrinogen mutation inherited from his father.

"I get it," Nick said. "You inherited this mutation from just one of your parents, so it's dominant."

"Duh," Greg interjected.

Martin shot a disapproving look at his eldest son. "That's right, Nick. You must have already learned something about inheritance in your biology class."

"Most of what we've learned is about peas and fruit flies, but I think it's pretty interesting."

As Greg rolled his eyes, Martin smiled, thinking it would be an easy sell to get Nick interested in the project he had in mind.

"Now, I don't want you boys to worry. You'll both be tested to see if you have the same mutation I have. If you have it, you will need to take the same medicine I take to prevent clots. I'm afraid you won't be able to participate in sports that will put you at risk for bleeding from injuries. No football or rugby, things like that."

"What about baseball?" Greg asked. "I'm not giving that up. No way."

"Baseball isn't as clear-cut. Let's wait for the results and decide later if you turn out to be positive. Other than taking one pill a day, you can have a normal life."

"Not playing baseball isn't a normal life. Not for me, anyway," Greg said, folding his arms across his chest.

"Look, Greg, at some point you'll have to learn that things don't always go your way. Knowing about the mutation now, if you have it, will save you from having clotting problems before they begin."

"Looks like Greg and I are fortunate that you discovered this, Dad," Nick said. "Sorry you had to go through all of this, but we're glad you're okay now."

"Thanks, Son."

"So now all Greg and I have to do is get tested. Doesn't sound like a big deal—"

Greg interrupted his brother. "We didn't need to have this big family meeting to tell us about this. I need to get going now. I was going to help Olivia with her homework tonight."

"How are you going to help her? You're not exactly a star pupil," Nick said. "You're just going to make out at her place. I know her parents will be taking Kyle to a karate match tonight."

"Shut up, asshole. If it makes any difference, I didn't know her parents would be gone. So mind your own business."

"Now, boys. This is no time to have one of your quarrels." Georgia said. "A little making out is okay, as long as you're both willing. No babies, though. Understand?" She looked from one boy to the other, and they each nodded their head in the affirmative.

"That'll be the day when Nick finds a girl to have sex with," Greg mumbled.

Martin ignored his son's last comment. "This, however, does not bring us to the end of our meeting. We are only beginning."

Greg and Nick eyed each other and shrugged in acquiescence.

"Of course my primary concern, when I learned of my defective fibrinogen, was protecting you boys. I've already scheduled you to be tested. We're lucky because I have connections to top-notch academicians, which afforded me the ability to find out what my problem is and what to do about it. But I started wondering, what about others? In addition to the sperm donor himself, the children of other couples he might have donated to, or any children of his own would be at risk. Each of his biological children has a fifty percent chance of inheriting this faulty gene. "

"So now you're worried about other people out there with this mutation?" Nick asked.

"Precisely."

"I don't see how you could find out about them. Unless the sperm bank this donor worked through kept records," Nick said.

"Now you're thinking like a real scientist, Nick. We're one step ahead of you, though. Grandma doesn't know the name of the sperm bank. But she does remember the name of the doctor who arranged it all. Unfortunately, he died a number of years ago, and his files were destroyed. There's no way to chase down the sperm donor and his offspring through records."

"Well, I guess we're done here, then," Greg said. "Can I go to Olivia's now?"

"Cool your jets," Martin said, irritation in his voice. "We're not done."

"I'm worried," said Nick. "Other people could be walking around with this mutation having no idea they're carrying a time bomb." He looked down at his feet and spoke softly. "A bomb that could be defused with just the right treatment."

"That's right, Son. But there is a way to tackle this problem."

"Really, Dad?" Nick said, looking up.

"Yes. Genetics."

"How are you going to sample everyone in the world for this fibrinogen mutation?" Nick asked.

"I'm not. But what I can do, what I have done, is look for half-siblings on genealogy websites."

Greg and Nick looked at each other. Then Greg spoke up. "So that's why you said we have relatives we didn't know about. Well? Do I have any long-lost aunts or uncles out there? I'm hoping for Mark Zuckerberg. Or Elon Musk. No, they're too weird. Warren Buffett. I'm hoping for him."

"I wish you could be serious," Martin said, giving Greg a stern look. "What I'm going to tell you is important. I'm not sure exactly how, or if it will be good or bad, but I had some twenty-five percent matches, half brothers and sisters I didn't know about."

"How many are there?" Nick asked.

"I don't have an exact number yet because I haven't eliminated all the duplicates at the different companies, but it appears to be about ninety."

Greg and Nick froze, staring at Martin as they appeared to be trying to imagine what having ninety new relatives would be like.

"Gee, Dad, are you sure there hasn't been some sort of mistake?" Nick asked. "That's an awfully high number."

"Your mother and I were quite surprised as well. Overwhelmed, but it all checks out. Each of the large companies I used came up with similar numbers of people. There's a lot of crossover with many of the same people popping up in different companies. Most of them live in this area. So, assuming they were all fathered by the same donor, the majority of them stayed in the area near where they were born. Locations of others who have moved away in all directions seem to be centered around this area, as would be expected."

"What do we do now?" Greg asked.

"I thought we could discuss that tonight. This is too important not to involve the whole family in decision-making. Remember, about half these people probably have the fibrinogen mutation I have."

"If it weren't for that mutation," Georgia said, "I think I'd be in favor of perhaps picking three or four to get to know. I don't know how you'd choose, but that would be reasonable."

"I've given this a lot of thought over the past few days," Martin said. "I think we should try to talk with as many of these relatives as possible. In person would be best, but phone or video chat would work."

"How about we send them each a form letter? Tell them they have the same biological father as you and need to get tested for the mutation that was just discovered?" Nick asked.

"That would be the simplest approach," Martin said, "but too impersonal. First of all, you need to consider that not all of these people are necessarily aware that the father they've known all their life is not their biological father. Not all parents let their kids in on that secret. It would be pretty traumatic to learn about it in a form letter. That's just too cold."

"I guess you're right, Dad. It still wouldn't be easy even if you met them in person."

"That's right, but we could ask questions to find out if they already know, and if they don't, we'd break the news to them gently. Next, I'd want to find out if they have another sibling who has the same sperm donor father. Infertile couples will sometimes try to use the same sperm donor for all their kids. If they don't know, their parents might. The gynecologist who arranged for my donor died a number of years back so that's a dead end. We can ask everyone we interview if their parents know the name of the sperm bank and donor number used for their artificial insemination. If they don't know, we can find out who the obstetrician was. He or she should have that information. That should allow us to track down all the donor's progeny, and hopefully notify the donor himself. There may be many sperm banks to look into. This is a very big, very unusual case. It's important to wrap this up quickly so as many affected people as possible can be notified."

"Where do you begin?" Nick asked.

"I'm glad you asked," Martin said. "Since you need an exciting project to work on for your biology class, I thought you could be my right-hand man for all of this. Maybe even more than that. You can do the interviewing, arrange the data, and have an award-winning class presentation. Especially if we can get some of the fibrinogen results in time to include."

"Wow, Dad, that would be very interesting. Do you really think I could help?"

"Absolutely. But we've got to get this up and running soon to try to make your deadline. How much time do we have?"

"My project is due in a little over two months."

"Then two months will be our goal. We should be able to get through most, if not all, of the matches by then. Whatever you don't finish by that time, you or I can do after you turn in your report. Tomorrow I'll call the people I've been in touch with and set up a group Zoom meeting for an evening later this week."

"I have a mock UN meeting Wednesday after school. Any other evening would be fine."

"Great. Now there's one other hurdle. Originally, when it was estimated only a few people would need to be tested for the fibrinogen mutation, Arthur said his grant money could cover all the costs of testing everyone involved. Now it looks like we'll need to run a lot more than expected, which will cost over two hundred thousand dollars. We need to raise a lot of money."

"Why are you looking at me?" Georgia asked.

"I was hoping you could help with fundraising," Martin said. "I'd get on my knees to beg, but I'm afraid that in my condition, I wouldn't be able to get up."

"You know I just signed on to run Jill's campaign for the state assembly."

"All you have to do is call in some favors to get the local stations to run notices as part of their public good mandate. They should be happy to do it."

"What do I tell Jill?"

"This will be short-lived, and won't take much of your time. You'll still be able to run another flawless campaign."

"I'd been planning to finish catching up on all those little things I didn't have a chance to do when I was taking care of you. Now—"

"I know, I know. I couldn't have recovered without you, and you deserve a lot of downtime before you start working those crazy hours you always put in when running a campaign. But you're needed here. I wouldn't ask if you weren't. This whole project, saving lives, depends on your participation. If there were anyone else I could ask I would." Martin knew he was pushing all the right buttons. He felt only slightly ashamed, manipulating Georgia with words like "need," "saving lives," and "if there were anyone else." But he really did need her. He wouldn't be shamelessly manipulating her if he didn't.

"Oh, all right. I'm in."

"One more thing. I need you to help me with something, Greg," Martin said.

Greg rolled his eyes. "What's that?"

"I'd like you to set up a private Facebook page."

"I thought you hated Facebook."

"I do. But this will be useful. Set up a page where all of us half-sibs can post things to each other. It will help us get to know one another without being too intrusive, and maybe we'll learn something useful. Who knows. As people on the list are notified, Nick can tell them about the page, and post updates about the testing. If they're interested in joining, it will be up to me or Nick to approve. Can you handle that?"

"No problem. Can I go to Olivia's now?" Greg asked.

"Sure," Martin answered. "She needs to get that homework done, and I can see how eager you are to help her."

Chapter 14

SEAN WAS PLEASED WITH HIS performance that night. *Swan Lake* was one of his favorites, and he'd absolutely nailed it that night as Prince Siegfried. He was wide awake when he got into his car for the short drive to his house in Brady Heights, a gay-friendly area of Tulsa, Oklahoma. There he would celebrate the end of a grueling week of performances with his husband, Vernon.

As he made the familiar drive home, he thought about how happy he was living there. At first reticent to move to an area he thought of as redneck, The Tulsa Ballet gave him an offer that was too good to turn down—an opportunity to become a principal dancer. Since Vernon could work anywhere the internet reached, they left their comfortable home in San Francisco and headed for Tulsa. It was a surprisingly accepting city, although there still were vestiges of the old, homophobic Bible Belt city. He occasionally felt uncomfortable, even threatened, but was comforted knowing he had never been physically attacked.

As he pulled into the driveway, he checked his watch. Almost midnight. While he waited for the garage door to open, a bullet hit him in the back of the head. His lifeless body hit the horn of his car, awakening several of his neighbors.

Two days later, Louisville, Kentucky, was the site of a similar homicide. The police investigations for both murders quickly went cold.

Chapter 15

THE NEXT MORNING BEFORE LEAVING for work, Martin emailed Oliver, Zoe, Cat, Daryl, and Brandon, asking if they could participate in a virtual meeting later that week, so everyone could get to know each other, and he and one of his sons could give them some important information. Throughout the day he checked for replies, while working on a grant proposal for converting cactus extracts into a source of clean energy, meeting with graduate students, and brainstorming with Dr. Stephen Bowditch, a junior faculty collaborator. Before he left work, he had heard from all the half-sibs he had emailed and set up a Zoom meeting for Thursday at seven p.m. All parties involved were enthusiastic about connecting with the others and learning what they could about their half-siblings. Although Brandon and Zoe had already contacted each other, they expressed interest in meeting the others.

That evening, Martin helped Nick design a spreadsheet on his son's laptop. He made columns for the half-sibs names, ages, contact information, and fibrinogen mutation testing—whether they had been notified about their risk, agreed to be tested, and status of testing. There was also space to include pertinent medical histories and the names of other half-siblings they knew about.

At the family dinner, as everyone dove into the roasted chicken Georgia had prepared, Martin was the first to speak. "I have to admit, I'm a bit nervous about meeting my half-sibs. Especially one of them."

"The exotic dancer you told me about?" Nick asked. "Sounds pretty iffy."

"You're probably right, Son, but I've learned it's best not to jump to any conclusions without evidence. At any rate, she needs to be informed about the dangerous mutation she may have inherited."

Greg rolled his eyes. "Sure, Dad. Just because she's a stripper—"

"Exotic dancer," Martin interrupted.

"Okay, exotic dancer. Even though she's one of those, we have to remember how superior our family is, so it would be wrong to conclude she's sleazy. After all, she's related to us, so her being an undesirable would be nearly impossible."

"That's not what I was saying. Let's just give her a chance. I'm not saying she's a brilliant upstanding citizen. Only that we shouldn't rush to judgment. Time will tell."

"I understand, Dad," Nick said.

Rolling his eyes again, Greg said, "You guys are so naïve."

#   #   #

Seven o'clock Thursday evening arrived with Martin and Nick sitting in front of the computer in the study. Zoe, Oliver, Daryl, Cat, and Brandon joined on time, and introductions were made. All commented about how surprised they were to find so many half-brothers and sisters, but none had contacted more than a few. Martin figured the others were doing what he was doing—looking at the features of everyone, seeing if they could detect any resemblance to themselves.

"Glad you could all make it," Martin said. He proceeded to speak a little about himself, then introduced his younger son. Nick smiled awkwardly and waved to the camera. Then Martin talked about his recent stroke, and that until recently, he hadn't been interested in learning about his biological father. "Something I learned recently changed all that. Later, I'll tell you about that, but first I'd like the rest of you to talk a little about yourselves."

Oliver wasted no time before chiming in. He described how he discovered his biological father was not the man who had raised him. He was forty-four years old, divorced with no children, and owned a shoe store.

He played baseball in high school and college and did a stint in the minor leagues. It wasn't long before he realized that he wasn't going to make it to the big leagues, so he relinquished his four-figure minor league salary and got an MBA. He still loved baseball and attended Boise Hawkes games whenever he could. At least four times a year he'd travel to Seattle to watch the Mariners.

Martin reflected on Greg's interest in baseball. *Must be some baseball genes in the family.*

After finishing his self-description, Oliver said, "I'm really excited because I have tickets to hear The Rocket speak on Friday. Anybody else going?"

"You mean The Rocket, the ultimate fighter?" Nick asked excitedly. "He's coming *here*?"

"Sure is. I'm a big fan of his. Especially because he has a funny nose like me." Oliver turned to the side so the others could appreciate the ski bump at the end of his proboscis.

"I see what you mean," Brandon said, chuckling. "I'll bet he got his from fighting, though."

"Not so. He was born with it. He's from around here, you know. He came into my shoe store about ten years ago, and we got to talking. Nicest guy. He noticed our similar noses and told me kids used to make fun of his when he was younger. Said that's why he got interested in fighting."

"Kids can be so cruel," Zoe said. "I'm a teacher and I see too much bullying, even with my high school students."

"Why don't you tell us about yourself now, Zoe?" Martin said.

An attractive blond with hazel eyes, she paused for a few seconds to collect her thoughts. "Okay. I'm Zoe and I'm related to all of you. I sound like I'm at an AA meeting, don't I?" Zoe paused again and chuckled. "I'm already acquainted with Brandon, so he already knows I'm thirty-six years old, and by day I teach high school math."

"If you're a teacher, you must be smart, too," Oliver said.

"I like to think I'm not stupid," Zoe answered. "When I was a teenager, my mom told me I was the child of an anonymous sperm donor. I'll never forget how shocked I was, and I began asking a lot of questions about my ancestors. Seems like it took a long time to get over it. I loved my dad, the one who raised me, but still, I had trouble wrapping my head around it for the longest time. I'm curious about my biological father but don't expect to ever find him. I had my DNA analyzed because I want to find out about my ancestry. I wasn't looking for relatives. I've been married for ten years to a wonderful man. We have no kids. My husband is an airline pilot, so he's gone a lot. Because of that, I've taken up stand-up comedy at night. So far, I've succeeded in getting a lot of boos and putting drunk people to sleep, but I'm not easily discouraged."

"Where will you be performing next?" Oliver asked. "I'd like to see you. Maybe we could all go."

"I'll check my schedule and get back to you. If you promise not to boo me."

"Promise," Oliver replied.

The next person to introduce himself was Brandon. A forty-two-year-old bespectacled accountant with short, brown hair, he spoke in almost a monotone. He described being told his biological father was not the man he knew as "Dad," but an unimportant anonymous person. He was five at the time and confused. Only later did he fully understand what it meant. He was never good at sports, but always liked working with numbers. "I guess I'm a stereotypical accountant," he said. "I'm a bit of a nerd and like working by myself in a quiet room. Sometimes I get excited when a new tax law is passed that will save my clients money. I'm married to an engineer, and we have two children in grade school. I must warn you, I like puns."

"I do, too," Martin said. "I wonder if it runs in the family. My wife doesn't appreciate them, and has banned me from making puns at home."

"There's no accounting for taste," Brandon replied.

"Ouch, that was a bad one," Oliver said.

"I warned you."

"Let's move on from our no-account accountant to Daryl."

"Sure," said Daryl, a young-looking man with auburn hair and a three-day growth of facial hair. "I'm thirty-two years old and live in a beautiful area of Washington state away from civilization. My closest neighbors are five miles away. I'm thankful for satellite internet because

I'm a software engineer and work from home. My sister wanted me to send off my DNA because our parents died, and we know we were both made with artificial insemination. She wanted to know if we both have the same biological father."

"Do you?" Oliver asked.

"Doesn't look like it. We have relatives in common on our mother's side, but none of the others are the same, and she's a twenty-seven percent match with me by DNA. In other words, she's a half-sib, just like all of you. My sister only has one half-sib on her paternal side. I already met him over Zoom. Seems like a nice guy. Her situation is much simpler than mine."

"That leaves us with Cat. Why don't you tell us about yourself, Cat?" Martin said.

"Okay," Cat said. A pretty brunette with a nose ring, Cat had a butterfly tattoo on her right shoulder exposed by her tank top. Although Martin found nose rings off-putting, he found her demeanor sympathetic and childlike. She wasn't anything like he'd expected an exotic dancer would be. Perhaps it was because of the blood connection, but whatever the reason, he took an instant liking to her.

"I'm the youngest one here. I'm twenty-seven years old, and my real name is Colleen, but I go by Cat. My story is different from all of yours. As Martin knows, I'm not respectable like all of you. I'm an exotic dancer."

"It's nice to know I have an interesting relative," Oliver said.

"You might say everything's relative," Brandon chimed in.

Cat continued. "Up until I was seven, I had the perfect childhood. I lived in a nice area of Boise with my mom and dad. My dad passed away from a heart attack, and everything changed. My mom sorta fell apart. She became distant from me. Never seemed interested in my grades, what I did outside of school, or who my friends were.

"She blew through my dad's life insurance payout, which probably wasn't all that much. When I was ten and she had to sell the house, I told her I missed Dad, and we wouldn't be poor if he was around. She said it didn't matter that he was gone, because he wasn't my real dad, my real dad was some random dude hired so she could have a baby—me. I was shocked and confused. Then we moved to a small apartment in a pretty sketchy neighborhood.

"Nothing much changed in my world until I was in the seventh grade when my mom married the super at our building. Mom seemed happier for a while, but it wasn't long before she and Rudy, my dear old stepdad, started drinking every night. He'd get violent and hit her. He didn't hit me, but he started . . ." Colleen seemed unable to continue, taking in several deep breaths.

"That's okay, honey," Zoe said. "I think we get the picture. You don't have to give us the details."

"Thanks," Cat said. "I was in pretty bad shape mentally by the time I started high school. My grades were slipping, and I cut class as much as I could. I started saving money, and in a few months, I'd saved over a hundred dollars so I could run away. Enough to tide me over for a few days. I'd heard it was easy to get a job as a nanny for rich people. I loved children, and all my living expenses would be taken care of."

"I can picture what happened next," Zoe said.

"Right," said Cat. "I got on a bus after school one day and rode out to the edge of town. It wasn't long before I met a slime bag named Big Al outside a soup kitchen. He promised to take care of me and get me a good job. I was young and dumb and trusted him. Fortunately for me, Big Al sent me out for a carton of cigarettes a few hours after I met him, and I was hit by a bus. I didn't think I was lucky at the time—I was in a lot of pain, with a broken thigh bone, two broken ribs, and a collapsed lung. Someone called an ambulance, and I was taken to the county hospital.

"I'd been raised Catholic, so when a nun came by to comfort me, I welcomed her. She put two and two together when I told her Big Al would take care of me after I was released. She arranged for me to go to a foster home in the area. It wasn't great, but it was better than the home I'd left. I enrolled in the local high school."

"How'd you get your daughter and become a stripper?" Oliver asked.

Martin was taken aback by Oliver's tactless question. "I think Cat's revealed enough about her past for one day," he said. "We should move on."

"That's okay," Cat said. "I'm an exotic dancer, not a stripper. Although I don't wear a whole lot when I dance, I always have some clothes on."

"My apologies," Oliver said.

"No problem. A lot of people don't think there's a difference, but I do," Cat said. "My life is an open book. Maybe not a book too many people would want to read, but I've done the best I could with the hand I was dealt.

"When I was a senior in high school, I knew I was about to age out of foster care, and I'd need to support myself. I started looking for a nanny job, like I'd planned to do when I first ran away. I found a job looking after two kids in a nice area of Boise. Right after graduation, I moved into the house. My own bedroom and bathroom and three meals a day were included. I didn't make a whole lot of money, but I made enough to buy whatever I needed. Everything was great for about two years. Then the parents, who were both lawyers, started having marital problems. I detected a coldness between them. They were real lovey-dovey when I first started, but that disappeared almost overnight. Often I'd hear yelling after the kids were asleep."

"I think I know where this is going," Oliver said.

"Right. The husband came into my room one night and sexually assaulted me. I didn't know what to do. He was an important, powerful man, and I figured no one would listen to me if I accused him of anything. After several assaults, I threatened to tell his wife if he did it again. He laughed it off and told me she wouldn't care. I told him he had bruised my arms and legs, and I had pictures. Again, he laughed it off and told me no one would believe me. I started looking for other nanny jobs. Meanwhile, I got in the habit of moving a heavy dresser in front of my bedroom door at night to keep him out. Less than a month after the assaults started, you guessed it, I was pregnant.

"Instead of feeling hopeless, I felt like I had power over him. I told him I was expecting his baby, I wanted to move out, and he'd better send me money, or I'd go to his wife and the police. A DNA test would confirm what he'd done. I'll never forget the look of horror on his face. Of course, he wanted me to get an abortion, but like I said, I was raised Catholic and wouldn't consider it. I wondered if he worried about others who would come forward if I pressed charges. Whatever the reason, he agreed to support me but threatened I wouldn't be safe if I ever double-crossed him and went to the cops. I found an apartment and moved out three days later. I felt sorry for his wife, who was very upset that I was leaving so suddenly. On the other hand, I thought she should have known what her husband was up to and done something to stop it."

"Is he Emerald's father?" Martin asked.

"Yes. Sometimes I wonder if I should have handled things differently. I hate that man, but because of him, I have Emerald. I can't imagine life without her. After she was born, I cut off all ties with him. I didn't want him to know where we were and come looking for his daughter sometime in the future. I'd passed by a so-called gentleman's club in the neighborhood several times and noticed a 'Dancers Wanted' sign in the window. I liked to dance, but when I applied I learned that I didn't have a clue how to dance the way they wanted me to. They liked the way I looked, so they had one of their girls give me lessons and then hired me. After a while, I was a pretty good dancer and was making a lot of money. The job's not respectable, I know that, but I don't really mind all those men looking at me. If someone tries to put his hands on me, one of the bouncers sets him straight pretty quickly."

"So Emerald's father got off scot-free," Brandon said.

"You could look at it that way," Cat said, "but he has to go through life knowing he has a beautiful daughter out there in the world, and he'll never have a chance to see her. In my opinion, that's a pretty big punishment."

"Does your mom know about Emerald?" Nick asked.

"Sadly, she died before Emerald was born."

The group was silent for a few moments before Martin changed the subject. He asked if any of them had possible half-siblings they'd discovered on other websites. After cross-checking with the information he had already obtained, Martin had six more names to add to his list.

Upon updating his information, Brandon asked, "What was the important information you were going to give us?"

"I was just going to talk about that," Martin answered. "The reason I became interested in chasing down relatives from my biological father's side is related to the stroke I had six months ago. Fortunately, I've mostly recovered." Then he described the testing he had undergone and the discovery of his fibrinogen mutation which could be managed with medication.

"Sorry about what you went through. I'm glad you're better now," said Oliver. "But what does that have to do with us?"

"The testing showed that I didn't inherit the bad gene from my mother. I got it from my father."

"Oh," said Brandon, Zoe, Cat, Daryl, and Oliver almost simultaneously, their eyes widened.

"Now I think you understand," Martin continued. "You are all at risk for having the same bad gene. Each of you has a fifty percent chance."

"I see," Brandon said. "Now what? What should we do?"

Martin saw the fear in his eyes. It's one thing to have sympathy for someone else with a serious medical condition, but a whole other thing when that someone is yourself. "No need to panic," Martin said. "The researcher will test all of you if you want. If you didn't inherit the gene, there's no need to do anything. If you did inherit it, you should take the same medicine as me, or a related one. Also, your kids should be tested."

Questions from the others came simultaneously.

"How do we arrange to get tested?"

"How much does the testing cost?"

"What's the test called? Is it covered by insurance?"

"If you want the test," Martin said, "tell Nick here, and the lab will arrange for someone to come to your home, collect blood, and do the test for free. It will be paid for by the research grant. Nick will be keeping track of everything, which is why I've brought him here tonight. If you test positive, you'll have to follow up with your own doctor to get the treatment you need. Fortunately, the medication isn't prohibitively expensive and should be covered by your insurance."

"Nick, I want the test," Brandon said. Zoe, Daryl, Cat, and Oliver quickly followed suit.

After that was settled, the participants engaged in a short session of small talk and ended the meeting. Although there was a bit of awkwardness in the encounter, they seemed to enjoy getting to know each other. Oliver stated he hoped he was negative for the mutation, a sentiment echoed by the others.

The following day after school, Nick phoned the contact person in Arthur's lab and arranged for Oliver, Zoe, Daryl, Cat, and Brandon to be tested. He arrived at the dinner table energized. "I've scheduled all the people from last night to be tested," he announced.

"Good job, Son," Martin said.

"I'm more excited about this than I expected to be."

"Maybe you'll catch the research bug like me," Martin said. "Research usually moves pretty slowly, but it's also exciting. I've never been involved in research like this, where there's some people I've met who will be directly helped by it."

"Maybe I'll go to medical school."

"I thought you wanted to be an anthropologist," Georgia said.

"I did. But this project is awesome. I'm thinking about changing what I want to do when I grow up."

"I'm glad you're keeping your mind open," Martin said, "but you've just started on this project. You don't need to decide anything right now. Or even next year."

"I'm serious about this. You'll see," Nick said, leaning in towards his dad. He turned to Greg. "How's the Facebook page coming along?"

"Geez, I just got the assignment last night. Haven't started it yet."

"Of course. You've been busy tutoring," Nick responded, gesturing quotation marks when he said "tutoring."

"Don't worry, you little brat. I'll have it up by this weekend."

"Great." Turning to his mom, Nick said, "It looks like we're going to need a lot of money to fund all the testing our relatives will want, if the response last night is any indication. I'm going to need your help getting the word out."

Georgia and Martin smiled at each other. Their younger son was taking charge in a way neither had anticipated.

"I'm glad to see your enthusiasm," Georgia said. "Try not to be too demanding of us, though. Remember what they say about catching more flies with honey."

Later that evening, Oliver phoned Martin. "Hey, Brother, I'd really like to get to know you better. I live by myself, so I get lonely a lot."

"Even at this late date, I'd like to get to know some of my half-siblings better, too," Martin said, choosing his words carefully.

"What I'd really like is a business partner I can trust. Since you're my brother, I know I can trust you."

Martin knew what was about to follow. Sure enough, after a little more small talk, Oliver announced, "I'm going to be expanding my shoe store. Normally I'd go to a bank to get a loan for the money I'll need, but I got to thinking. I've got a brother I didn't even know about a month ago. I'd like to offer him the chance to invest in my expansion project and make some money off of it for himself. What do you say? You'd be a part-owner of the new store, which I'm sure will be very successful."

Martin had wondered how long it would be before a less fortunate relative asked for financial assistance. He gently deflected the generous offer, telling Oliver he wished him luck, but had far too many bills to think about investing. "I'm late on my car payments," he claimed, even though he had never taken out a car loan in his life.

Feeling tense, Martin played Sade's "Smooth Operator" on his saxophone. That soothing tune in particular was his go-to sound when he needed comforting.

Chapter 16

RANSOM WAS ALL SMILES AS he headed to the subway stop for the
Line 2 train. He enjoyed the one-hour ride to his home in Hell's Kitchen, a
renovated brownstone he shared with his wife and two young children.
He recognized a youthful volunteer from the Bronx Zoo animal hospital who
approached him with a smile. "Congratulations, Doc," she said. "That was
the most exciting thing I've ever seen."

"Stick around, and you may be lucky enough to see something even
more impressive," Ransom answered, turning away as the train arrived.
Scooting into a seat, he looked forward to reflecting on the day's activities.
He closed his eyes to relive the moment he inserted the arthroscope and saw
the loose fragment of knee cartilage that had been causing the problem. He'd
carefully sewn it back in place and sutured the incisions he had made. This
was the third such surgery he'd performed, but he'd still been a bit nervous
until the eighteen-foot-tall patient awoke from general anesthesia. After all,
it wasn't every day he operated on a giraffe, and the anesthesia was the most
dangerous part.

He thought about how he would broach the subject the next time he
saw his neighbor, an orthopedic surgeon. The neighbor's tallest patient had
probably been no more than six-feet four—six feet six, tops. And he was
limited to bones and cartilage, whereas Ransom performed a wide variety of
surgery on all kinds of animals.

He seemed to arrive at Grand Central Station more quickly than usual.

He rose from his seat and joined the swarm of commuters exiting the car. Squeezing between others at the doorway, a single dull popping sound rang out, but no one seemed to notice. On the platform, as the crowd he was in disbursed, Ransom's lifeless body fell to the ground. He'd been fatally shot in the back of the head.

Two more men and three women were killed in two boroughs of New York City over the next week. All died from a single bullet to the head. Detectives in Manhattan and Brooklyn came up empty-handed.

Chapter 17

THE FOLLOWING WEEKEND, MARTIN AND Nick met in the study, where they went over the spreadsheet. Under the column headed "Date Testing Discussed," Nick had entered the date of the previous Zoom session next to the names of the five half-sibs that participated. Checkmarks were by their names in the column headed "Wants Testing." Dates for scheduled blood draws were already entered for each.

"Looks good, Son," Martin said. "Very organized. I'm impressed—I'm glad you're running this project."

"It's taking a little longer than I thought it would, but it's worth it. This is a lot more interesting than my regular homework."

"I think it's time we had another Zoom meeting. I'll let you pick out six more names and set it up. I'd like to have it by the end of the week."

"Sure, Dad. You'll be at the meeting, won't you?"

"I'll be at this one, but after that, you'll be on your own."

"Okay. By the way, when will Greg and I get the results of our tests back?"

"It takes about two weeks after your blood is drawn, so it will be about another week. Since everything is being done in a research lab, not a commercial lab, the timing is a little unpredictable. Don't worry, whatever the result, you'll both be fine. You just may need to take the medication, and stay away from activities with a high risk of injury."

The following Wednesday, Martin sat in on the Zoom session Nick arranged. Nick managed to arrange for six half-sibs to attend. Martin was proud of how well his son conducted the meeting. He was also relieved to be able to pass the bulk of the work to him. During the encounter, Martin amused himself by studying the faces of the participants. Two of them had cleft chins like his. Another had a nose bump similar to Oliver's. He took a liking to one of the participants, Andy Miller, when he mentioned both he and his wife were optometrists and owed the success of their marriage to the fact they could see eye to eye.

Several days later, Martin was notified by a technician in Arthur's lab that Greg and Nick had each tested negative for the defective fibrinogen gene. Martin was relieved. They had lucked out. He shared the news with Georgia and each boy as soon as he returned from work that evening.

All were in good spirits around the dinner table. "The bad gene ends with me in this branch of the family," Martin said.

"That's good news about fibrinogen, but I'm sure we inherited a lot of other lousy genes from you and Mom that weren't tested," Greg said.

"Lousy genes, maybe," Martin said, "but probably nothing that will kill you at a young age."

"With that good news, I think I'll take up free climbing," Greg said.

"No you won't," said Georgia. "You won't be doing any free climbing as long as I'm around."

"How's the Facebook page?" Martin inquired.

"Glad you asked. I've set it up and you can start telling people to sign up."

"Got that?" Martin asked, turning to Nick. "You can start telling everyone to sign up for the Facebook page. Only people who are proven to be half-siblings by DNA can join." Turning to Georgia, he asked, "I know you're busy, but have you had any time to look into raising funds for this?"

"It's going to be tough. I wanted to run a public service announcement, but the local stations won't do it. They say it doesn't qualify. To advertise it ourselves would be costly. It would probably make more sense to privately pay for additional tests, rather than run an ad. I'll make a few phone calls to my wealthiest donors and see if I can get them to donate something, but given all the other worthwhile causes out there, I doubt you'll get enough to test everyone."

"I've lined up eight more people to be tested," Nick said. "So far, everyone wants it. I spoke to someone in the lab, and she said there was enough money for just a few more after that. Anyone else who wants the test will have to pay for it themselves, but it's expensive—Forty-five hundred bucks."

"Almost all of the people we've contacted so far have good jobs and are probably comfortable financially," Martin said. "Still, they may not want to pay for the test themselves. There's going to be a lot more half-siblings of mine that will need the test, and if they're positive, their kids will need to be tested, too. I'm still discovering more of these half-sibs as time goes by. There could be two hundred more people that will need to be tested. It could cost a million dollars." He looked at Georgia. "What would you say—"

"Stop right there," Georgia said. "No way are we going to spend our nest egg on this."

"I knew you'd say that. Still, I felt I should ask. Let's revisit that topic if we can't find outside funding."

"Meanwhile," Nick asked, "what do I tell people I contact after the last free testing slot has been taken? At the rate I'm contacting people, that'll be in a day or two."

"Ask your mother," Martin answered.

Nick had learned to avoid pursuing a topic his parents disagreed on and let the subject drop.

Following breakfast the next day, while getting ready for work, Martin started to think about all the half-siblings that had been identified and wondered how much he should get to know them. How obligated should he feel to ensure that everyone who wanted the test was able to get it? Although wary at first, lately Martin had started to think he would enjoy becoming involved in the lives of his long-lost relatives, as he was with family on his mother's side. These newly discovered half-sibs might expand the circle of people his sons could depend on in the future. With a large number of matches, however, it was unlikely that he could develop a meaningful relationship with all of them. He felt closest with those he had met on the first Zoom call, knowing more about them than the rest. Furthermore, he had developed a soft spot for Cat and had decided to check in on her periodically whether or not she tested positive for the gene mutation, to see if she needed help.

Oliver, on the other hand, had validated Martin's concern for relatives seeking to gain financially from their blood connection. Georgia was right. He shouldn't sacrifice their savings—a potential lifeline for their sons—so all these strangers could be tested. Perhaps it would be best if he didn't try to get to know any of them better. Yet he couldn't ignore the fact that they were his blood relatives. Could he really turn his back on them? He decided to check the Facebook page frequently to keep in touch.

When he reached his office, Martin started his routine of checking emails. He usually received a slurry of messages overnight from the administration, companies that wanted his attention, colleagues seeking his opinion about something or the other, and graduate students wanting to meet with him to discuss their data. As he began to answer the emails requiring a response, he thought about his biological father. He had suppressed all thoughts of him in the past, knowing his identity was confidential. Now he wondered if he could find him. Did he want to? What sort of person would intentionally father so many children? Did he have delusions of grandeur, thinking his DNA was so special, he was doing a favor to improving the human race? Did he ever attempt to find any of the children he had fathered? Did he have a clue about his potentially lethal mutation? Had that mutation killed him yet? If not, would he want to meet him?

After fulfilling his obligation to answer emails, he called Dean and got right into the reason for his call. "Can you think of a way I can use all the DNA matching information to find out who my biological father is?"

"I was wondering how long it would take before you asked. Of course, if he'd submitted DNA to one of these genealogy sites himself, he would have popped up as a fifty percent match already. I assume that hasn't happened."

"Precisely. Chances are he already died."

"There is another avenue you can try. It may not find your dad, but it's worth a try. You may have noticed that some individuals post their family tree."

"I noticed that option, but have never looked into it."

"Some people spend a lot of time tracing their relatives back as many generations as they can. They use DNA match information, as well as other information they gather from different sources, such as family history they learn from relatives or, for the more serious ones, archived material they chase down.

"You could look for your father by checking your half-sib's family trees. If someone has it filled out on both the maternal and paternal sides, that person is either very resourceful or is part of the sperm donor's recognized family. If you're lucky enough to find such a person on your list of half-sibs, he or she could lead you right to your dad.

"I'd be careful, though. Some family trees are flat-out inaccurate. Also, be aware that if you do identify a recognized offspring, that person may not have a clue about their father's generosity when it came to sperm banks. In fact, he or she might be somewhat traumatized by learning about it. I suspect, though, if that person has noticed all these twenty-five percent matches, they've already reached out to some of them and know what their dad did."

That evening, when Martin met with Nick in the study, his son was holding his spreadsheet, fidgeting with a pen. He bit his lip as he sat down.

"Something wrong?" Martin asked.

"Yeah. I got an email back from a woman on the list. Actually, the email was from the woman's husband." He paused and shifted in his seat.

"And?"

"He said his wife had died a month ago from a blood clot in her lungs. What should I do?"

"How old was she?"

"Forty."

"That's a real shame. But it's very important. You should find out if she had kids. She probably had the mutation, and her kids could have it. You need to write back so you can order tests if needed."

"I got his phone number but don't know what to say. Could you call?"

Martin sighed but reminded himself Nick was only fifteen years old. He'd have to take care of the difficult discussions himself. "Okay. Leave the information with me and I'll call."

Nick already had the information written on a Post-it note and handed it to his father.

"I'll take care of this," Martin said, "but I need you to ask all the people you contact from now on if they have a genealogical family tree. I'll look for family trees posted on genealogy sites by people who have already been contacted."

Instead of working on a paper he was planning to submit to *The Journal of Organic Chemistry*, Martin called the husband of the deceased woman and determined that they had two teenage children. He'd ask Nick to arrange for their tests the next day. Then he spent several hours exploring the available family trees of the half-siblings Nick had already contacted. It was a dead end—he didn't come across one paternal relative.

Tired and frazzled, Martin noted the time as he walked to the kitchen for a glass of water. Everyone was asleep, leaving the house quiet with the exception of the refrigerator. He sat at the kitchen table, nursing his water while he thought about what to do next. Sure, Nick might come up with the name of someone who could be his father, but realistically, the chances were slim. He had a burning desire now to find out who the man was, not only to learn about his roots but, if still alive, to chastise him for knowingly fathering so many children.

A thought crossed his mind. He remembered considering the possibility for a moment during the first Zoom meeting with his relatives but had forgotten about it. They'd spoken briefly about Oliver's nose, which was similar to that of the ultimate fighter, The Rocket. The following Zoom meeting included another half-sib with the same nose shape. The Rocket was from their little corner of the world. That raised an interesting possibility: The Rocket could be another half-sibling. He might even be the recognized son of the high-volume sperm donor.

It was too late to relax by playing the saxophone without waking the household. Martin didn't sleep well that night.

Chapter 18

THE SOUND OF A TWIG breaking interrupted Wynona's train of thought, taking her away from the images in her head as she tried to capture them in the Word document on her computer screen. The whoosh of the wind outside relaxed her. *No one in their right mind would be walking around outside in this weather.* She felt safe in her bungalow, hidden by the dense trees of the forest in the remote area of Oregon where she was most comfortable. Visitors were not allowed. Even the drivers of delivery vehicles knew to leave their cartons at the end of her long driveway. Occasionally a passer-by would make off with her supplies before she got to them, but it was worth the sacrifice to avoid contact with the outside world.

She walked to the nearest window and peered out. Seeing no signs of life in the moonlight, Wynona returned to her desk and resumed typing. Another sound, perhaps an opossum or raccoon walking over some twigs. Just to be sure, she reached into the desk drawer to her right and pulled out her pistol. Carrying it in her right hand, she walked to another window and peered out. Before she had time to react, the moonlight revealed a dark form, and the glint of a gun pointed at her head, just on the other side of the glass. A single shot rang out, scattering the raccoons nearby. Her novel would remain unfinished for eternity.

Two more people were shot to death on remote properties in rural Oregon and Washington over the following three days. It would be a while before their bodies were found.

Chapter 19

AFTER CHECKING HIS EMAIL AT work, Martin googled The Rocket. He learned the UFC fighter had been born in a nearby town to a middle-class couple. His mom was a paralegal, his dad a social worker. He'd gone to the local public high school and attended community college for a year before dropping out to pursue his ambition of becoming a mixed martial arts athlete. In three years he had earned enough money with a part-time warehouse job to pay for training. Working out incessantly, he slept in his car most of the time. When he started to compete, he earned little or no money for each fight, but soon proved to be a worthy opponent and began to earn enough money in UFC competitions to enjoy a comfortable middle-class life. Along the way, his power and quickness earned him the moniker "The Rocket." Once he was popular enough to win product endorsements, the big bucks started rolling in.

He had an older brother and a younger sister and was close to his siblings and parents, who he helped out financially. Nowhere was there mention of him or his siblings being conceived by a sperm donor. *Doesn't rule it out, though.*

Looking at images of The Rocket, Martin could appreciate the bulbous ski bump at the end of his nose, similar to the two half-sibs he'd met over Zoom. How many people had such a nose? Martin had no idea. Looking at the few pictures he could find of Rocket's parents and siblings, he found no obvious similarities in their appearances. His sister looked Asian and was likely adopted, providing some support for the notion that Rocket's dad might have been unable to father a child.

Martin wondered how he could contact a celebrity like The Rocket. He found the fighter's website and scrolled through it. The fighter's logo, a sleek red rocket with circular streaks around the length, gave the illusion of a spinning rocket. The logo appeared on each page of the website which was full of photos and videos showing some of The Rocket's moves, including his famous Rocket choke and Rocket twister.

Pages listed awards won, the latest being the middleweight championship, which he had defended multiple times. His schedule of future events and the charities he supported, most of which were medically related, were also displayed. An online shop to buy T-shirts, sweatshirts, shorts, and other fan paraphernalia had numerous items for sale, even a bobblehead in his likeness. A link to a site selling tickets to upcoming events was yet another way for his followers to spend their money. Martin had heard of ultimate fighting, and may even have heard of The Rocket, but until then had no inkling what a big business it was.

He finally came to a page where he could fill out a form to contact The Rocket. What would he say? He thought about the best way to word his message. Should he use his own natural language, or would he have a better shot at receiving a reply if he wrote like a fan, using lots of "yos" and "dudes?" He convinced himself that if he tried to sound like an ultimate fighting follower, he'd make an ass of himself. He wrote a note in his natural voice:

Dear The Rocket,

I'm from the Boise area and recently learned that you are too. My biological father was a sperm donor, and I inherited a dangerous mutation from him causing my blood to clot abnormally. I have reason to believe you may be related to me because you are from this area and share some physical characteristics with children of the same sperm donor. I would like to discuss this with you if you are the child of a sperm donor. Knowing how to treat the abnormality caused by the mutation could be lifesaving if you inherited it, too.

Martin left his personal email address at the end of the message. After proofreading the note three times, he pressed the send button. Looking at the time, he realized he'd spent over an hour looking into the popular ultimate fighter. The professor pushed away thoughts of The Rocket and began editing an article for the *Journal of Organic Chemistry*.

Throughout the day, Martin checked the email on his phone. No message from The Rocket. He figured it might be days before The Rocket would see it. He'd have to wait patiently.

That evening at dinner, Martin told his family about his research on The Rocket, the charity work he does, the awards he's received, and the merchandise for sale on his website. They were perplexed at Martin's new interest in ultimate fighting until he mentioned his suspicion that The Rocket might be another long-lost half-sib, and that he'd sent him a message to that effect.

"Dad, that's pretty lame," Greg said. "Someone like The Rocket's never gonna believe you're not some sort of wacko. He'll probably never see the message anyway. Celebrities have people who answer fan mail for them."

"I have an idea," Georgia said.

"I was hoping you would," Martin answered.

"I'm going to be doing an event for Jill next week to raise money for a regional medical center in her district. You mentioned some of the charities The Rocket supports. Since he supports medical causes, it won't seem strange if I contact him about lending assistance to our fundraiser. He probably gets asked to support things all the time.

"You can do that?" Nick asked.

"I have my ways. I'll just reach out to him directly through his publicist. I do things like that often."

"I always knew you were good at what you do," Martin said.

The following afternoon, Martin checked his private email at work and noticed a reply from The Rocket.

Thank you for your interest. I always enjoy hearing from fans. You make all the training I do seem worthwhile. I hope you're taking good care of yourself with exercise and a good diet.

All my best,
The Rocket.

Greg was right. The message he'd sent the day before was answered by a staff member who probably didn't even read it. Surely, The Rocket would never lay eyes on it. He hoped Georgia could work some of her magic and get his attention.

At dinner that evening, Nick was excited. Excited and a bit upset at the same time.

"Oliver Feinberg's test results came back today," he said. He paused while his parents and brother looked his way and gave him their full attention.

Finally, Martin asked, "Well? Aren't you going to tell us what they found?"

"He tested positive."

"Too bad," Martin said. "How did he react when you told him?"

"I haven't told him yet. I guess I didn't think about that part of the study. I just pictured myself giving people the good news that they were negative. I don't want to tell Oliver he's positive."

"You want me to tell him?" Martin asked.

Nick looked down at his plate. "Um, yeah, I'd like that."

"You should have thought about that earlier. You know, roughly half the people tested will be positive." Martin paused, as Nick squirmed in his seat, continuing to look at his plate. "How about you listen while I tell him? Then you can do the next ones."

"Good going, Bozo," Greg said to his brother. "Now Dad has to do your work for you."

"Let's get this over with right after dinner," Martin said.

"Okay."

"Doesn't anyone want to know about my day?" Georgia asked, looking at Martin beseechingly.

"Of course, dear," Martin said. "We're dying to know, aren't we, boys?"

Nick and Greg nodded yes, as they each mumbled, "Sure."

"For starters, I approved the design of a flyer that will be sent to every voter in Jill's district. We barely have enough funds to pay for them, but after they're sent out next week, we should get more money in so I can order lawn signs."

"That's very exciting, Mom," Greg said, faking an exaggerated yawn.

"Oh, and I accomplished one other thing I think is pretty important."

"Don't tell me—you found some high school kids willing to go door to door soliciting votes, so they get school credit for community activity," Greg said.

"Well, no, but that's a good idea. High school kids. They're easy to dupe into doing a lot of free work." She paused for effect before continuing. "I spoke to The Rocket's manager today."

"I knew you could get through to him," Martin exclaimed.

"Her. His manager is a woman."

"Sorry. What did *she* say?"

"She said she'd met The Rocket's father before, and never thought about whether or not he was The Rocket's biological father. They don't look alike, but that's nothing suspicious. She will ask him about it the next time they speak, probably in a few days. She'll also ask him if he'll make an appearance or at least lend his name to the fundraiser Jill's spearheading for the hospital. Healthcare, especially in rural communities, is a key concern of his. He's in training and has no public fights scheduled for close to three weeks, so he could spare some time if he's interested."

"That's promising," Martin said. "If we can get him involved in this fibrinogen problem, that could be a big boost. He could help us raise enough money to get everyone tested."

"If he publicizes this," Nick said, "there's no telling how many more people will get themselves tested at one of the genealogy sites to see if their biological dad is this mega sperm donor. They may know their mom used a sperm bank, or they just may wonder. A bunch more half-sibs may turn up, meaning they'll need to run even more tests."

"Good point," Martin said. "Although it may seem frustrating to have new names turn up continuously, we need to stay focused on what we're trying to accomplish—informing everyone who might be at risk for the mutation so they can be tested. Saving lives is what it's all about."

"You're right, Dad. It's just that I have only so much time before my project is due in school."

"Don't worry about that. You can turn in the results for what you have when it's due. You could still work on the project over the summer to finish everything if you want."

"I'll want to do that."

After dinner, Nick sat next to his father as he dialed Oliver's number. Martin was dreading a phone call with Oliver, not wanting to be hit up again to invest in his company. He put the phone on speaker, and Oliver answered after a few rings. "Hey, Brother, good to hear from you. I was just about to watch *Field of Dreams* for the hundredth time on Netflix. Do you have my test results back, or did you reconsider about investing in my shoe business?"

His worst fear realized, Martin ignored the investment question and answered, "I have your lab results." He reminded Oliver that a positive test only meant he'd have to be treated, and the treatment was effective.

"Sounds like you're preparing me for the bad news."

"I wouldn't put it quite like that, but yes, you do have the mutation. You'll be getting something in the mail in the next few days. It will describe the abnormality in your gene for fibrinogen. You can get in touch with your physician now, or wait until you have the written report. Do you understand?"

"I'm afraid I do. I'm a bit disappointed—I hoped I was negative for the mutation, but I'm thankful that I've been warned about this danger. Now that I think of it, if you hadn't contacted me, I could have a major stroke, maybe even die, any time. I'll get on this right away. Still want to keep in touch, though."

"Sure, we'll be in touch," Martin said. *I'll give you a call the next time I have a few hundred thousand dollars I need to get rid of.* He capped off the evening playing Pink Floyd's "Money" on his saxophone.

Chapter 20

RAQUEL LEFT HER ATTORNEY'S OFFICE in Seattle, optimistic she had a good case. Her boss in the marketing department of Microsoft, a married man twenty years her senior, had been harassing her with unwanted advances and crude innuendos. She had complained to HR, but it had been months, and the harassment continued. Her attorney had sent a formal letter to the Microsoft legal department, and one of their attorneys had spoken to the perpetrator.

He had denied the allegations, so Microsoft legal had backed off. They didn't know that Raquel had documented everything with dates and times and recorded some of the encounters. Her attorney warned her to be careful, as she had seen men like that react with violence. Driving home, Raquel was confident she could defend herself, as she carried a Glock pistol in her car and had another in her home.

She reached the house she shared with her roommate in Issaquah, a suburb of Seattle. As the garage was full of boxes and miscellaneous items the women were storing, Raquel parked in the driveway as usual. It was pitch black out, and Raquel was thankful her roommate had turned on the porch light. As she exited her car, she heard a noise from across the street. Thinking of her attorney's warning, she turned to retrieve her gun from the glove compartment but never reached it. She fell to the ground dead after a bullet shattered the back of her skull.

Two similar murders took place in the following two days, the first in Seattle, the second in nearby Vancouver, British Columbia, Canada. Investigations into the cases quickly went cold.

Chapter 21

MORE FIBRINOGEN GENE TEST RESULTs trickled in the next week. Each evening at dinner, Nick reported on the most recent reports from Arthur's lab.

"Are you finding it easier to talk to the people who are positive?" Martin asked.

"I'm getting used to it. I like giving people good news better, though."

"Understood. That's normal."

"I still have more of your half-sibs to call about getting tested, but there's no more money to do it. I haven't called any new people for a day, waiting for you to tell me what to do."

"From now on when you call people you should tell them they have the option of paying for the test themselves or waiting until we have funding, which could take a long time."

"Before you do that, I have some news that might change things," Georgia said, smiling.

"Did you hear back from The Rocket?" Nick asked.

"I did. He called me himself. Your instincts were right on," Georgia said, looking at Martin. "His biological father was a sperm donor. Now that he knows about the genetic disease he may have inherited, he's very interested in getting the test."

"Damn. Just when the lab ran out of money for testing," Nick said.

"No problem. I told him the funds are depleted and we're working on raising more. He volunteered to pay for the test himself."

"Shouldn't we submit his DNA to one of the ancestry sites first, to see if he's even related?" Nick asked. "He could be the son of a different sperm donor."

"Good thinking, Son," Martin said. "It's true that just because he has a nose similar to other descendants of this donor, he's not necessarily a relative of ours. However, given that he's from this area, it's quite plausible he's part of our group, so I think it makes sense to skip the ancestry sites and go directly to testing for the mutation. Especially since he's not interested in finding his long-lost relatives. It would be best not to delay testing him for the mutation since he could be very helpful with fundraising."

"That's great. I'll arrange for someone to come out and get his blood," Nick said. He paused a minute, and added, "But I don't know how to contact him."

"I'll give you his contact information after dinner," Georgia said. "If he's positive, he'll pay to have his three kids tested."

"I wonder if he's ever been contacted by his biological father," Martin said. "The donor might see a resemblance and want to connect with him since he's rich and famous."

"He never said anything about that, only that he had no interest in connecting with him," Georgia said.

"Could you ask him?" Martin asked. "I'm running out of avenues to identify this mega sperm donor."

"I'll be talking to him in a few days about participating in our fundraiser. He wanted to learn a little more about the proposed hospital and get back to me. I could slip in a question about his biological father then."

After dinner, Martin was looking through family trees on an ancestry website, coming up with nothing helpful, when his cell phone rang. To his surprise, the name Colleen Leopold appeared on his caller ID. *I hope she's not going to hit me up for money. I like her, but that would disappoint me.* He answered.

"This is Cat," the caller said.

"I know."

"Um, you're probably wondering why I'm calling."

"I am." He tried not to sound too cold but was determined to fend off her pleas for money.

"I'm really sorry to bother you, but I didn't know who else to call."

Here it comes. "Is something wrong?"

"The couple I worked for as a nanny—the one where the husband raped me—well, they came to my apartment today."

"They? I thought they got a divorce already."

"To my surprise, they've gotten back together. I'm not sure if they never went through with the divorce, or they got divorced and then remarried, but they're married now. They're all lovey-dovey again. The husband told his wife about Emerald. She believes I seduced him, and thinks Emerald looks just like her perv husband. Fortunately, she doesn't, but that's what his wife kept saying. Now they both want Emerald back and will pay me five thousand dollars to give her up. If I don't, they said they'll make my life miserable. They'll go to court where they're sure to win. They think they'll have no problem proving I'm an unfit mother."

"What did you tell them? Are you going to give Emerald to them?"

"Of course not!" Cat exclaimed. "I would never give her up. Not for a million dollars. I told them that. The woman bent her knees and got close to Emerald. I think she tried to kiss her, but Emerald bit her on the shoulder. Then the woman said she knew where I worked. I don't know how they got my address or found out where I work, but I know they have a lot of connections high up in government and things like that. They said there was no way any judge would let Emerald stay with me once they learned I work at the Exotic Bunny Club."

"I can certainly understand why you're upset," Martin said, "but I don't have any expertise in legal matters."

"I was just hoping you could give me some advice. I need to move so they can't find me, and I'm afraid to go back to my job, cause they could track me down there too. I know you're smart and you know a lot of people. I was wondering if you knew someone who could offer me a job, so I could find a new place to live. I can do anything, but I have to be able to take care of Emerald. Perhaps a childcare job, where I could bring my daughter along. I know the law school at the university provides pro bono legal advice, so

I'm going to contact them. But I need to move ASAP. That's my top concern right now."

"Let me talk to my wife, and I'll get back to you soon," Martin said. He felt conflicted. He had a soft spot for Cat. She seemed so helpless and vulnerable, yet surprisingly resourceful. She hadn't asked him for money—only assistance in landing a job. On the other hand, he didn't want to be taken advantage of or put his family in any danger on the off-chance she was a sophisticated grifter. After all, she'd been around the block a few times.

He found Georgia at the kitchen table, typing on her laptop as she often did after dinner.

"Remember that young woman, Cat, I told you about? The one with the young child?"

"Sure. You said you liked her, and she tested negative for the mutation. Why?"

"She just called me, and it seems she's in trouble. The couple she used to work for visited her today. They're back together and want the girl. Made all sorts of threats. They have her address and know where she works, so she wants to move right away and find a new job. Do you have any ideas?"

"I can tell from that look in your eyes that you want to help her out. You're probably even thinking we should put her up here."

"The thought did cross my mind."

"But you don't know her very well, do you?"

"Only that she's my half-sister, and she's in trouble."

"Tell you what. I'll call Jill. She has connections with the police in her area. I'll see if she can run a background check on Cat. If she comes up clean, she can stay here for a few days. We can set up the large Aerobed in the laundry room for the two of them."

Martin hugged his wife. "I knew you'd know what to do." He wrote down Cat's name, Colleen Leopold, and her age. "Let me know as soon as you hear."

Martin returned to his study to continue the search for his biological father. It was nearly eleven p.m. when Georgia interrupted him. "She checks out," she said. "No criminal record."

"So she can stay here?"

"For a few days. I'll see what I can do about finding her a job and a permanent place to live. She's going to need some legal help too."

"She's already looked into getting pro bono help at the law school."

"She's resourceful. I like that."

"She is related to me, you know."

"I won't hold that against her." Georgia paused. "But seriously, if I detect any suspicious behavior, she'll have to leave."

"Understood. I'll call her now and get that Aerobed pumped up."

"I'll tell the boys."

Georgia told Nick first.

"That's so cool," he said. "She seems really nice. It'll be interesting getting to know someone who's like those people we see on cop shows."

"Right, society's underbelly. Those people are not as glamourous and interesting as they may seem on TV."

"I get that, Mom. It's not like I'm stupid."

"I know that, dear. I hope she turns out to be a wonderful person, but let me know if you notice anything off about her, especially if things go missing."

"Sure," Nick said as he rolled his eyes. "And I'll be sure to tell you if she has an AK-47 or someone's severed head."

After having a similar discussion with Greg, Georgia found Martin in his study. "I think the boys are looking forward to your half-sister's visit. Let's hope for the best."

Cat arrived at their front door after midnight, parking her ten-year-old Ford Fiesta against the curb in front, behind Greg's Toyota Corolla. Carrying her very sleepy daughter, she was pulling a small suitcase, bulging at the seams. Martin was struck by how attractive she was, more so than she had appeared during their zoom session. She was tall and thin, with dark brown hair in a thick braid almost reaching her mid-back. If she could dance at all, he could see why she made a lot of money from tips at her previous job, even though she wasn't particularly well-endowed.

"Thank you so much for letting us stay here," she said quietly, so as not to wake Emerald. "I don't know what would become of us without your help. I'd hate for Emerald to have to live in my car."

"I hope you can get on your feet soon," Georgia said. "Right now it's late and we need to get to sleep. I'll show you where you'll be staying. It's only a small space in the laundry room, but you won't be staying long, I assume."

"I'm sure it will be fine."

Martin grabbed Cat's suitcase and took up the rear as the young mother followed Georgia down the hall. "Here it is," Georgia said when they'd reached the laundry room. "There are sheets, pillows, and towels in the cabinet over here, and the bathroom is down the hall."

"I noticed it," Cat said. "I'll get us set up in a jiffy. We don't want to bother you." She gently put Emerald on the Aerobed, for the first time exposing her face to Martin and Georgia.

"She's adorable," Martin said, meaning every word.

Chapter 22

CAITLIN ENTERED HER CONDOMINIUM, STILL shivering. It was colder than usual at this time of year, even for Minneapolis. Instead of walking, this morning she had taken her car to her job at the Walker Art Center, where she was a curator.

Although the thermostat was set to sixty-eight degrees, she turned on the gas fireplace and stood before it to stop her shivering. Finally warm enough to remove her wool scarf, coat, and knit hat with a pom pom on top, she headed to her kitchen to set up two wine glasses and snacks in preparation for Zach's visit in an hour. Tonight was a night for celebration—she had finally landed that large donation of artwork she'd been working on. She had jumped into action as soon as she heard the wealthy art collector was planning to downsize.

Standing on a stepstool to reach the wine glasses, she smiled as she remembered receiving the signed document that afternoon promising delivery of the items. Her thoughts were interrupted by a slight creaking sound. Had Zach let himself in earlier to surprise her? Before she could turn around to check, a bullet pierced her skull, and she fell to the floor.

Over the next week, three similar homicides took place in the greater Minneapolis-St. Paul area. Several people were suspects, but all were released.

Chapter 23

THE NEXT MORNING ARRIVED TOO soon for Martin. He was in the middle of an intense dream about Cat and Emerald fleeing from an evil man. He was trying to save them, but as often happens in dreams, was never quite able to help them and was in constant grave danger himself. Waking was somewhat of a relief, but he was tired, as was Georgia. When they arrived in the kitchen together, Cat had already made coffee and Emerald was eating a bowl of Cheerios.

"I hope you don't mind," Cat said somewhat sheepishly. "Emerald was hungry, so I went ahead and gave her something for breakfast."

"Of course," Martin said. "While you're here, please help yourself to food. We weren't expecting company, so we'll probably have to go shopping soon. You'll have to tell us what you like and don't like."

"We're not fussy eaters. We try to eat healthy but like pretty much everything. If you want, I could make dinner for you tonight. One thing my mother taught me was how to cook a few things. I have a great chicken recipe."

Georgia and Martin looked at each other and half smiled. "That'd be great," Georgia said. "You could write down what you need, and I'll pick it up later."

"The chicken has to marinate for several hours so I'll get everything needed this morning. If I don't buy too much, I'll be able to use my debit card. . . "

"I won't hear of it," Georgia said. "You'll do me a big favor by doing the shopping." She looked through her wallet, removed some twenty dollar bills, and handed them to Cat. "Luckily I went to the ATM two days ago. Here's eighty dollars. If you could pick up some extra milk and whatever cereal you and Emerald like for breakfast, that would help. Is that enough?"

"That'll be plenty for everything."

"Maybe the boys and I could swing by your apartment to collect your stuff this weekend," Martin said. "Could we take your CR-V, Peaches?"

"No problem. I won't need it Saturday morning."

"We wouldn't be able to take your furniture, but we could bring back most of your other things."

Cat smiled. "That would be awesome. My furniture isn't worth keeping but Emerald is already missing her toys. I still have my key. I'll call the manager and let him know I'm moving out and you'll leave the key. I'm paid up till the end of the month. He can keep my deposit."

"He could send it here," Georgia said.

"I don't want to give him this address. He'd probably give it to my old boss when he comes looking for me, and that would cause you a whole lot of trouble."

Emerald finished eating her breakfast and stood by her mom, who picked her up and held her in her lap. "She's a bit shy," Cat explained, as Emerald buried her head in her mother's chest, "but it usually doesn't take long for her to warm up to new people."

"Well, look at that!" Martin said, staring at Cat's left hand which was holding Emerald.

"Is something wrong?" Cat asked.

"Not at all," Martin answered, smiling and holding up his left hand. "You have the same curved pinky I have."

"Interesting," Cat said. "Must be a family trait."

"We must have gotten it from our father. My mom doesn't have it, but Nick does."

"I've only run across a few other people with the same thing. It's not common. Except in our family, I guess." Cat smiled. "Doesn't bother me at all."

"Me neither," Martin said. "My mom asked the pediatrician about it when I was younger. The technical term is clinodactyly. Sometimes it's associated with other things, but often it's just something of no consequence you can inherit from your parents."

"I didn't know that, but I guess it's further proof that we're related."

"Not that our genetic match isn't enough," Martin replied.

Later that day, as he sat in his office, Martin reflected on his interaction with Cat that morning. He wondered if he was getting too soft, but felt she was a good person who he could trust. She'd just had a difficult life. Her resourcefulness was impressive. He remembered the expression, "I never met a con artist I didn't like." That's why they were successful. Still, he didn't see her as someone who would take advantage of him. She was his half-sister, after all, although she felt more like a daughter to him.

Over the next few days, Martin and his family adjusted favorably to Cat's presence. She was always pleasant and upbeat despite her predicament and insisted on making most of the dinners. With her around, the kitchen was cleaner than normal. As her mother had predicted, Emerald warmed up to the family and was soon entertaining them with her childish antics and constant questions. Greg tried to teach her to play T-ball in the backyard with an old set from his youth he found in the garage, and Nick, who had recently watched *Squid Game*, enjoyed playing red light/green light with her, but with less drastic consequences for mistakes. When the weekend rolled around, Martin and the boys picked up toys, books, clothes, and personal items from Cat's apartment. Emerald was overjoyed to be reunited with her toys.

The following Monday, after meeting with his graduate students, Martin thought about asking Georgia if they should consider allowing Cat to stay with them longer. Sure, their house wasn't set up for a long-term guest, but they could park their cars in the driveway like many of their neighbors, and set the mother and daughter up in the garage. The extra money they spent on food wasn't much but was well worth it considering how much Cat helped around the house. He'd noticed Georgia being more relaxed and energetic since Cat had arrived, as she'd been freed from a lot of the household chores she always insisted on doing herself. He was thinking about how to best approach Georgia with a proposal to let Cat stay, maybe even give her a salary so she could buy clothes and incidentals when his cell rang.

Surprised to see Georgia's name on the caller ID as she rarely called him at work when she was working on a campaign, he answered.

"I wanted to talk to you privately, away from the house," she said.

"Is it about Cat?"

"Yes, how'd you know?"

"I had a feeling." Martin's heart sank, expecting Georgia would order him to send Cat to a homeless shelter that evening.

"I found a job for her today. A volunteer working on Jill's campaign needs a live-in nanny. She's well-to-do and seems very nice. She's married to an older man and is quite attractive, so I don't think Cat would find herself in the same predicament as before. Since the woman lives in the farthest part of Jill's district, she'd be almost two hundred miles away from here, so Cat's previous employer would have a hard time finding her. They'd never accidentally run into her way out there."

With a lump in his throat, Martin said, "It does sound like the ideal job for her."

"I wanted to tell you about it because I'm feeling guilty."

"Why?"

"Because I don't want to tell her about it. You may think I'm crazy, but I've come to appreciate everything Cat does around the house."

Martin's gloom lifted. There was hope.

Georgia continued. "I've been thinking we should perhaps let Cat stay with us permanently, at least several months. I've come to trust her—even like her—and she's been such a help to me. I really enjoy having Emerald around the house, too. What do you think?"

"I couldn't be happier. In fact, I was sitting here thinking about the best way to ask you if you'd consider letting her stay with us longer."

"Wow," Georgia said. "I'm glad we're so on the same page. I think we should pay her something too."

"If you insist." Martin smiled to himself.

"I only wish I hadn't heard about the other job offer."

"Let's tell her about the nanny position, then ask her if she'd like to stay with us instead. You can put your finest spin on our offer. You're good at that."

"I'll give it my best. We should ask the boys what they think first, though. I think they'll be happy about it. I'll talk to Nick about it. You can talk to Greg."

Martin arrived home that evening, anticipating the conversation they'd have with Cat, hoping she'd opt to stay with them. The first thing that met his ears was the sound of small feet running and excited squeals. Nick was playing a high-stakes game of hide-and-seek with Emerald.

After hanging up his jacket and putting his briefcase in his office, he headed down the hall to speak to Greg, but couldn't avoid overhearing a conversation in hushed tones behind the door to Greg's room, a door which was slightly ajar. Cat was telling Greg, "It's weed."

"Yeah, my dad might kill me if he saw me with it."

Martin was seething.

Cat answered, "It can be our secret, then. But I suggest—"

Martin could hardly control his anger. He wanted to burst into the room and throw Cat out immediately. But there was Emerald to consider.

He walked away quietly and sat in the kitchen, waiting for Cat to leave Greg's room. A few minutes later, when Cat joined Emerald and Nick in their game of hide and seek, Martin marched down to Greg's room.

"I heard Cat trying to get you to try some marijuana," he said.

Greg's face turned red. "What are you talking about?"

"Don't play dumb. Half-sister of mine or not, I can't allow someone to stay in my house who's going to try to turn my kids into pot heads.

Greg chuckled. "Were you listening to the conversation I just had with her?"

"Yes. I came to your door with the intention of telling you something, but I couldn't help but overhear your conversation."

"You always tell us not to judge things too quickly. I hate to be the first to tell you Dad—don't kill me, but I've been smoking weed with my friends since I was a high school sophomore."

Martin fell silent and stared at Greg incredulously for a few seconds. "I had no idea."

"Yeah, Dad. I think you've been in a bit of denial. It's not like it's a big deal, though."

"It is to me."

"Well, my grades haven't suffered."

"Yes, you've managed to maintain a mediocre GPA."

"Good enough for what I want to do. Anyway, it's not like I'm gonna start doing heroin or something, and I don't smoke cigarettes or vape tobacco. Me and my friends just like to get together and have fun. I thought Cat was cool, and I invited her to smoke with me, but it turns out she's not as cool as I thought."

"She doesn't smoke marijuana?"

"That's what she said. She told me she wouldn't tell you, but I should stop. Fat chance. So, what did you want to talk to me about?"

The tension that had been building in Martin's shoulders dissipated. Now he was more convinced than ever that Cat would make a great addition to their household. "Your mom and I were thinking about having Cat and Emerald move in more long-term. We could fix up the garage for her and keep the cars on the street."

"Hey, that's a great idea. Even if she's not all that cool."

Martin told Greg of the other job offer but hoped Cat would decide to stay with them.

That night, before shutting off the lights to go to sleep, Martin turned to Georgia. "Do you think Greg has ever tried marijuana?" He wanted to break the news of his discovery gently.

"He smokes it with his friends at least once a week."

"You knew that already?"

"Of course. I didn't want to tell you. I wanted you to find out for yourself. He told me about your conversation earlier."

"What else is going on that I'm ignorant of?"

"Absolutely nothing I can think of. And no, Nick doesn't smoke weed. Not yet, anyway."

"It's illegal. He could get into serious trouble."

"I'm not going to turn him in. Are you?"

"Of course not, but where does he get it from?"

"You know those trips he takes every few months to Huntington, just over the Oregon border?"

"I thought he was visiting someone."

"He is. He's visiting a guy who sells weed. Don't forget you used to like to get high when we were in college."

"That's just because you were a bad influence on me."

Chapter 24

THE SUN WAS STILL LOW IN the sky when Justin checked his watch during his morning jog along the Brushy Creek Trail near his home in Round Rock, Texas. He noted his time was the best yet since he'd broken his leg in a skiing accident during the last trip to Aspen with his buddies. His mind wandered back to his decision to move to Round Rock seven years earlier when he began working at the headquarters of Dell Computers located in this suburb of Austin.

Now that he had a wife and two small children and no longer worked at Dell, he thought this might be a good time to move to a different location if they were ever going to move—before the kids started school. Uprooting them would be more difficult then.

Round Rock was still a desirable place to live, but it was growing quickly, and he worried that the nature of the town would change. With his own successful electronics company in Austin now, and a wife who was an artist and could work anywhere, he thought about other towns in the area they might move to. He started going through a list of possibilities in his head but didn't get far before being struck down by a bullet that smashed through his skull and entered his brain.

Three similar executions took place in the Austin and Houston areas over the next five days. No persons of interest were identified.

Chapter 25

AFTER EMERALD WAS ASLEEP, GEORGIA and Martin met with Cat and told her about the job offer in rural Idaho, as well as their proposal to refurbish the garage so she and Emerald could live there comfortably. The choice was hers.

Cat's eyes teared up. Martin feared she might cry, but she didn't. "Thanks so much," she said. "You've both been so wonderful to me. I don't know what to say."

"Just let us know when you've made up your mind."

The next morning, Martin and the rest of the family were greeted with pancakes for breakfast. Cat was busy flipping them on the griddle while keeping her eye on Emerald. Martin wondered if this was her way of saying thanks for everything, but I'm taking the job two hundred miles away.

Martin's eyes met Georgia's as they silently communicated their uncertainty. When all were seated at the table, Cat spoke.

"I hope you all like pancakes."

"We do," was the reply from all whose mouth wasn't full at the moment.

"I've really enjoyed living here and getting to know all of you," Cat continued.

Here it comes. Thanks so much, but I'm going to take the other job.

"Being with all of you has made me appreciate more than ever the value of family. I know we're not really close. I'm only a half-sister to Martin and a half-aunt to Greg and Nick, but you're the only family I have now. The other job sounds good—really good—and I thank you for that. But you're family, and I'd rather stay with you, if that's still okay."

Martin let out a deep breath. "Of course, it's still okay. We'll get busy and clean out the garage. Then we'll order you some beds and other furniture."

"If you move the cars out, I can start cleaning it today. Emerald and I just need one double bed. We're used to sleeping together. I'm really excited."

"So are we," Georgia said.

That evening, Martin and the boys went through all the boxes in the garage and sorted everything into piles to be disposed of, taken to Goodwill, or distributed to various closets and shelves in the house. Cat and Emerald slept in the garage on the Aerobed for the first time.

The following day, Martin woke up with a smile. Things were falling into place. True, he hadn't made progress in finding his biological father, but Nick was doing better than expected overseeing the half-sibling project. Despite devoting a lot of time looking into his family tree, Martin's research and related activities at the university were going well. Cat and Emerald would be staying to help out and provide that intangible warmth provided by family. He'd already accepted the fact that his elder son smoked marijuana and had been doing so for a while.

At dinner, Georgia smiled as she delivered more good news. "I found out today that The Rocket will not only participate in the hospital fundraiser, he's also going to pay to test all the relatives who need it in the future."

"That's wonderful," Martin said. His expression suddenly changed to one of alarm. "Hey," he shouted as he scooted his chair back. "What was that?" He looked under the table only to see Emerald, who had quietly slithered to the floor and was now poking his ankle. Martin laughed as he picked Emerald up and sat her on his lap.

"Did Emerald poke you?" Cat asked, her face turning red.

"Sure did. No big deal, but it caught me by surprise."

"I'm so sorry. She did that to me a lot at home. I guess she feels comfortable here now, so she wants to poke all of you." Cat turned to Emerald and admonished her gently.

"Nick used to tie our shoelaces together under the table," Martin said. "Although it irritated me at the time, now that the boys are grown up—sort of—I find those types of antics refreshing."

"She can poke my ankles all she wants," Nick said. "Considering all the things I did when I was her age, I can't complain. About The Rocket paying for the testing—that's a load off my mind. I can't wait to tell everyone who's been waiting to get tested. It'll make it easier for me to speak to the half-sibs I haven't contacted yet."

"The Facebook page is very popular amongst my half-sibs," Martin said. "I check it every few days. Sometimes even post something myself."

"You're welcome," Greg said, drawing Martin's attention to the fact that he hadn't thanked his eldest son.

After an uncomfortable delay, Martin muttered "Thanks, Greg."

Saturday arrived, and Georgia went shopping with Cat and Emerald. She ordered furniture and purchased sheets, towels, a princess bedspread selected by Emerald, a full-length mirror, toys, and clothes for the child and young mother.

By the time they returned to the house, Martin was directing two men on where to set up the bed they were delivering.

"I don't remember the last time I had so much fun," Georgia confided to Martin.

"I might take that as an insult. I thought you had a pretty good time last night."

"I already forgot."

"No problem. I'll refresh your memory tonight."

Georgia smiled.

The rest of the weekend was spent setting up the garage. The desk and sofa Georgia had ordered hadn't arrived yet, but there was still plenty to do with what they had already. Conveniently, the laundry room and a half bathroom were located near the garage. Cat and Emerald would need to share the boys' bathroom for showering, but they planned to do that in the mornings after Nick and Greg had gone to school. Emerald made fast friends with a boy her age who lived up the street.

Sunday evening, after Martin and Georgia had retired to their bedroom, Martin commented, "It's hard for me to think of Cat as my sister—she seems more like a long-lost daughter. And Emerald seems like a grandchild."

"This is good practice for us, for when Greg or Nick have kids."

"We should try to practice not to spoil Emerald."

"That'll be tough."

Monday morning was the usual lively event, only with a little more energy than usual. Cat was especially cheery as she refilled Martin's and Georgia's coffee cups.

"You don't need to do that, Cat," Georgia said. "Why don't you sit and have breakfast with us? You're family. We appreciate you helping out, but this isn't a Downton Abby type of situation. We're all equals. All equally trying to make our way in this crazy world."

"I enjoy helping," Cat said. "But this morning I have an ulterior motive."

"What's that?" Martin asked.

"I was going to ask you for a ride to the university because I don't trust my car to drive that distance. I'm getting it serviced tomorrow, but today I have a meeting with a law student about my situation with Emerald. We can take an Uber back."

"All you had to do was ask," Martin said. "I'd be happy to take you."

"I don't know how much a law student is going to help you," Georgia said. "I'll ask Jill if there is a lawyer on staff who knows of a good family law attorney."

"I can't pay for that."

"Let's not worry about that now. Meanwhile, go ahead and keep your appointment."

Martin drove Emerald and Cat to the University and parked in his reserved spot. He pointed out the direction of the law school and proceeded to his office.

That evening, over a dinner of lasagna and salad prepared by Cat, Martin noticed Nick being unusually quiet. Even more disturbing, he hardly touched his food. A growing teen, he usually ate more than everyone else except Greg.

"Something bothering you, Nick?" Martin asked. "You're not eating much. Don't you feel well?"

"I just had some bad news today."

"Sorry to hear that," Georgia said. "You should have said something earlier. Was there a problem at school?"

"No. It's this project. I found out that another relative died recently. His name was Kurt Slocum."

"There's a lot of people who might have this bad gene," Martin said. "Now there's two people we know of who recently died from the mutation. Others may have already died, and there may be more out there who we'll never find through genealogy sites, since most people don't participate in them."

"That's all true, Dad, but this person I just found out about today didn't die from the mutation. He was murdered."

The table grew silent, as all eyes were on Nick.

"What happened?" Greg asked.

"He was killed in front of his house while he was in his car. Shot in the back of the head."

"Geez," Cat said. "Let's talk about this later." As she spoke, she eyed Emerald excessively, indicating the ensuing conversation would not be suitable for her delicate ears.

"Got it," Nick said.

"On a more pleasant note," Georgia said, smiling, "I got the name of an excellent family law attorney today. Tomorrow I'll give her a call and see if she can help Cat."

"Thanks so much," Cat replied. "The law student I saw today wasn't a whole lot of help. He said I might be able to maintain custody of Emerald, but since I never filed a police report against my employer, and they have a lot of money, it would be a difficult fight for me. Hiding from them will work for a while, but it is likely they will hire a detective, and I'll be found."

"Why do you need a lawyer, Mommy?" Emerald asked.

"There are some people who are trying to cause a problem for me, sweetie."

"You mean those bad people who came to our apartment?"

"Yes."

"I didn't like them."

"Don't worry, honey. We're safe here."

Emerald smiled and finished her dinner.

After Emerald was asleep, Nick met with his parents to discuss the latest death around the kitchen table. Greg, always interested in a story about murder, joined them.

"Kurt lived in Greenwood Village, which is a suburb of Denver. The police have no idea who did it," Nick said. "It seemed like a random shooting. Nothing was stolen. The man was an engineer who worked at a big mining company. He had a wife and two young kids. No known enemies. It happened about a month ago and the wife just emailed me about it."

"I'll get in touch with the wife," Martin said. "Those kids need to be tested. I don't want you to have to deal with a grieving widow, Nick."

"Thanks, Dad."

"There's something else I've been thinking about that we need to consider with this study. We really need to expand our search for all the kids this super donor fathered. Our approach isn't going to cut it. A lot of people will be overlooked. I'm going to hire an attorney to contact the sperm banks in the area and ask them to turn over the name of my sperm donor. Once we have that, we can ask the banks for a list of the other children he fathered."

"Can't you just get that information yourself, Dad?" Greg asked.

"There are three sperm banks within fifty miles of here. I called each one, but none would divulge any information. There are laws against that, and they are adamant about protecting the identity of their donors. I explained that my mother was never given the name of the sperm bank used, or the donor number, and lives are at stake because of his genetic condition, but they wouldn't budge."

"Maybe the attorney I found for Cat can help with that," Georgia said.

"Good idea, I'll ask her. The laws are pretty strict about protecting donors, but I'm hoping that a lawyer might strike some fear into the sperm bank administrators for being so lax and allowing the donor to father so many children. Once I get his name, the lawyer should be able to get a list of all his progeny from sperm banks in the area."

A few days later, Cat and Martin were contacted by a junior lawyer from the law firm Jill had referred Cat to. Each explained their individual predicaments in great detail so the main attorney could analyze their cases. The following Monday, Martin and Cat walked into the toney law offices of Constance Jackson and were greeted by the cheerful receptionist, who offered coffee.

Cat and Martin each opted for a cup of black coffee, which was served quickly. As they sipped, they had a chance to look around the office, tastefully decorated with watercolor paintings and objects d'art. The receptionist appeared busy typing on her computer and answering phone calls. Ten minutes later a smartly dressed woman around fifty years old, with gray hair and a no-nonsense look, appeared from the hallway with an outstretched hand.

"Dr. Starling and Ms. Leopold, I'm Constance. Pleased to meet both of you," she said as she shook their hands. "Why don't we go to my office where we can discuss your issues."

They followed Constance past several closed doors and a small conference room, into an office decorated in similar colors and style to the reception area. A large desk with a solid front faced the door, and two comfortable chairs stood opposite. Adjacent was a small couch. Martin and Cat each sat in a chair.

"Thank you for seeing us on such short notice," Martin said.

"Jill insisted, so I made room. Jill and I go way back. Despite some of her crazy progressive ideas, I'm still very fond of her. She's like a sister. I've had a chance to look into both or your cases. Colleen, let's start with you."

"Please call me Cat."

"Okay, Cat. Your situation is hardly unique. I myself have had at least a dozen similar cases over the years. Of course, there are always differences when you get down to the details."

"I really couldn't bear it if they took Emerald from me."

"I understand. I'm a mother too. Since the couple involved hasn't taken any formal legal action yet, we don't have any complaints to answer at the moment."

"But if they find me, I'm sure they'll hire an attorney to get Emerald."

"Most likely. I didn't mean we shouldn't do anything. Now is the time to get research done and prepare for them to make the first move. From what I know, you're in a fairly good position."

"Oh?" Cat said, smiling.

"I have a pretty good instinct about these things. Often, people with money threaten those without the same resources, hoping to bully them into cooperation. Or, they hire a lawyer to attempt to railroad an adversary who doesn't have funds to mount a good legal defense. You don't fall into either of these categories because you have me, and I'll make sure you have a strong defense against any of their attacks."

"I don't have much money."

"Don't worry. I'll take your case pro bono. That means I won't charge you."

Cat smiled. "OMG! That's so awesome. I feel guilty, having your help without paying you, but since it's for Emerald's good, I will gratefully accept your services."

"Spoken like a loving mother. Fortunately, your case should be easy to win if they ever do file papers to take custody of your daughter. Your previous employers were divorced a few years ago, and I was able to get a transcript of their court documents. The wife accused her husband of forcing himself on you and testified she had seen your bruises. Unless she wants to be charged with perjury, she won't be in a position to recant that testimony. In addition, the husband has been accused of making unwanted advances and manhandling three women at work. Once I bring this to their attention, I doubt they will pursue custody."

"But what if they do? They seemed pretty determined."

"They'll lose in court. It will take more of my time, but this is a straightforward case, and there is little chance they will prevail. No competent attorney would let his or her clients pursue such a case. Especially high-profile clients like them. Their reputations would be ruined."

Cat let out a sigh of release. "I can't tell you how worried I've been. Now I feel so much better."

"Glad to be of help." Constance turned to Martin. "Your case is a bit more complicated, with some unique aspects."

"I was afraid of that."

"That's not to say I don't have some ideas."

"I was hoping you would." Martin listened intently as Constance continued.

"As I understand it, you are not so much interested in learning the identity of your biological father as you are in learning the identity of the other children he fathered."

"That's true. Although I am curious to know something about the man whose DNA I'm carrying around, the identity of all his offspring is a much higher priority."

"Most people in cases like this, where a party wants to learn about their biological parents when those records have been sealed, are dissuaded when they talk with the agencies involved in their adoption or insemination. However, when those parties hire an attorney and petition the court, each case is treated individually. The outcome depends on the approach of the attorney, as well as the disposition of the judge involved."

Martin shifted in his seat. "Are you saying it's a bit of a crapshoot?"

"It can be. I would suggest pursuing an avenue where the sperm banks may be more likely to cooperate. I'd start by asking the banks if they have a record of supplying a specimen to your mother's doctor. They shouldn't have a problem with that, as sperm banks have no obligation to hide the identity of physicians who have used them. I can have someone on my staff inquire at all the local banks and those within a hundred miles. There aren't many. It may be that we find donations arranged by this doctor at only a single sperm bank, since they usually only use one. Then we'll have only one sperm bank to deal with."

"Makes sense."

"We'll ask that bank to check if your mother is listed as a recipient of one of the samples received by that doctor. I imagine she will be. She may need to sign a document giving the sperm bank permission to disclose that information. Will she do that?"

"I'm sure she would."

"Great. This shouldn't take long. Once we identify the sperm bank involved in your conception, we will suss out how cooperative they are in identifying the sperm donor after receiving a letter from my law offices. Sometimes these entities capitulate without a fight. Let's hope that happens in this case. If not, we can start legal proceedings. If we fail to identify the donor that way, we can try to identify him at another facility assuming the mother of one of your half-sibs will sign a release form."

"I can start looking into that now. I would bet I'll be able to find others in our group whose mother will cooperate."

"Okay. I'll have a letter typed up this afternoon for your mother to sign. Please leave her address with the receptionist, and tell her to expect the letter soon. The faster she gets it back to us, the quicker we'll be able to approach the sperm banks. I'll notify you after we've located the facility used by your mother's physician, and find out how they respond to our initial letter."

After shaking hands again, Martin felt buoyed by his meeting with Constance. On the way out, he left his mother's address with the receptionist and called his mom to alert her to the importance of signing and returning the letter she'd be getting soon.

Chapter 26

LOIS PUNCHED HER TIMECARD AND exited the pizza joint through the back door to enter the parking lot. Sitting in the driver's seat of her Hyundai Elantra, she took a moment to massage her feet. *Eight hours on my feet. I don't know how much longer I can do this.*

She slipped the key into the ignition and started the engine. As usual, she berated herself during the twenty-minute drive to her parents' house. How could she have fallen so far? Thirty-seven years old, and the only place she could afford to live was the house she grew up in outside of Boise.

Lois told herself she should have appreciated the fat job she landed after college, writing code for a startup company, a company now worth over three hundred million dollars. She would have had stock worth oodles by now. Instead, she started using coke, then meth. Losing her job due to poor performance should have been a wake-up call. Instead, that call didn't come until she'd been sentenced to five years in prison for grand larceny and possession of a controlled substance. At the time, she was focused on getting money from the jewelry heist she and her then-boyfriend tried to pull off so they could score more meth. What she really needed was to get clean. How could she have been so stupid?

Prison had straightened her out, all right, and she was thankful her parents hired an expensive attorney to get her released after serving only two years. But now, even with a degree in computer science from Northwestern, her criminal record rendered her essentially unemployable. The only jobs open to her were the ones nobody with other options would take. If only someone in the computer programming business would give her a second chance.

It was dark by the time Lois arrived home. She parked on the curb in front of the house and reached for the door handle. Her last thoughts were of starting her own software company before a bullet struck the back of her head, and she crumpled against the door.

Four more people in the greater Boise area were murdered by a single bullet in the head over the following week. The area's most experienced homicide detective, Bradly Hunter, was assigned to lead the investigation.

Chapter 27

SEVERAL UNEVENTFUL DAYS WENT BY. More lab results came in, which Nick added to his spreadsheet. The fifty-fifty distribution of the fibrinogen mutation held firm.

When Martin arrived home the following Wednesday, Nick met him in the entryway as soon as he entered the house. Distress was written all over his face.

"What's up, Nick?" Martin asked.

"I got The Rocket's results today."

"I take it from the look on your face it's not good news."

"Right. He tested positive. I don't want to be the one to tell him."

"I understand. I'll have your mother call and ask him to call me."

"This is a big deal. He'll have to quit fighting if he takes the medicine."

"True. This will be life-changing for him. If he's a smart guy, though, he will have realized a while ago he won't be able to fight forever. He's already close to forty years old. Hopefully, he's already considered what he's going to do after he can no longer win fights, or he's injured too badly to compete. That day will just be arriving sooner than expected."

"And his kids. Don't forget to ask if he wants his kids tested."

"Of course." Martin smiled, reflecting on how vested his son was in the project, taking the lead in ensuring all the half-sibs were appropriately tested and notified.

The call from The Rocket came the next morning, while Martin was in his office. Georgia had given him The Rocket's number, so he identified the caller when he checked the caller ID. He'd never considered himself any sort of fan, but Martin's stomach tensed. Deep in his subconscious, he must have been intimidated, if only slightly, at the thought of speaking to a celebrity.

"Mr. Rocket?" Martin said upon pressing the answer icon.

A slight chuckle at the other end was followed by "Name's Elmer. You can call me that. The Rocket is just my professional name."

"I figured you hadn't been named Rocket at birth. I just didn't have another name for you."

"My parents had a sense of humor, or so they believed. Our last name was Fudge, so they thought it would be funny to name me so my full name sounded like Elmer Fudd. As I was growing up, I failed to see the humor, although many of my schoolmates did. But that's water under the bridge." Rocket paused before continuing. "I suppose you know why I'm calling."

"I do. I'm afraid you tested positive. You have the mutation."

After an awkward silence, Rocket spoke. "I was afraid of that. I had an injury a few years ago. I broke my left radius—one of the bones in my arm—or, more accurately, someone broke it for me. The doctors told me I had some abnormal clotting around the fracture, and they had to go in and clean it out so it would heal properly. They didn't seem to think much of it at the time, but when I heard I might have a mutation that could cause abnormal clotting, I thought it was likely I had it."

"I'm not a doctor, but that makes sense to me. Your physician will likely recommend you take a blood thinner."

"I know, and she'll probably tell me I need to find another line of work. She tells me that all the time anyway."

"The way I see it, it's just a question of time before you'd have to give up fighting. It's a young man's sport."

"A foolish young man's sport, to be more accurate."

Martin laughed. "It's not something I would do even if I were twenty years younger, but it looks like it's worked out pretty well for you up to now."

"Can't complain. But I'm not crazy. I've been thinking about the next chapter in my life. One thing I've toyed with is becoming a motivational speaker, stressing a healthy diet, exercise, and good health care. I might start by writing a memoir. I've been approached about running for congress, but I don't think I have the stomach for that. I'm sure I'd be tempted to bash in a few heads in my first week if I were elected. Whatever I decide, I'll need to be on that medication you take. I also need to get my kids to be tested. I have three—a boy and two girls."

"How old are they?"

"They're between six and ten."

"They're young, so they're not at risk for a clot now. No one seems to know exactly when the risk goes up, but probably between the teenage years and my age when I had the stroke, forty-three."

"Talking to you, I feel motivated to get more involved with your effort to notify all who might be impacted by this gene. Since I've had an interest in health for many years—after all, my success has required me to be as fit as possible—and I'm a well-known person affected by this gene, it makes sense that I take an active role in getting people tested. I already told your wife I'd pay for everyone who needs to get the test."

"She told me and we're very appreciative of your generosity. If you're serious about becoming a motivational speaker for people interested in pursuing a healthier lifestyle, this might be a good way to get your foot planted squarely in the door."

"I was thinking about that too."

"It would be fantastic to have you actively involved in identifying all those at risk. Why don't you think about it, and get back to me? Let me know what you'd be interested in doing."

"I don't need to think about it. In my line of work, I need to make split-second decisions. I'd like to help."

"In addition to finding my half-siblings through DNA, we're working on identifying the sperm donor now. I know the doctor who arranged for my mother's pregnancy died, and I'm told his records were destroyed. I've hired a very good lawyer to try to find out which sperm bank handled the transaction."

"You need to know a lot more than just which sperm bank was involved."

"I know. My attorney suggested starting with identifying the sperm bank and going from there. This may take quite a while. A lot depends on the judges who will ultimately make rulings."

"I understand. Confidentiality agreements can really hold things up. Tell you what. I'll pay the attorney's fee, and if you need to hire a private investigator, I'll pay for that too. In the meantime, I can hold some rallies and give talks to raise awareness in the general population. I'm sure there are people affected who, like me, never had their DNA analyzed at one of those genealogy sites."

"Precisely. There may be distant relatives of the sperm donor who have it—after all, he got it from an ancestor unless it started with him. Many people have abnormal blood clots, so unless there is a clear familial inheritance pattern, they'll never know the reason."

"Being able to warn people before they have a serious problem will be big," The Rocket said.

"I'll talk to Georgia about pairing you with her candidate so you can speak at her rallies. But you should have rallies of your own."

"I'll talk to my PR lead about that. First, I'll have to announce my retirement from fighting and talk to my physician about the best treatment for me."

"You're not wasting any time."

"I'm usually on a pretty tight schedule. My people are used to that."

Chapter 28

MARTIN WAS ANIMATED AT DINNER that night, talking about his earlier conversation with The Rocket. "He's going to change everything," Martin said. "He's going to help me find more relatives at risk. Talking to him wasn't anything like what I expected. He's very friendly and easy to talk to. Even sounds intelligent."

"What did you expect?" Georgia asked.

"I thought he might sound like some sort of barbarian. You know, a lot of grunting noises."

Georgia laughed. "You probably learned what his real name is."

"That's right. Elmer Fudge."

The boys looked up, stunned expressions on their faces. "You've got to be kidding," Greg said.

"Does that sound like something I could make up?"

"Guess not."

"I'm sure Jill will be happy to include The Rocket in as many of her rallies as he wants to participate in," Georgia said. "He really draws in the crowds."

"I hate to be the bearer of bad news," Nick said, "but I found out something disturbing today."

"Oh?" said Martin. "Something about the study?"

"Yeah. A few weeks ago I contacted another half- sibling, but she never wrote me back. I sent a follow-up email and just heard back from her mother."

"Another death from a clot?" Martin asked.

"Another death," Nick answered. "But not from a clot. The woman was murdered. Shot while in her car in front of her house. Shot in the head, to be specific. There are no suspects."

"That sounds similar to the previous murder," Greg said. "Remember? The guy that was shot inside his car in front of his house. I wonder if these murders could be related in some way."

"I was wondering about that myself," Nick said. "I thought if I mentioned it, you might think I'm crazy."

Martin remained silent as the muscles in his chest tightened.

"Let's talk about this after dinner," Georgia said, eyeing Emerald who seemed oblivious as she played with a doll.

After dinner, Martin, Georgia, and the boys gathered in the living room.

"What do you know about this?" Martin asked Nick. "Do you know where she was, or if there are there any suspects?"

"I didn't ask, but this one's local. She lived outside of Boise. I looked for some information online, but didn't find any more details." Nick paused before continuing. "Are you in danger, Dad?" he asked. "Maybe someone is going down the list of all the half-sibs and killing them. Someone else could have a list just like mine."

"Even if someone had the names of all my half-sibs who appear on genealogy sites, they wouldn't have their addresses," Martin said. "The sites don't make that information public. It's not even on our private Facebook page. Your computer is the only place where the addresses are stored. Remember, we contacted the people on my list, and only got their addresses after talking to them. Nobody's contacted me to get our address. Other than Cat, of course."

"I hate to break this to you, Dad, but there are other ways to get addresses," Greg said. "Still, I agree. It's pretty far-fetched to think someone is trying to knock off everyone who's in this half-sib group. What would be the purpose? Anyway, the chances anyone in this family would be next are pretty slim, as there's a whole lot of half-sibs and only two people have been murdered."

Martin turned to Nick. "Give me the name of the local victim and the town she lived in. I'll follow up. It's probably just a coincidence, but it's possible the two victims knew each other. They could have become acquainted a while ago through the genealogy sites they used. If the murders are related, the local police shouldn't be treating them as isolated events."

Before retiring for the night, Martin played "Smooth Operator" on his sax, hoping to cast off some of his concern. It didn't work. He could have brushed off two home robberies where murders had taken place. But two people shot in the head while sitting in their cars outside their homes? He hardly slept that night.

The following day, Martin called the police department of the town the recent murder took place in. He'd never been to the small city but knew it was an upper middle-class area twenty-five miles away. He gave his name and said he was seeking information on the murder of Lois Bishop. His query was answered with, "Let me transfer you."

After a series of beeps, a man with a gruff voice answered. "Detective Hunter here. I understand you are asking about the murder of Lois Bishop."

"That's right. Do you have a suspect? Is there anything you can tell me about the investigation?"

"Are you a relative?"

"I'm her half-brother."

"When did you last see your half-sister?"

"I haven't actually met her. I only know about her through a genealogy site."

After a short silence, the detective said, "I'd like to talk to you. Can you come down to the station?"

Martin was taken aback by the question but wanted to find out what he could. "When would you like me to come?"

"How about now?"

"I have a busy day planned, but I could move things around. How would three thirty work for you?"

"That'll be just fine." Detective Hunter gave Martin the address of the station, then added, "I'll see you then. Ask for me."

Something about Hunter's voice bothered Martin. He sounded friendly enough, but the friendliness seemed forced. *Probably my imagination.* The rest of the day dragged on for Martin, who was anticipating what he might find out about the murder. He imagined the police had a lot of information. After all, he was invited to visit the station. There was probably so much evidence, including pictures and/or diagrams, it couldn't all be explained over the phone. Foremost on his mind was the possibility the two murders of half-sibs were related. He hoped there was no basis for such a concern. Martin arrived at the police station two minutes early. His heart was racing as he walked up to the receptionist and asked for Detective Hunter.

Soon, a heavy-set man with salt-and-pepper hair dressed in blue pants, a white shirt, and a black tie appeared. "Mr. Starling, I presume," he said. His expressionless face left Martin feeling a bit uneasy.

"That's me," Martin answered.

"Shall we go into one of our quiet rooms for privacy?" the detective asked.

"Sure," Martin said. His discomfort increased as the officer ushered him into a small, unwelcoming interrogation room. Four uncomfortable-looking chairs were arranged around a beat-up rectangular wooden table. Cameras were mounted on two corners of the ceiling, and electronic equipment was secured to the middle of the table.

"Have a seat," Hunter said, gesturing towards the chairs as he closed the door.

Hearing the click of the latch made Martin even edgier. He tried to stay calm by asking himself what he had expected. Did he think the detective would take him to a coffee shop or a picnic table? Of course not. Maybe an informal discussion across the desk. That wouldn't have afforded them any privacy. This was probably just standard procedure. He took the seat nearest the door. Not that it made any difference—he knew that if Hunter wanted to detain him for some reason, there would be no escape. Not from a police station.

"You don't mind if I record our conversation, do you?" the detective asked as he reached for the recording apparatus.

"No problem," Martin said, simultaneous with Hunter pressing the record switch to the on position. *What have I stepped into?*

"Can I get you something to drink?" Hunter asked, a fake smile on his face as his eyes appeared to study the professor from head to toe.

Martin thought Hunter was trying to appear friendly, but the detective's demeanor did nothing to set his mind at ease. "Some water would be nice."

Hunter disappeared momentarily and returned with two water bottles. He handed one to Martin, then wasted no time in getting the interview started.

"You say you are the half-brother of Lois Bishop. Is that correct?"

"Yes, but I only recently found out about Lois—"

"And you'd never met her before. Is that right?"

"Right. I only recently found out we were related and hadn't had a chance—"

"Did you read about her murder in the newspaper?"

"No, I only found out recently through my son. He—"

"How old is your son?"

"He's fifteen."

"What's his name?"

"Nick. Nicholas Starling." Martin felt sweat starting to trickle down his forehead. The last thing he wanted to do was focus attention on his son. He would need to tread carefully with this detective, who appeared impatient, perhaps because he was suspicious about his, or perhaps even his son's, involvement. He cleared his throat before saying, "I don't see how this has anything to do with answering my question about the investigation."

"I'd say you're about six feet, or six feet one."

"Six feet."

"And your son? How tall is he?"

"He's still growing, of course. I'd say he's about five-eight. What does that matter?"

"How did Nick learn about Lois's murder?"

"He was trying to contact her when—"

"So Nick learned Lois was your half-sister and tried to contact her for some reason. Is that correct?"

"Technically, what you're saying is true, but please allow me to elaborate. I recently discovered I have a lot of half-siblings I didn't know about before. My son, at my request, tried to contact them and in doing so, learned Lois had been murdered. I'm wondering if you have any suspects or a motive. We recently learned that another half-sibling who lives in Colorado was also shot and killed. I know this may sound far-fetched, but we're wondering if the murders are related and if other half-siblings are in danger."

"As far as we know, the murder of Lois Bishop is an isolated event."

"What about suspects?"

"Can't say, but I anticipate we'll be able to solve this case before long. Before I forget, I want to ask you about your car. Is that your black Audi in the parking lot?"

"Yes, it is," Martin answered, feeling somewhat confused.

"How do you like it? I'm looking to buy a new car myself."

"So far, it's been okay. Had a little trouble with the electrical system, but got that fixed."

"Do you have any other cars?"

"My older son drives a junker, a 2005 Toyota Corolla, and my wife drives a Honda CR-V. It's been a very reliable, comfortable car."

"You don't say. I've been seriously considering getting one of those myself. A silver one."

"That's the color she drives. I don't think you can go wrong with a CR-V, if it's the right size for you."

"Thanks," Hunter said. "You mentioned an older son. How old is he?"

"Greg is seventeen. I'm not sure—"

"How tall is Greg?" Hunter's tone was flat.

"He's about my height." Martin was baffled by the direction the interview was going. Hunter's lack of expression gave no hint about what he was thinking.

The detective's questions continued. "Do you have any guns in your house?"

"Just a single pistol." Martin thought he detected a slight change in the detective's expression, as if he'd said something to pique his interest.

"Do you know how to shoot it?"

"Sure. I've used it at the local gun range a few times. I haven't done that for several years though, now."

"How's your aim?"

Martin chuckled nervously. "Pretty good, actually. I guess I'm a natural."

"Oh?" the detective looked at him expectantly, as if waiting for Martin to continue.

"My dad used to take me with him when he went hunting. I was really close to him, so I enjoyed going, but I never took to hunting the way he did. When I was twelve, he handed me a rifle and told me to shoot a rabbit about thirty feet away. I aimed at the rabbit's eye. The bullet went right through its eye and he died. I hadn't been prepared for that. Not killing an animal. Took me a while to get over it. I continued to go on hunting trips with my dad, but never hunted myself after that."

"How about your kids? Do you ever take them for target practice or hunting?"

"They've never shot a gun. I don't like guns but keep one for protection. Frankly, I'm not sure if I'd be able to use it if someone broke into our house. I keep the thing locked up where the kids can't get to it."

"Where is the key?"

"I have it hidden in my bedroom. Under the mattress."

"Excellent hiding place. I'm sure no teenager could possibly find such a well-hidden key." Sarcasm dripped from every word. Hunter excused himself and left the room, closing the door behind him.

Sweat streamed down Martin's forehead as he waited for Hunter to return. Although he was gone for only a few minutes, it seemed like an eternity. When the detective finally returned, Martin said, "Look, I came here just wanting information about the murders of my half-siblings, and to find out if the police had thought the murders might be connected, especially since the victims were related by blood. I wasn't expecting to be interrogated like my sons or I were suspects. If you're not going to answer my question, I'll leave."

"I'm afraid I can't let you do that."

Martin's shoulders tightened. "You're going to arrest me?"

"You're not under arrest, but I will detain you, at least until officers can get to your home to inspect your weapon."

"Do I need to call my lawyer?"

"That's up to you. Depending on how guilty you or your son is, you might want to. Officers are on their way to your place right now. If your gun doesn't match the caliber of the bullet that shot Lois Bishop or anyone else, we'll have to let you go. But that doesn't mean you're innocent."

Did I hear him correctly? Did he say, "anyone else?" Martin's eyes jumped from the detective to the door, back to the detective. "Don't you need a warrant?"

"They got an emergency warrant."

"You said 'anyone else'. What did you mean by that?"

"What do you think it means?"

"Have there been others murdered by the same person?"

"What do you think?"

Martin was now less frightened, and more irritated by the detective's game of answering questions with another question. If there were multiple murders committed by the same person, there was no way he or his children could be suspected. They had no motive, and most likely had solid alibis.

"I don't know what to think, frankly. Neither me nor my sons had anything to do with any murders. I'm just trying to find out about my murdered half-siblings and find out if there are any suspects or known motives."

An officer tapped on the window in the door to the interrogation room, and Hunter slipped outside to speak to her. He returned a few seconds later. "Looks like you're in luck. Your gun isn't the same caliber as the weapon that killed anyone in recent unsolved cases. But that doesn't clear you or your sons. Do you have other children?"

"Just the two boys."

"Your housekeeper seemed very protective. That's what our officers reported. She didn't want to let them in. Read the warrant very carefully. Wanted to call you or your wife before allowing them in, but they wouldn't let her, of course."

"She's not our housekeeper. She's my half-sister."

Detective Hunter looked up, his head tilted, and his brow wrinkled. "Another half-sister?" he asked. "What is this, some sort of cult?"

"Not at all. Let me explain. I had a devastating stoke over half a year ago."

"You look pretty healthy to me, despite walking with a cane."

"That wasn't the case after my stroke. I went through a lot of rehabilitation. But as you can see, I still need this," he said, lifting the cane.

Still looking skeptical, Hunter said, "I suppose everything you just said can be verified by your medical records."

"Absolutely."

"Okay. So you had a stroke. That doesn't mean you couldn't have shot someone."

Martin felt his face turn red and his chest tighten. *Stay calm. This cop seems crazy, like he thinks me or one of my kids might have killed these people. I'll have to explain everything to him carefully.* Trying to sound collected, Martin began his narrative. "Let me give you some background. Luckily, I have connections in the academic world, and the cause of my stroke was revealed by a research lab. Turns out I have a rare genetic condition predisposing me to blood clots. I need to take medication so I won't have another stroke. I've always known that my mother had to use a sperm donor to get pregnant with me. When I discovered this rare mutation, I felt an obligation to find out if I had half-siblings who would also be at risk for blood clots. I thought I might have one or two. The doctor who arranged the sperm donation for my mom died a number of years ago, and his records are no longer available. I tried contacting local sperm banks, but they were no help."

"They have laws preventing disclosure of information regarding sperm donors."

Martin interpreted the comment as an indication Hunter might be starting to believe him. "Precisely. I was getting nowhere so I decided to try ancestry sites. A lot of people find relatives that way."

"So that's how you discovered your half-siblings? After they had already been murdered?"

"They must have been murdered after sending their specimens to the ancestry site. I discovered not only them but many others. You can only imagine how surprised I was to find out I have almost a hundred siblings. And these are only the ones who have searched for relatives on ancestry sites. There are likely many more."

"How did you learn Ms. Bishop had been murdered?"

"Her mother responded to Nick's email to her."

"And the other one?"

"My son found out from his wife after he emailed him." Martin went on to explain that Nick was contacting all the half-sibs and arranging for them to be tested for his high school biology project.

"I suppose you have proof for everything you're telling me?" Hunter asked.

"Absolutely. We even have a celebrity who has this mutation. He's from around here and was also conceived via a sperm bank."

"Who's that?"

"Since he's been public about it, I suppose there's no harm in telling you. Are you familiar with The Rocket?"

For the first time, Detective Hunter wore a genuine smile. He slapped the desk as he exclaimed, "Damn, sure am. I'm a big fan."

"Well, he happens to be my half-brother. He clearly got the half with the muscles." Martin laughed nervously.

"This job just gets more and more interesting every day. I suppose I should talk to him just to be sure what you're telling me is true. Tell you what. Why don't you write down where I can contact your doctor, The Rocket, and anyone else who can corroborate what you've told me."

After Martin had written down the phone number of The Rocket, his personal physician, and Constance Jackson, he got up to leave.

"We'll be in touch," Hunter said. "It will take a few days to check all of this out. I suggest no one in your family leave the country."

"You said there were other murders."

"There are always other murders. You may not be aware, but the police departments in Idaho communicate with each other in case there are related cases in different areas. There are no cases similar to that of Lois Bishop. I would know."

Hunter's lack of eye contact made Martin suspect he was lying. But, more importantly, he wondered if he considered him a person of interest.

Chapter 29

WALKING THROUGH THE FRONT DOOR of his home that evening was especially sweet for Martin. He was greeted with the savory aroma of a roast of some sort and a hug around his thighs from Emerald. *So much better than spending the night in jail.* He paid particular attention to all the details around him—the comfort of his living room, the sound of the TV as his boys and Georgia watched the news, the plastic unicorn on the floor of the kitchen.

He joined his wife and children in the dining room that functioned as a den to watch the last half of the local news. A car accident in which two people had been seriously injured, a residential fire, and the closure of a local restaurant chain were the main stories he heard. As Georgia clicked the TV off with the remote, she commented on the news story at the top of the program. "Looks like The Rocket wasted no time in deciding to quit fighting. He made the announcement earlier today. They must have spent at least ten minutes showing footage of his press conference and interviews with disappointed fans."

That'll go a long way to convince Hunter I was telling him the truth. The conversation around the dinner table was more animated than usual that evening. Topics included Cat's description of the officers retrieving the firearm, Greg's narrative of an impressive play he'd made in baseball practice, Nick's progress with his half-sibling project, Georgia's optimism from the latest poll results for her candidate, and Martin's description of his trip to the police station, including Hunter's mention of other murders.

"Just because the detective said there were no related murders doesn't make it true," Greg said. "The police don't have to tell you anything about an investigation."

"That goes along with the fact that he didn't tell me much of anything. All I know is he seemed to think I had something to do with Lois's murder or knew something about it."

"Cops are always suspicious of people who ask about a murder investigation, especially if they aren't related to the victim," Greg said.

"I said I was her half-brother."

"He probably doesn't believe you. You'd never even met her."

I seem to have opened up a can of worms when I asked about the murders. Now Hunter thinks me or one of my kids, maybe all of us, had something to do with it. Martin told himself that despite the detective's absurd suspicions, he couldn't possibly have evidence against any of them, so he decided to keep the details of his detainment to himself for the time being, not wanting to worry his boys.

After dinner, Martin called Elmer Fudge to alert him to a potential phone call from Detective Hunter. The following morning, he spoke to Constance Jackson and described his visit to the station the previous evening.

"As you know, I'm not a criminal attorney, so I can't give you much advice. All I can tell you is, don't talk to the police without representation. I have an acquaintance who is very experienced in criminal matters. He's earned acquittals in several high-profile cases, including murder cases. Matthew Douglas."

"I know that name."

"Many people do. I'll get you his information."

Martin took Mr. Douglas's phone number but had no intention of calling him. *This guy's going to charge a fortune. Probably cost at least a quarter million minimum if he represents me—money I'm on the hook for myself.* Martin slipped the small piece of paper where he'd jotted down the attorney's name and number into his wallet, on the off-chance he found himself in a desperate situation. That evening, the professor didn't play his saxophone. He hardly slept that night.

The next day was uneventful. Martin's uneasiness wasn't mollified by knowing he carried the contact information of a top-notch criminal attorney in his wallet. Nick continued to contact half-siblings and collect data on the testing of others. Checking the Facebook page that evening, Martin noted several members commenting about Lois Bishop. Although none of them knew her personally, they expressed shock and sorrow at her loss. The professor's heart skipped a beat when he read that another half-sib who lived in the area, Barney Gibbert, had been murdered ten days earlier. *Counting Kurt Slocum, that makes three half-sibs murdered. If I go back to the detective with this information, would it help? It's not like I have any idea who the murderer is, but he'll think at least one of us is guilty, for sure.*

A good night's sleep became a distant memory for Martin, as he spent the next night tossing and turning.

Over dinner two days after his dad visited the police station, Nick reported he'd contacted Lois's mother and learned that his half-aunt had been a waitress in a local pizzeria. She'd been shot as she got out of her car in front of their house. "Cops had gotten videos of the murder from two security cameras on their street," he said. "The murderer wore a long black tunic, is right-handed, and never exposed his face. And get this—the cops did some fancy calculations. They used the angle of the cameras and the location of the shooter and figured out he's six feet tall, plus or minus a half inch or so. That's gotta help, right?"

"I don't know how much," Martin said. "There are a lot of men who are the same height."

Nick chuckled. "So, Dad, that makes you and Greg suspects, doesn't it?"

Georgia, Greg, and Cat laughed but Martin could only force a partial smile. *Hunter had the height of Lois's murderer when he questioned me, and probably had the height of Barney's assassin, too. Probably both murderers were around six feet tall. That's why Hunter was so obsessed with finding out how tall my sons and I are. Greg and I could be suspects simply because we happen to be around six feet, and I had to open my big mouth and inquire about Lois's murder.*

Martin was on edge the following weekend. Every time he heard the familiar Marimba ring of his iPhone, his muscles tensed until he determined the call wasn't from Hunter, or Greg informing him he'd been arrested.

Late Monday afternoon Elmer phoned. "I just had a strange call from your Detective Hunter," he said. "As you warned me, he asked me a lot of questions about you and your kids, and wanted to know if there was any truth to what you told him about this genetic disease."

Martin detected an uneasy pause. "And?" he said, after a few uncomfortable moments.

"I told him what I knew. But then I got to thinking. Sorry, man, but he raised some questions I just can't ignore."

"Like what? Everything I've told you is the truth."

"How do I know you've been completely level with me? I'm not sure we're even half-siblings. I've never sent a specimen to a genealogy company. And I know this may sound crazy, but how can I be sure this fibrinogen test result I got is legit? I never got an official report from a recognized medical laboratory. Just some supposed research lab I've never heard of says I have this mutation."

"Why would I lie to you about something like that?"

"Maybe to get money out of me. You've already succeeded, if that's what you've been after."

"The only money I've gotten has been to pay for the testing."

"How do I know that? You could be scamming me into thinking I'm paying for testing that's not actually happening. Or maybe you want me to quit fighting."

"Why would I want you to do that?"

"Maybe you have a thing against ultimate fighting. I know some people think it should be banned. Maybe you're backing someone who's an aspiring fighter and you want me out of the picture. I don't know why, I just know it's starting to not feel right."

"That detective put some crazy thoughts into your head."

"He thinks you and one of your kids are linked to some murders."

"He told you that?" Martin felt his face flush.

"He said you fit the profile."

"What did he mean by that? Both of us fit the profile, or just one of us?"

"I don't know, man. He wasn't very specific."

"Why would he tell you all of this?"

"I'm someone familiar to him, so he thinks he can trust me. I have a reputation for discipline, honesty, and charity work with my fans. He wants me to help him prove that you're a murderer."

"Why would either of us want to murder anyone? How would murdering people be linked to finding half-siblings with a treatable genetic disease?"

"Hunter thinks you've started some sort of cult. You convince people they're related to you and get them to do things. Like you got me to donate money and quit fighting. Maybe some people get suspicious, and you kill them."

"Don't you see how crazy that sounds? Lois, the half-sister whose murder was the one I asked Hunter about, worked in a pizza joint. What could she possibly do for me? Comp me some extra toppings? I've never even been to the place she worked in."

"Just because I can't answer all these questions doesn't make me trust you."

"What can I do to convince you that I'm telling you the truth?"

"I don't know, but the only reason I'm calling you now is to give you a chance to convince me you're legit. I believed you all the way until Hunter called. Now I have to wonder if you could just be a very, very good con man. But I was raised to be fair, so I'm giving you a chance to prove you're on the up-and-up."

Martin thought for a moment. He needed to come up with evidence to convince Elmer he'd been completely truthful with him. "Ah," he said. "I just thought of a good way to convince you I've been nothing but honest."

"Okay, shoot."

"Do you trust commercial companies that test DNA?"

"I suppose I do."

"Pick any company you want that tests for family relationships, like paternity and siblings. The turnaround time for those tests is much faster than for a full genealogy assessment. We can both submit samples at the same time. You can send a sample under any name you choose. If these samples come up with a twenty-five percent match with each other, indicating we are half-brothers, would that convince you?"

"I suppose it would. What about the fibrinogen mutation? How will I know I really have that?"

"I'll give you the name of the doctor who runs the lab that's doing all the testing. You can look him up. He's a highly respected academician. You can talk to him if you want. You could even visit his lab. It's up to you how much you want to investigate whether or not he's legitimate."

"Okay, okay. Let's do the DNA test. That'll be enough."

Elmer picked out a company and ordered two test kits. Martin met him at a hotel, and they collected their specimens simultaneously. Elmer mailed them to the company, and they waited, knowing it would take over a week to get the results. Martin was sure Elmer had the mutation. But was he a half-sib? It was possible he was a more distant relative who had inherited the gene from a common relative several generations removed. Martin's concerns were partially allayed knowing Elmer was the product of artificial insemination from a donor in the same area where he himself had been conceived. He'd just have to wait.

Chapter 30

TIME MOVED SLOWLY FOR MARTIN. He tried to immerse himself in his work, but his mind kept wandering to his meeting with Hunter. He noticed people in cars parked on his street a few houses away. Had there always been people parked on the street? Was this a police stakeout? Was it an assassin looking for another half-sibling to murder? Was he becoming paranoid?

At dinner two days after Martin and Elmer had submitted their DNA samples, Greg mentioned, "I think someone was following me when I went to Tucker's house after the game. Some dude parked on the street pulled out behind me when I left the parking lot and parked a few houses down from Tucker's house."

"What kind of car was it?" Martin asked.

"A white Crown Victoria. The kind used by undercover cops a lot. That's why I noticed it."

Martin was relieved the car was more likely to be driven by a cop than an assassin. "Was he there when you left?"

"Yeah. I was only there about forty-five minutes, and I noticed the dude was still there. He didn't follow me back home, though. I lost him with a U-turn."

"Let me know if it happens again, not that there's much I could do about it. How'd the game go?"

"We kicked their ass. I threw a no-hitter. Second time this season."

"That's really impressive," Georgia said. "But if I find out you were smoking dope with your friend and then drove home high, I'm going to kick your ass."

Looking guilty, Greg didn't respond.

The following morning, Martin received a call from Constance Jackson. "We were able to get all the sperm banks withing five hundred miles to cooperate with a combination of sweet-talking and orders from two local judges," she said. "They all checked their records, but none found any accounts for Dr. Kirby Sanborn. He never got donors through any of them."

"Damn! Now what? Looks like we've hit a dead end."

"Not quite. There's one more avenue we could explore. This may be a very unusual case, similar to one I had ten years ago. It calls for a different approach. I think we should look into this Doctor Sanborn more closely. He may be the sperm donor."

Martin gasped, then was silent a moment as the meaning of his attorney's words sunk in. "Are you suggesting he fathered all of these children himself?"

"Right. It's happened before."

"So you think the sick asshole who fathered all these children was Dr. Sanborn himself."

"Everything is pointing to that conclusion."

"Son of a bitch." Martin slammed the top of his desk. "Ouch," he said as he cradled the phone in his neck while squeezing his now aching right hand with his left. "Jeez, this is just hitting me now. Doctor Sanborn could be my biological father. I'm not sure if I should hate him or love him."

"I suggest we try to nail down his involvement."

"How? He died over twenty years ago. When I first started on this project, I visited his old office—my mom remembered where it was. There's a new practice there now, a weight-loss clinic. Nobody who works there knows anything about Sanborn. The space has changed hands several times. It was a family practice office before the weight-loss clinic took it over four years ago. There were no old records or computers on the premises when they moved in."

"My investigator has other ways of obtaining information. Dr. Sanborn may be survived by a wife, some children, or other relatives."

"I tried looking for his wife but got nowhere."

"My investigator, Fatima, sometimes amazes me with how she discovers things. It may take her a while, but be patient. If Dr. Sanborn had a wife, she'll find her. If the wife died, she'll find his children or other relatives."

Martin felt hopeful as he wished Constance luck and ended the call.

The next days were intense, as Martin's thoughts bounced from concern about the police investigation, the car that followed Greg which was probably not the only tail tracking the movements of his family and himself, the DNA studies with Elmer still pending, and the investigation into the whereabouts of Dr. Sanborn's wife. Not to mention keeping up with the demands of his work, and the normal family goings-on.

The dinner conversation Thursday night was animated. Both boys were excited the weekend was near. Cat had made a delicious lemon chicken dish, and all were enjoying her home-baked chocolate chip cookies afterwards. Emerald was entertaining the others by singing and dancing while eating a cookie and waving a pink magic wand. The joyous mood was interrupted by a loud banging on the door.

"Anyone expecting someone?" Greg asked.

"Not me," replied Georgia. The others responded in a similar manner.

"I'll see who it is," Greg said, standing up. He marched out of the kitchen, to the front door. Raised voices, Greg's and another male's, reached the kitchen. With loud footsteps, Greg returned to the kitchen, followed by a uniformed officer. All expressions of joy and levity Greg had been experiencing moments before were drained from his face. "Dad," he said. His voice was barely louder than a whisper as he motioned over his shoulder towards the officer with his thumb. "This guy has a warrant to search the house."

The room fell silent, until Emerald, seeming confused, rushed to Cat, crying. As Cat comforted her daughter, Martin rose and spoke to the officer. "What's this all about?"

"We have a warrant to search the premises."

"Your people already did that. They found my gun and it was clean."

"We're going to do a more extended search now."

"What are you looking for?"

"Can't say. But I have several officers with me, and we intend to look for several objects. One of my men will stay with all of you in here while the others conduct the search. I have to ask everyone here to remain in this room."

Martin glared at the intruders and took his seat, resisting the urge to shove the officers out the front door.

Greg reached for his phone and pressed the number of a contact.

"I'll have to ask you to put your phone away. No phone calls."

"I was just going to call my girlfriend and tell her I'll be late."

"Sorry, that will have to wait. It shouldn't take us more than a half hour to search the house. You can call then and apologize if necessary."

Greg slipped the phone back into his pocket and sat down in his usual position at the table. The rest of the family remained seated, waiting in silence as officers began to make their way through the house, speaking in hushed tones. The sounds of drawers and doors opening and closing surrounded them. Fifteen minutes later, two officers wearing vinyl gloves were in the kitchen, searching the contents of all the cabinets and drawers. Others were in the garage.

Finally, it was over. One of the officers came into the kitchen holding an evidence bag. "We're taking this navy hoodie we found."

The officer who had been waiting with them in the kitchen sounded disappointed when he said, "Sorry for the inconvenience. You can get back to your evening." As quickly as they had entered, the officers disappeared.

"What was that about?" Nick asked after the front door slammed shut.

"They're looking for evidence that we were involved in Lois's murder," Martin said.

Georgia, Cat, and the boys looked at him in horror. None appeared able to speak.

"Don't worry," Martin said. "They're grasping at straws. They obviously didn't find anything of importance. I think the detective in charge doesn't have any good leads, so he's getting desperate."

"That hoodie is probably mine," Greg said. "You don't have a navy hoodie, do you, Nick?"

"Nope. Must be yours."

"Shit," Greg said. "They're probably going to test it."

"What for?" Georgia asked.

"I don't know. Maybe DNA. Maybe gunpowder. Maybe pollens that are only found in one place. That's what they do on those forensics shows I watch. I just hope they don't test it for marijuana."

"I doubt they'd test it for that," Martin said.

"What do we do now, Dad?" Nick asked. "What if they plant something on his hoodie? Even if he's a jerk, he doesn't deserve going to jail."

"Don't worry about that," Georgia said. "They wouldn't do anything like that."

"Don't tell me not to worry. After all, it's *my* hoodie they took," Greg said.

"I have the name of a hot-shot criminal defense lawyer," Martin said. "I didn't think I'd need him, but the events of tonight have changed my mind. I'll contact him in the morning. We may not be able to afford him, but I'll worry about that later."

Chapter 31

"LAW OFFICES OF MATTHEW DOUGLAS."

Martin felt relief just hearing the receptionist's voice. He hadn't slept much the night before but was at last on the verge of getting some much-needed help. Martin introduced himself and told the receptionist he had been referred by Constance Jackson.

The professor answered a series of questions, then was placed on hold. After being forced to listen to country western music over the phone for several minutes, he was greeted by a loud voice with a slight southern accent.

"So, Constance Jackson sent you to me. She's a great gal. Are you a friend or relative of hers?"

"I'm a client of hers on another matter. It's not exactly related to the matter I'm contacting you about."

"Not exactly? Why don't you tell me about it? First, I'll need to get a retainer from you to establish attorney-client privilege so you can speak to me in confidence."

Martin grimaced. "How much will that be?"

"Let's start with a thousand dollars. If I don't need to do anything, I'll give it back, minus any incidental charges, like our conversation today. If I take the case and it goes to court, well, it'll cost you a whole lot more. If you give me your credit card number, you can tell me all about your case now."

"It's a deal." Martin told him his Mastercard information, then filled him in on the discovery of his half-siblings, how he came to learn about Lois

Bishop and other half-sibs who had been murdered, and what had transpired with the police.

When Martin finished, Mr. Douglas was quiet for a while. Martin remained silent as he heard the sounds of the attorney typing on a keyboard. After a few minutes, Mr. Douglas broke the silence with a series of questions. "Are you being blackmailed by anyone?"

"No, never."

"Are you having an affair, or have you had one in the past?"

"Absolutely not. No time for that," Martin said, followed by an uneasy chuckle.

"What about your wife? Do you suspect she is having an affair or had one in the past?"

"Why, no. I trust her completely."

"What about your kids? Have they had any trouble with the law, or been disciplined at school?"

"No, they're both good kids. Never been in any kind of trouble."

"What about drugs? Are you or is anyone in your family involved in drugs? By that, I mean using or selling."

Martin hesitated a few seconds before answering. "I found out recently that my older boy uses marijuana. He doesn't sell it, though."

"Was he ever arrested for it?"

"No. Not yet anyway." Again, Martin laughed nervously.

"If someone were to check into your finances, would they find any large additions or withdrawals?"

"No, although our Mastercard bill last month was a bit larger than usual because we fixed up the garage for Cat and Emerald."

"I hope you're telling me the truth about everything," Mr. Douglas said. "I have a pretty good sense about these things, and I believe you. I know only a fool would hold back from his attorney, and I doubt a fool could have worked his way up to being a chemistry professor at the university. The police likely have some information that makes them suspect you and your son. Probably more than you just asking about the case, although that might have been enough at first to raise the detective's dander. Things may be uncomfortable for a while, but we should be able to get you and your boy out from under the veil of suspicion pretty quickly.

"In the meantime, I'll send you my fee schedule and some of my cards. Make sure the detective sees one of those cards if he meets with you in the future. Might make him tread a bit lightly. If he does try to question you again, do not answer him without me being present. If any other officer tries to question you, be sure to call me and don't tell them a thing until I arrive. Tell your wife, kids, and your half-sister Cat the same thing."

Disconnecting from the call, Martin closed his eyes for a few seconds and let out a deep breath, allowing a sense of relief wash over him.

At dinner, Martin relayed his attorney's instructions.

"Let's hope it doesn't come to that," Georgia said. "I sure hope they find out who the murderer or murderers are soon."

"Makes me curious about what Lois, Kurt, and Barney were up to. I also wonder if there were other victims. Maybe they were involved in something together, like selling drugs or extortion," Martin said, thinking about the questions Douglas had asked him earlier.

"You'd think the cops would know if that were the case," Greg said. "They've probably already checked their finances. The spouse is always a prime suspect until he or she is ruled out."

"Lois wasn't married. What worries me is the police sometimes start off on the wrong foot, suspecting someone for the wrong reason and not pursuing other leads," Martin said.

"Like that movie, *Richard Jewell*, where the FBI thought that security guard set off a bomb at the Atlanta Olympics," Greg said.

"Exactly. Fortunately for him, his innocence was eventually recognized, although he suffered greatly from the intense investigation and negative publicity he received from the accusation. I'm more worried about people who, like Richard Jewell, are wrongly accused, but are later convicted because the truth never sees the light of day. We don't hear about the mistakes that are made if they are never discovered."

"Well, the Richard Jewell case was a long time ago," Greg said. "Things are different now."

"Just because it happened before you were born doesn't mean some things aren't the same. I still remember the case very clearly. People got railroaded back then, and they can still get railroaded today."

"There's often a car parked down the street at night ever since they raided our house," Georgia said. "The car changes, but someone is always sitting in it. I wondered if it was someone trying to gather information about Jill's campaign—looking to see who might be visiting me. Now I wonder if it's the police."

"I haven't noticed anyone following me," Martin said.

"Me neither," Greg said. "Not since that time after the game. Of course, if they're good at tailing someone, they won't be noticed."

"Let's hope it's a journalist trying to dig up something on Jill," Martin said. "Not that there's anything he or she will find here. It's not as if police departments have enough money to follow suspects twenty-four-seven, anyway. Not unless they think they're very important."

"I can't imagine they think anyone here is important," Georgia said. "They've already searched this house twice." After pausing a moment, she asked, "Any news about the DNA you and Elmer sent off?"

"Not yet. Don't expect if for days."

"How about the detective that works for Constance Jackson? Any information about the wife of your mother's doctor?"

"Haven't heard a peep."

Georgia turned to her younger son. "Nick, how are you doing with your genetic testing project? Do you still have more people to contact?"

"It seems like I get a few more names each week, but I'm almost all caught up. I just have four names right now that I'm waiting to hear back from. Lots of tests for the fibrinogen mutation are still pending, though."

"Isn't anyone going to ask me about how Jill's campaign is going?" Georgia asked, looking at everyone around the dinner table.

Everyone spoke up with their own version of "How's it going?"

"Her numbers look good, but it's still early. I sure hope The Rocket's DNA proves he's your half-brother, Martin, because he's been lukewarm about endorsing Jill's healthcare ventures ever since that cop spoke to him. His full-bore participation would be a real boost to her campaign."

"Nobody's hoping he's my half-brother more than me," Martin said.

After dinner, Martin headed out to Rosie's, a bar in a seedy area about ten miles from his house. The Potato Heads often performed there, and they'd be performing that night. He'd played with them in the pianist's living room a week earlier for the first time since his stroke. They'd urged him to join them at Rosie's and jam with them as little or as much as he wanted. He took Georgia's car as usual when he went there, not wanting to park his Audi in the exposed parking lot. As he pulled onto a main street, he noticed a car that had been parked down the street following two cars behind. After a quick U-turn followed by a left into the parking lot of a popular restaurant, he saw the tailing cop or assassin continue straight past him. Feeling invigorated, he smiled as he pulled back onto the main road and headed to Rosie's. Worry quickly set in, as he wondered why he was being followed. Murderer? Police officer? The latter was preferable, but why would the police suspect him of anything?

Walking through the door of Rosie's, his concerns evaporated as he was greeted by his bandmates and a noisy, spirited crowd. He'd forgotten how much fun it was to perform in front of a live audience, even for just the two numbers he participated in.

The house was dark when he returned home after eleven p.m. Passing by Greg's door, he heard what sounded like muffled laughter. *He's got a girl in his room, but that's the least of my problems.* The levity he'd felt at Rosie's quickly dissipated, and Martin was left with worry of impending doom. He didn't sleep well that night.

Chapter 32

DETECTIVE HUNTER CUT THE HEADLIGHTS and stepped out of his Crown Victoria. Floodlights illuminated the street and officers already on the scene milling around. A policewoman was comforting a middle-aged woman sobbing on her front lawn, near the body of a man face down, his legs splayed on the driveway next to a silver Toyota Camry, his head resting on the adjacent lawn. The driver's door was open, and two officers were outlining the corpse with the numbered yellow A-frame markers associated with crime scenes.

Moments later, a truck bearing the markings of the medical examiner pulled up. Two investigators jumped out, walked around the area briefly, pulled on shoe coverings and vinyl gloves, and hovered around the victim.

As Hunter approached the scene, he stuffed his large hands into a pair of gloves and stopped briefly to slip paper booties over his shoes, struggling to keep his balance as he stood on one foot, then the other. Once his shoes were protected, he walked towards two officers talking. "Who's in charge?" Hunter asked.

"I am, Detective," one of them answered.

"Okay, Potter, what do you know so far?"

"Not much. The wife was waiting for her husband to come home. She went outside and found him like that." Potter pointed to the dead man. "Penny's going to talk to her now. She seems to develop a good rapport with women. If we're lucky, she'll get some useful information."

"If this is like all the earlier cases, the wife won't know anything helpful."

"I know, and so far it's looking like the others." Potter pointed to the curb on the opposite side of the street from the body. "It appears the shooter stood there, about fifty feet from the victim. An empty casing, similar to the ones we've seen before, was found on the asphalt. Again, must have used a silencer."

Hunter walked over to the Medical Examiner, squatting next to the deceased. "How long do you suppose he's been dead?" he asked quietly, so as not to be heard by the distressed woman nearby.

"Considering his temperature and the ambient temperature, about one hour, possibly ninety minutes."

"Thanks." Hunter looked around and found Potter again. "You'd better go to every house around here and collect all the surveillance recordings," he told him. He looked up and down the street as far as he could see with the illumination provided by the floodlights. "This looks like a pretty nice neighborhood. A lot of these houses will have Ring or some other recording system. We need to pay close attention to events starting around two hours before your arrival."

"You got it."

Hunter took his time walking around the area, studying the scene assiduously while taking care to avoid stepping on anything that might be evidence. Crime scene technicians had arrived and were busy photographing the body and surroundings. The shell casing was being bagged when Hunter approached and asked to inspect it. Using gloved hands, one of the technicians retrieved the casing from the bag and held it out for Hunter.

"Looks like a forty caliber, same as the others," he said.

"Yeah, single casing, opposite side of the street from the victim," the technician answered. "Looks almost exactly the same as the Bishop and Gibbert cases. I was called in on both of those. I'll bet it's the same guy that killed them and the others."

"We'll know for sure after we have a chance to view footage from surveillance cameras and compare bullets."

"I'm sure it will match all the others," the technician said.

Hunter looked up and noticed Officer Penny Hassan escorting the victim's wife into the house. Several minutes later, Hassan reappeared. After looking around for a few seconds, she spotted Hunter and walked over to him.

"What did you find out?" Hunter asked.

"The victim's name is Ansel Montoya. Wife is Christina Montoya. He was thirty-nine years old, a dentist with a local practice. Wife said she spoke to him three hours ago, before he left work. She knew he'd be working late that night because he had a patient with an emergency. He sounded his usual self, asked if she needed him to pick up anything from the store on his way home. No known enemies. No disgruntled patients that she knew about. Heard nothing until she tried to call him on his cell because dinner was ready, and he was late. She'd opened the kitchen window to let the steam out and heard his phone ring. When he didn't come into the house moments later like she expected, she went outside to investigate. That's when she found him. Never heard a gun discharge. She ran to a neighbor, who called 911."

"Does she seem credible?"

"Yes. Her story sticks together. I told her you'd want to talk to her. Just knock on the door. She's sitting in the kitchen with the lights off."

"Is anyone coming to stay with her?"

"No kids, but her sister is on her way. She's a few hours away by car."

"Good. She shouldn't be alone." Hunter walked to the front door and knocked. Christina Montoya let him in and led him to the dark kitchen. The smells of fried chicken and freshly baked cookies made Hunter hungry.

"Can I turn on a light?" he asked. Once permission was granted, Hunter found a switch and flipped it on. Pots and pans were on the stove, and the kitchen table was set for two. Christina, hair disheveled and eyes red, sat in one of the chairs not facing a place setting; Hunter took a seat opposite her. The scene immediately told him that the victim's wife, unless a very industrious mastermind, couldn't have murdered him. What woman would go to the trouble of laboring all day in the kitchen, only to have her cooking go uneaten? The pile of used tissues on the table told him she'd been crying.

Hunter began his questioning, covering the same particulars transmitted by Officer Hassan. Once he established the consistency of Christina's answers, he probed further.

"Did your husband ever indicate he was in danger at any time in the past?"

"Never."

"Any trouble with neighbors or relatives?"

"None."

"Any idea who would have done this?"

"No. Everyone loved Ansel. I know, people make jokes about how much they hate going to see the dentist, but his patients really loved him. When we'd go out to eat or go shopping, they'd stop and talk to him. Same with other dentists we ran into. They were fond of Ansel too. I can't imagine he had any enemies."

"Any financial problems? Is there a chance he owed money?"

"I take care of our house finances. We're in very good shape. Our house is almost paid off, we have enough money saved to pay for a year of expenses, and Ansel's retirement account has done well. He was talking about retiring when he reached fifty-five, but I guess that will never happen now." Christina burst into tears.

"I'm sorry, but I have to ask. Have you had an affair with anyone outside of your marriage?"

Christina looked up, eyes wide as she ran her fingers through her hair. "Never! How can you ask such a thing?"

"I'm terribly sorry. We want to catch your husband's murderer, but I have to ask these questions so we can focus on finding the perpetrator. One more unpleasant question—is there any chance your husband was having an affair or was being blackmailed for anything?"

Christina took a deep breath and let it out slowly. "No. We were very happily married. We traveled a lot and had a full life. He had no time for an affair. I always knew where he was, and he knew where I was. There's no way he could have paid off any blackmailers, because, as I told you, I handled the finances. I'd know if money were missing."

"Any idea at all who may have done this?"

"Like I said multiple times before, no."

"Do you own a gun?"

"My husband had one. I never used it. Don't know how."

"May I see it?"

Christina sighed. "I'll see if I can find it." She disappeared down a hallway, returning a few minutes later holding a shoebox. "It's in here. I don't like to touch it," she said, handing the container to Hunter.

The detective opened the box and inspected the contents. Still wearing gloves, he picked up the thirty-two-caliber gun, rolled it over in his hands, then removed the clip and examined it. "Doesn't look like this has been fired recently."

"My husband's the only one who ever fired it, and he hasn't been to the shooting range in over five years."

Hunter placed the gun back in the box and set it down on the table.

"I want you to find whoever did this," Christina said, tears welling in her eyes again.

"We have every intention of finding the person or persons responsible for your husband's death, and hitting him with the full force of the law. If you ask me, a cold-blooded killing like this deserves the death penalty. Still legal in this state, I'm happy to say."

"I was never in favor of it before, but my husband was, and now I have to admit, I've changed my mind. If you ask me, lethal injection is too gentle. I'd like to deliver the death penalty to whoever did this myself, but it wouldn't be by lethal injection."

"I hear you," the detective said. He fished a card from his pocket and handed it to Christina. "Here's my card. If you think of anything—and I mean anything—that might be helpful in finding your husband's murderer, don't hesitate to call. Now, I'll find my way out."

Hunter stepped outside and blinked, the police lights momentarily unbearably bright. Half the officers were gone, and the body of Ansel Montoya had been removed, leaving behind markers of the body's previous position on the driveway. Technicians were collecting samples of debris in the area, while others swabbed the car and driveway for DNA samples, and dusted for fingerprints.

Hunter took out his flashlight and turned it on, not wanting to overlook anything that might be hidden in a shadow. Stepping around technicians busily gathering evidence, he first inspected the vicinity where the body had been, slowly aiming the light at the entire driveway surface, the nearby grass, and finally, the victim's car, inside and out. Nothing stood out to him. *They're probably wasting their time collecting those samples.*

Next, he walked to the area where the casing had been found. If this murder had been committed by the same man who had killed previously in a similar manner, his car, a silver Honda CR-V with stolen license plates, would have been parked nearby, just behind the location where the casing was found. He carefully shone his light on the asphalt, walking slowly along a path adjacent to where he figured the driver's side of the murderer's car had been. After taking a few steps, he stopped and squatted, intently focusing on a small area that he lit up with his flashlight. His body tensed. *Could this be it, the clue we've been waiting for?*

Not wanting to appear too excited, like a rookie who'd found his first piece of useful evidence, he stood and turned around, careful not to step on the area of interest. He hailed one of the medical technicians over.

"What is it, Detective?" she asked.

"Be careful where you step," he said as he turned around, squatted again, and pointed to a small spot on the asphalt. "See that?"

The technician crouched down facing ninety degrees from him and stared at the asphalt. "What is that? A fiber?"

"It's a damn mosquito! A squashed little motherfucker."

The technician was silent a few seconds, then swallowed nervously. "I don't understand. What about it, sir?"

"Look, there's a bit of red," Hunter said impatiently. "That means blood. I think this mosquito bit our murderer, who then squashed it just enough to decommission it, and left it here on the road. Look, one of its legs is moving a little."

"I still don't get it. You think there's enough blood there to do DNA analysis?"

"You bet I do," Hunter said, unable to suppress a smile. "It's been done before—DNA extracted from blood sucked up by a mosquito can be analyzed to solve a crime."

"So I should collect it?"

"You have to ask? Of course, you should collect it. This could be our big break. Be careful and get everything off the pavement. If we can get a good DNA sample from this, I'll be indebted to that mosquito forever. I'll never kill another one. Well, maybe not for another month, anyway."

Hunter left the scene feeling an adrenaline rush, his pulse racing and his sense of awareness heightened. *We're gonna get you now. You and whoever else in your depraved family is involved, Professor Starling.*

Chapter 33

THE FOLLOWING DAY WAS TOUGH for Martin. Two of his graduate students had gone to a party the night before and been involved in a car pileup. Both were seriously injured and would be out for over a month. Not only did he feel bad for the students, but the accident would set his research back. Another lab would now likely beat him to publication on that matter. He almost hated himself for being so distraught over losing out on publishing first, rather than only being concerned for his student's well-being.

The chairman was pressuring him to work on the oil company project. He figured he wouldn't be able to put off a confrontation with him much longer. A paper he had submitted was returned, with a comment stating he needed more documentation of his findings. He didn't agree and was deciding whether to do the extra experiments or submit a counterargument.

Still no word from any of the private investigators working his cases or from the company analyzing his and The Rocket's DNA, although it was too early for that. Georgia called to remind him to pick up a washer at a hardware store on the way home so he could fix the kitchen sink. Meanwhile, the weight of the investigations into the deaths of Lois Bishop and Barney Gibbert were heavy on his mind.

After work, Martin picked up the washer and returned home. Georgia and the boys were watching the local evening news, while Cat was in the kitchen with Emerald, cooking and reciting the exciting adventures of the three little pigs and Goldilocks.

As he sat down, the newsreader began to speak of the murder of Ansel Montoya, a dentist in a nearby suburb, the previous evening.

"That name sounds familiar," Nick said. "Is he a friend of yours, Dad?"

"Never heard of him."

"What about you, Mom."

"Don't know him either. We all go to the same dentist, Dr. Nash, so there's no connection there."

As the story unfolded on TV, they all listened. The victim lived in an upper middle-class community and was just outside his parked car in the driveway when he was shot in the head. There were no leads so far, but the police hoped to learn something from surveillance cameras in the neighborhood.

"Sounds like Lois Bishop and Barney Gibbert," Martin said. "I hope the cops don't believe we're responsible for all the murders."

Nick jumped up. "I think I know where I've seen that name before. Ansel Montoya."

"Where?" Georgia asked.

"I'll let you know in a sec. I just want to check to see if I'm right." Nick disappeared into his room for a minute, then returned. "I've got it!" he said. All eyes were on him as he panned the room. "He's on the list. He's one of the half-sibs. I contacted him two weeks ago, and his DNA results are pending."

Silence filled the room. Only the sound of clanking pots and pans and Emerald skipping in the kitchen were audible.

Finally, Martin broke the silence. "This is very strange. It could be a coincidence, but doesn't it seem unlikely that three similar murders in the area happen to involve my half-sibs? There's four similar murders if we count the death of Kurt Slocum in Colorado."

"I'll say," Georgia said. "Maybe these people were connected previously, possibly through the genealogy site. They could have been involved in something dangerous."

"I suppose that's possible," Martin said. "But from what we know, these people don't seem to be the criminal type.

"Except for the charges the dentist makes," Greg said.

"Seriously," Martin said, unamused by Greg's comment, "perhaps I should notify Detective Hunter about this. Knowing there are four murder victims on my half-sib list might send his investigation in a different direction. Maybe he could offer us some protection, and get off my back."

"If you talk to him again, it could make him more suspicious," Georgia said. "He might wonder if you just made this list up to throw him off. I can't imagine he'd send officers to watch us and everyone else on the list. There's not enough money. For some reason, he seems to have a bug up his ass about you. You'd best leave him alone. Don't poke the bear."

"There may be even more related murders, from what he said. I'd sure like to know if they, too, were half-sibs."

"Call your criminal attorney in the morning," Georgia said. "He should be able to advise you."

Martin felt uneasy as they sat around the kitchen table for dinner. Cat served her mother's recipe for vegetarian lasagna which had quickly become a family favorite. The familiar comfort food with salad and garlic bread soon relaxed the tension in the air. Not wanting to discuss murder in front of Emerald, the family's conversation quickly changed to lighter subjects, including the weather, Major League Baseball, and whose turn it was to mow the lawn that weekend.

As they were finishing their meal, Georgia said, "I don't want you boys taking off now. I planned a little celebration." She smiled at Martin, who looked around nervously. "It's okay if you forgot, dear. I know you have a lot on your mind."

"I get it," Nick said. "It's your anniversary. How come you guys didn't go out for dinner like you usually do?"

"I didn't want to give your father any more anxiety by making a big deal about it. It's not like we were just married, you know."

"You still deserve the best, Peaches," Martin said, looking at Georgia. "It's not easy being married to me, especially now."

"I'll be the judge of that," Georgia said as she left the table and headed down the hall. The room remained quiet until she returned carrying a small gift and card which she handed to Martin. "You should know what this is. You'd better guess right."

"Could it be a vial of titanium by any chance?"

"Well done," Georgia answered as Martin read the card.

"Show us the card, Dad," Greg said.

"Not till you're older."

"You always say that."

"And I always will, because you'll never be old enough."

The small amount of levity seemed to relax everyone for the moment. Martin opened the present, and held up a two-inch vial filled with chunks of a silver metallic substance, labeled "#22 Ti."

"What's that for?" Cat asked, looking confused.

"Why don't you explain it, Greg," Martin suggested.

With all eyes on him, Greg took a sip of water and began to speak. "Legend has it that on their first wedding anniversary, Mom gave Dad a vial filled with hydrogen, the first element in the periodic table. Although hydrogen is a clear gas, and the vial looked empty, it was labeled #1 H, so Dad asked her what was up. Mom told him she was going to get him a vial of the element with the atomic number corresponding to their years of marriage for every anniversary. He says that's when he knew he'd married the right woman."

"I have to look up the correct element every year," Georgia said. "This year is titanium, atomic number twenty-two. He keeps the vials in his office on a special stand I had made so the chemicals can be arranged just like they are in the periodic table."

"I was wondering what that was," Cat said. "I saw the vials on the ledge in front of the picture window. Silly me, I thought they were bottles of spices you sprinkled in tea or water."

Martin, Georgia, and the boys laughed. "One more thing about those vials," Georgia said. "Martin didn't believe the first vial I gave him was really full of hydrogen. He thought I was making some sort of joke, and just had room air in it. Before I could stop him, he lit a match and opened the vial. It lit up like the Hindenburg because hydrogen is very flammable. Burned his eyebrows, but he was okay. I had the bottle refilled with hydrogen, and he's never doubted me since."

"That's when I realized that not only was she the right woman for me, but she was a woman of her word."

Light chuckles erupted around the table as Martin began to sing "Peaches on My Mind" to the tune of "Georgia on My Mind." Finished singing, he reached into his back pocket and produced a small box wrapped in silver paper adorned with a red bow which he handed to Georgia.

Georgia's mouth fell open as she slapped her hands against her cheeks before taking the gift from her husband.

"You didn't really think I forgot?" he asked.

"I didn't think you remembered or had time to buy me anything." She tore through the paper and opened the box. Looking inside she gasped, then held up a solid gold bangle bracelet with a dozen small, embedded diamonds. After the *oohs* and *aahs* had subsided, she slipped the bracelet on her right wrist and stretched her arm out, admiring her new bling. "I love it," she exclaimed, as she got up and hugged her husband.

More *oohs* and *aahs* ensued as the happy couple kissed, stopping only when Greg remarked, "Get a room."

Cat was about to serve ice cream and a cake decorated with HAPPY 22ND ANNIVERSARY for dessert when there was a loud knock at the door.

"Is anyone expecting someone?" Georgia asked.

A resounding "No" emanated from the others.

"I'll get it," Greg volunteered. "I'll bet it's some Latter-Day Saints. I like to give them a bad time."

"Okay, Greg, just don't take too long. Your ice cream will melt," Georgia said.

All listened as Greg opened the front door. Instead of being offered a free copy of *The Watchtower*, the voice of a man announcing he had warrants to collect DNA from Martin Starling and Greg Starling was heard in the kitchen. Martin ran to the door. "What's going on?" he bellowed, looking at the uniformed cop he recognized from the night the house had been searched. Standing next to him was a woman with a lanyard hanging around her neck, identifying herself as a forensic technician.

"Like I was telling your son, I have warrants to collect DNA samples from you and your son here," the officer said. "It will just take a few minutes."

"What the hell is wrong with you guys?" Martin asked. "Greg, come inside. You," he said, looking at the unwelcome visitors at the door, "wait here. I'm calling my lawyer." He slammed the door in their faces. Then, walking towards the kitchen, Martin dialed his attorney, as Greg followed behind. The professor hyperventilated waiting for the call to be answered, then yelled at the person at the exchange who finally greeted him. "This is Professor Martin Starling. I need to speak to Mr. Douglas. Now. I've got a cop at my door with a warrant, and a technician itching to get DNA from me and my son," he yelled.

"Hold on a minute sir," the soul on the other end answered. After several minutes, the familiar voice of Matthew Douglas came on the line. "Sorry it took so long to connect. I'm at a charity event. What's going on?" he asked.

Martin explained the situation. Douglas asked him to read the exact wording of the warrant, so Martin traipsed back to the front door and asked to see it. He read the document to his attorney, who said, "Looks like all is in order. You'll have to cooperate, or they'll arrest you. If you get arrested, that will only delay things, but you'll likely need to give up your DNA eventually. If you're innocent, I suggest you comply."

"As I said before, we're innocent."

"This could be a good thing. If the police want to test your DNA, they probably have a DNA specimen from the perpetrator now. It will take time, several days at least, weeks if they don't rush this, but I think they'll give this priority. Eventually, the DNA will clear you, so let them take samples from you and your son but don't answer any of their questions."

"Okay, we'll do it," Martin said to the officer.

"May we come in? It will be easier if we do this inside. Otherwise, your neighbors can see everything."

Martin invited the officer and forensic technician into the living room. The woman swabbed the cheeks of Martin and Greg, carefully putting the swabs into separate, labeled collection tubes when complete. All the while, the officer made small talk, sneaking in questions, like asking where they had been the previous evening. Martin remained cordial but refused to answer, and told his children to be quiet. When finished with the collection, the officer and technician thanked Martin and Greg for their cooperation and left.

Georgia came into the living room carrying a container. "Martin, I want you to teach me and the boys how to use this thing," she said, lifting the gun from the metal box where it was stored.

Chapter 34

"HEY, BRO. LOOKS LIKE YOU were being straight with me." Martin had answered the call from Elmer with trepidation while hoping for vindication.

"The results are in?"

"Sure are. Just this morning. It's official—you and I are brothers. Half-brothers, but that's just a detail. Sorry I got bamboozled by Detective Hunter. That guy really thinks you are trying to pull one over on me about being related, and you are guilty, guilty, guilty."

"He told you that?"

"Sure did. I'd say he's convinced."

"I was afraid of that. For some reason, he's certain that me or my son are murderers and we're some sort of crime family. I can't figure out why he jumped to that conclusion, just because I asked about the murder of one of our half-sisters."

"I got the feeling there's more to it than that, but he wouldn't say."

"None of us have even met the woman. The only reason I called the police station is because there were other half-siblings who'd been murdered. We wanted to know if they'd made the connection, and if there were any suspects. That's the extent of our association with her. I was surprised Detective Hunter asked me to come to the station. I wish I had refused."

"I don't know if that would have helped."

"Now the situation seems even worse. Another half-brother was recently murdered. Shot in the head outside his home. You probably heard about it on the news. Ansel Montoya."

"Yes, I did hear about that. He's a half-brother?"

"He is. I'm afraid I'm seeing a pattern here, and it's frightening. These half-sibs could have been mixed up in something shady together, or someone may be targeting all of us for some unknown reason."

"That does sound scary. I have a good security team. But you and the others should be careful. Meanwhile, I want to do more to notify others who are at risk for this mutation we have. Any luck identifying our sperm donor?"

"No, but my attorney has a good hunch. She suspects the donor is the doctor who did the insemination. There's no record of my mother's doctor receiving specimens from any sperm banks within several hundred miles. His name was Kirby Sanborn. Died some years ago. Do you by any chance know the name of the obstetrician your mother used? If my attorney is correct, it was the same doctor. She thinks he used his sperm for all my half-sibs. He must have been some sort of sicko."

"I'll ask my mom if she remembers the name of her doctor. If it's Kirby Sanborn, then I think we have our answer. That could simplify things. All we'd need to do is get a list of the patients he inseminated, and try to track down their children."

"Easier said than done. He died before everything went electronic. His old paper records were likely destroyed or stored in an unknown place. Right now, my lawyer's investigator is trying to find his wife. I don't know if she's still alive."

"Is there anything I can do now to help out?"

After thinking for a moment, Martin replied, "It might help if you called Hunter and told him we really are related."

"I'll give it a try, although I can't guarantee he won't still suspect you."

After disconnecting from the call, Martin let out a sigh of relief and reflected on the good news. He was in his office at work, due to meet with a post-doctoral fellow in a few minutes. Nonetheless, he logged into his account at the company where Elmer had sent their DNA samples. He verified that he and Elmer were a twenty-seven percent match, consistent with being half-brothers. He himself obviously hadn't inherited the genes for competitive combat.

That evening, Martin shared the news about Elmer with the rest of the family.

"We were already pretty sure you two were half-brothers," Georgia said. "I'm not sure this changes anything."

"I'm hoping this information coming from The Rocket himself will cause Hunter to reconsider the thrust of his investigation. Not only do I want him to lay off of us, but I want him to find the real killer."

"Sometimes when someone is tied to their idea, it takes a whole lot to dissuade them," Georgia said.

"Right," said Nick. "There's a guy in my class who is convinced the earth is flat. My teacher showed him maps and pictures of the Earth from outer space, but he's still a flat Earther."

After dinner, Martin went to his office, where he received a text from Elmer.

I called Hunter today. Told him about genetics results, proving you and I are half-brothers. Thanked me for the info but said there was compelling evidence against you. Wouldn't tell me what. Sorry. I confirmed my mom's doc was Kirby Sanborn. Hope that helps.

Martin pumped his fist when he read the last part. "Yeah," he said, the words heard by no one but himself. He found Nick in his room doing geometry homework.

"I have a new assignment for you. I should have thought of this before."

"What is it, Dad?"

"I'd like you to ask as many people on the list as possible if they can find out the name of the doctor who performed their mom's artificial insemination."

"What does that matter?"

"I think all the mothers may have used the same doctor, and I think that doctor, well, is the biological father of all these people."

"Eww. Does that mean what I think it does?"

"'Fraid so. I just learned that my mom and Elmer's mom used the same doctor."

"I'll get on it tomorrow after school, Dad. I'm all caught up contacting people on the list until more names get added. Most of the DNA studies on them have been done. I won't include any more in my official school biology project, so I'll be done with it soon. It won't take me too long to write it all up."

"More than a week ahead of schedule."

Nick smiled. "Yeah. I'll probably be the first one in my class to turn in their project."

Martin returned to his study, where he received a call from Elmer.

"I have an idea," Elmer said. "I want to get word out to all our half-sibs who haven't connected with any ancestry websites, people who aren't on your list. They need to be tested too."

"I'm working on finding out who else Dr. Sanborn inseminated. Unfortunately, the path is cold, and it may take a while."

"Then you should like my idea. I want to publicize the hell out of this. We can start locally, then go nationally to reach people who have moved away. I want to put out public service announcements and paid advertisements to notify the public that if they are the product of artificial insemination performed by Dr. Kirby Sanborn in Boise, they need to be tested."

"That's a great idea, but not everyone's going to know the name of their mother's doctor."

"But we'll reach the people who do know. That's worth something. Meanwhile, you can continue to chase down the names of Sanborn's patients by other means."

"We may be inundated with people who know their biological dad was a sperm donor, but don't know the name of the doctor who did it, and can't find out because their parents are dead, or don't remember."

"Don't worry, I'll cover the testing cost."

"I'll ask my friend Dean, the one who started me on this whole genealogy rabbit hole, to help. He can test people who don't know if their mom was Sanborn's patient, to determine if they are my half-sibs. Only my half-sibs will be tested for the mutation. That will cost less than testing everyone for the mutation first. His company is taking off now and a lot of his genealogy testing is currently automated."

Martin slept better that night than he had for some time. Elmer was on his side, and he had more evidence that the treating doctor had used his own sperm to inseminate the mothers of all his half-sibs. Finding the insemination records might prove difficult, but at least they had a starting place now. Hopefully, Constance's investigator would locate the wife of the late doctor soon, and she might know where to find the old records. He racked his brain, trying to figure out why Hunter was so convinced he and his sons were guilty. What evidence could he have? No matter how hard Martin thought about it, he came up blank. He was comforted knowing the DNA analysis would clear Greg and him, assuming they had a good DNA specimen from the real murderer.

Martin was feeling pretty optimistic until at breakfast, after checking that Emerald wasn't within earshot, Georgia said, "Don't forget about teaching all of us how to use that gun."

Thoughts of a murderer lurking out there someplace, possibly plotting to murder him, invaded his thoughts. "Let's all go to the range this weekend. How does that sound to everyone?"

Cat looked confused.

"Georgia and I have decided everyone in the house should learn how to shoot the gun I've been hiding in my bedroom for years. That includes you, Cat, if you're willing. Perhaps Emerald can play with her friend down the street while the rest of us go to the shooting range."

"I'll do it if you want me to."

"Good," Georgia said. "Let's do it Saturday. Two in the afternoon. The weather will be good."

All agreed.

When the weekend came, after Cat took Emerald to play with her friend, they all piled into the CR-V and Martin drove them to the shooting range, several miles away. He began by giving a lesson in gun safety before everyone took turns firing the weapon. Four hours later, Georgia, the boys, and Cat knew how to load the gun, turn the safety on and off, and fire. All were able to at least hit the targets at the shooting range. While Martin's accuracy was impressive, the skill of the others left a lot to be desired.

"We'll keep the gun on a high shelf in the kitchen, where anyone other than Emerald can get to it. I'll take the clip out and leave it next to the gun."

"Let's hope no one ever needs it," Cat said.

"I think it's time we installed an alarm system in the house," Georgia said.

"Good idea," Martin answered. "I'll call on Monday. Should have done it years ago."

The weekend dragged, as Martin grew uneasy with every noise, from dogs barking in the neighborhood, to the sound of tree branches swaying in the breeze, and Cat cooking in the kitchen. He noted Georgia jump when a next-door neighbor slammed his fence gate closed.

The one bright spot for Martin was reading over Nick's biology report, which he was going to turn in the following week. The professor couldn't have been prouder of his younger son who had organized the data clearly, and written an in-depth, well-thought-out discussion.

"Don't worry, Dad," Nick said as his father handed the papers back to him. "I may be done with the school report, but I'm going to stay with the project until it's complete."

Martin felt himself almost tear up. *That's my boy.*

The following Monday, Martin received a call from Constance. Fatima, her investigator, had spoken to a friend of hers in Huntsville, Alabama, and learned of an unsolved murder in that area that seemed similar to the half-sibling murders. The victim, Brooke Metcalf, who had been a managing director at the NASA Space Flight Center, was not on Martin's list of genealogy matches. He wondered if she was a half-sibling, and if the murder was linked to the others. There was no way to know with the information Fatima had gathered.

Shortly after the call, Franklin Brothers Security came to install the state-of-the-art security system Martin had recently ordered for the house. As the technician was explaining all the features, showing the family members how to turn the alarm off and on, Martin thought *if this doesn't prove our lives have changed for the worse, I don't know what does.*

Chapter 35

THAT EVENING, MARTIN DROVE NICK to a video recording studio in a small town outside of Boise. Located in a strip mall where most of the retail space was empty, they parked directly in front of a storefront and went inside. Each was wearing jeans and a sport coat over a grey T-shirt.

"You with Elmer Fudge?" the middle-aged woman behind the counter asked, looking at the computer screen before her.

"We are."

"Please wait there," she said, pointing to a row of folding chairs along one wall. "Nobody gets in until I get the credit card from Elmer. He'd better be here soon, or I'm gonna lock this place up. Is that guy rich or something? He's paying me and my staff an extra five hundred each to stay late so you all can do this after we close."

"I didn't know that. But he has means," Martin said as he and Nick took seats. *This isn't what I expected.* Martin looked around the desolate room painted olive green. *I guess this is what Elmer meant when he said he'd found an out-of-the-way place to avoid making a scene.*

"Who's that?" Nick whispered, pointing to the single photograph hanging on the wall, a tan, withered, elderly man atop a white horse. He was decked out in a white cowboy outfit with a V-shaped red fringe across the front, reaching from shoulder to shoulder. Above the fringe were appliqued blue stars. More fringe and stars adorned the cuff area. The patriotic look was completed by a white cowboy hat with a red and blue horizontally-striped hatband.

"He looks familiar," Martin quietly remarked to Nick.

"Why that's Wyatt Boudreaux," the woman behind the counter said, undeterred from interrupting her customer's private conversation. "He was a big rodeo star back in his day. When he retired, he opened up this studio. He also happened to be my grandaddy."

"You must be proud," Martin said, not knowing what else to say. He was relieved upon seeing a black SUV pull up next to his car. A burly man stepped out of the driver's side, and Elmer, dressed similarly to Martin and Nick, exited the other.

The driver opened the door to the studio, and Elmer walked in.

The woman behind the desk stared, speechless as her eyes widened and she ran a hand through her hair. After a few beats, she managed to sputter, "Why, why you're The Rocket, aren't you?"

"'Fraid so," Elmer said as he walked to the counter.

"I'm such a big fan. Why didn't you tell me it was you that was coming? I woulda told my kin and my neighbors so they coulda met you."

"That's why I didn't tell you. I want to keep this very low-key, so I used my real name."

"You mean your real name's Elmer?"

"Sure is."

"Well, I'll be a monkey's uncle." She ran her fingers through her hair again, before asking, "Hey, are you really gonna stop fighting?"

"I am."

"Damn. Well, could I get your autograph?"

"Sure," Elmer said. "Would you like me to sign as The Rocket, or should I use my real name?"

The woman looked around the counter and found a crumpled piece of paper. She straightened it out and ran the side of her hand over it before handing it to Elmer. "The Rocket would be just fine. And you can address it to me, Josephine," she said, holding up a pen.

"My pleasure," Elmer responded, as he grabbed the pen and wrote a quick note. When he was done, he looked up at her. "Now don't tell me you're a relative of Wyatt Boudreaux."

Josephine blushed. "I'm his granddaughter."

"I'm impressed," Elmer said. "I was a big fan of his growing up. Now, is everyone ready?"

"It's just me and one other guy. He's back there waitin' on you."

"You want my credit card?" Elmer asked, taking out his wallet.

"Oh, yes, if you don't mind. I almost forgot."

After swiping the card, Josephine led the party back to one of the two studio rooms, each the size of a small hotel room. Three lightly-padded swivel chairs were towards the rear of the room, in front of a solid green wall. A video camera mounted on a wheeled tripod stood in front. As they walked towards the green wall, a row of bright lights attached to the ceiling lit up the area brightly.

A man with a shaved head and scraggly beard walked towards them, bringing with him the strong odor of cigarette smoke. "Well I'll be damned," he said. He turned to Josephine. "Why the hell didn't you tell me The Rocket was coming? I'da brought some of my people to meet him."

"Please don't call anyone, or I'll have to cancel," Elmer said. "I want to get this done quickly and leave. I don't want any attention."

"Don't you worry about a thing, Mr. Rocket," Josephine said, giving her employee a disapproving look. "We're nothin' here if not professional."

"Okay," Elmer said. "Let's get started. How about if I take the chair on the left, you take the middle chair, Martin, and Nick, you take the one on the right."

Martin and Nick agreed, and each took their respective chairs.

"I'm sure you've been practicing this at home," Elmer said, "but let's do a dry run. Remember, two minutes. That's all the time we have."

"Sure, we worked on it yesterday," Martin said, looking at Nick who nodded in the affirmative.

"It'll start with us sitting here, and a man's voice which Josephine here will add later will say, 'And now, an important message from The Rocket.' You got that, Josephine?"

"Sure do. Already told Leon I needed him for a voiceover, and he's ready."

"Good. Now the camera closes in on us, and I start. Here goes." Elmer shifted in his chair, smiled, and looked straight at the camera. "Greetings. In case you don't know me, I'm the Ultimate Fighter Middleweight Champion The Rocket, and I want to share something with you that's very important. Not long ago, I discovered that I had a half-brother, Professor Martin Starling, who is sitting next to me. I shouldn't have been terribly surprised by that, as I knew that I was born through the miracle of artificial insemination. My dad, a wonderful man who unfortunately died a few years back, wasn't able to father children, although he was a man's man in every other way. My parents desperately wanted a child, so they chose what they thought was their best option. I always knew I had been conceived that way growing up, but always considered the man who raised me to be my real dad.

"Although I'd never given it any thought, in retrospect, it made sense that my biological father could have fathered another child or two. All that came home to roost when I was contacted by Martin here, who was also conceived through artificial insemination, and told me I was his half-brother. Frankly, it was a really nice surprise. In addition to the wonderful sister I'd known all my life, I had a brother! Who wouldn't want that? Unfortunately, the story doesn't end there. Martin, why don't you fill these nice folks in on what you told me."

"Sure," Martin said. "I had a devastating stroke about half a year ago. Fortunately, I had excellent medical care. I survived and have made a remarkable recovery. It took a lot of time and hard work, but I'm close to where I was before the incident. I'm lucky I have connections in the academic world. A very smart researcher in San Francisco discovered that I have a rare mutation that makes my blood clot more easily than it should. My stroke was the result of an abnormal clot that formed in my brain. Currently, the mutation I have can only be detected in this scientist's research lab. Now that I know I have this mutation, I take a medicine that should prevent me from having an abnormal blood clot in the future."

"Why are you here today to tell your story? What do you want the good folks out there watching to know?" Elmer asked.

"Since my abnormal clotting tendency is caused by a mutation, people related to me may have inherited it too. If I had known about it earlier, I would have been on preventative medicine, and wouldn't have gotten the stroke.

It could have been worse—I could have died, been mentally debilitated, permanently wheelchair-bound, or lost a limb, depending on where the abnormal clot formed. I knew I didn't inherit the gene from my mother because I had her tested, so I must have inherited it from my biological father. I had reason to believe that you, Rocket, were related to me."

"I'm thankful that you contacted me to warn me I had a fifty-fifty chance of inheriting the mutated gene. You arranged for me to have a simple blood test, and I learned that I do, in fact, carry that bad gene, same as you. I have started the medication, a blood thinner, and will be on it for the rest of my life. It will no longer be safe for me to participate in fighting, but that's a small price to pay for my health. Is there anything else of interest you learned?"

"I figured I might have a few half-siblings I didn't know about, as my sperm donor may have had a family of his own, or he may have donated sperm to other couples wanting children. I signed up with a few of the genealogy companies helping people find relatives to see if anyone would pop up."

"Did they?"

"I'll say. I learned that I had almost a hundred half-siblings out there. Those were just the ones I learned about because they registered on an ancestry site."

"So our biological father was pretty busy!"

"Yes, he was."

"What are you doing for these siblings?"

Martin turned to Nick and patted him on the arm. "I've recruited my son, Nick here, to contact every half-brother and sister we learn about and arrange for them to be tested."

"How's that going, Nick?" Elmer asked.

Nick smiled as he had been instructed. He started talking, his voice shaky at first, but the delivery became smoother as he proceeded. "I have a spreadsheet of all the names of my dad's half-siblings, and I've been contacting each of them. I explain why I'm calling, and ask if they want to be tested. So far, they all do. I arrange for someone to come to their house and collect a blood sample. When I get the result, I contact them. If they are positive for the bad gene and they have children, I arrange for their children to be tested, because they have a fifty percent chance of being affected. Anyone positive is directed to contact their physician to get the proper medication. There are probably many more people out there who should be tested, but they never signed up with an DNA testing website, so they're not on my list."

"That's right," Elmer said. "If you know you are the product of artificial insemination that was performed in the Boise area, or if you suspect that is the case, but you never submitted a sample to a large ancestry site, you might have the mutation. I urge you to contact Nick so you can be tested. The website, clotting disorders dot com, has Nick's email address and a form you can fill out. The website is on your screen now. If you think you may have been conceived through artificial insemination, please don't hesitate to contact Nick or fill out the form. I think this is so important, I am paying for all the testing myself. Nick here is generously donating his time. Thank you and God bless."

Martin, Nick, and Elmer relaxed as they sat in silence for several moments.

"Well?" Elmer asked, staring into the studio.

"That was over two and a half minutes," Josephine said. "You need to cut out more'n thirty seconds."

They spent the next hour running through the script repeatedly, each time eliminating a few words and avoiding pauses. Finally, when they had recorded a smooth presentation exactly a hundred and twenty seconds long, they agreed they were done. Elmer settled the bill with Josephine and left, followed by Martin and Nick.

As they walked out the door, Josephine shouted, "I'll have this ready for you to approve in two days."

Three days later, the notice appeared on local stations all across Idaho, as well as in some large metropolitan areas in other states.

In a matter of days, over fifty names had been tentatively added to Nick's list. Only after DNA proved they were half-sibs did the names make it to the active roll, which brought an invitation to join the Facebook group.

Chapter 36

DETECTIVE HUNTER THREW HIS PEN at his desk and glared at the officer facing him. "What do you mean, he said we don't have enough evidence?"

"Sorry, sir, that's what the judge said." The officer looked at the floor before continuing. No one in the department enjoyed talking to Hunter when he wasn't getting his way. "He said you need to wait for the DNA analysis. If you're wrong, it would be very embarrassing, and the county might get sued. We should have the information in less than a week. If there's a match, he'll issue it."

"What about the people that might be murdered between now and then? Did he think about them?" Hunter yelled. "We've got to get this guy locked up. And probably his kids and his wife too. I suspect they're all involved, I just don't know how."

"Maybe if that hoodie had shown something . . ."

"These guys are smart, so it's not surprising there was nothing useful found in his house, but as soon as he called about Lois Bishop, I knew he was connected. He had no reason to even know her, so why else would he be sniffing around, trying to find out about our investigation."

"He didn't ask about the five others in the area who had been murdered by the same gun, in the same way."

"Maybe he didn't want to seem too obvious."

"He says she was a relative."

"Half-brother who never knew her. Easy to make up."

"Did you look into that?"

"I didn't have to. I interviewed her mother right after the murder and asked for a list of relatives. His name never came up. Hell, the professor even admitted to being a sharpshooter. And that curved pinky of his matches the pinky of the assassin I saw in two of those videos. A clue no one else noticed, I might add."

"True, but the judge says lots of people have a curved finger, and you don't know for a fact that he's such a good shot. He might just have been bragging."

"I had Lambert go to the shooting range after the whole family went there. The target he used had nothing but bullseyes."

"Okay, he's a good marksman, but that doesn't mean he killed anyone."

"We know the professor took off in the Honda CR-V and ditched his tail the night Montoya, the dentist, was murdered."

"But we don't know where he went. No witnesses saw him at the crime scene. He might have an alibi."

"I'm sure he's got people who will lie about him being elsewhere, or he went someplace and slipped out to murder Montoya, then returned. He'll have an alibi, all right, but it will be a load of crap."

"About the Starling's CR-V—it has a dent on the left fender that didn't show up in any of the surveillance recordings."

"But it's the same make and color as the car the murderer drives. Those recordings are grainy, just not clear enough to show the dent."

"Well, the judge wasn't convinced. And the license plate screws were dirty and rusty—didn't look like the plates had been swapped out recently."

"Like I said, these guys are smart. They've figured out a way to steal plates and attach them to the car without removing the old plates, or they rub mud on the screws each time they put their plates back on. Look, we know from our experts in crime scene analysis that the triggerman, or men, is the same height as Starling and his older son. The younger kid is involved in some way, keeping some kind of records. I haven't yet figured out what the mother does, but she had to know they're using her car. Coincidence about the professor going out the night of Montoya's murder, the height of him and his son, Greg, the mom's car, Starling's curved finger, his claim to be related to Bishop and Gibbert, and his poking around about our progress? I don't think so. If I had a nickel for every guilty person who pokes around, I'd be a rich man."

"The judge says the height of Starling and his son could just be a coincidence. Lots of people are six feet tall. You don't even have a motive."

"I don't need to know the motive. I just know they're guilty. Why do you suppose the whole family went to the shooting range for target practice this weekend?"

"About that—they didn't use a gun the same caliber as the one used in the murders." The officer backed away slightly, as if she expected Hunter to punch another hole in the wall.

"Of course not," Hunter yelled, making a fist. "They suspect they're being followed so they practiced with a different caliber gun."

"What about The Rocket? He's a half-brother of the guy, and he's got this weird mutation. He's convinced the Starlings are innocent."

"I think Professor Starling has The Rocket hoodwinked. I don't know what the professor's angle is, connecting with his long-lost celebrity half-brother, and claiming others are his half-siblings, but he's the criminal mastermind behind all of this. I've been a homicide detective since you were in diapers. I can feel these things. That judge needs to respect my years of experience. It was me and me alone who solved the Cook murders, the Crescent Lake massacre, and the Highway boxcutter killings, to name a few. I have an instinct about these cases that never lets me down. I should take a picture of all the awards I've gotten and send it to him." Hunter stared angrily at the officer, picked up the letter opener on his desk, and smashed the point into the desktop, adding to the nicks in the wood finish from previous desktop assaults.

"Well, it's not up to me, sir," the officer said nervously. "I'm only the messenger. The judge says you have to wait for the DNA analysis."

"Let's hope nobody else is murdered as we're sitting around waiting, while the judge cleans his belly button."

Without responding, the officer turned and left the room, leaving Hunter to sulk alone. Moments later, all could hear the familiar sound of a fist penetrating the wall of the detective's office.

Hunter thought about Karl Kemp, the first murder case he solved after he became a detective. He'd wanted to arrest Kemp, only to have a judge refuse to issue the necessary warrant. Within a week, Kemp had murdered two more innocent people. Hunter had promised himself he'd never again fail to protect the public.

For the rest of the day, the detective concentrated on other cases. A murder committed during a convenience store holdup, and a woman was strangled—probably by her husband, who had been arrested previously for being drunk and disorderly. Nothing with the challenge and gravity of the serial killers at large. He left work that evening and headed for home, still seething about the judge's decision.

Hunter's condominium, a one-bedroom unit in a middle-class area, was anything but cheerful. He had a TV, a stained beige sofa, a plastic coffee table, and two folding chairs in the living room, the latter purchased just in case a rare visitor stopped by. The heavy curtains were closed, letting in little light during the day. By keeping them shut, he didn't need to bother closing them in the evening. No pictures hung on the walls, only a corkboard to which newspaper articles about crimes he had solved or was working on were pinned. The only other wall features were holes in the plaster, four in the living room, and one in the bedroom, where Hunter, in fits of rage, had punched the walls.

The kitchen cabinets were sparsely occupied by glasses and dishes for four, as well as cans and packets of food, heating being the only preparation needed before eating. The few pots and pans he had were rarely used, the microwave being his go-to kitchen appliance. As he walked to the kitchen sink for a glass of water, Hunter detected a strong, musty odor. Looking around, he spotted an open loaf of bread with mold flourishing on the front piece. Swearing under his breath, he sealed the bread loaf and placed it outside the front door to dispose of the next time he left his unit.

The detective walked to the bedroom and emptied his pockets of his keys, wallet, and pen, placing them on the small computer desk next to the dresser. He smiled a bit as usual as he looked at the pen, a gift from the only person in the world who loved him, his mother. She'd explained it was what was called a tactical pen, with a point strong enough to break glass, and a small knife blade that shot out the top at the touch of a button. He doubted the knife blade could do much damage and laughed to himself when she told him she thought the pen might save his life someday, even suggesting he carry it with him in place of a gun. His mother had been a strong anti-gun activist for as long as he could remember. Clearly, she had no idea what his job entailed or how safely and effectively he could use his firearm if need be. Nonetheless, the pen wrote smoothly, and he carried it in his pocket whenever he went out.

His mother had never wanted him to go into law enforcement, hoping he'd become a pilot, teacher, doctor, or just about anything else. But she understood why he'd been drawn to the profession. He'd wanted to be a police officer ever since her husband—Hunter's father— had been murdered in a carjacking when her son was ten. Mentally sharp but suffering from arthritis, she now lived in an assisted living facility in Kentucky.

Hunter sat on the queen-size bed and bent over to remove his shoes and put on his slippers, which he kept just under the box spring. *Damned homo judge. Just like a female judge. A judge who was a real man would never hesitate to lock this dangerous guy up. He'd be more concerned about keeping the public safe than worrying about making sure all the paperwork looked perfect.*

The bed was the only furniture he had taken following his divorce five years prior. After ten years of marriage that had produced no children and few joyous times, his wife had decided to move on. Since then, the only person to have slept in the bed was himself. Looking around, an observer might conclude that Detective Hunter had no life, but they would be wrong— he was living the life he loved, and it centered solely around his job as a homicide detective. Nothing else mattered much.

The detective, comfortable in his slippers, walked to the living room where he picked up the Samsung remote control, turned on the TV, and sat on the sofa. After finding the right channel, he went to the kitchen to get his evening meal, then returned to the couch where he balanced a bowl of microwaved chili on his right thigh, and sipped on a bottle of imported beer, the only thing he splurged on. It was time for *Blue Bloods*, one of his few guilty pleasures. He identified strongly with the characters in the show, their frustrations, and their triumphs.

Twenty minutes later Detective Danny Reagan was chasing down a criminal when Hunter's cell phone rang. Checking the caller ID, he determined that the watch commander was calling. *Damn, I really should get a DVR. These interruptions always come at the wrong time.* He answered tersely.

"Now don't be mad at me, Brad. I know you're gonna say told you so and all that, but remember, I'm on your side. It's the damn judge that's fucked everything up."

Hunter breathed deeply. "I don't know what you're talking about. Would you stop making excuses and tell me why the fuck you're calling me?"

"He—or they—struck again."

Hunter screamed into the phone. "Goddamn it. I warned them. I knew this would happen."

"I know. Remember, I told you not to be mad at me."

"Right. Sorry. I'm just so pissed off."

"I don't blame you. Now let me tell you where this happened. Currently, it's being investigated by the locals. The victim is a thirty-six-year-old white female named Darlene Sparrow. She was a physical therapist with two young children. Found by her husband inside her car. Looks like she was shot in the head while waiting for the garage door to open. The local police will be contacting you tomorrow with all the evidence they've collected and will send over copies of the surveillance videos they collect. So far it looks exactly like the others."

"Did our stakeout see anyone leave the Starling house earlier?"

The watch commander paused before answering. "I'm afraid there was no car out there tonight. Budgetary problems. They're only authorizing a stakeout every fourth night or so."

"Unbelievable assholes," Hunter yelled.

"Believe me, I begged, but couldn't get a car out there tonight."

As always, Hunter insisted on seeing the crime scene for himself that night. The watch commander gave him the address and the detective left immediately to drive the thirty miles to the destination, dumping the moldy bread in the garbage chute on the way out. Again, the crime had been perpetrated in an upper-middle-class neighborhood, now with yellow crime scene tape in front of a two-story gabled house with a manicured lawn. He noted a single light on in the home and imagined the husband trying to comfort his children while in the depths of despair himself.

The detective exited his car and inspected the area with the aid of his flashlight. He found police markings in the area where the casings had been found but saw no evidence of blood or anything else that might have DNA. That dead mosquito from the last case was just a lucky find. Professor Starling was careful. If he'd been locked up this wouldn't have happened. Hunter imagined that no one else in the family would have gone out on their own and done this.

He was getting ready to leave when a middle-aged man exited the house and walked down the driveway.

"Excuse me," Hunter said, as he displayed his badge. "Are you Mr. Sparrow?"

"No, I live across the street. I imagine you're here about the murder."

"Right."

"I was just keeping Kyle company. He's in pretty bad shape, but he insisted I leave. His sister will be arriving tomorrow morning to help out with the kids and make arrangements."

"Did you know these people well?"

"We've been neighbors for about eight years. Me and my wife have been pretty close with them. Lovely couple. Can't figure out who woulda done this."

"Did they get along well?"

"You mean with each other?" Hunter nodded in the affirmative. "Absolutely. We used to joke about what lovebirds they were, even though they weren't exactly newlyweds."

"I understand the victim was a physical therapist. What does her husband do?"

"He's an orthopedic surgeon. She worked in his office. Would have driven me crazy to work with my wife, but those two seemed to enjoy working together."

Hunter left, convinced that the husband, usually a prime suspect, hadn't murdered his wife. It was that degenerate family who had once again inflicted terrible pain on innocents for some reason so far known only to the Starlings.

Chapter 37

THE FOLLOWING EVENING, MARTIN AND the rest of his family sat before the TV to watch the news as Cat prepared dinner. A cloak of somberness had overcome them, and they'd fallen into a pattern of watching the local evening newscast together before dinner. All listened as the newsreader began the next story.

"There has been another in the bizarre string of murders that has afflicted the area. Last night, the body of Darlene Sparrow, a thirty-six-year-old married mother of two, was found in front of her house by her husband. The victim was in her car, and it appeared she had been waiting for the garage door to open when she was taken down by a single bullet to the head. This appears to be the eighth in a series of murders locally that seem to be connected. Police are reaching out to other areas to see if there are similar cases in those communities. No suspect is under arrest at this time, although the police are following an active lead, for which they haven't provided any details. Meanwhile, people are cautioned to be careful and check out their surroundings, especially in front of their own homes. If any suspicious cars or people are noted, you are advised to call the police immediately."

Once the segment was concluded, Martin and the other family members looked at each other in silence. Martin was the first to speak.

"I was with Elmer and Nick last night, making the public service video. Elmer and the people at the studio can vouch for us."

"I know you were there, too," Georgia said. "But you don't need to convince me you're innocent. Just that detective. We don't know what time the murder took place. It could have been after you left the studio."

"I was texting Olivia," Greg said. "We texted back and forth for hours."

"But you can text from anywhere," Georgia said. "The police could probably locate the tower you pinged off of if they wanted to, but I'm not sure they're interested in finding the truth."

"A good defense attorney could, though," Greg said.

"I'm not sure that would help," Martin said. "The cops could argue you had someone else write those texts."

"They'd never find that hypothetical person because he doesn't exist," Greg answered. "I sent them myself."

"Just because they couldn't find that person doesn't mean he doesn't exist. A prosecutor can offer all sorts of arguments to sink a good defense."

"I'm afraid your alibis won't hold up to a cop who is convinced you're guilty," Georgia said. "Let's hope that DNA analysis gets finished soon."

"At least now we know the police have connected the local cases we know about, and some we didn't know about," Martin said. He turned to Nick. "Check to see if Darlene Sparrow is on your list."

"I don't have to. I remember her name because she's been active on the Facebook page a lot during the past few days. She recently tested positive for the mutation and was asking lots of questions about that. Her kid's tests are pending."

"Don't try to convince me that this is just a coincidence," Georgia said. "Someone has a list like the one we have of all your half-sibs, and he's killing them."

"It appears more likely with every new murder," Martin said. "That reminds me—when I came home tonight the alarm wasn't on. We didn't spend all that money on a new alarm system to have it ignored. You all need to be more conscientious. Set it each time you go in and out."

"Sorry, Dad," Greg said. "I think I forgot to set it after I got home from practice. I'll do better."

"I hope so," Martin answered. "The safety of everyone in this house depends on it. You're almost eighteen years old. It's time you acted more responsibly."

The professor tossed and turned all night. He noted Georgia getting up several times to walk around the house. "What are you doing?" he asked.

"Checking on the kids and Cat. I keep hearing noises."

"Just the wind and the house creaking."

"Hope so." He didn't want to let on that the sounds were making him anxious too.

Breakfast the following morning was a solemn affair. Everyone seemed tired from a lack of sleep, despite having slept later than usual, even for a Saturday.

Trying to lighten the mood, Martin asked Greg, "What are you and Olivia doing this weekend?"

"We're not getting together this weekend." Greg's tone was somber.

That was the first instance Martin remembered the two not spending time together on a weekend when they were both in town since they'd started dating months earlier. "You two splitting up?"

"I don't know. She texted me this morning that her dad says she can't see me anymore. He's a police officer and thinks we're all involved in these murders, so I've been banned."

"I can't believe it," Georgia said. "There's no evidence, and no one here's even been charged. None of our names has been released to the papers."

"That doesn't mean people don't know," Greg said. "Seems everyone at school is aware we're under some sort of suspicion."

"What do you mean? How do they all know?"

"Word spreads pretty fast. There's kids at school who seem to know everything because their parents are cops, and they tell their friends. I didn't want to worry you any more than you already were. Besides, you can't do anything about it. Since we're on the subject, I want to let you know I don't plan to go to my graduation."

"This is getting out of hand," Georgia said. "I wish you'd brought this up before. I won't hear of you missing your graduation. That detective is ruining our reputation, not to mention our lives. A few people in Jill's campaign have been noticeably stand-offish. I wonder if people think I'm living with a bunch of murderers, or somehow involved myself. I'll bet that's why Ruby from down the street didn't wave back when I saw her gardening in front of her house yesterday. I know she saw me."

"Another thing, while we're talking about it, "Nick said, "my English teacher kept me after class two days ago to ask me if I had any family problems I wanted to report. I told her nothing was going on, but she asked me the same thing three times. I didn't want to be late for my next class, so finally, I just left. It was awkward."

"I shouldn't be surprised by this," Martin said. "I know people are talking behind my back. My secretary, Ruth, has been doing a good job of keeping me informed. Seems Stephen Bowditch is the only faculty member who's been standing up for me. I guess everyone else thinks I'm capable of being a serial killer." Martin looked around the table from one face to the next before continuing. "I'm glad we got all of this out in the open. I thought I was the only one people are suspicious of, and it pains me to see that the rest of you have been suffering in silence. Unfortunately, I'm afraid we're all going to have to just suck it up until our names are cleared. Until then, we've got each other."

After dinner, Georgia approached Martin in his study. "Are you at all concerned about your job security?" she asked.

"I didn't want to worry you, but the dean asked me a few days ago if I wanted to take some time off, and leave Stephen in charge. Since I'm tenured, he has no grounds to sideline me. I told him I intended to continue working without interruption."

"Do you think Stephen is trying to push you out to advance himself?"

"Not a chance. He told me the chairman had asked him to take over, but he'd refused. I believe him. He doesn't see himself as a leader because he lacks the confidence he should have. He's a really smart guy, and I've been encouraging him to take on more responsibility. In time, I'm sure he will."

"Maybe you should speed things up for him. Take some time off now. I can tell the strain is getting to you."

"The last thing I want to do is appear to be hiding. Once the DNA studies clear all of us, things should get back to normal. Speaking of DNA," Martin said, lifting the blue folder he had been studying, "That second son of mine has done a fine job on his biology project. I can't believe he put together such a detailed, well-thought-out report. I hardly helped him at all."

Georgia smiled. "I always knew my second son was special. My first one too." Georgia left the study, the smile on her face replaced by a worried look as she walked down the hall.

When Martin arrived at work the following day, he noticed he was greeted with less enthusiasm than usual, even sensing some of the staff grimacing at each other behind his back. The extra deference he had been receiving on account of his cane had dissipated. The professor reasoned that if he were in their shoes, he might react the same way. After all, how could anyone be sure he wasn't a serial killer? He was mild-mannered and generally kept to himself, similar to many serial killers that have been written about over the years. If someone told him another member of his department killed people on the side, he just might believe them.

Doing his best to ignore the frosty reception, he sat at his desk and went through his emails. When he'd dispensed with most of them, he answered a call from Constance Jackson.

"We've located Dr. Sanborn's wife, Agatha. She's remarried and lives in Jupiter, Florida. Agatha divorced the doctor two years before he died suddenly, then changed back to her maiden name, Laurier. She remarried several years later, and her last name is now Diaz. Fatima has arranged for a phone call with Agatha tomorrow at seven a.m. our time. She had agreed for you and me to join the call. I'm hoping you can make time for that call tomorrow morning."

"Absolutely. I don't normally leave for work until much later than seven."

"Let's hope Agatha can help us out."

Before hanging up, Martin shared with Constance his concern about the murders of his half-siblings.

"Interesting," Constance said. "I've read about those murders in the news. I don't know what to make of the fact that some of your half-siblings have been victims, but if there's one thing I've learned, it's that inexplicable events usually make sense in time."

Martin was up early the next day. The time for the phone call arrived with Martin sitting at his desk in the study, staring at his cell phone, a list of questions to ask in front of him. Finally, the moment arrived, announced by the familiar Marimba ring of his iPhone. He answered using the speaker phone setting.

The awkward business of making introductions for several people over the phone was expedited by Constance. On behalf of herself and the others, she thanked Agatha for agreeing to speak to them and got down to business.

"I understand you divorced Dr. Sanborn two years before his death."

"That's right. He was a very difficult man—brilliant, but mean and unforgiving. He was in good health when we divorced. Despite his challenging personality, I never would have deserted him had he been in failing health."

"Do you know how he died?" Martin asked.

"Massive blood clot to the lungs, a pulmonary embolism, I was told."

"Do you know what brought on the blood clot?" Martin asked, fairly certain his pulmonary embolism was the result of the fibrinogen mutation he'd generously shared with so many people.

"No one ever gave me a reason. He hadn't had any heart problems, cancer, surgery, or infections—I know sometimes they can cause people to get clots." Agatha sniffled, then started to speak. "Our daughter . . ." her voice trailed off, as if she were unable to continue.

"Are you okay, Agatha?" Constance asked.

A few moments later, Agatha answered, "Yes, I'm okay. You'd think that after all these years I could talk about our daughter without breaking down."

"There's nothing worse than losing a child," Fatima said.

Agatha sniffled again and began speaking. "We didn't lose her then, but she came close to dying from a serious bacterial infection when she was two. She developed blood clots in her legs, and they had to amputate both of them below the knees."

"Sorry to hear that," Martin said, thinking the unfortunate child had likely inherited the mutated fibrinogen gene from her father, giving her a proclivity to form abnormal blood clots. "Do you have other children?"

"No, only Naomi. There were complications with her birth and I had to have a hysterectomy. Kirby was very upset. He'd always wanted to have lots of children. I wanted a big family, too, but quickly learned to live with the fact that we had only one child. Kirby couldn't adjust, but he wouldn't hear of adoption. I think he thought his DNA was so special, if he couldn't father more children himself, he didn't want any more."

"Sounds narcissistic," Constance said.

"I hate to speak ill of the dead, but he was the definition of a narcissist. If only I'd recognized that when I was young and fell for him."

"Do you know what happened to Dr. Sanborn's office files after he died?" Constance asked. "We're very interested in finding them because we have reason to believe they contain the names of people who need to be notified about an important issue regarding their health. Even though the records are old, the matter was only recently discovered."

"Oh, dear. It sounds terribly important. Did Kirby do something wrong to endanger these people?"

"No, but some of his patients need to be notified. We want to look through his records to identify them."

"I'm sure he kept meticulous files. He was just that way. I'd like to help, but I don't know what happened to the records after his death. He never remarried and had no siblings, so Naomi took care of his estate after he died."

"I'd like to speak to her," Constance said. "She might know where the files are. Can you check if she'd be willing to talk with us?"

"I wish I could, but I don't know where she is. I'm not even sure if she's still alive."

"It's important," Martin said, "because not only do we need to find those files, but from what you've told us, I think she may have a dangerous medical condition that needs to be treated—a clotting disorder like what Dr. Sanborn had."

"I'd love to help, but I don't see how I can. Naomi had such a difficult life. Despite the amputations, she was able to master walking and running with her prostheses, but kids made fun of her when she started school. She became withdrawn and started to do poorly in her classes, even though she tested high on intelligence tests and had a remarkable memory. To make matters worse, Kirby was very disappointed she wasn't a star pupil and took every opportunity to ridicule her. The bastard told her he cared more about his creations—that's the word he used when he spoke of the babies born from the artificial inseminations he performed—than he did about her. After the divorce, I went through a series of therapists to try to help Naomi, but they all failed. Four years ago, she tried to kill herself with pills. Fortunately, I found her in time and paramedics saved her. She was discharged from the hospital to a very nice psychiatric facility I paid for. She was furious with me for saving her. She escaped the facility, and I haven't seen her since. I hired a detective two years ago, but she was unable to find her and thought Naomi had succeeded in committing suicide. I refuse to believe she's dead, though. I don't think I could bear it. Now, to make matters worse, you think she could be in danger from more blood clots."

"Yes, I believe Dr. Sanborn had a pulmonary embolism because he had a defective gene, which he passed on to her," Martin said.

"Goodness," Agatha said. "You think if Naomi is alive that she's in danger?"

"Yes," Martin answered. "But there's a treatment. Just one or two pills a day could save her life."

"She's suffered so much as it is," Agatha said. "I hope she calls. I have no other way to find her."

"I hope we can locate her. We'd also like to notify other relatives of your husband, so they can be tested for the disorder," Constance said.

"Kirby had no relatives other than Naomi. No siblings. No cousins, even. His dad was an only child and died just a few years ago. His mother, who died of a stroke when he was young, had a brother, but he had no kids before he died of AIDS."

"Do you know anything about the health of the doctor's grandparents?"

"All of them lived at least to their late eighties."

"That's good to know," Martin said. "Since the doctor's mother had a stroke, but her parents lived a long time, she was probably the first to have the mutation. Only her progeny would have it, so the mutation probably hasn't spread beyond Dr. Sanborn's children."

"So just Naomi is at risk, then," Agatha said.

"You've been most helpful," Constance said, not wanting to add to Agatha's anguish by telling her about their suspicion that Sanborn had fathered many other children. "Thank you for your time. If you think of anything else that might be helpful to us, please contact me."

Once the call had ended, there was a moment of silence before Constance remarked, "If I wasn't convinced before, I am now. This crazy doctor fathered all these kids. Why else would he refer to them as his creations, and say he cared more about them than about Naomi?"

"We need to get all the names of the people the police suspect were murdered by the same assassin as Lois Bishop," Martin said, "and we need to confirm that all the victims are Dr. Sanborn's kids. But who would be killing them, and why?"

"We're no closer to getting the list of all the mothers Sanborn impregnated," Constance said. "We need to find Naomi if the poor thing is still alive. She may know where Sanborn's records are, and her life is in danger—from her medical condition, and maybe from this assassin."

"I suppose I'm a target, too," Martin said. "And because I participated in that video warning people they might have the mutation, the murderer knows what I look like."

Nothing about the conversation with Agatha Diaz eased Martin's anxiety. He hadn't slept well in weeks, his once healthy appetite was replaced by a constant queasiness. Days earlier, he'd needed to tighten his belt a notch. Whereas he'd had a few gray strands on his head at the time of his stroke, he now had salt-and-pepper hair, heavy on the salt. He tried to keep a brave front for his family, but it was getting harder every day.

Chapter 38

"DO YOU THINK GREG AND I are on the list?" Nick asked Martin. "Or Mom?"

"If I knew what the motive was, I might be able to answer you better, but from what I know, only the children of the doctor have been targeted. If we could get the police to cooperate, rather than hound us, we would know for sure."

"So what do we do now?"

"We wait. I wait. Meanwhile, we all need to be very careful."

"What about what other people are saying about us?" Nick asked.

"What about it?"

"What can we do about it? Kenny's mom won't let me come over to their house."

"I can't believe that," Georgia exclaimed. "Why, I'm going to call her up and give her a piece of my mind."

"You need to keep every piece of that you have," Martin said, receiving the expected glare from his wife. "Really, honey, it's best if we ignore this. We'll be vindicated soon, I'm sure, and everyone will be impressed with how well we conducted ourselves. Impressed, and at the same time, ashamed of themselves. Meanwhile, it's a losing proposition to argue with these people who are jumping to conclusions. Look at our politics. Once people have their minds made up, it's almost impossible to change them until there is overwhelming evidence. Often overwhelming evidence isn't enough."

"Okay, I won't call her today," Georgia said, "but I won't stay silent forever. Meanwhile, I'm worried you might get shot outside our home when you return from work."

Starting that evening, either Nick or Greg, armed with the family gun in full view, stepped outside to greet their father when he came home from work. Cat rarely went out in the evening, but if she did, someone would similarly meet her outside. Two days later, Martin had floodlights installed to light up the front of his house and the adjacent street. Several surveillance cameras captured all the nearby activity. That evening, the family celebrated Greg's eighteenth birthday. They went through the motions of a cake and presents, but there was little joy.

The anxiety that gripped the Starling family was shared by others in the community, as the series of homicides was discussed on the local news. The murders were reported as random, the work of a perverted individual or group of individuals. The general public was unaware they probably would never be the target of the assassin.

"The discussions on our Facebook site are getting rather heated," Martin said to Georgia as they were preparing to retire that evening. "Some members are worried about the number of people from our group who have been murdered. Few think it's just a coincidence. Several have posted concerns about me and Nick collecting names and starting the Facebook page. They know we have access to it, so their wording is vague, but I worry that some of my half-sibs are starting to suspect us of being involved in the murders, and may be having private communication away from the Facebook page."

"Hopefully, the police will get your DNA results soon and exonerate you."

"Before that happens, though, I wonder if I should address the issue on the site, talk of my concern that we are being targeted, and warn them to be extra careful."

"No need. The public has been warned. Your half-sibs should take the same precautions as everyone else. I don't know if you'd be doing anyone a favor by sharing your concerns and making everyone on the site paranoid."

"Paranoid like us?"

"Well, yes."

"I'd say we're being more careful than we would be if we thought this was a threat to the general public. If another person on the list gets murdered and I didn't try to warn them—"

"I know, you'd feel terrible. I see your point. You can post your concerns in the morning."

"I hope it doesn't backfire. If Hunter finds out, he'll think I'm trying to deflect attention from myself." Martin paused before continuing. "I'll have to take that chance."

"I knew you'd say that."

"Of course, if I'm not exonerated before another murder, a murder which I'm afraid is going to happen sooner or later, we may start seeing some trouble from my half-siblings. Not to mention more unpleasantness from our neighbors and the boys' classmates."

"You're right, I'm afraid. I didn't want to tell you, but someone wrote something nasty on our garage door. Fortunately, they used chalk and I was able to hose it off."

"What did they write?"

"Don't feed the serial killers inside."

As Martin sat on the bed, his head in his hands, Georgia took a toothpaste box from under the bed and handed it to Martin. "Greg, for all the faults you think he has, is concerned about you. He wanted to give this to you so you could relax."

With one eyebrow raised and his head tilted to the side, Martin shook the box. Too light to contain a tube of toothpaste, he felt something lightweight inside. He opened the container and turned it upside down over the bed. Five neatly-rolled doobies fell out.

"Before you object, I want you to just try one. You're wound up so tight, I'm afraid you're going to have a heart attack. And here," Georgia said, retrieving something else from under the bed, "I've got a bag of Cool Ranch Doritos. That was always your favorite back then, and you could stand to put on a few pounds."

"I guess I don't have much to lose," Martin said as he lit a joint with a match Georgia handed him. He slept better that night than he had in quite some time.

Before work the next day, Martin logged into the Facebook site. Zoe Clyburn had posted the date and time of her next stand-up performance, to be held in three weeks at a small venue near Boise. Two members had already posted that they'd be attending. Martin responded that he, too, was looking forward to the event and meeting some of his half-sibs in person. Then he posted his concerns about the serial killer in their area targeting people like them who had been fathered by Dr. Sanborn. He urged everyone to take particular care when arriving home in the dark. He also mentioned that he had gone to the police with his concerns but to his surprise, rather than helping, the detective leading the investigation considered him and one of his sons to be suspects. He expected to be cleared soon by DNA samples they had willingly provided. He didn't know if the murderer chose his victims from their Facebook page, but he cautioned everyone not to share the list of site members with anyone on the outside. He didn't see Greg at breakfast that morning. He had left early for an appointment to have his senior graduation photo taken.

That evening, Martin pulled into the driveway next to Georgia's car. Although it wasn't quite dark yet, he called Greg on his cell phone and asked him for protection while he exited the car. Once he saw Greg at the front door holding a fully-exposed pistol, Martin stepped out of his car. He was about to slam the driver's door shut when he heard the sound of footsteps running towards him.

He looked up at Greg, standing in the doorway holding the gun in his right hand, but appearing frozen. *Damn. He can't handle this. He's just a boy. I should have carried the gun in my car so I could protect myself.* He kept his eyes on Greg, hoping to see him snap into action. Instead, his son continued to stand in a catatonic state. Martin's muscles tensed as he waited for the fatal bullet from the unknown assassin. He shut his eyes tightly, as he thought of Georgia and the boys going on without him. He wished he could tell them how much he loved them, that he knew they could go on to live happy, successful lives without him.

Seconds after he first heard the footsteps, he was still standing, awaiting his demise, when the sound of rubber-soled shoes hitting the pavement approached closer than he had expected. A moment later he felt both of his arms being grabbed firmly. He opened his eyes and looked to his right and left. Half of him was relieved to see he was straddled by two uniformed officers. The other half was terrified—not of being shot dead on the spot, but of being arrested. If for some reason his DNA hadn't freed him, he feared he was beyond help and might be spending a lot of time, perhaps all the time he had left in the world, behind bars.

As one officer took his cane and cuffed his wrists behind his back, the other patted him down. Martin started to lose his balance, but one of the officers held onto him and began to speak. "Dr. Martin Starling, you are under arrest for the murders of Darlene Sparrow, Ansel Montoya, Barney Gibbert . . ." the list went on. The combination of relief and horror Martin felt prevented him from fully grasping everything that was being said. As he was escorted away, Martin yelled to Greg, "Call Matthew Douglas."

Sitting in the back of the police cruiser alone, hands uncomfortably restrained behind him, Martin's heart pounded as sweat snaked down his face. *How can this be happening to me? I'm innocent. They can't have any solid evidence against me unless it was fabricated. I'm sure Hunter is behind this. He's had something against me ever since I spoke to him on the phone. But why?* These thoughts occupied Martin's mind during the half hour drive to the precinct house. Meanwhile, the two officers sitting in the front seat of the police cruiser chitchatted about their kids, seeming oblivious to Martin's plight.

When the vehicle finally came to the police station, the driver steered the car to the back of the building and stopped before a wide opening. A security grille hung from the top, preventing the cruiser from proceeding farther. "Looks like someone intercepted our radio message again," one of the officers said, looking at the group of two dozen reporters and photographers that were waiting. Martin lowered his head as lights flashed and the journalists shouted questions.

"Why'd you do it?"

"Did your whole family help you?"

"Are you the leader of a cult?"

The officer in the passenger seat got out, pushed the closest members of the media out of the way, and punched a code into the adjacent keypad. The grille rose, allowing the driver to enter a large barren space with a cement floor inside the building. Once inside, the metal barricade lowered, and the voices of the yelling reporters became muted and difficult to understand.

One of the officers opened Martin's door, and directed him to stand. He re-cuffed him so both of his hands were in front, then offered him his cane, which had been placed in the trunk during the ride. As Martin grabbed the cane the officer warned him, "Don't try anything funny with that cane, or we'll take it away." He then grabbed his prisoner's upper arm and led him from the car through a set of glass doors at the opposite end of the space.

Martin found himself in a large room with a half dozen sheriff's officers milling around, most behind a high wraparound counter. A female officer approached and waved a small device slightly larger than a cell phone around his body, moving the cane out of the way as needed. When it hovered near his front right pants pocket, the device emitted a high-pitched beep. Holding the device in one hand, the officer retrieved keys and change from Martin's pocket, then said, "Okay. He's good to go."

The officer who had been escorting Martin then guided the professor to the counter, where a uniformed deputy sheriff asked him a series of questions, entering information into the computer before him as he proceeded. After another pat down, this more thorough than the previous one, Martin was led to a brightly lit area where he was positioned in front of a large ruler painted on the wall, which he recognized as the type behind subjects of mug shots. A placard with his name, birthdate, current date, location, and arrest number was shoved in his hand. A voice yelled out, "Look here."

Martin looked up and was briefly blinded by a flash of light as the moment was captured in perpetuity by the camera several feet away.

"Turn to the side," the voice shouted.

Martin complied, and a second image was recorded. Wasting no time, the officer escorting him again grabbed Martin's arm and guided him through a set of wooden double doors into a room about the size of a bus, with several fixed wooden benches. A pudgy officer in full uniform wearing vinyl gloves waddled over to Martin. "I got this," he said to the deputy who had been leading Martin around.

"Sure thing," the now-familiar deputy sheriff said, then turned and exited the room.

"Remove all your clothes," the portly deputy said.

"Can I call my lawyer?" Martin asked, barely recognizing his own voice, which was dry and cracking. He worried that Nick hadn't called his attorney as he had requested.

"You have to be fully processed first," the deputy answered. His voice was cold. "Then you can call."

As the officer stood close by and stared, Martin sat on a bench and removed his shoes, placing his cane nearby. He felt his face flush from embarrassment as he fiddled with his belt.

"Hurry it up," the deputy sheriff ordered.

Martin swallowed hard, then tried to mentally remove himself from the awkward situation. He disrobed down to his briefs, slowly folding his clothes to stall for time as he progressed.

"Those, too," the deputy said, staring at Martin's crotch.

Looking at the floor, Martin pushed himself to standing with his cane and removed his underwear, thankful he had worn a pair of navy briefs that morning, so any stains, if present, would be inconspicuous. He placed them atop his clothes just before the officer scooped them up and placed them in a labeled box. "Come with me," he said.

Martin walked with the officer through another wooden door into a brightly lit room with a row of showers. "Bend over," the deputy said tersely.

Already humiliated more than he'd ever been before, Martin complied as he tried to think of better times. When he felt his testicles being groped, then a finger invading his most private orifice, he was jarred back to the present. After it was over, Martin wondered if the officer had put on a fresh pair of gloves. He had been too traumatized to notice.

"Take a shower," the deputy sheriff said.

Glad the worst was over, Martin showered, after which he was handed gray prison garb which he happily put on. He was pleasantly surprised that he wasn't assaulted with a spray of delousing powder as he'd seen in many movies.

Once dressed in his new, or at least new to him, threads, another deputy sheriff escorted Martin to the open door of a small room. The aroma of a burger and fries made him feel hungrier than he had been seconds before.

A familiar voice from within said, "Come in and take a seat."

As Martin entered the room, he saw Detective Hunter waiting inside, looking like a cat ready to swat around the mouse it had just caught. "You're probably hungry," he said, cracking a sneer that Martin figured was his attempt at showing a friendly smile. As Martin took a seat opposite him and placed his cane nearby, Hunter said, "I brought you some food. If you want to eat, all you have to do is talk to me."

Martin looked at the inviting fast food in front of him, tempted to speak to Hunter for an hour if only he could eat the meal before him. Invoking every ounce of self-control he had, Martin said, "I want to speak to my attorney."

"We can resolve this more quickly if you and I can have a conversation now. It might take quite some time before your attorney can get here. Probably not until tomorrow or the next day."

Although enticed to do whatever it took to satisfy his hunger, Martin repeated his request, "I want to speak to my attorney."

Hunter shook his head, and said, "You're gonna regret this. I'm trying to help you out, here. You sure you want your lawyer?"

Martin nodded in the affirmative. "Yes, I want my lawyer. I believe you need to stop questioning me now."

"That's the way it usually works on TV. However, there's no recording of this conversation, so who's to say what happened?" After pausing a moment, Hunter added, "I see I'm not going to get anywhere with you." He then asked for the name and city of Martin's lawyer and made a call on his cell. Moments later, he received a text with Matthew Douglas's number. He dialed the number on the landline phone in the room, then handed the receiver to Martin.

After Martin spoke to his attorney's answering service and waited on hold for what seemed way too long, Douglas picked up.

"I hear you've been arrested," Douglas said.

"How did you know?"

"Your son called."

"I wasn't sure he'd remember to do that. He seemed pretty upset at the time."

"He sounded stressed when I spoke to him, but be assured that he called. I'm in my car right now. Hang tight, I'm on my way to the jail. Try to relax."

Easier said than done. Martin hung up reluctantly, wanting to stay connected to Douglas, his only hope at the moment, as long as possible. Hunter was gone, and seconds later a guard came to lead Martin to his quarters, a short walk away. The cell was a small room, about the size of the cargo space in a small U-Haul truck. The drab gray cement walls did nothing to boost Martin's spirits. As he stared at the toilet, sink, and cot, his chest felt hollow. The clank of the metal door slamming behind him brought him to a new low. With not much choice regarding where to sit, he took a seat in the middle of the cot and rested his head in his hands, feeling the metal support under the thin mattress hard against his buttocks.

Martin had barely moved over the next half hour, before hearing the sound of a key in the lock. He looked up in time to see a sheriff's deputy open the door. "Your lawyer's here. Stand up."

As soon as Martin pushed himself to standing, the jailer affixed shackles, connected by chains, to his wrists and ankles. "Follow me," he said.

Finding it difficult to walk with the limitations imposed by the chains and his handicap, Martin shuffled alongside the deputy, leaning heavily on his cane. Despite the overwhelmingly bleak state of affairs, he felt some optimism at the prospect of speaking to his attorney. Someone on his side in this godawful place.

Douglas was waiting in the same small room Hunter had been in when Martin arrived. Rather than wearing an expensive pin-striped suit, the attorney was dressed in jeans and a blue T-shirt. The professor took the seat opposite his lawyer, and his escort left. He didn't go far, though, as Martin noticed him observing through a window in the closed door.

Douglas started the conversation. "How are you holding up?"

"I feel like I'm in a state of shock, but I suppose I'm doing as well as can be expected." He paused for a moment, then asked, "What the hell happened? Why did I get arrested now? They couldn't have gotten any more evidence against me."

"Does the name Zoe Clyburn mean anything to you?"

Martin thought for a moment. "Yes, she's one of my half-sisters. I spoke to her soon after I started collecting the names of my half-siblings. A group of us was planning to see her perform her comedy act. Don't tell me . . ."

"Yes. She was murdered last night, same as the others."

Martin gasped and put his head in his hands. Barely seeming to notice, Douglas continued. "On my way here, I made a few phone calls and learned that Detective Hunter questioned her husband last night. He asked him if he knew you, and he said he hadn't heard of you. This morning, her husband called Hunter back and told him he'd seen your name when going through some of his wife's emails. Given the danger to the public the killer poses, the judge gave the okay to arrest you, knowing that you and the victim were acquainted. If more deaths could have been prevented by arresting you, even though there wasn't an airtight case, all hell would break loose, and he'd be in big trouble. For that reason, he decided it would be best to lock you up. It was assumed that you are the ringleader, so without you, neither Greg nor anyone else in your family would do any more killing."

"Can I get out on bail? I don't know how long I can tolerate this place without going bonkers."

"I don't think a judge will set bail for you, not with you being charged with serial murders. You'll have to hang in there. Remember, the DNA results will be coming in any day now. Meanwhile, I brought you a few things."

Douglas reached into his briefcase and took out packages of junk food, a newspaper, and three John Grisham novels. "I grabbed these when I left home—thought they might make the time pass a little quicker."

"Thanks. And thanks for coming out at night to see me."

"I don't do that for most of my clients, but," the attorney said with a smile, "I figured you needed to see me tonight."

Martin was brought back to his cell, where he ate the candy bars and Cracker Jacks brought by Douglas. He alternated between trying to sleep and reading one of the legal thrillers in his possession. The client in the Grisham novel had been arrested for a crime he hadn't committed. Martin was pretty sure the protagonist would be exonerated by the end of the novel. If only he could be as certain about his own fate. He found himself longing for Mary Jane.

Chapter 39

"WHAT THE FUCK ARE YOU talking about," Detective Hunter yelled into the phone. "What you're telling me is impossible. You screwed up. I'm sending the leftover sample to another lab. What do you mean you don't have enough left?"

The detective slammed the phone down, then picked up the receiver and slammed it down again just as a newly-hired detective entered his office to discuss a homicide that took place during a carjacking the previous day. "Everything okay?" she asked, biting her lower lip.

"Just got a call from the director of the forensics lab. He said the blood from the mosquito I found at the Montoya crime scene isn't an exact match to Starling."

"You've got to be kidding," the younger detective said, cradling her jaw in her right hand.

"Wish I was. He said our suspects, Starling and his older son, are excluded. Both of them. According to that moron, there isn't even enough sample left to have it retested elsewhere."

"What're you going to do now? You can't let Starling go, or the killing will continue."

"I've been advised that when I feel like this, I should count to ten." Hunter took in a deep breath and exhaled as he quickly counted "onetwothreefourfivesixseveneightnineten." He turned to grab his jacket on the coat rack behind him. "Now I'm going to the lab to give that asshole a piece of my mind." Seconds later, he was out the door.

Detective Hunter knew the way to the county crime lab well. A forty-five-minute drive from the station, he'd been there many times over the years. Hunter missed the old lab director who had recently retired. He'd been there as long as the detective could remember and always assured Hunter that he kept up with the latest technological advances in DNA testing strategies that had taken place over the years. The lab had never been the first to adopt anything but had conformed to the latest standards in a timely manner. In Hunter's opinion, the new director, a young Hispanic man who had trained at a fancy eastern college, was an unknown quantity. Always skeptical until proven otherwise, Hunter didn't know the new director well enough to trust him. The man's minority status, allowing the county to check a box for diversity, and east coast credentials, didn't help.

Honking at cars, and flipping the bird at other drivers did little to tamp down the heat under his collar. When Hunter parked his car in the crime lab parking lot, he was still fuming. He rushed out of his car, through the building's glass doors, and marched up to the receptionist sitting behind a desk near the entrance.

The young woman with spikey green hair looked up and displayed a fake smile. "Why Detective Hunter, so nice to see you."

"Love what you've done with your hair," he said sarcastically.

"Really? I almost had it dyed orange. What do you think? Do you think I should change it to orange?"

They could have gone on like that all day, each qualifying for an Oscar in over-acting as they'd been doing for over a year, ever since they'd both been disciplined. The incident bringing on the HR investigation started after the receptionist had thrown a coke in Hunter's face in response to a snide remark he'd made about her attire being inappropriate. Both were deemed guilty of unacceptable behavior, with Hunter's remark causing a hostile work environment, and the young woman overreacting a tad.

Realizing he didn't have a lot of time to waste, Hunter said, "I want to speak to Rivera. Now."

"One moment, please," the receptionist said, twirling her green hair, an action Hunter interpreted as an attempt to annoy him. She picked up the receiver of the phone on her desk, pressed a button on the phone, and began speaking softly. The conversation went back and forth a few times, so Hunter assumed she wasn't just informing Rivera someone was here to see him, she was likely saying something derogatory about him. She chuckled and hung up. Turning to Hunter, she said, "He's free now. You can go back. You know the way."

"Aren't you supposed to offer me a cup of coffee?"

"Would you like some coffee, Detective Hunter?" the receptionist said, her voice mockingly sweet, her visage displaying an exaggerated, obviously phony, smile."

"Why, yes, I would. Sugar, no cream."

"I'll bring it to you momentarily. Maybe the sugar will improve your disposition."

Hunter walked past rows of white lab benches cluttered with test tubes, reagents, specimens, chemical hoods, and equipment. Technicians dressed in white lab coats, safety glasses, masks, and white or purple nitrile gloves were scattered throughout, busy pipetting, weighing, mixing, writing in notebooks, typing on computers, and talking. As he approached the bank of offices at the rear of the room, a dark-haired man stepped out of the largest and greeted him.

"I think I know why you're here," Dr. Rivera said, smiling. "It's about the Starling case, is it not?"

"You're damn right it is."

"I wish you hadn't hung up on me earlier. I might have been able to save you the trip, but since you're here, let me get the technician who originally ran the samples. Meanwhile, have a seat." Rivera motioned to the chairs across from the desk in his office and ventured into the lab area. Moments later, the receptionist came to deliver a hot cup of coffee, placing it on the desk in front of Hunter.

"It's very hot," she said. "It would be a shame if you spilled it in your lap." She turned to leave just as the director returned with a young bespectacled woman with noticeable acne, her frizzy red hair cut short. She wore a clean, white lab coat and held a notebook under one arm.

"This is Detective Hunter, Lisa," Rivera said, as the woman took the seat next to Hunter. "He was hoping the DNA recovered from the mosquito found at the scene of the Montoya case was an exact match with our suspect, Dr. Starling, or his eldest son. Can you walk him through your findings?" Rivera turned to Hunter and said, "This is Lisa, one of our finest technicians. She looks younger than she is—she's actually been here over eight years. I reviewed all the work of our DNA technicians for the past two years when I took this position and found her to be the best. Lisa's work and documentation are impeccable. That's why I chose her to run these samples. I knew how important they are."

"Well, I hope she can explain how a DNA sample from the murderer only partially matches the sample he left behind. Hunter leaned towards Lisa and added, "Explain that, and you get a gold star."

Lisa, looking uncomfortable, scrunched her shoulders and upper torso and leaned away. A moment later, using her sleeve, she wiped away a drop of Hunter's spittle that had landed on a sliver of her exposed bare wrist on the opposite arm.

Rivera nodded encouragingly at Lisa, who was looking up at him. "Lisa is a bit shy," he said to Hunter. "I'm working with her to improve her communication skills. Once she has more confidence, she'll be a dynamite witness for us, so please give her your full attention. Now," he said, turning back to Lisa, "the floor is yours. Don't worry. Detective Hunter is a bit gruff, but he doesn't bite. Not to my knowledge, anyway."

Lisa swallowed as she placed her notebook on the table, facing Hunter and herself. She sounded like a child, as she began to page through the notes. "These pages all deal with DNA extraction and quantification." She stopped on a page and pointed to some numbers. "I tested the blood from the mosquito, and cheek swab cells from your suspects, Dr. Starling and his son Greg. My goal was to compare the DNA profile from the blood in the mosquito to the suspects to rule them in or out. I also tested DNA from the victim, just in case the mosquito blood was from her, and not the perpetrator."

Hunter squirmed in his seat as he sipped on his coffee. "You sure you got the right specimens?" he asked.

"Yes. Everything is barcoded, and I always visually check twice for confirmation." Lisa paused. Hearing no objection from Hunter, she continued. "You can see here that the amount of DNA extracted from the cells of Dr. Montoya, Dr. Starling, and his son was relatively high, while the DNA extracted from the mosquito sample was much lower, barely detectable. I knew there wouldn't be much, so I used practically the whole sample. Frankly, I wasn't certain there'd be enough, but fortunately, it was sufficient for the next step."

Lisa turned the page, where more numbers were displayed.

"Hold on a minute, there," Hunter said. "You said you used practically the whole sample. That seems a little careless. Maybe if you'd used everything you had, your results would have been different."

"That's not true. The results we get aren't dependent on the amount. We either get a result or we don't. I decided to risk getting no results on a few of our markers in order to have a little sample left over. Knowing how important this sample was, I didn't want to rule out the possibility of future analysis using a more sensitive technique. If need be, the remainder can be sent to a lab capable of analyzing tiny amounts of DNA, something crime labs aren't set up to do."

"Aha!" Hunter said. "So you could send some of the mosquito blood DNA to a lab that knows what they're doing."

"We can't just send a specimen from a criminal investigation to a lab that doesn't follow chain of custody procedures," Rivera said, raising his voice as he eyed Hunter coldly. "Any results would be thrown out of court. Besides, as you will see, Lisa's results are quite conclusive. They may not be the results you want, but they are rock solid." Lowering his voice and speaking calmly, he turned to Lisa. "Please go on."

Lisa bit her lip before proceeding. "All the samples went through amplification as part of the testing process. You're probably familiar with that—polymerase chain reaction, or PCR."

"Unfortunately, not only am I familiar with it, but thanks to all the crime shows on TV every criminal with half a brain knows about it and avoids leaving even trace amounts of DNA behind. The disposable glove industry is doing very well these days due to advances in fingerprint and DNA technology."

"No doubt about it," Rivera said. "Your suspect, or suspects, certainly know about DNA evidence and have been careful not to leave any behind. We tested all the casings from these crime scenes and haven't found any DNA. No foreign DNA was found on or around any of the victims or the areas where the perpetrator's car was parked. It was your quick thinking that gave us the only DNA sample we have," Rivera said, his voice calmer now, if not friendly.

"Just doing my job," Hunter said. *Nice try, but buttering me up won't win me over.*

After getting a smile and a nod from Rivera, Lisa continued. "During testing, we get what we call a DNA fingerprint—we look at the DNA in thirteen specific areas of the genetic material. Each such DNA fingerprint can be compared to the DNA fingerprint from another person. What we're looking at is the number of times short sequences of DNA are repeated. These areas have been selected because the number of repeats in these regions varies a lot between unrelated individuals. Although one area may match between random people, the chance of all thirteen matching is astronomically small, usually one in billions, depending on the specific number of repeats at a particular location on the DNA."

Lisa flipped through the notebook until she landed on a page with a number of graphs running vertically. "Here we have the fingerprints of the DNA from the mosquito, Ansel Montoya, Martin Starling, and Greg Starling." Lisa ran her finger down one of the graphs, pointing to the peaks rising from the straight line. "Each of these spikes represents the number of repeats, usually around four, detected in the sample at a specific DNA location. The results are really quite astounding."

Hunter clenched his fists as he resisted grabbing the notebook and flinging it against the wall. *Astounding. Is that the word they use these days when they're covering up for their incompetence?*

"Before Lisa continues," Rivera said, "I want to warn Detective Hunter here that I didn't get a chance to tell him about all of our findings over the phone before our call was interrupted. I'm sure he'll be as surprised as we were." Rivera again nodded at Lisa to continue.

"The findings of the DNA fingerprint comparisons are here," Lisa said, paging through more graphs, until she found a table. "This chart summarizes our findings. First, I want to point out the results of the amelogenin testing."

"Never heard of it," Hunter said.

"It's a fairly new type of test Dr. Rivera introduced to the lab. It's run along with the DNA fingerprinting I told you about. With this type of testing, we can determine the gender of the individual."

"Does that take into account people who think they were born into the wrong sex?" Hunter asked with a sneer.

"Well, no," Lisa answered, ignoring Hunter's attempt to inject his irrelevant feelings about transgender individuals into the conversation. "This determines the gender they were born with, as defined by their sex chromosomes." She pointed to a line of data at the top of the chart. "You can see that Dr. Montoya, Dr. Starling, and his son, of course, tested as male. Each has an X and a Y chromosome. Our suspect tested as a female. She has no Y chromosome, only X."

"What the fuck!" Hunter said. "Impossible. Serial killers like this are always male. The murderer the night of Montoya's killing was six feet, like the professor. That would rule out almost all women. This highfalutin amalgam testing, or whatever you call it—"

"Amelogenin," Lisa and Rivera said simultaneously.

"Whatever. Call back the previous lab director. Have him look this over. I trusted him, but you woke, young people with your new, fancy ideas—I don't think you know what you're doing."

Dr. Rivera's face turned red, and he breathed in and out a few times before speaking. "I didn't want to air our dirty laundry, but I'll tell you this much: the previous director was behind the times, and, frankly, cut corners. We're going over some cases now that may have been compromised. I've made it a priority to modernize this lab. I can assure you we are using the most up-to-date techniques. Lisa didn't show you, but she ran all the controls required, and every one of them came in within range. Her results are valid. The blood in the mosquito is from a woman. Whether or not that woman is the perpetrator is for you to determine. To get anywhere in solving this case, we have to trust each other. For all I know, that sample was from a mosquito you found a mile away from the crime scene. Or from something you found in a public restroom."

"Okay, okay," Hunter said. "Message received."

"Now, Lisa," Rivera said, "why don't you show our friend the rest of your results."

Lisa looked around nervously before continuing. "Getting back to the DNA fingerprinting, here you can see that when we compare the DNA of the mosquito blood, Dr. Starling, and Dr. Montoya, each sample matches the other two by approximately twenty-five percent."

"So Starling matches the mosquito DNA?"

"Only twenty-five percent. That excludes him from being the source of the mosquito DNA. He'd have to be a one hundred percent match to be considered the source."

"What about the Starling boy?"

"Greg Starling is a fifty percent match with Martin Starling, as predicted, and a twelve and a half percent match with the mosquito and the victim. He is also excluded. But the partial matches indicate genetic relationships. Although I was confident in my findings, the results were so startling, I repeated all the testing. That's why it took twice as long as it should have to finish the report. As expected, the findings were exactly the same the second time around."

"Maybe the samples were cross-contaminated," Hunter said. "I've seen that before."

"Look," Dr. Rivera said, leaning towards Hunter, his eyes glaring, "this was a well-run study. I trust Lisa's work completely. If the problem was contamination, the peaks of the contaminant would be smaller than the others, and there'd be extra peaks. The sort of thing even a rookie should figure out."

"I've seen that happen in this very lab before, and it wasn't picked up at first. Only when examined by an outside lab hired by a defendant."

"I understand your suspicions, but the sloppiness of the previous administration isn't tolerated by me. I run a very tight ship, and the mediocrity you experienced before is a thing of the past. Our quality control procedures have improved significantly. Before you criticize the work product here, I suggest you learn some basics, so you don't sound like an idiot." By the time he'd finished speaking, Rivera's face was red, and his hands were in fists.

Hunter stood and looked like he was going to punch Rivera. "Look, asshole, I know this guy, Starling, is guilty. Or his son. Or both. You're right, I don't know much about this DNA crap, but I do know that you're not making sense. We don't report a twenty-five percent match on fingerprints. That would be bullshit. If a perpetrator is reported to have blond hair, we don't describe suspects with light brown hair as being a twenty-five percent match in hair color."

Hunter reached for the half-full cup of coffee on the desk in front of him as Rivera balled up his fists and started to walk around his desk, towards Hunter. "Please!" shouted Lisa, "I wish the two of you would grow up."

Hunter turned and saw tears in the young woman's eyes. Her distress and apparent desperation snapped him out of his rage and sent notions of shame to the forefront of his consciousness. *Onetwothreeforufivesixseveneightnineten.* He breathed deeply and sat down, now feeling calmer. "Sorry, Lisa," he said. "I see now that Dr. Rivera is a hothead like me."

The two men laughed nervously, as they both sat in their seats. In calming down, Hunter realized that perhaps he didn't have all the answers and should listen to Lisa explain the findings. Maybe, just maybe, Rivera and Lisa knew what they were talking about. As difficult as it was, he needed to keep an open mind. He wanted to nail Starling and/or his boy for the murders, but only if they were truly guilty. Looking at Lisa, Hunter said, "I'm sorry I started to lose it there. I shouldn't have behaved that way. Please continue with your explanation, and tell me what you make of this twenty-five percent match of the mosquito blood with Martin Starling, and half of that with his son."

"First, allow me to explain something. DNA matches are much more precise than things like fingerprints or hair color. The exact amount of matching DNA can be calculated. Approximately ninety-nine-point-nine percent of DNA is the same in just about everyone, but the other tenth of a percent has genetic variability. We test those areas. Although the technology changes somewhat with time, we now have a robust method for comparing DNA between people, with only a small amount of DNA in these locations shared by unrelated people. That amount that can be quantitated. A twenty-five percent match indicates a fairly close relationship."

"Like how close? Brothers? Cousins? Children?"

"Parents and children share roughly half their DNA, or fifty percent. Like Martin Starling and his son."

"That's what I thought. In the past, I've had to hunt down a few people trying to escape paternity support payments."

"Similarly, full siblings share half of their DNA with each other. The mosquito blood, however, shares twenty-five percent of its DNA with the professor as well as the victim."

"What do you make of that?"

"A twenty-five percent match shows these specimens come from people related by being grandparents, grandchildren, aunts, uncles, nieces, nephews, or half-siblings with each other. We've nicknamed the person whose blood was in the mosquito 'Skeeter Mosquito.'" Lisa chuckled nervously before continuing. "Since Skeeter is a female, she could be the grandmother, aunt, niece, or half-sister of Dr. Montoya and Dr. Starling. Dr. Montoya had no siblings, so he had no nieces. I don't know about Dr. Starling. Given the close ages of Dr. Starling and Dr. Montoya, I think it's most likely those two were half-siblings. I'm told the perpetrator didn't move like an elderly person. Although that's a soft call, I would guess she is a half-sister of both Dr. Montoya and Dr. Starling. The Starling boy's match, twelve and a half percent, is exactly what you would expect from the son of Martin Starling who, again, is a twenty-five percent match with the others."

"What about CODIS?" Hunter asked, referring to the Combined DNA Index System, the FBI's DNA database. "Did you check for a match there?"

"Sure did. So far, no match for either Dr. Montoya, Skeeter, or either of the Starlings."

"This is a most unusual case," Rivera said. "I've never seen a case involving three half-siblings."

Hunter rubbed his chin, his eyes not focused on anything in particular. After a few moments, he spoke in a voice softer than his usual intensity. "Starling first came to my attention when he inquired about the murder of Lois Bishop. He said he wanted to know if we had any leads because she was his half-sister. He also claimed a murder victim in Colorado was a half-brother. He said he had a lot of half-siblings and was concerned someone was targeting them. I didn't buy it. His story seemed so contrived, I thought he was fishing. So often, guilty parties come up with all sorts of reasons why they want to know how an investigation is going so they can keep tabs on things. His wife drove the same kind of car as the murderer, and he and Greg were the same height as the killer as calculated by our analysts. He was an excellent marksman and I noticed he had a curved pinky like the murderer. Seemed like a perfect fit. Then, later he ditched a police tail the same night of Darlene Sparrow's murder." Hunter hung his head. "Everything pointed to him. Damn. Could the Starlings be innocent? How could I have been so wrong? Maybe there really is something to this crazy half-sibling thing."

"We can certainly help explore that possibility. Get us DNA from all the previous victims of this killer or killers," Rivera said. "Look, we're all after the same thing. Catching the criminal. It's easy to convince ourselves of things when there is enough evidence to look convincing. But we need to explore all angles to be as certain as possible and re-look at things when we get more data. It's difficult to admit when we're wrong. If you were wrong, that's water under the bridge. From now on, we'll move forward. We'll work together to solve these cases."

Rivera stood up from his seat and held out his hand. Hunter rose and shook it.

"I'll have samples from the other murder victims sent to you. Meanwhile, I suppose I should have Professor Starling released from prison."

"I think that in light of this evidence, that would be best. I imagine you'll ask him about any other half-sibs he might have. We could test them, too, against Skeeter. If we're lucky, we'll get a one hundred percent match. A fifty percent match would be from a full sib of Skeeter."

"He did mention something about having collected information about a lot of half-sibs he recently discovered through some of those ancestry sites. I discounted it at the time."

"If he's totally innocent, he might cooperate and lead us to the perpetrator," Rivera said.

"If he's innocent, he won't know who the perp is."

"But Skeeter, or possibly a complete sibling of hers, may be on his list. It's just a matter of testing his half-sibs. It could lead you to Skeeter directly."

Hunter left the crime lab dazed. Instead of driving back to the station, he went home and downed two beers. *I really fucked up. Rivera's right, damn it. I'm going to have to trust that asshole. I'll have to work with him to catch this motherfucker.*

Chapter 40

MARTIN HEARD THE SOUND OF the key in the door. He was hungry and hoped it was time for lunch. The door opened, and he noted the prison guard was empty-handed.

The professor's pulse quickened. *Damn. I wonder what he wants. If Hunter wants to question me again, I'm going to insist on getting some food.*

"This is your lucky day, Professor," the sheriff's deputy said.

"Oh?"

"You don't know?"

"Know what?"

"You just got a get-out-of-jail-free card. You're going home."

Martin didn't remember feeling this elated since he was a young boy on Christmas morning. "You're not kidding me, are you?"

"Nope. C'mon, let's go."

Martin grabbed his cane and stood. The guard led him to a counter where paperwork was being filled out, and he was told to sign for receiving the clothes and other items that had been confiscated when he was first arrested. Before leaving his signature on the form, Martin phoned Georgia.

"I'm getting out," he said.

"Thank goodness. When?"

"Now. I don't know what happened, but I want to get out of here as fast as I can before they change their mind."

"I'm home now. I'll leave right away. It should take me forty-five minutes to get there.

"I'll be waiting for you."

Martin was so excited while getting dressed, he missed the leg hole of his pants three times, almost toppling over despite being supported by his cane. *Get a hold of yourself.* He closed his eyes and took three long, deep breaths. He started over, carefully putting one leg into the appropriate pant leg without incident, then the other. Once his pants were zipped, he donned his shirt, socks, and shoes. When the deputy finally opened the door for him to walk out into the sunshine, he was unaware of the smile on his face.

Martin found a bench conveniently situated near the jail exit, where he could wait for his ride. A young man with long, greasy brown hair was seated at one end. He was wearing a tank top exposing an elaborate array of tattoos covering at least his upper chest and right arm. The decorated youth looked Martin up and down as he took a deep drag from his cigarette, seeming to assess how dangerous the professor with a cane, dressed in khaki pants and a striped button-down shirt, might be. Not wanting to stand, Martin sat on the opposite end of the bench to avoid as much second-hand smoke as possible.

"You just get out?" the young man asked.

"Yes."

"Me, too. This time they just got me for drunk and disorderly. Bar fight. I was lucky—my old lady got the meth I was selling out of my pocket just as the cops arrived." He turned to Martin as if looking for an expression of shock and awe on his face before continuing. "I'll bet you was arrested for passing bad checks or something like that. Am I right?"

"No. Murder." Martin took a moment to bask in the instant respect his comment brought him.

"Damn," the man said, shaking his head from side to side. "Never woulda guessed. Did you do it?"

"They just let me out. What does that tell you?"

"You got yourself a good lawyer."

Martin was relieved when a husky blond woman in leathers on a Harley pulled up and his bench mate hopped on the back. "See you around," the man said to Martin as the motorcycle engine roared on take-off.

Martin nodded in response. Glad to be alone, he paged through the emails on his phone, stopping every few minutes to look around and breathe in the fresh air. He was reading a message from the chemistry department chair when he heard a car pull up and stop, the engine still running. He looked up to see his wife's CR-V. Without thinking, he raced to the driver's door of the car where Georgia got out, and they embraced for a long time.

"Okay, let's get going," Georgia said. "This isn't the best neighborhood."

"You're right," Martin responded. "I hear this is where prisoners go when they're let out of jail." He got into the passenger seat, and his wife drove away.

"Hope you're not mad," Georgia said, "but I called your secretary yesterday and told her you had a bad cold and might need to miss a few days of work."

"I'd almost forgot about work, with everything else that's going on. Did she believe you?"

"I don't think so. She seemed quite concerned, more than she would be for a minor illness like a cold."

"I'm sure she'll interrogate me when I return. Thanks for calling her." Then Martin recounted the events of his nightmare retreat at taxpayers' expense. By the time they were five miles from home, Martin had brought Georgia up to date, including the conversation with his fellow released prisoner.

"I've got some news. Overall good news, but I'm not exactly happy about it," Georgia said.

"Now you've got me curious. And a little frightened."

"Nothing to be frightened about. Constance called Cat. Emerald's father has agreed to give up all paternal rights to Emerald. He's no longer a threat."

"What happened?"

"Seems his wife threw him out again. He's now jobless on account of multiple harassment complaints, and no longer has an interest in being Emerald's dad. I don't know if he even sees his other kids now. Constance says she thinks he's drinking a lot. Seemed drunk when he signed the papers, and said he was going to live with his sister in Albuquerque."

"Cat must be delighted. But I think I know why you're not happy about it. Cat's going to want to move out, isn't she?"

"Exactly. She said she loves living with us, but she really wants to find her own place. I'd feel the same if I were in her shoes. I told her she should stay with us until she can get a good job and find a nice place to live. She seemed open to that."

"Unfortunately, I don't think that will take very long. But we can't hold her back."

When they got home, they were greeted by Cat and Emerald. The boys were still at school. Martin congratulated his half-sister on her legal victory and took a long shower. He called his secretary and after a brief interrogation, confessed he'd been arrested.

"I knew something was up," she said. "I didn't believe you were sick. Where are you now?"

"I'm home. They saw the error of their ways and let me out."

"That must have been horrible—spending the night in prison."

"The accommodations left a lot to be desired. I'll be glad to get back to normal. I'll be coming in to work soon."

"Are you up to it?"

"Works well for me.

"Thank goodness," she said after groaning at the pun. Then she whispered, "There's a man here who insists on seeing you."

"What's his name?"

Whispering again, she answered, "He says his name is Detective Hunter."

Chapter 41

FOLLOWING THE RULES HADN'T BEEN working out for Martin lately. Before leaving for work, he took down a box from his closet and found a shirt he'd bought on a family vacation years ago. The musty odor didn't dissuade him from trying it on.

Georgia chuckled when she saw him. "I haven't seen that in years. Still looks good on you."   Upon reaching the chemistry department, Martin had to pass in front of his secretary's desk to reach his office. He took a deep breath and approached with trepidation, knowing Hunter would be lying in wait for him there, probably with a brand-new arrest warrant. He nodded as he walked by Ruth, who raised her eyebrows upon seeing him, and gave him a big smile. As expected, his nemesis was lurking, pacing in front of the small reception area.

"Dr. Starling," Hunter said as Martin drew nearer, slowing his stride and leaning more heavily on his cane.

Unable to avoid the man looming in front of him, the professor responded coldly, "What brings you here?"

"I need to speak to you about something. It would be best if we could talk in your office."

Knowing there was no escaping the detective's tentacles, Martin retrieved keys from his pocket and opened his office door. *It would be preferable if he arrested me inside my office, out of sight of the others. Maybe he'll allow me to walk out on my own volition, without handcuffs.* Hunter followed him inside and took a seat in front of Martin's desk without being invited. Seeing that, Martin wasn't sure what to do. He walked around his desk, took his usual seat behind it, and stood his cane up nearby.

"I owe you an apology, Professor," Hunter began. "We were able to collect DNA which we think came from the murderer of Ansel Montoya. Neither you nor your son Greg is a match. That's why you were let out."

Martin felt almost dizzy from the relief those simple words provided. *Neither you nor your son Greg are a match.* He closed his eyes and let out a deep breath.

"I knew that would be the case."

His cheeks flushed, and looking down at the desk, Hunter continued. "I confess, I got off on the wrong track."

This detective may be an asshole, but at least he's got the balls to admit he's wrong. Martin almost felt sorry for him. "I appreciate it's hard to admit when you've been wrong," he said. "It sure took long enough to get the DNA test done."

"Government lab. Lots of backup, you know. I did ask them to prioritize the testing as this is such a big case. It turns out the murderer of Dr. Montoya is a female."

"That's a surprise."

"I almost couldn't believe it when I found out, since female serial murderers are rare, and almost never use firearms. Many are nurses who kill their patients. Others kill for money or revenge. Also, the height of the murderer or murderers is taller than most women. We all just assumed it was a man. However, DNA analysis of the sample we collected shows it's from a female."

"I always considered myself very open-minded when it comes to what women can do, but now I see room for improvement when it comes to imagining serial killers," Martin said.

"The real reason I came here today is because I want to talk to you about the results in a little more detail. If I remember correctly, you mentioned you'd recently discovered several half-siblings."

"More than several," Martin said, wondering if Hunter finally suspected his half-siblings were being murdered for some reason. "More like close to a hundred fifty as of now."

"Can you tell me about that? How did you find them?"

"I used genealogy sites."

"How long ago did you start?"

"Close to three months ago. I wanted to find my half-siblings so I could warn them they may have inherited the same potentially lethal mutation I have that caused my stroke. I inherited it from my biological father who was a sperm donor. It appears he was a physician who performed many artificial inseminations with his own sperm. What he did was unethical and probably illegal. But that's irrelevant now. He's dead, so he'll never have to answer for what he did."

"How many of these half-siblings have you met?"

"Cat's the only one I've met in person. I've talked to a handful of others by phone and over Zoom. My younger son took over the task of finding these relatives and having them tested for the mutation so he's more familiar with most of them."

"Do you think any of these half-siblings would have a motive to kill?"

Martin's head jerked back slightly. *Odd question.* "No. Why do you ask?"

"The blood specimen we tested not only came from a woman, but it came from a woman who is a half-sibling of you and Ansel Montoya."

Martin's eyes widened as he sat speechless, while Hunter's revelation took hold in his brain. *Could it be that one of his half-siblings, one who he or Nick had talked to and was a participant on his Facebook page, was the murderer?* After a few moments, he began to speak. "I don't know what to make of that. I've known for a while that someone is murdering my half-siblings. Since I first spoke to you, I've learned of other half-siblings on my list who have been murdered—Darlene Sparrow, Ansel Montoya, Zoe Clyburn, and Barney Gibbert. It can't be a coincidence, and I've been wanting to know if other half-siblings of mine have been murdered in a similar way. My whole family and many of my half-sibs have been frightened. Someone is going after us, the children of this renegade doctor. I've wondered why someone would want to target us, but I never thought the murderer was one of us."

"Needless to say, I'd like to find out which one of your half-sisters is guilty. Would you cooperate with the investigation and give me your list?"

"I'll help in any way I can. I'm sure I want to stop this more than you do. I have more than one list. There's the list of all the matches I have on genealogy sites, as well as a growing list of people who believe they may be the offspring of this doctor. Those people are responding to the notices The Rocket has on TV and in newspapers. That list has gotten quite long, and only about a quarter of them have been tested. Those that are proven to be half-sibs are added to the list of matches and participate in a private Facebook group. There is also a private eye looking into possible related murders in other areas. If you remember, I mentioned the murder of a half-brother in Colorado when I first came to your office."

Hunter looked down, his face momentarily turning red with embarrassment at having ignored this important piece of information. "What did your investigator find?"

"She's found a handful of cases that looks similar, although we haven't been able to determine if they are half-siblings. Her investigation relies on connections she has in other police departments. It would probably move along much quicker if it went through official police channels."

"We can look into that. Meanwhile, are there any females on your list that strike you as odd or suspicious?"

"It would be hard for me to believe that any of the people I've spoken to could be responsible for this, but I can't rule out the possibility that the murderer is one of the women on my list. She probably identified her victims by finding matches on ancestry sites, like I did. Perhaps you could get the DNA data of the women on my list directly from the genealogy companies and compare it to your DNA profile of the murderer."

"Even if we could get a warrant to do that, it probably wouldn't help. I don't understand everything about DNA testing, but I do know that those genealogy companies don't use the same technique as crime labs to analyze the DNA. Genealogy companies use techniques that look at different areas because they're looking for distant relatives and ethnic origins. In crime labs, we're looking to include or exclude suspects, which doesn't require the same sort of testing. So trying to compare data from a genealogy site with our results is like comparing apples and oranges."

"Yes, that would be futile," Martin said. "I would suggest you send a portion of the blood you have from the murderer to at least one of the large ancestry sites and see if they have a match."

"I'm told we don't have much of the original blood sample left."

Martin thought for a moment. "I have a friend who runs a new ancestry site. He's a professor at my college and is the person who got me started using genealogy companies. He has the ability to run any type of analysis you need. He analyzes DNA from ancient bones and teeth, so he has to make many copies of the DNA in specimens with very little material. I believe he'd be able to amplify the DNA in your remaining blood specimen and get the type of data used by ancestry companies. Then you could send that raw data to any of the genealogy companies to see if they have a match in their files."

"I'll call my good friend Dr. Rivera at the crime lab and see if he can arrange to do that. There may be some legal hurdles, but I'll let him deal with that. Meanwhile, I'll set up a tip line. Hopefully, something useful will come of that. Also, I need you to call your friend with the ancestry company and find out how quickly he can do what we discussed."

Hunter hadn't said "please" before his last request, but Martin didn't mind.

"By the way, Professor," Hunter said, "I like your Hawaiian shirt. When I was in college, my professors were all too stuffy to dress like that."

Martin called Dean as soon as the detective left. Then he ordered a half dozen Hawaiian shirts to be delivered to his home. His wardrobe needed a reboot.

Chapter 42

DINNER AT THE STARLING HOUSE that night was festive. Martin was glad to be home, the nightmare of being confined to a cell behind him. Nick had gotten an A on his biology project, and Greg said Olivia was going to be coming over later.

"She's going to sneak out of her house," he said. "Her parents still don't want her associating with me, so that's the only way we can get together."

Georgia and Martin looked at each other inquisitively. Finally, Georgia spoke. "Normally, I wouldn't approve of you conspiring against the parents of another child, but you're both over eighteen now, and Olivia's parents are jerks. Just don't give me any details."

"Okay. I won't tell you about how I figured out how to bypass the house alarm so Olivia can come and go through my window without setting it off."

"Don't do that," Martin said, an angry expression on his face. "She can come in through the front door here like everyone else. We need the alarm to be set at all times—don't bypass it. The safety of everyone here depends on it. Hopefully, once word is out that I've been cleared, her parents won't object to you two seeing each other."

"She's come in through my window before. She's too embarrassed for you to know she's coming over. Doesn't want anyone here to see her."

"I forbid it," Martin said. Looking at Greg, he sensed his son was planning on bypassing the alarm anyway. "I mean it, Greg. Don't fool around with bypassing the alarm."

An uncomfortable silence followed as Greg pushed the food on his plate around and sulked. Finally, Cat spoke up. "I found a job that's almost perfect," she said. "I'll be working in a bookstore not too far from here. The pay isn't great, but it will be enough for me and Emerald to live on, and I'll get a big discount on everything in the store. They sell children's books, and I can have the ones that don't sell for free, so I'll be able to get a ton of books for Emerald."

"Congratulations, Cat," Georgia said.

"I'm sure you'll be glad to get your garage back," Cat said.

"I hope you won't be leaving us too soon. We're all going to miss you." Martin and the boys nodded in agreement. "Of course, you can take all the furniture we bought for you since we won't have room for it here once we change your room back to a garage. We'll help you move, but let us know if there's anything else we can do to help."

Cat looked uneasy as she looked down. "There is something you could help me with. I really appreciate everything you've done for me. My job will be Tuesday through Saturday. I found a preschool for Emerald near the bookstore. I checked it out and it seems perfect. I hate to ask, but since the preschool is Monday through Friday, I'm having a hard time figuring out where I can take Emerald on Saturdays. They said I could bring her to the store on weekends occasionally, but I needed to make other arrangements. I was wondering . . ."

"You want us to watch her on Saturdays?" Georgia asked with a smile, her eyes wide.

"Well, I was wondering if that would be possible. I could come here to clean up and do the shopping on Mondays, even prepare dinner if you want."

"If we want?" Martin asked sarcastically. "Of course we want. We'd love to watch Emerald. Also, we've grown very accustomed to your cooking. Apologies to Georgia, but we'd look forward to having a meal of yours once a week. And, of course, we'd want you and Emerald to join us."

Cat let out a long breath and smiled. "That would be great. I'd miss our dinners with all of you. So would Emerald."

"How soon do you think you'll be moving?" Greg asked.

"I start work in a week. I found a small house for rent about five miles from here. Three bedrooms, two baths, and a fairly modern kitchen. It would be perfect for Emerald. There's a backyard with a swing set. The owner liked Emerald, and said she'd hold it a week for me."

"Sounds perfect," Martin said. "Why don't you just take it?"

"One problem. It's a little too pricey for me—"

"We could help you with that," Martin volunteered. "Couldn't we?" he looked to Georgia for approval.

"Of course. Don't let the opportunity pass you by."

"Thanks for the offer, but I figured if I could get a roommate—another woman—she could help out with the rent. I'd pay two-thirds and she'd pay one-third. Then I could do it on my own. I'd have to be sure she was compatible. I wouldn't want someone who was always entertaining strange men. She would have to be someone quiet and stable."

"I have an idea," Martin said. "You can put the word out on our Facebook page."

"Great idea," Cat said. "I'll write something up tonight and post it after Emerald's in bed."

Thinking about his earlier discussion with Hunter, Martin added, "I'd like to meet her first." He'd want to be sure she wasn't around six feet tall.

#   #   #

Hunter spoke to Dr. Rivera about sending the remainder of Skeeter's specimen to Dean's lab, DNA Discoveries. Rivera agreed to speak to Dean but Googled him and his company before calling. He found numerous impressive academic articles regarding DNA amplification and analysis techniques. The lab director then called Dean to discuss the possibility of sending Skeeter's remaining blood specimen to DNA Discoveries for the purpose of processing it so he could submit her DNA information in a form that could be used by commercial genealogy sites.

Dean explained the procedures he planned to use, starting with amplification of all of the suspect's DNA. This would be followed by the technique used by genealogy companies called single nucleotide polymorphisms, or SNPs, analysis, whereby thousands of sites throughout the chromosome, areas where there are a lot of genetic variabilities, are sequenced. He confirmed that his lab was set up to sequence the large number of SNPs used by genealogy sites. Impressed by Dean's knowledge and list of publications, Rivera expedited clearance from the legal department that set up chain of custody procedures to use at DNA Discoveries. The minuscule but precious sample of Skeeter's blood was delivered by special messenger to Dean's lab within forty-eight hours. Time being of the essence, technicians were ready to start processing the precious specimen as soon as it arrived.

While technicians at DNA Discoveries were amplifying Skeeter's DNA sample, another man was murdered outside his home while sitting in his car, waiting for the garage door to open. As in the other cases, he was shot in the head with a single bullet, the assassin appeared to be six feet tall, and no evidence other than a casing devoid of DNA or fingerprints was left behind.

The victim, a thirty-seven-year-old attorney, was not on Martin's list. Hunter had blood from the victim sent to the crime lab so Lisa could analyze it. Two days later he learned that the latest victim was Skeeter's half-brother.

The following day, Dean's lab completed the SNPs analysis of Skeeter's blood, and uploaded the information to three large ancestry sites using the name "Skeeter Mosquito." By the following day, over one hundred matches had been reported in the twenty-five percent range. These corresponded to Martin's list of half-sibs previously identified on genealogy reports. There was no hundred-percent match, which would have indicated an identical twin or a previous submission to an ancestry site by Skeeter herself. Likewise, there was no fifty-percent match, which would have indicated a parent or full sibling.

Meanwhile, letters went out to all the names on Martin's list, warning them they might be targeted by the assassin. Public service announcements narrated by The Rocket were played in many large cities. Police departments were inundated with calls about suspicious people spotted in neighborhoods, as well as people asking for additional police protection which wasn't forthcoming. Callers were informed repeatedly that they'd need to hire their own protection if they wanted it. Despite being strapped for money, most departments in the Boise area, the area where most of the people on the list lived, put a few extra police on patrol at night. Gun sales shot up nationwide.

As word got out, the coldness experienced by the Starlings dissipated, replaced by sentiments of sympathy, and statements like "I knew you couldn't be involved." Olivia was still forbidden to associate with Greg because her parents feared she could be caught in the crossfire should there be an assassination attempt on her boyfriend, despite the grandchildren of Dr. Sanborn not being considered targets. So far, only his children had been victims.

Georgia and Martin got in the habit of smoking a joint together in the bedroom once or twice a week. Martin thanked Greg and gave him cash to buy extra weed the next time he visited Huntington but made him promise not to tell Nick. The professor no longer got funny looks from his colleagues when he came to work in what had become his new fashion statement—a Hawaiian shirt.

Martin, Georgia, Cat, Emerald, and Nick attended Greg's graduation. All went according to plan, despite the general pall over the ceremony brought on by Martin's presence, and concern over a possible assassination attempt. Ten police officers stationed around the venue did little to allay fears. After the ceremony, Greg went to an all-night party and slept until two pm the following day.

Martin, Georgia, and the boys were disappointed when Cat found the perfect roommate through the secure Facebook site. A half-sister named Sarah Knightly had recommended a cousin of hers, the daughter of her mother's brother. Martin confirmed with Dean that Sarah was only a twenty-five percent match with Skeeter.

Sarah wrote that her cousin, Caroline, was a quiet, single woman. She currently shared an apartment with a friend who was getting married and needed to find a new place to stay. She was around twenty-five years older than Cat and worked nearby in the library.

Cat met Caroline at a coffee shop and learned that the older woman spent most of her time in her room, at her job, or keeping company with her mother who lived in a nursing home. She got most of her meals from local restaurants and knew all the best take-out places. She seemed nice, not too chatty, and fit the bill perfectly. Caroline moved into the rental house three days later, ahead of Cat.

The following weekend, driving a van they'd borrowed from a neighbor, Martin and the boys arrived at Cat's new rental, a modest twenty-year-old tan stucco ranch house, similar to the other homes in the neighborhood. They began moving Cat's possessions from the van into her new home, meeting Caroline briefly when she emerged from her room to see what the commotion was about. The new roommate seemed pleasant enough, a dowdy-looking woman with thick glasses who wore baggy clothes, her long gray hair in a neat bun.

Meanwhile, Dean submitted Skeeter's data to more genealogy companies. There were no hundred-percent matches, nor were there matches of fifty percent, which would have identified a full sibling or parent. They were no closer to identifying her. Dean called Martin with the disappointing news.

"What about more distant maternal relatives?" Martin asked. "If we could identify them, maybe they would lead us to her."

"Unfortunately, aside from her half-sibs, all of Skeeter's matches are below two percent. Some of those are probably from her dad, and his relatives wouldn't know anything about all these half-siblings made by artificial insemination. Figuring out which ones are Skeeter's maternal relatives, and chasing them down, could take a lot of time."

"What if we compared the distant matches of Skeeter with my distant matches? Any that are the same will be from our father. Once we eliminate those, we'll only have maternal matches. That could help. Although the relative would be distant, if they know things about their genealogy, he or she might be able to identify the murderer or her mother."

"That could work, although when looking at distant relatives, you may find that a match may show up with one relative, but not another. That's because there's some randomness involved in how genetic material is distributed."

"Let's give it a try. I'll explain this to Hunter and ask him to look through the data."

Following a short discussion, Hunter agreed with the plan, and Martin sent him the information he had on the distant relatives of himself and Skeeter. Hunter began the task of crossing off all the relatives Skeeter had in common with Martin, as these would be paternal, not maternal matches they were interested in. After cross-checking the first thirty, Hunter realized that the large majority of matches were paternal, as he had eliminated all but one.

Hunter passed the information onto Martin, who identified that single remaining name in the family tree of another half-sib. The relative was therefore paternal, and wouldn't be helpful. After some discussion, Hunter and Martin agreed that with the large number of paternal distant relatives, this approach was impractical. They would need to cross-check possible maternal matches against the family trees of other half-siblings, which would take too much time with their small staff.

With no other leads in the case, Hunter slept more poorly than usual. His days were spent fielding calls from police departments, both in Idaho as well as other states. He even got calls from politicians, including the Idaho governor, asking about the status of the investigation. Each night, Hunter drove to the home of one potential victim in the area and waited, hoping that random luck would allow him to catch the murderer as she was preparing to strike. Each night he was disappointed.

Over the next two weeks, five more people in the Boise area were murdered in the same way. Two of the people were on the list, while the others weren't. DNA from the victims not on the list showed them each to be a twenty-five percent match with the others.

Two days later, a man came into the same police department Martin had visited, claiming to have seen the murderer. After a short wait, he was escorted to Detective Hunter's office.

"How do you know you saw the perpetrator?" Hunter asked.

"My mom had artificial insemination with Dr. Sanborn like the others, so I suppose he's my biological dad. When I drove home last night, a silver Honda CR-V was waiting a few houses down the street from my house. I saw someone sitting behind the wheel, which made me suspicious. I drove past my house and shot at the driver. Scared her away. She turned the car around and sped off." Hunter checked the list of half-sibs Martin had given him. This man's name wasn't on it.

"Did you ever send your DNA to a genealogy site? Hunter asked.

"Never."

"Did you ever talk to anyone about being a child of Dr. Sanborn?"

"I only recently shared that information with my wife, and I know she wouldn't tell anyone."

"How do you suppose the shooter might have gotten your name?"

"No idea."

"Did you get a good look at her?"

"No, it was dark."

"Are you sure it was a woman?"

"Not from what I saw, but I'm sure it was the murderer everyone's looking for. Why else would someone be sitting in a parked car in front of an empty house? I happen to know the people who live there are out of town."

"License plate?"

"Didn't get it. It was dark."

"I'll check with the neighbors—see if there is surveillance video. You're lucky you didn't kill anyone. The driver could have been an innocent person who was lost or visiting someone else on your block. I should arrest you, but instead, I'll give you a warning. Don't do that again."

"What else could I have done? Wait to be shot? I was standing my ground."

"I understand your frustration, but from what you said, you weren't being threatened."

The man thought a moment. "I'm pretty sure I saw her holding a gun. Maybe she was only going to steal my car. Whatever she was doing, she was a threat."

"Next time it might be best if you call the police."

That evening, before setting out on his night watch, Hunter went home to reflect on the facts of the case and relax over a bottle of beer. After taking his first gulp, he got a call from his mother. Usually ignoring her calls, he picked up this time.

"Bradkins," she said, using the name she had called him ever since he could remember. "I'm so glad you decided to answer. I've missed you."

"Sorry, Mom. I've been busy. Big case."

"You always have a big case."

"This one's different. There's a serial killer who has murdered a lot of people. I need to stop her."

"Her? That must be the case I heard about on the news. I hope you can stop her, but you know, if she's caught, there will be another one after that and another after that."

"Right. But I can only deal with what's going on now."

"I worry about you being under so much pressure all the time. I wish you'd find a companion, someone to help you relax."

"Like another wife?"

"Well, yes. You can't go on like this forever."

"That wife thing didn't turn out too well for me."

"I know, but you're older now. Perhaps you're ready."

"Gotta go now. I'm getting a call from dispatch."

There was no call from dispatch and Hunter felt a tinge of guilt as he disconnected the call. He finished his beer and left to stake out another potential victim.

The following day, Hunter reviewed surveillance videos from houses in the neighborhood of the man who had shot at the silver Honda CR-V. He was able to make out the vehicle's license on one. As in the other cases, the plate was registered to a different car. A gun was visible in the driver's hand for a moment, but Hunter doubted the man who fired the shots had seen it. Studying the videos several times, the detective was at a loss to describe the driver, the features obscured by a combination of darkness and a hoodie pulled tightly around the face. He reran the recording from one of the houses multiple times, concentrating on the car moments before it took off. Watching it the tenth time, he was convinced: the bullet shot by the man claiming to stand his ground had made a hole in the front right headlight, near the edge.

That evening Hunter visited Martin's house. Georgia answered the door.

"I have a warrant to inspect your car," Hunter said, holding out the paperwork.

"It's parked on the street," Georgia said. "All you have to do is look."

"I already looked at the part I'm interested in, the right front light. But I need to remove the glass, and look behind it. See if there's any evidence of a bullet hole."

"Knock yourself out," Georgia said, turning around and slamming the door behind her.

Using a tool he had brought with him, Hunter removed the glass from the light in question. Seeing no evidence of damage, he replaced the glass and rang the bell at the front door again. This time Martin answered. His face was red, and he took a deep breath as if he were about to scream at Hunter.

The detective held up one arm, flexing his hand. "Don't say it. I know you're mad, but I just needed to be absolutely certain. Although our murderer drives a silver Honda CR-V the same model as yours, I can now prove it's a different car from your wife's. Someone shot at the murderer's car last night and hit the light. I needed to be sure there was no damage behind the glass on your wife's car since the broken glass could have been replaced this morning."

"Did the driver get away?"

"Unfortunately, yes. We're still no closer to catching her. Although some people are putting up resistance, like the fellow who tried to shoot her last night, she's still succeeding in killing more victims."

"I was just about to call Dean. He texted me that he had another idea for tracking down Skeeter through her maternal relatives. If you want, I'll put him on speaker, and you can listen."

"I'd love to."

Martin escorted Hunter into his study, put his phone on his desk, and called Dean. He explained that he was on speaker, and Hunter was listening.

"I'd sure be interested in hearing a good idea right now," Hunter said.

"I was watching my wife sort the wash this morning," Dean said. "White in one pile, colors in another. It got me thinking. Unless we're very unlucky, the murderer has a normal number of blood relatives on her mother's side."

"How will that help?"

"As you know, we all get half our DNA from our mother, and half from our father. With a known sample of Martin's DNA and a known sample of his mother's, I could sort his DNA into two groups, DNA from his mother, and DNA from his father, like my wife sorts the laundry."

"How would you do that?" Martin asked.

"I could analyze your mother's DNA and identify the sequences you got from her. The remaining sequences would be from your biological father, Dr. Sanborn. That would give me half of the doctor's sequences since you have about half of Sanborn's genetic material, which was distributed to you randomly. The same holds for all your half-siblings. Half their DNA is from Sanborn, but none will have exactly the same half as you. If the analysis were repeated for several of the half-siblings, namely subtracting their mother's sequences from their own, I could identify the DNA sequences contributed by Sanborn for each. Then I could put all the information regarding Sanborn's DNA together, and come up with the composition of most of his DNA. Once I do that, I could subtract the DNA information on Sanborn from Skeeter's DNA information. That would leave only the DNA Skeeter inherited from her mother, which would be half of the mother's total DNA. I'd be sorting Skeeter's DNA like my wife sorts the wash. I already have a program that could do all of the analysis needed."

"Brilliant," Martin said. "I see where this is going."

"Right. Once I have the mother's DNA information, I could load that onto ancestry sites and get you a list of relatives related only on the maternal side. The father's relatives would be eliminated. The maternal relatives, even if fairly distant, might provide some useful information regarding the identification of Skeeter's mother."

"Sounds complicated," Hunter said, "definitely above my pay grade. But if you think it will help, I'm all for it. I'll have to get Dr. Rivera to agree."

Chapter 43

DETECTIVE HUNTER BROUGHT A LARGE box of donuts to the crime lab and stood in front of the receptionist's desk. "Something smells good," the young green-haired woman remarked.

"Are you flirting with me?" Hunter asked.

"Hardly. I just want a donut."

"Glad you told me, because you made me so uncomfortable with your remark, I was just about to call HR and file a complaint. Now, if you're not too busy, tell Rivera I'm here. By the way, these donuts are for the DNA analysts. You know, the people that do the real work around here. You can check with Rivera later to see if he'll let you have the crumbs after the technicians finish them."

The receptionist stuck out her tongue, then made a quiet call. She hung up and told Hunter that Dr. Rivera was expecting him. The detective walked through the lab, noticing technicians in their white coats looking busy as usual. There was less chatter than he was used to seeing. *Rivera seems to be running a tight ship like he said.*

A female technician was leaving the director's office when Hunter arrived. Rivera was standing behind his desk as Hunter scooted past the exiting woman.

"What have we here?" Rivera asked, seeing the box Hunter was carrying.

"I passed by a donut shop on the way here and thought, 'What the hell. I should bring these hard-working lab scientists a treat. Might help make up for the fact that they have such a terrible boss.'" Both men smiled.

"On behalf of the staff, let me offer my thanks. One moment and I'll take these to the break room," Rivera said. "They'll probably be gone by the time I get back here."

The director left momentarily, leaving Hunter to look around. He noticed a pile of journals on the desk, and a picture of Rivera with a young, beautiful dark-haired woman. Both were wearing parkas, smiling while holding skis atop a mound of snow. For a moment, Hunter felt a pang of envy, and regret that he had no outside life, nothing to look forward to should he become unable to continue working.

Rivera returned quickly. "What can I do for you today?" he asked.

"I spoke to Martin and Dean last night. Dean told me about an interesting approach to finding our perpetrator. I want to pass it by you to see what you think. I want your cooperation so we're all working together."

"Good idea," Rivera said, "although I imagine if the idea came from Dean, it's solid."

Hunter explained Dean's idea about trying to find Skeeter's mother and suggested Rivera call him with any questions.

"It sounds like a clever idea," Rivera said. "It could develop into a pretty useful technique down the line. I'll give Dean a call for more details, and if it all checks out, I'll send him the leftover samples I have from victims."

"Great. Meanwhile, I'll try to locate the victims' moms and arrange to collect samples from them if they're willing, so you can start to develop Sanborn's DNA data."

The two men shook hands, and Hunter left. He walked through the lab and found Lisa, busy entering data into a computer. "This is for you," he said, handing her a small box tied with a red ribbon. "I'm a man of my word, and you deserve it." He walked away as she started to open the gift, a gold star pendant on a chain. He turned in time to see a smile cross her face.

Next, he stopped by the break room and noted that the box of donuts was empty. When he passed by the receptionist on the way out, he said, "If you hurry, you can get a donut. There's one left." Out of the corner of his eye, he saw her get up and rush towards the break room. He smiled, happy he had driven the two miles out of his way to Jonnie's Donuts.

Later that day, Rivera sent Hunter a list of ten victims whose DNA was already in the crime lab, available for Dean to analyze. Hunter went down the list and determined which had a mother living in the area. The first five he contacted agreed to submit their DNA. All were eager to do whatever they could to catch the killer of their children. DNA from Martin and his mother were also included, for a total of six pairs of DNA specimens from which Dean hoped to determine Dr. Sanborn's DNA profile.

Technicians at DNA Discoveries prioritized characterizing the DNA samples received from the crime lab, as well as samples from the mothers, as they arrived. Dean stood by the computer terminal to check the results as determinations of the paternal contribution of each DNA sample were being performed. Although the program had been tested on specimens where the maternal and paternal DNA data was already known, this was the first time it had been used on a sample in which the information on one of the parents was unknown.

Dean called Martin and Rivera after the analysis of the first sample was complete to let them know the program had run smoothly, and he now had information on half of Sanborn's DNA. Within twenty-four hours, his lab had extracted Sanborn's DNA profile from the remaining five samples. The results from the six partial DNA determinations of Sanborn were then combined into one report, duplicate data was discarded, and a ninety-eight percent complete profile of the prolific father remained.

Finally, Sanborn's contributions were subtracted from Skeeter's DNA information. They now had a fifty-percent DNA profile of the perpetrator's mother six days after the project was begun.

Dean called Rivera, then Martin, with the news. "Hopefully, we'll get some significant maternal matches which got buried in the large number of paternal matches," he told Martin. "Rivera will be loading the information to several sites today. We may have some hits tomorrow. Then the real work begins."

"That should keep Hunter busy for a while."

"He's going to work closely with Rivera, who will advise him about the genetic relationships, and who it makes sense to pursue. Hunter will provide the gumshoe expertise—looking up records, finding out where they all live, interviewing them for more information, things like that."

"Has Hunter ever done anything like this before?"

"I doubt it. This is the first time that crime lab has participated in hunting down a criminal through a relative's DNA."

"Can't say I love the guy, but he's starting to grow on me. I won't tell him, though. He can probably detect it." Dean groaned as Martin continued. "Of course, even if he does identify the murderer's mother, we still may not be able to find the murderer. The mother might be dead or out of the country. She may be unwilling to say where her daughter is."

"I know. We're still a long ways from finding her."

Chapter 44

HUNTER WAS AT HIS DESK, going over the list of Martin's half-sibs, trying to decide which house he would monitor that evening in hopes of catching the murderer. His cell phone rang, and the caller was identified as Mario Rivera. Weeks earlier, that same caller ID would have conjured up thoughts of punching the lab director in the face, but instead, he found himself smiling, rushing to answer the call. Two days earlier Rivera had told him that Skeeter's mother's DNA information had been uploaded to several genealogy sites. "What's up, Rivera?" Hunter asked.

"I have some potentially good news. We got five hits on the mother."

"How close?"

"Almost two percent. Since the matches are with only half the mother's DNA, that's consistent with close to a four percent match with her complete DNA, which would be a first cousin once or twice removed, or a second cousin."

"First cousin twice removed. What's that? The grandchild of a first cousin?"

"Either that or the descendent of a great-great-grandparent. Since the matches are all in their thirties, they are probably related through a grandparent or great-grandparent."

"These relationships are very confusing," Hunter said.

"I know. That's why I'm staring at a family tree diagram as I'm talking to you."

"That makes me feel a little better."

"Conveniently, three live in the area. I'll give you the contact information I have for them, and you can follow up by interviewing them and searching public records as needed. Hopefully, you'll be able to get enough information to compile a list of people who might be the mother of our perpetrator."

"With so few of them, it's no wonder they were washed out by the large number of Sanborn's relatives."

"Right. He must've had some relatives with very large families. Much fewer on the maternal side. If we're lucky, at least one of these will break the case."

With five leads to the mother of the murderer, Hunter was encouraged. He found out everything he could on the matches by checking DMV and police records. They all had Facebook pages, where two listed genealogy research as being a "passion." Although he couldn't understand why so many people wasted their time on Facebook and revealed so much about themselves, he was thankful for it. He learned who was married, how many children they had, where they'd been on vacation, and what their favorite foods, TV shows, books, and movies were. Unfortunately, none mentioned a distant cousin whom they suspected of being a serial killer.

The detective wasted no time contacting the three relatives who lived locally, and setting up a time to question them about a person of interest in a police case. It was his experience that most people want to help police find criminals if they were guilty of a crime they disapproved of, such as murder.

During each interview, Hunter revealed he had reason to believe the person they were after was a distant relative, and slowly worked into asking them for their genealogy information. All three people he spoke with were happy to cooperate. Each had a family tree going back at least three generations, and included first and second cousins, up to twice removed. One had third and fourth cousins. Many of the relatives were deceased, and a lot of diamonds, squares, and circles for possible relatives not yet identified were blank, squares representing males, circles representing females, and diamonds representing relatives of unknown gender.

Since Skeeter's mother hadn't been identified using commercial genealogy testing, Hunter homed in on people represented by diamonds or circles, who might be the murderer's mother but hadn't been identified through DNA. These were people expected to have around a three to six percent DNA match with the relatives of Skeeter's mom he questioned. In his notes, he referred to them as the four percenters.

The interviews were tedious, with each distant cousin going into more detail about irrelevant relatives than Hunter wanted to know. He was able to get some information about a quarter of the people on family trees who hadn't been identified by genealogy. Some were unlikely to be Skeeter's mother, being too young, too old, or having other reasons for being ruled out, although they might provide information useful for the search. Twenty-two were not ruled out as Skeeter's mother. He also jotted down the names and contact information of two elderly relatives who were still alive, a possible great-aunt and great-uncle of Skeeter.

Midweek, Hunter flew to Texas to interview a maternal relative in Texas, asking the same questions of her. Similar to the others, she had cooperated, with long-winded answers to his questions but had provided the detective with three more candidates for Skeeter's mother.

Upon Hunter's return, fifteen messages were on his desk about unsolved murder cases around the country that fit the description of those in Boise. About half the victims were on Martin's list of half-siblings. He arranged for specimens from the others to be sent to his crime lab so Rivera could confirm they were half-siblings.

That Friday, the detective was in his office, staring at the list of twenty-five people who might be Skeeter's mother. Some had been on the family tree of everyone he had interviewed. Others had only been on only one. He had the name, age, and location of only three. Eighteen were associated with a name only. Four were identified only as a diamond on family trees—not even their gender was known.

Hunter knew that searching for progeny of everyone on his list, looking for live births of females would be slow. Many were out of state. Figuring out which birth records could refer to Skeeter would be daunting, even with the resources he had available as a police detective.

He tried to contact a possible great-uncle of Skeeter's mother but soon learned he was out of the country and couldn't be contacted. His third wife, however, knew enough about the family to inform Hunter that three of the women on the list had no daughters, and could therefore be eliminated. That left twenty-two.

The next person he contacted, a possible great-aunt in her late eighties, claimed to be hard of hearing and insisted on speaking to him in person only. Hoping for a breakthrough, Hunter made an appointment to see her. As he parked in front of her modest house in a semi-rural area, he took note of the front yard full of weeds and chipped paint on the front door. He knocked and was greeted by an elderly, pleasant-looking woman with short gray hair, wearing a loose cotton dress and slippers.

"Detective Hunter?" she said, smiling. Hunter nodded. "Please come in."

She escorted the detective to a small living room with furniture wrapped in clear plastic.

"Please have a seat and make yourself comfortable. I'll be right back with some refreshments."

Hunter started to speak. "Please don't go to any bother on my . . ." but before he could finish, she was gone.

Several minutes later the octogenarian returned carrying a tray with cups, tea, coffee, and two kinds of freshly-baked cookies. *She's going to try to talk my ear off.* Hunter had been around long enough to know the signs. Lonely woman, probably a widow, expecting a visitor, spends hours baking and preparing for the guest. Insurance salesman, reverse mortgage broker, or police officer—it didn't matter. It was a warm body she could talk to, and she was going to make it last as long as she possibly could.

Resigned to spend the next hour at least talking to the woman, often needing to shout so he could be understood, Hunter helped himself to coffee and sampled each type of cookie the woman had made. As he tried to insert questions about any great nieces she might have, Hunter's hostess dominated the conversation with talk about her late husband, her children, and grandchildren, and a trip she had taken to London with her husband twenty years earlier.

By the time he was able to extract himself, Hunter was mentally worn out, but he had the name of a grand-niece in the area he hadn't known of before. She was in her thirties and provided the detective with information about two more women who could be Skeeter's mother. He and his team spent a full day trying to locate them. Just following this one branch of the family tree, Hunter realized, was going to be quite time-consuming.

Three days after sitting in the living room of the elderly woman, eating her freshly-baked cookies, a woman was murdered in the parking lot of a supermarket after dark. The victim, Fiona Prescott, was a thirty-five-year-old housewife and mother of two. While the attack wasn't recorded on video, a witness described seeing a silver car, possibly a Honda CR-V, peel away after the gunshot. A spent shell, similar to the others, was on the asphalt about fifteen feet away.

Hunter called a meeting of the task force.

"She's getting more brazen," he said. "This one took place in a public parking lot."

"Brazen, but careful," another officer said. "It was dark, with few people around. This wasn't even caught on camera."

"I think we can expect more like this," Hunter said. "This woman is a good shot. Hasn't missed her target once, as far as we know. Always just one casing. Never more than one shot heard. Kelso, why don't you check military records? Look for a female with combat training, possibly sniper training, who was dishonorably discharged, living in the area. Morse, I'd like you to check all the gun stores in the area. There's probably a lot that carry these bullets. See if anyone remembers a woman purchasing them, possibly in large quantities. Get a copy of any video from such a transaction. Any other ideas?"

"How's the tip line working?" another officer asked. "I heard some people are unable to get through."

"That's right. I've asked for more money so we can handle more calls. Unfortunately, the tips we've been getting haven't been helpful so far. If I didn't know it before, I know it now; there's an awful lot of people around here who wear black hoodies."

"Yeah, people wearing black hoodies out in public are probably innocent," the lone female officer on the task force said. "The murderer is no idiot. She probably only wears the hoodie when she's about to kill someone."

"Good point," Hunter said. "We should probably exclude anyone who wears a hoody when they're walking around in public." The others chuckled. "Unfortunately, we have to follow up on all these leads. We've been wasting a lot of time, while our murderer seems to be killing people more frequently, and with this last one, with more boldness. It's almost as if she's in a hurry to kill as many as possible."

Two days later, Hunter learned that, as expected, Fiona Prescott was the half-sister of the others. The pressure was on. Reporters came by or called him every day. What had started as an occasional irritation, was now a daily occurrence. Lately, contact from five or six journalists a day was commonplace. The public was clamoring for more protection. Hunter spoke to The Rocket, asking him to reassure the public the police were doing everything they could.

"Everything they can do isn't enough," The Rocket said. "You don't know who this is or what she looks like. Those grainy images you run on TV haven't been much help. People are still being killed. From what I hear, the public doesn't think you're doing anything. Just waiting for her to slip up. They think you're sitting around, waiting."

"We're doing a lot behind the scenes. We just can't talk about it." There was no way Hunter was going to let the public know they were trying to hunt down the perpetrator through DNA and questioning her maternal relatives. If the murderer knew that, she might start knocking off relatives on her mother's side. It was best if she never learned the police had a sample of her DNA.

If he could figure out a motive for the murders, he might have a better chance of finding her. Jealousy? Hatred? It didn't appear the murderer was acquainted with any of her victims, and certainly not all of them. While each was at least comfortably middle class, it would be hard to come up with a reason she would be more jealous of them than non-relatives. How could she hate them if she didn't know them? A love triangle was out of the question with all those people, both men and women, of varying ages. Money? There was no evidence any money from the victims was being left to anyone other than close family members, mainly spouses and children. Information? She was never seen questioning her victims, trying to get their PIN numbers or passwords before resorting to murder. The motive was evading him. There had to be one—these were not thrill murders. In those cases, victims were chosen randomly by the killer whose reason for killing was to fulfill their sick itch for gratification through murder, often involving torture and collection of a trophy from the victim.

The other piece of the puzzle was how the murderer got the names of her victims. She hadn't revealed her DNA information publicly, although she may have submitted samples, and kept her information private on genealogy sites. If so, her name wouldn't be revealed to others, but she would get the names of relatives who made their information public. In that case, she could have a list of relatives similar to Martin's. Getting private information from a genealogy company would be difficult for Hunter, if not impossible, due to privacy regulations. He thought about having their legal department start the process but rejected the idea. If she had submitted DNA, she wouldn't have used her real name and demographic information. Since she had murdered half-siblings who were not on Martin's list, at least some of her information must have been coming from elsewhere. But where?

Hunter fell asleep mulling this over in front of his TV, a beer in one hand and the TV remote in the other. He was still sitting in his chair when sunlight made its way through the curtains and hit his face before six a.m. Awake, he went to the bathroom and looked in the mirror. He looked even worse than he felt. *You've got to think of something. People are dying.*

Chapter 45

HUNTER WAITED UNTIL SEVEN-THIRTY A.M. to call Martin. "I need an up-to-date list of all your half-sibs. Have you added any names since I got the list from you?"

"Names keep trickling in now that so many people are getting tested. The number of confirmed half-sibs is over two hundred."

"I'd like to come by now to look at your laptop with all the information about your half-siblings," he said.

"The computer belongs to my son."

"I need it. Ask him or tell him. I need to look at it this morning." Hunter thought a moment, then added, "Please. I want to compare the names on his computer with the names of all the people we believe were murdered by Skeeter. I want to confirm that not all of the victims were identified by genealogy sites."

"Okay, you can come by now. Nick is camping with the family of a friend, but his computer is here," Martin answered.

Hunter was at Martin's front door, a large envelope under his arm, thirty minutes later. The house was quiet, as Georgia had left for work, and Greg was still asleep. The two men sat at the kitchen table, studying Nick's laptop. A list of all the victims nationwide the assassin was credited with murdering, pulled from the large envelope he'd brought, was in Hunter's left hand.

Hunter slowly scrolled down Nick's spreadsheet, crossing out names on his list as he read them on Nick's computer.

When he got to the end of the list, Hunter lowered his head and sighed heavily. "Looks like there are thirty-two murder victims that still don't appear anywhere on your list. Even if your computer was hacked, there has to have been another source of the names."

"There's a few notes down here," Martin said, scrolling down further. "These are just miscellaneous things either Nick or I entered that don't directly relate to the people on the list. Maybe Nick added the names of some half-sibs awaiting their genealogy test results here for some reason."

The two men read Nick's notes about who to contact to arrange testing for the mutation, then technical notes about how the test was performed.

Contact information for Constance Jackson and her investigator was next. That was followed by the name of the prolific doctor, Kirby Sanborn, and his date of death.

Then came the name Agatha Diaz, followed by "Naomi" in parenthesis.

"Hold on," Hunter said. "Agatha. That's not a very common name. Where have I seen that before?" He was silent as he placed his left elbow on the table and leaned forward, resting his chin on his left hand. Martin studied him for the next minutes, unsure what to do. Finally, Hunter raised his head and smacked his forehead with the palm of his left hand. "I know where I saw that name," he said as he thumbed through papers in the large envelope. Pulling one page out, he said, "Here. Agatha Laurier. Does that name mean anything to you?"

"How'd you get that name?" Martin asked.

"She was identified as a second cousin by two of the distant matches with Skeeter's mom."

Martin smiled. "I have some good news for you."

Hunter looked up as his pulse quickened.

Martin continued. "As you know, Kirby Sanborn was the doctor who fathered me and all my half-sibs. I found that out through an attorney and her private investigator."

Hunter felt his chest about to explode. *Tell me what you know, already, before I wring your neck.* It was difficult, but he managed to appear calm, showing only his friendliest smile.

"The investigator learned that before Sanborn died, his wife divorced him. She remarried, and her name is now Agatha Diaz. But I remember that after her divorce before she remarried, she used her maiden name, Agatha Laurier. Not a common name at all. That second cousin you learned about is probably Sanborn's ex-wife."

Hunter sat in stunned silence several moments, as Martin wrinkled his brow, appearing deep in thought. Finally, Hunter spoke. "You think she's our murderer?"

"No. Remember, half of Skeeter's DNA is from Sanborn. But the murderer could be their child, Naomi Sanborn. If she's around six feet tall. And she's not dead."

Hunter jumped up and started walking around the room, gesturing wildly with his arms. "This is big. Sanborn's daughter. Wow! All we have to do now is get her address and arrest her. I can't believe it. We could have her in custody by the end of the day, and close the case." Hunter was breathless as he let out an excited whoop.

"I'm afraid it's not going to be quite that simple," Martin said.

Hunter sat down, the excitement drained from his face. "Why's that?"

"First of all, there's the height. Six feet is pretty tall for a woman."

"The shooter may be six feet, but a second person, a woman, could have been crouched down in the car. She has to be the ringleader. After all, they're going after her relatives. I don't know why, but we'll find that out later. Ninety percent of the time, when we catch one, he or she will roll over and give up the other."

"You're going to offer her a deal?"

"That's not up to me. Even without her cooperation, all we need to do usually is get the cell phone or computer of the person in custody, and the other names will be revealed."

"Before you get too excited, there's another problem, and it's a big one. It won't be easy to locate her. Her mother has no idea where she is. Agatha even hired a private detective, but she couldn't find her and thinks Naomi might be dead. If we can show the blood sample you have is from Agatha's daughter, that means she's very much alive." Then Martin relayed everything he had learned about Naomi from her mother.

"We need to get DNA from Agatha," Hunter said. "The methods used by

DNA discoveries to get Skeeter's mother's DNA information haven't been properly vetted. If we can prove she's her mother using standard techniques, then we have a national manhunt on our hands. A hunt for Naomi Sanborn."

Chapter 46

SITTING AT HIS DESK, HUNTER thought about the best approach. Should he call Agatha Diaz? If he asked her to volunteer a DNA sample after explaining that her daughter, Naomi, was suspected of being the mastermind behind a serial killer, would she cooperate? Perhaps he should get a court order to be served in Florida. That would be complicated due to paperwork. It would make sense that if Naomi wanted to kill people, she'd have someone do the dirty work for her, possibly someone with military sniper training.

He mulled over his options, aware that time was passing, and lives were at risk. He unfolded the paper Martin had given him with Agatha's phone number and placed it on the desk in front of him. He picked up the desk phone and dialed. Agatha answered.

Hunter introduced himself, stating his name and position in the local police department. He thought it would be best not to disclose the exact reason for his call. "We're looking for your daughter because there is reason to believe her life is in danger from an inherited blood clotting disorder."

"I learned about that a while ago from a lawyer and her client trying to find out about my ex-husband, Naomi's father. Like I told them, I don't know where she is or even if she's alive, but of course, if she's still alive, I hope you can find her so she can get the medication she needs."

"We'd like to have a picture of her, as recent as possible, to help us find her. You've never been notified that she'd died, have you?"

"No, I haven't. But I wonder if she might be a Jane Doe buried in some unmarked grave."

"Let me help. I've found a number of people who'd been given up for dead." Hunter didn't feel good, blatantly lying to this probably very nice woman, but he had to do what needed to be done.

"That's so good to hear," Agatha said. "I have a nice picture I took of Naomi four years ago before she disappeared. Give me your email address and I'll send it to you."

After giving Agatha his email address, Hunter asked about Naomi's height, weight, eye and hair color, as well as any distinguishing birthmarks. Brown eyes and dark brown hair, five foot six, one hundred forty pounds, with no distinguishing marks. She'd fit unnoticed in any crowd. Only her leg prosthetics were unusual. Her height ruled her out as the shooter. Hunter also confirmed that Agatha had no other children, either male or female.

Satisfied with the information he'd gotten so far, Hunter wanted more, information that might help him locate her or uncover a motive. "I know her father, Dr. Sanborn, died some years ago. Did he leave her much?" If she had a hefty inheritance, she could easily travel anywhere.

"The bastard didn't leave her a dime. She always relied on me for support. Kirby had inherited money from his father, who made a fortune from a family-owned large mining company. I believe he had over fifty million dollars when our divorce was finalized."

Hunter whistled. "That would be worth quite a lot today."

"You may be thinking I'm a rich woman, but I'm not. I never got any of that money. Since it was an inheritance, he was able to keep all that money separate from our community property. I never saw him spend much of it. When I divorced him, I knew what I was potentially giving up, but it wasn't worth being in a miserable marriage to be rich."

"If he didn't leave the money to Naomi, who did he leave it to?" Hunter asked.

"Charity. Naomi was devastated when she found out he left all of it to strangers rather than her, his own daughter. Kirby had told me he was leaving everything to charity, but I hoped he was lying. He liked to play cruel games and wouldn't show me his will, so I was never sure. I had warned Naomi not to expect anything from him, but I don't think she believed me. I'm not sure if Kirby ever told her about the money directly, or if she found out from the lawyer after he died. It would have been just like Kirby to tell her himself and emphasize the fact that she wasn't getting anything."

"To your knowledge, did the attorney distribute the money as Dr. Sanborn requested?"

"That's what Naomi told me happened. She handled Kirby's things after he died. I know you're wondering—did the attorney really give all that money to charity, or did he keep it himself?"

"The thought did cross my mind," Hunter said. "It wouldn't be terribly difficult for a dishonest attorney to launder all that money and give it to himself if no one was looking closely."

"I thought that might be the case, but I never looked into it. All I knew was Naomi wasn't going to get that money. I didn't want to upset her further, so I didn't bring it up again or investigate."

"How was it that Naomi took care of her father's estate after he died if they were on such bad terms?"

"I don't think there was much for her to do. Kirby's attorney took care of disbursing the money according to my ex's wishes, but he hired Naomi to do some odds and ends having to do with the estate. She took care of liquidating his furniture, office contents, and car. He paid her as an executor because, I think, he felt sorry for her. At least she got some money out of it."

"Do you have the name of the attorney who handled the doctor's estate?" Hunter asked, making a note to refer the case to experts in financial crimes if he discovered any evidence the attorney had embezzled the money meant for charity. It wouldn't be unusual to find money as the motive for murder.

"Yes. Kirby used the same attorney we'd used before the divorce. Let me walk into the next room to get you his name and contact information." As she continued to speak, the sound of footsteps and doors opening and closing came over the phone. "I keep all my old papers in a file cabinet in the attic. Hardly ever need to access it. Damn. This drawer is stuck. I wish my husband were here, but he's gone to Argentina on business for two weeks." She paused as Hunter stayed silent. After letting out a loud grunt, the sound of a file drawer sliding open met Hunter's ears. "Here it is," Agatha said moments later, "now I remember. Reginald Beaufort." Agatha gave him the phone number and address she had for Mr. Beaufort years ago. "Honestly," she said, "I have no idea if he's still practicing."

Hunter thanked Mrs. Diaz for the information, then phoned the Jupiter, Florida, police department to ask for a favor. He spoke to a sergeant who agreed to send an officer to the Diaz house on the next garbage collection day to pick up items from the trash for DNA analysis.

After that, he dialed the number for Reginald Beaufort's law offices but was met with a message stating *This number is no longer in service.* Not wanting to waste time, he called a junior member of the task force and asked him to locate the Beaufort law office or find out who had taken it over. Meanwhile, he would continue his practice of watching the house of one potential victim every night.

Within the hour, Hunter had received a digital image of Naomi Sanborn. Looking younger than her current age of forty-eight, she had medium-length wavy hair, dark in color with small streaks of gray. Neither beautiful nor homely, she had the kind of face that was easy to forget. He wrote a description to accompany the photo and issued a statewide BOLO—be on the lookout. It stated she was a double amputee, five-foot-six, and might be accompanied by a six-foot-tall man. The make and color of the car seen at the crime scenes, as well as the admonition that she and her partner should be considered armed and dangerous, were included.

Late the following afternoon, the officer assigned had located the law office of Reginald Beaufort II, who had taken over the practice of his father several years earlier. Hunter called Mr. Beaufort and explained he needed to inquire about the estate of Dr. Kirby Sanborn, who had died over twenty years earlier.

"My dad's paperwork isn't as organized as I'd like," the younger Beaufort said. "But I should have that paperwork in the archived files. I'll have my secretary check and call you back."

Hunter was restless as he waited for the callback. He looked up Beaufort's home address and determined he lived in a solidly middle-class home, not the sort of residence a multimillionaire would be expected to live in. Hunter concluded it was unlikely the attorney had been the recipient of ill-gotten gains from Sanborn's estate.

Next, the detective checked on the results of the BOLO. There had been a few possible sightings, but none had panned out. *She's probably changed her appearance anyway.*

Three hours after Hunter had contacted him, Beaufort called him back. "I think there's something strange about this case."

I could have told you that. Instead of revealing his thoughts, Hunter replied, "Why do you say that?"

"I can't find his file. My secretary noticed bent tabs in the files around the area where Sanborn's file should be. She thinks it looks as if someone had thumbed through the area quickly. She showed me, and I agree. That got me thinking. I'm not sure if it's related, but my office was broken into over a year ago. A window had been smashed, and a security tape showed a person in a hoodie crawling through the window. A few things had been messed up, but nothing seemed to be missing. We rarely go into these old files, so it's quite possible the burglar took the Sanborn file, but we never noticed."

"I take it there were no fingerprints or other evidence left behind."

"You guessed it."

"Do you have any knowledge about what was in the file?"

"I'm afraid not. If the deceased died over twenty years ago, it's likely his estate was settled well before my dad died. We only keep records for our protection in case someone later claims fraud or negligence on our part."

"Did your father ever talk to you about the Sanborn estate?"

"No. He wouldn't—attorney-client privilege. When Dr. Sanborn died, I was still in high school. Can I ask why you're so interested in the will of someone who died so long ago? Was there a problem I should be aware of?"

"You've probably heard about the serial killer on the loose."

"Sanborn! I should have figured it out when you asked me about his file. I never suspected one of my dad's clients was the doctor who had all those kids who are now being murdered for some reason. Geez… I've read about the murders, but never thought I would be involved in any way. Why all the interest in the will?"

"To tell you the truth, we don't know what the motive for the murders is, and I'm trying to find out. I thought there might be something in the will that would shed some light on it." Hunter didn't want to let on that he suspected the money Sanborn left to charity was embezzled, and the murders were somehow related to that crime. How they were related was another question.

"Sure. If I discover that missing file or learn anything that might be useful, I'll let you know. I sure hope you catch the guy."

Sitting at his office after the call, Hunter closed his eyes and held his head in his hands, his elbows propped up on the desk. *What could she have been after, getting ahold of the old man's will? It's a bit late to contest it. I doubt the courts could force whatever charity received it to send it back. It's already been spent. Unless Beaufort has it tucked away. In which case, why not extort Beaufort for whatever money is left? Why murder her half-siblings?*

Chapter 47

THE FOLLOWING DAY, DNA SAMPLES from the garbage can of Agatha Diaz were delivered to Dr. Rivera in a biohazard bag via Federal Express. Technicians in Florida had collected DNA from a 7Up can, a bandage with a large spot of blood, and an old toothbrush.

Rivera asked Lisa to drop what she was doing and work on confirming that at least one of the specimens was a match to the partial DNA profile they had derived for Skeeter's mother and a half-match with Skeeter. He spoke to Hunter and promised they'd be processed as quickly as possible.

Before the end of the following day, Hunter received a call from Rivera telling him he had just uploaded the results to the crime lab's secure website. Hunter could almost hear Rivera smiling over the phone as he refused to give him the results, instead telling him to check for himself.

Hunter logged onto the site, his hands shaking so much he misspelled his password several times before succeeding. As soon as the results were displayed, he let out a hoot. All three specimens from Florida were a perfect match with their derived profile of Skeeter's mother and a fifty-four percent match with Skeeter. This meant Agatha Diaz was Skeeter's mother. Since Agatha had only one child, Naomi, they now had the name and face of the person behind the killings.

Hunter sat back and reveled in his accomplishment for a few moments. No motive yet, but he hoped that would come later. Early the next morning, when it was nine a.m. in Florida, Hunter phoned Agatha. He knew there was no easy way to divulge what her daughter had been up to. Over the years, he'd developed his own procedure. Whether by phone or in person, he'd ask the loved one to sit down, then in one short sentence, tell them the bad news. He did the same with Naomi's mother.

After an audible gasp followed by moments of silence, Agatha spoke, her voice shaky. "I don't know whether I should be overjoyed or a basket case. You tell me my daughter is alive. I thought she was probably dead, so I should be overjoyed. Yet at the same time, you tell me she's behind all these killings. How is a mother supposed to feel about that? Naomi's had a rough time and sometimes seemed to be in a dark place. But she was never violent, and I have a hard time believing she did what you've accused her of. I surely can't be happy she's suspected of these things."

"I know it's difficult to imagine your daughter is guilty of these murders, but the evidence against her is strong. If she contacts you, or you learn where she is, it's important you contact me. Unless she turns herself in peacefully, it's possible she'll be killed by a police bullet. You'll be doing her a favor by helping us find her so we can bring her in peacefully."

"I understand. But that doesn't mean I like it."

"Like anyone else, she'll have a chance to hire an attorney and prove that she's innocent. You might consider looking for a good defense attorney now. That way if she contacts you, you have something to offer her." Hunter doubted even the best attorney could do much for Naomi, but he wanted to give Agatha time for the reality to sink in.

The hunt for Naomi began in earnest the next day. The information distributed in the Idaho BOLO was now shared with police departments nationwide. The Rocket appeared on TV and begged Naomi and her accomplice to turn themselves in. He posted a fifty-thousand-dollar reward for anyone who led to their capture. Agatha also sent messages to Naomi over the airways, telling her she was worried she would be killed if she didn't surrender voluntarily. She promised to help in any way she could and provide her with the best legal defense. The killing had to stop.

The phones of the tip line were constantly backed up, ringing incessantly from callers all around the country. Despite the increased capacity Hunter had arranged for recently, the call volume overwhelmed the system. Whatever her motive, Naomi had to know she was wanted. If she continued the killing, she would be caught. If she stopped the killing, she would be caught.

From the thousands of calls that came in, one conversation from a Colorado prosthetist caught the attention of authorities. The contents of the discussion moved up the chain of command quickly and were passed on to a local sergeant who called Hunter within the hour.

"What the hell is a prosthetist?" Hunter asked the sergeant.

"I was told it's someone who makes prosthetic limbs for people. Like when someone loses an arm or a leg, a prosthetist makes them a fake one."

"Hmm. I never thought about it before, but I suppose people need prosthetic devices to be fit to the unique shape and exact location of the amputation site. That's probably why I've never seen them at Target."

"I have his number. You might want to call him yourself. He said the woman you're looking for looks like a past patient of his. She went by a different name, but he's sure it's her. Both her legs were amputated below the knee when she was a young child. He said some other things I didn't follow, but it might mean more to you."

Hunter took the name and number of the prosthetist and made the call. It was picked up in two rings. "I was hoping you'd call soon," the prosthetist said after Hunter introduced himself. "I remember this woman not only because she was a double amputee—I've seen a number of them, mostly referred from the Veterans Administration—but because she had a very strange request."

"Tell me about it," Hunter said, thinking someone might want to hide a gun or a knife in a fake leg, a clever way to conceal a weapon when going through airport security or any other sort of metal detector.

"She had me make two sets of prosthetics for her. One set kept her at her usual height, five foot six. The other made her taller, six feet. She told me she wanted to play tricks on her friends. Frankly, she was so odd and humorless, I found it hard to believe she had many friends."

"Of course!" Hunter said as he thumped his forehead. "She's the shooter and the mastermind. I should have figured it out. She's a double amputee. She could change her height by using different fake legs. That long tunic she wears when she's jacked up to be six feet hides where her knees bend. That would give it away. This information will greatly assist us."

"Glad I could help."

"How long ago did you make these legs for her?"

"I checked my records. She picked them up two years ago."

"Do you know where she is now?"

"I haven't seen her since she got her prosthetics. They fit her perfectly, so she didn't come back for any adjustments. At the time, she was living in a small town nearby. I have that address, but don't know if she's still there."

"Not even her mother has seen her since before then, so you're the best source we have about what she looked like. Do you remember the color of her hair?"

"It was purple when I saw her, but I doubt she was a natural purple head." He laughed at his own joke.

"That tells us she's not averse to dying her hair. Any markings—scars, piercings, or tattoos you remember?"

"She had a weird tattoo on her right shoulder. Looked like a poorly drawn house. Frankly, when I saw it I thought it might have been a swastika she had re-made into something else. I've seen that before. Some people around here get Swastika tattoos, then regret it. I always think that no matter what attracted them to that despicable symbol in the first place, it's good they no longer want it."

Hunter got the last known address of Naomi Sanborn from the prosthetist and thanked him for his help. He felt remorse for hounding Martin so long. It was an unlucky coincidence that he and his boy were approximately the same height as the murderer appeared wearing her prosthetics. He'd never make that mistake again, although he doubted a similar situation would present itself in the future. Now his top priority would be finding Naomi. He wasn't sure if knowing there was only one fugitive out there rather than two made it easier or harder to find her.

There hadn't been a murder since Naomi's name and face had been plastered all over the country. Hunter hoped she had decided to stop murdering, perhaps had even left the country. He wanted the satisfaction of arresting her himself, but if his work so far led to a halt in the killings, that wouldn't be a bad consolation prize.

The detective spoke to the lieutenant at the Colorado police department nearest the address he was given by the prosthetist. He explained he was looking for Naomi Sanborn, the murderer who was the focus of a nationwide manhunt. Her last known address was in his jurisdiction, and he asked the officer to stake the place out until he got there the next day.

"That's a pretty bad area," the lieutenant said. "This is a poor county, but that particular section of town makes most other areas around here look damn good. I'll put two men on it tonight."

Hunter planned to get an emergency warrant from the judge who had originally turned down his request to arrest Martin. With the information he had now, he was confident the judge would cooperate. Although he doubted Naomi still lived there, he wanted to be the one to knock on the door if she hadn't moved. He could only imagine the satisfaction he would feel, clicking handcuffs around her wrists, and kneeing her where it would hurt most in the process. He didn't want to take a chance the local police would rob him of that.

The following morning, Hunter received permission from his captain to go to Colorado for the purpose of finding Naomi. Then he phoned Agatha and asked her to look through her daughter's bedroom to retrieve items that would be likely to have Naomi's latent prints. He cautioned her not to touch them directly, but to handle them with gloves or tissue. Next, he phoned the local police and asked them to have Naomi's items collected and sent to him.

He picked up the warrant for Naomi Sanborn's arrest and was on a plane to Grand Junction that afternoon with a layover in Phoenix. He checked two firearms in his luggage, in compliance with TSA rules.

That evening Hunter drove his rental car two and a half hours to the small town where Naomi had lived two years earlier. He found a Motel Six-like lodge a few miles away, its most notable feature an excellent view of the freeway. After grabbing a six-pack of beer, a hot dog, and a bag of popcorn at the local Kwiki Mart, he settled into his room. Sleep came late and ended at six-thirty a.m. with a loud fight involving the couple next door.

Hunter dressed in a white shirt and khaki pants before heading to the address given him by the prosthetist. As expected, the apartment building was in a run-down area inhabited by a mixture of working-class people,

Hispanic and white. A few young children played in a nearby field, watched by their young mothers.

Hunter knocked loudly on the door of the apartment. A dark-haired man in a rumpled white T-shirt and boxer shorts opened the door as he wiped the sleep from his eyes. Seven men in sleeping bags were in various stages of awaking. The man at the door spoke English poorly, but the detective learned that he and his roommates were from Guatemala and worked in a nearby sawmill. They'd lived there almost a year, and Hunter suspected they had immigrated illegally. The man gave the detective permission to search the premises, but he only found seven other Guatemalans, mostly women. There was no sign of Naomi and all the residents denied knowing who she was.

Disappointed but not surprised, Hunter showed the picture of Naomi to a group of three young women he found outside the building. One didn't speak English. None recognized her. Walking in the area, he showed the image to several men and women. The ones who understood English denied ever seeing her before.

Hunter returned to his hotel where he dressed in jeans and a T-shirt, fitting in with the blue-collar neighborhood. He dined on bad coffee, eggs over easy, and bacon at a nearby greasy spoon. Although he didn't smoke, tobacco being the one vice he'd given up years ago, he rolled a pack of Marlboro's in his shirt sleeve. He hadn't done that since he'd left the military years earlier, but the skill came back to him quickly. He grabbed one of several copies of the picture he had of Naomi, and headed out.

Ten minutes later, he stumbled upon a pool hall. Given the relatively early hour, ten-thirty a.m., he was surprised it was as busy as it was. Most of the patrons were men with shaved heads, appearing to range from late teens to mid-sixties. Several hard-looking women wearing skimpy clothing were mixed in. Almost everyone was holding a beer can and smoking a cigarette, while a quarter were playing pool.

As Hunter stood in the doorway, the noise quieted. Soon, everyone was staring at him. *Looks like I stepped into the hangout of a gang or militia group.* He noted the swastika tattoos visible on most of them, some displaying the vile symbol on their face. *White supremacy militia.* He'd been in dicey situations before, but was always reassured by his ability to pull out his police badge to get people to back off. In Colorado, though, he wasn't an officer—he was just like every other civilian.

"Hi, y'all," Hunter said, trying to sound like a country bumpkin. A country bumpkin might be ridiculed, but not killed. "Am I interrupting something?"

A short, muscular man heavily covered in tattoos of swastikas and devils stepped up. "This is a closed party."

Hunter glanced sideways at the man behind the bar, who busied himself by wiping down the counter, avoiding eye contact.

"Sorry to bother y'all, but I'm lookin' for someone. I been lookin' for her for a while now. I work on a farm in Idaho. Don't have much, but this woman stole a necklace from my wife. Wasn't worth anything, but it's all her mom left her, and I just want it back. Ain't interested in pressin' no charges, nothin' like that. Any of you seen her?" He held up a picture of Naomi. "Names Naomi. Don't know her last name."

Several of the men came closer to get a better look. "We know her," one of them said. Two others nodded in agreement.

"Know where I can find her?"

"Good luck with that. She used to run with the Righteous Whites, a group in these parts. Ain't seen her for a while, though."

"Where can I find these Righteous Whites?"

"They kinda keep to themselves. Got a compound in the woods, not too far from here." After the man drew a map to their location, he added, "I'd be a bit careful goin' there. They don't take to strangers." He looked around at his buddies, smiling, "They ain't friendly like us." As if on cue, the others laughed.

Hunter returned to his motel, where he loaded his guns, put the Glock in an ankle holster, and a diminutive nine-millimeter J-frame revolver in the small pocket of a pad that went around his waist. Although uncomfortable with the gun compressing his belly, the padding was thick enough the firearm would be undetectable in a pat-down. He checked himself out in the full-length mirror attached to the bathroom door. Although his image appeared wavy due to the low quality of the glass, he was satisfied he looked like an ordinary dude out for a drive.

Following the crude map drawn in the pool hall, Hunter drove along a windy road for a half hour before coming to a wooden barricade blocking traffic. A "No Trespassing" sign was prominently displayed. Despite that, he drove off the road to get around the obstruction. After motoring another half mile, a large wooden building popped into view.

For a moment, the detective wondered if he should call his mother to say goodbye before parking his car in front of the building. As he was getting out, three men dressed in military camouflage appeared, each armed with a rifle. Hunter raised his arms as he assumed a standing position.

Chapter 48

"WHO ARE YOU AND WHAT do you want?" one of the men yelled at him. Aside from a Swastika on his face, he had two teardrops tattooed below the lateral edge of his left eye, indicating he'd been in prison and had murdered two people. The way the other men looked at him, he appeared to be the leader.

"Geez, sorry to come here without an invite," Hunter said, "but I wanted to talk to y'all about something. My name's Brad Hunter. Some boys in town told me you might know something about a lady I'm lookin' for. I didn't know no other way to talk to you other than to just come here. I didn't have a phone number or nothin'."

"Who you lookin' for?"

"Someone goes by the name Naomi. Don't know her last name." He gave the same reason he was looking for her as he'd told the men in the bar earlier.

"Don't know anyone named Naomi, do we boys?" the man asked, looking at the other two. They shook their heads in agreement.

"Let me show you her picture. She mighta used a different name here." Hunter reached into his pants pocket, causing the men to get closer and point their guns directly at his head. He stopped and looked up. "I just wanna show you her picture."

"Okay. But go real slow. One move we don't like, and we'll shoot yer head off."

"Got it." Hunter removed the photo a little at a time until it was completely out of his pocket, then held it up. "I'd really 'preciate it if you could tell me if she was here, and if you know where she is."

The leader nodded towards one of his men who was wearing a red baseball cap backward on his head. He lowered his gun, walked towards Hunter, and took the photo. He studied it for a few seconds, then passed it to the man in charge and raised his gun again. After perusing the picture for a short while, the leader held it out so the third man could look at it. Keeping their eyes on Hunter and their guns pointed at his head, the three men stood together and spoke quietly amongst themselves.

Finally, the leader spoke up. "We know her. Goes by Dawn Kennedy now. But she ain't here no more."

"Any idea where she went?"

"You sure ask a lot of questions." As soon as those words were spoken, the men grabbed Hunter and patted him down. The man wearing the baseball cap found the ankle gun.

"I knew it!" the head man said, as the other two wrestled Hunter to the ground. Pointing Hunter's gun at his face, he asked, "You with the gover'ment?"

"No. I don't mean to cause you no trouble. I was warned to be careful in these here parts. I don't even know how to shoot that thing."

The leader put his own gun down, removed the clip from Hunter's Glock, and put the bullets in his shirt pocket before kicking the pistol away.

"Search him better, guys," the man said to his underlings.

The two men lifted Hunter's shirt and discovered the pad holding his other firearm. It didn't take long for them to find the weapon it was concealing. One of the men tucked the gun into the left rear pocket of his pants. They reached into Hunter's back right pocket, retrieved his wallet, and removed the credit card and the fifty dollars it held. Tossing that to the side, they went through Hunter's other pockets and found his keys, cell phone, and pen, then threw them on the ground near the other items.

"Looks like we got us a little problem," the leader said. "I don't know who you are exactly, but I doubt you're lookin' for Dawn because she stole a necklace from your wife. She's one of us now. She's family. We took her in when nobody else would help her. She damn near killed herself with drugs. Woulda died if one of ours boys hadn't found her."

"She was on drugs?"

"She wasn't no addict. She was trying to kill herself. Lots of people around here feel pretty down and out, so we help 'em. That's one of the ways we get new members. After we found Dawn we took her to the clinic, and she recovered. She wasn't depressed no more, just knowing there were folks like us who cared about her. Gave her a second chance.

"She told us she had a plan, but had run out of ways to get it done. We was just what she needed because all she had to do for her plan to work was learn how to shoot a gun. We took her in and one of our boys taught her all about how to use a gun real good. She's a better shot than any of us now. A real natural. Now she's off on that secret mission of hers. Left about two years ago. I don't know where she went and don't care 'cause we all trust her. When she left, she promised she was gonna come back with a whole lot of money. Even gave us a date, which is just about another year or so from now. I'm only telling you this because I know you won't tell no one else."

"You're right. I won't. Your secret's safe with me. I won't even look for her no more if you don't want me to."

"I know you won't tell nobody, and I know you won't look for her no more because my buddy over here's gonna kill you." He looked at the man on his right and nodded. "Just get it over with quick, then meet us back at the canteen. We'll drive out to the pond later and dump him there."

The leader and the man with the baseball cap turned and walked back to the building, leaving Hunter with their buddy who had tucked the detective's small J-frame revolver in his pants. "This is gonna be real fun," he said aiming his rifle at Hunter's head, his smile revealing crooked yellowed teeth.

Hunter was surprised at how calm he felt. He'd been in dangerous situations before, but none where he'd been as helpless as he was now, with a gun pointed at his head, the gun being held by someone who had been ordered to execute him.

What flashed through his mind wasn't his whole life, but rather the opportunities he'd missed. All this time he could have had a fuller life, with a wife, family, and friends. Although he'd enjoyed his work as a detective and was proud of what he'd accomplished, he always looked forward to having a more balanced life in the future. He regretted that given the situation at hand, it was too late.

"Can I call my mom?" he asked. "I want to say goodbye. Please. I'm all she has."

"I love the way you people beg for things when yer about to be kilt."

"You don't really want to kill me, do you?" Hunter asked, although there was no doubt in his mind that the man holding the gun would enjoy blowing his head off. He wasn't afraid, but he'd do his best to stall his execution, hoping a sheriff might drive up any moment and put a stop to it. *For all I know these guys pay the sheriff off. Maybe the sheriff's even a member. I wonder if I could reach into this guy's pocket, pull out my revolver, and shoot him before he shoots me.* Hunter mulled this thought over in his mind, waiting for his would-be executioner to turn around, if even for a moment, giving him the opportunity to grab the gun. That wasn't happening.

"Let me at least stand up so I can die like a man," Hunter said, slowly raising himself to all fours.

"You stay right there. Far as I'm concerned, you ain't no man."

A shadow moved across the dirt Hunter was settled on, and his captor glanced up to see a large turkey vulture riding a thermal overhead. With little time to think, Hunter grabbed his tactical pen, laying in the dirt just over two feet from his right hand. He extended the blade with a touch of a button, and jumped at the man, jabbing him with all his might between his fourth and fifth rib just to the left of his sternum, where his heart was. The man had a startled look as Hunter pulled his pen away, the action followed by a gush of blood coming from the small hole he'd made.

Frozen for a moment while he marveled at how effective the knife blade was, Hunter quickly gained his bearings and sprang into action. He grabbed his keys and cell phone and sprinted back to his car, not turning when he heard the sound of the man falling to the ground. He started the engine and drove down the dirt road backward, not taking the time to turn the vehicle around until he'd skirted beyond the obstruction in the road. The tires screeched as he floored the accelerator, his mind not yet caught up with what had just transpired. His adrenaline was still pumping as he pulled into the parking lot of his motel.

Hunter sat in the car a few minutes, taking in deep breaths and rehashing the events that had taken place at the compound. Still in the vehicle, he called his mother.

"Is everything all right?" she asked.

"Everything's fine. I just hadn't spoken to you for a while and wanted to see how you're doing."

"I'm doing just fine. Would love to see you, but I know how busy you are."

"I'm working a big case now like I told you, but I hope to wrap it up soon. After that, I'll come visit you. In fact, if this case drags on, I'll come to see you anyway. In six months, tops."

"That'd be great. There's a lady down the hall who has an adorable daughter. Her husband died a few years ago and I think she'd be perfect for you. I know you never like me to try to find someone for you, but you're not getting any younger and it's time you settled down. Again."

"Okay, Mom. Find out what you can about her and maybe I'll let you introduce us."

"Really? This doesn't sound like you, but I'm going to hold you to it."

After disconnecting from the call, Hunter found a maid who let him into his room. He shoved his belongings into his luggage and checked out. With no identification or credit card, he had a kerfuffle at the airport but calls to his captain smoothed the way for his return.

The following day Hunter was back in his office, thinking about the case. He was no closer to knowing where Naomi, or whatever she was calling herself now, was. Knowing she'd had weapons training convinced him she was acting alone. If her motivation was money, as his new acquaintances at the compound had indicated, he needed to find out the details. What money, and how was she going to collect it? Did she need to murder all her half-sibs to get it?

Chapter 49

REPORTS OF NAOMI SANBORN SIGHTINGS continued to pour in from as far away as Waikiki Beach and the Everglades. The afternoon following his return from Colorado, Hunter received a hairbrush, two pens, and a half-used tube of toothpaste, each in its own evidence bag, from the Jupiter Police Department. He drove these to the crime lab himself, where multiple well-preserved latent prints were found. The hairbrush was then sent to the DNA lab, where hairs were removed. DNA from the hair bulbs was then processed to be compared with Skeeter's DNA, for more irrefutable evidence of the murderer's identity.

The latent fingerprints were loaded into IAFIS, the Integrated Automated Fingerprint Identification System, to look for matching prints in the system. Copies were distributed nationwide, to compare with prints of people suspected of being Naomi. This would potentially allow for quick identification.

Over the next several days, Hunter received information about numerous calls that came into the tip line. Local police were sent to investigate all but obvious hoaxes and psychic leads, such as witnessing the suspect enter a spaceship, or envisioning her at a certain location in a dream. In many of the credible cases, the person sighted had touched objects that could be tested for fingerprints. None matched Naomi's. As the search went on, more murders nationwide were linked to Naomi, and she continued to murder more people in the Boise area, three or four a week. All victims were Martin's half-siblings—some were on his list, and some weren't.

Meanwhile, still keeping a watchful eye and being scrupulous about setting the house alarm, Martin and the family enjoyed spending Saturdays with Emerald, and having dinner with her and Cat on Mondays. Cat enjoyed her job at the bookstore and was writing a children's book in her spare time. Her daughter was soaking up knowledge in her preschool program and making friends.

"How's that roommate of yours?" Georgia asked one evening.

"Seems nice enough, but pretty much keeps to herself as expected," Cat answered. "I was going to ask you about her, though. She wants to write a book about the murders. She's already found an interested publisher."

"That doesn't sound like a good idea."

"I didn't think you'd be in favor of it, but Caroline's been asking me about it a lot. Says her cousin, Sarah Knightly, wants her to do it because it might help find the murderer."

"How would it help?" Greg asked.

"She thinks a lot of people don't keep up with the news. Not reliable news, anyway. She'd like a book to get out there ASAP so the public will get interested and help find Naomi. Also, I think she needs the advance she can get for the book so she can afford the rent. She's having some financial problems because of her mom's expenses. I sure don't want her to move out."

"If she moves out, Cat, don't worry, we'll help you."

"I really want to take care of Emerald and me by myself."

"Well," Georgia said, looking around, "we can't stop her from writing a book, if that's what she wants to do."

Cat smiled. "She'd really like to meet all of you and get more background before she accepts the publisher's offer. She wants this to be a serious, accurate book."

"I don't think it would hurt to talk to her," Martin said. "Why don't you invite her to dinner here next week?"

"That's a good idea," Georgia added. "Now that I think about it, we should have reached out to her earlier. From what you've told me, she's probably very lonely. We've been so preoccupied with everything that's going on, I didn't think to invite her over before. We could tell her some of what we've been through and answer some questions."

"Thanks so much. I'll find out what days will work for her. She'll have to tell her mom she won't be visiting her until late."

#   #   #

More tips poured in. Suspicions were eliminated with fingerprint comparisons when they were available. DNA testing of the hairs in Naomi's hairbrush confirmed that her DNA was an exact match to Skeeter's.

Days later, a call was forwarded to Hunter from a tip line in Utah. A plastic surgeon had important information for him. Hunter dialed the office of Dr. Simone Barrister, introduced himself, and asked to speak to the doctor.

Hunter was placed on hold for what seemed an eternity before the doctor answered. "I think I operated on Naomi Sanborn a year and a half ago," she said. Dr. Barrister stopped for a moment before continuing. "No, I'm sure I operated on her."

"I see you're a plastic surgeon. Did you change her appearance?"

"I'm afraid I did. Those pictures you're showing don't look like her now. I changed the shape of her eyes and nose and did a brow lift. She told me she had a violent ex-husband and needed to change her appearance. I've done that for several women in the past. I'm known in the area for doing that, so I had no reason to doubt her."

"Damn. I wish you'd called before."

"I wanted to, but I checked with my attorney. He told me if I called you it would be a HIPAA violation. I finally decided I couldn't sit by while she goes around murdering people, so I'm calling now. If it's a HIPAA violation, let the government arrest me. I think it's important you let the public know she no longer looks the same."

"Can you send me a current picture of her? I know you plastic surgeons always take before and after pictures of your patients."

"Unfortunately, I don't have one. I was going to take her picture at a follow-up appointment, but she absolutely wouldn't allow it. Had a fit, she was so worried her ex-husband would see it."

"Can you work with a police artist?"

"I don't think that would be useful. It's been over a year. I have so many patients, I can't be sure about my memory of her after the surgery. I have a photo of her before the procedure, though, and it's the same woman I've seen on TV. She also had lower extremity prostheses, although I only saw her use the ones that made her average in height. I checked all my notes before calling the tip line. I have no doubt it was her."

After ending the call, Hunter put his head in his hands and took three deep breaths. He counted to ten but felt no relief. Only after putting his fist through the wall did he get a modicum of relief. With no accurate photo of the suspect, she would be hard to catch indeed. He called in a junior member of the team and had her retract the photo they had from circulation and distribute a notice that the photo that had been disseminated was old, and the murderer likely looked quite different currently. He couldn't bear to do it himself, but he continued to monitor the house of one potential victim in the area each night, hoping to catch Naomi in the act.

One evening as he prepared to do this, he parked near the house of yet another half-sib, a thirty-eight-year-old woman who lived alone. The house looked deserted, the mailbox overflowing. No lights were on, but there was a car in the carport. He took his flashlight to look in the windows but saw nobody. All was in order, except there was a bunch of brown bananas, long past their prime, in a bowl on the kitchen counter. He phoned the local police and learned that the resident, Sarah Knightly, had been reported missing almost a month earlier. A search of her house had produced no evidence. Only a computer appeared to be missing, as an ethernet cable attached to a computer modem was disconnected at the far end, laying under the desk near an indentation in the rug the size of a computer tower footprint. An old VGA cable dangled from the computer screen on the desk above. Police investigating her disappearance had found that Ms. Knightly had taken an Uber to the Boise Amtrak station shortly before her reported disappearance. She had told the driver she was going on a long vacation, and the case was closed.

#   #   #

Caroline arrived at the Starling's house promptly at six-thirty the following Monday carrying a small bouquet. She was dressed in a pair of baggy black pants and a beige top. The food was being kept warm on the stove when Cat and Emerald greeted her at the door.

"I noticed a white Crown Victoria car across the street with a man inside. Is that some sort of police guard by any chance?" Caroline asked.

"Sure is," Cat said. "I think the detective on the case feels bad about how he treated the professor at first, so he's arranged for the house to be guarded as much as the budget allows."

Cat ushered Caroline into the dining area where the Starling family was waiting. After introductions were made, Georgia thanked her guest for the colorful blooms and put them in a small vase in the center of the kitchen table. She reached for Caroline's shoulder bag, offering to place it on the side table next to Cat's.

"I'll keep it with me if you don't mind," Caroline said, pulling her purse close. "Sometimes my allergies act up and I like to keep my inhaler with me."

Everyone sat around the table, which was slightly crowded with seven people. Caroline put her hands together and spoke quietly, saying a prayer before eating. As the food was passed around, people served themselves and spoke sparingly until Georgia asked Caroline about her plans to write a book about the murders.

"I think it could help everyone involved," Caroline said. "Everyone except the murderer, of course. Cat probably told you I spoke to a small publisher in Chicago about it, and he's very interested."

Throughout the rest of the meal, Caroline asked questions about how each member of the family felt about the situation, how worried they were, and how the murders affected their everyday lives. The discussion became lively at times.

Over dessert and coffee, Caroline asked how they kept track of all the half-sibs, their testing, and results. As Martin explained the spreadsheet they kept, Caroline asked detailed questions about all the data they collected on genetics, genealogy, and fibrinogen mutation results.

"I'm having a hard time picturing how you organize all that information.

Do you suppose I could see your spreadsheet, just so I could describe it to my readers?" she asked. "Thinking about it now, I think that's what I'm going to focus on in the book. Seems to me everything you're doing centers around that. It would really help if I could just see the brains of the operation."

Martin turned to Nick. "Why don't you get your laptop? We can show her. Just don't show her the names and contact information in the left columns."

Nick excused himself and returned shortly with his laptop. Martin used it to show Caroline how the data was organized. "It's been three weeks since we've added the name of a new half-sib, and we believe we probably have every last one of them listed. We've also noted all who have been murdered."

"How many have been killed?"

"About sixty-five that we know of so far."

"I'd like to include those names in my book. Do you suppose I could borrow your computer so I can write them down?"

Martin was taken aback. "I can't let you have this. It has all sorts of personal information, like addresses and mutation status of both living and deceased relatives. I can't risk that getting into the wrong hands accidentally, but I'll be happy to email you the list of murder victims after dinner. Those names are already public."

"Any chance you can tell me about the police investigation?" Caroline asked as Martin put the computer aside. "As I understand it, you've been involved."

"Very peripherally," Martin said. "All I know is they're working really hard trying to catch the murderer and stop the killings. I don't think the police have told me everything they know."

"I'll bet you're right."

After a little more small talk, Caroline thanked everyone for their help, Georgia wished her luck with the book, and she left.

"Thanks so much for helping Caroline," Cat said to Martin as she began to clear the table. Seconds later, Emerald tugged at her mother's skirt hem. "What is it, dear," Cat said, bending over to get close to her daughter's upturned face.

As Emerald whispered into her ear, Cat gasped. Her expression changed from that of an adoring mother to a woman who had just heard some terrifying news. All eyes were on her as she stood up. "Emerald just told me she thought Caroline was weird."

"That's probably an understatement," Greg said with a chuckle.

"This is important. Emerald said that when she poked at her ankles under the table, they felt funny, and Caroline didn't move. It was like she couldn't feel Emerald's fingers even when she poked her harder and harder."

"Hey, where's my laptop?" Nick yelled, interrupting the conversation.

"I put it right there on the counter," Martin replied.

"Well, it's not there now! See?" Nick was pointing to a bare space on the kitchen counter, biting his lip and looking like he might cry.

"It couldn't have gone far," Cat said, walking around the kitchen, lifting the few items on the counter.

"I'll bet Caroline took it," Martin said, looking around, a panicked look on his face.

"Yeah, I could tell she was really disappointed you wouldn't let her borrow it," Greg said, looking at his father.

All fell silent until Martin started speaking, his tone deadly serious. "I don't understand how this could have happened, but I think it's no accident that Caroline wound up as Cat's roommate. I'll bet she's Naomi. That's why she didn't react when Emerald poked her—she was poking her prosthetics. Hunter recently found out she'd had plastic surgery, so we don't know what she looks like. She may be having difficulty getting the addresses of some of the half-sibs. May even be missing some names, so she set out to get Nick's computer. I'm surprised she didn't shoot me, Cat, and the rest of us while she had the chance."

"She noticed the undercover cop car," Cat said. "Asked about it when she walked in. I didn't think about it at the time, but she was probably sizing up the situation. If that car hadn't been there, we might all be dead by now."

Georgia raised her hands to her cheeks. "She probably had a gun in her purse. She wouldn't let it leave her side."

"I'm calling Hunter right away," Martin said. He turned to Cat. "I want you and Emerald to stay here tonight."

Martin went into his study for privacy but was followed by Georgia. His chest was tight, and he was hyperventilating as he pressed the number for Hunter's cell phone. It didn't take long for the detective to answer. "You got something?"

"She was here," Hunter said. His throat was so dry his voice was croaking.

"Who was there?" Hunter sounded impatient.

"Naomi. The murderer. She was here," Martin said, his voice stronger.

Hunter was silent several beats before responding. "You're telling me Naomi Sanborn was in your house?" he yelled.

"Yes, I'm sure it was her. She stole Nick's laptop. I think she wanted our spreadsheet because she wanted to get the addresses of all the half-sibs."

"Where is she now?"

"She was living with Cat. I'll explain all that to you later. If you want to find her now, go to Cat's place. Naomi just left here and is on her way." He gave Hunter the address, and they all sat in the living room as Emerald played with a doll.

"I'm so sorry," Cat said. "It's all my fault for bringing her here."

"There's no way you could know what Caroline was going to do," Georgia said in her most comforting mom voice.

"Lucky everything's backed up," Nick said. "But I'm going to need a new computer."

"We'll get you a new one," Martin said. "Find something online and I'll order it for you. No doubt, it'll be faster and have more memory than the one she took."

No more words were spoken as they waited for word from Detective Hunter.

Chapter 50

HUNTER'S HEART WAS PUMPING. HE hadn't felt this alive in a long time. As he dashed out of his condominium to his car, he called two of his associates to meet him at Cat's house. It took only seconds for him to grab the siren from his trunk and secure it to the top of the car.

Squealing out of the parking lot, he barely missed the couple walking from their car. *Get ahold of yourself.* That self-awareness was fleeting, all but forgotten as he activated the siren and sped towards his destination, feeling a surge of power as cars pulled to the shoulder to let him pass.

Twenty minutes later he screeched to a halt in front of Cat's house. His associates hadn't arrived yet, but he couldn't wait. The house was dark, with no cars in the carport. He exited his vehicle, careful not to slam the door and possibly warn the fugitive from justice who might be inside. With his flashlight in hand, he peered into the front windows. Seeing nothing, he shone his light inside. No signs of life.

He heard the other officers drive up, less than thirty seconds apart. After rushing to the curb as they parked, he motioned for them to be quiet. They got out of their cars without making a sound and approached Hunter. In a hushed voice, the detective told them he hadn't seen anyone in the house yet, but they should check all the windows. Each assessed their assigned area, entering the backyard through an unlocked gate. Minutes later they spoke into their shoulder radios. No one had been spotted inside.

"Time to enter," Hunter whispered. He directed one officer to remain behind the house, while he met the other at the front door. "I got permission from the lady who rents the place to enter without knocking." After trying the door handle and finding it locked, he ran to his car and retrieved a black metal battering ram.

"You sure this is okay?" his colleague asked.

"If it's not okay, it damn well should be," Hunter responded as he backed up, holding the ram parallel to the ground. He ran towards the door screaming, before reaching the target in three long steps. With a thud, the ram bashed into the door near the handle, breaking the doorframe. The door swung open, and Hunter aimed his light into the living room.

After looking around and seeing no one in the immediate vicinity, Hunter and the other officer rushed in. Finding no one to confront them, they dashed through the house, Hunter taking the left side, the other taking the right. They met at the back door, where the third officer was waiting.

"Looks like no one is here," Hunter said. "Goddamn it. Shit. I thought we had her." He turned on the nearest light and cursed some more, resisting the urge to slam the fist at the end of his right arm through the plaster of the closest wall.

"Maybe we can find something useful if we search the house," one of the officers said.

"Sure. Let's do that," Hunter agreed. "I'll bet she's long gone, though."

Together, the officers went from room to room. Nothing seemed out of place. In one bedroom, a princess bedspread covered a double bed. Several colorful posters of Disney cartoon characters decorated the wall. Children's clothes filled a dresser, while toys and books were neatly held in bookcases and storage bins.

Another room had a queen size bed with a colorful bedspread. Inexpensive, yet fashionable clothes were in the closet and dresser. Magazines were stacked on the nightstand next to the bed, jewelry and makeup occupying most of the dresser top. The walls were adorned with posters of art by Georgia O'Keefe, Van Gogh, and Klimt. By comparison, the third bedroom looked to be inhabited by someone from Sparta. The twin bed was made up with white sheets and a beige quilt. Three pairs of dark pants and two off-white blouses hung in the closet. In the dresser were two sweaters, one grey, one black, and several pair of women's cotton underwear. The walls were bare.

"This must have been her room," Hunter said. "She probably keeps most of her things in her car in case she needs to make a quick exit. I'm sure she's not coming back." He called the professor and updated him.

"Damn," Martin said. "So close."

"Happens. If we hurry, we still could catch her. Can you give me a description of what she looks like now?"

With Georgia's help, Martin did the best he could, describing her glasses, hair, features, and general build.

"Ask Cat what kind of car she drives."

Seconds later, Martin answered. "She drives a silver Vespa locally. Keeps a car in a garage someplace. Claims to be afraid of break-ins if she leaves it on the street."

"Smart."

"Any chance Cat has a recent picture of her or knows her license number?"

After a short delay, Martin answered "No" to both questions.

"Keep your doors locked and your alarm on," Hunter said. "I doubt she'll be back, but you never know."

After completing the call, Hunter contacted dispatch and asked them to notify all police in the Boise area to be on the lookout for Naomi, relaying the description Martin had given. The following day, fingerprints and DNA samples from the Spartan bedroom confirmed what they all knew: the renter occupying that room had been Naomi Sanborn.

The following day, officers dug up the backyard of Sarah Knightly's residence. The decomposing body of a female was found in a shallow grave behind rose bushes. Comparing notes with Martin, Hunter concluded that Naomi had murdered Sarah and used her identity to gain entrée into the private Facebook. She was then able to offer up herself as the perfect roommate for Cat.

A police sketch artist met with Cat to produce a likeness of Naomi. Unable to accurately describe Naomi's eyes which had been hidden by glasses, Cat did the best she could. The resulting image, although far from perfect, was widely distributed. Now that her new face had been revealed,

Hunter hoped Naomi would stop killing. Not that he would stop looking for her. Bringing her to justice still loomed large in his mind.

The owner of the house had the damage left by Hunter repaired and installed an alarm system. Shortly afterwards, Cat and Emerald moved back in. Not wanting to take in another roommate after the trauma caused by the last one, Cat accepted payment from Martin and Georgia for cleaning house and preparing dinners on Mondays.

Three days after dining with the Starlings, Naomi struck again. This victim was in Bend, Oregon. The modus operandi was the same. Although the victim wasn't on Martin's list, DNA analysis performed over the next few days proved that she was a half-sister.

Hunter was at home when he received word of the latest murder. He retrieved a cold beer from the refrigerator and took a swig. *There are so many brothers and sisters. She can't kill every last one of them, can she?*

Chapter 51

THE DETECTIVE ANSWERED HIS PHONE. "Detective Hunter here."

"I've got some information I know you're going to find very interesting." Reginald Beaufort II sounded out of breath as he spoke.

Hunter had been at his desk at the precinct mulling over some of the leads that had come in regarding the sightings of Naomi. He had all but forgotten about the attorney who had taken over the practice of Reginald Beaufort, the man who had handled Dr. Sanborn's trust. "I can use all the help I can get. Do you know where Naomi is?"

"No."

"Didn't think so." Hunter's tone overflowed with derision.

"I don't know where she is, but I know why she's doing it."

Hunter stood at his desk, silent for a moment before he spoke. "Did I hear you right? You know why she's murdering all these people?"

"I do."

"Don't make me pull it out of you," Hunter said, his voice raised. "Tell me already."

"My dad was somewhat disorganized, but bless him, he set up a tickler system."

"A what?"

"A tickler system. To remind him of things he has to get done on certain dates. Usually, they're set up on a daily and monthly basis, but Dad had a number of things planned far into the future. I thought everything he had in his tickler file had been completed two years ago. Today, my administrator told me there was one task left, that I was supposed to start working on today. The last item in that tickler file. I took a look at it yesterday and found some very interesting information."

"I'm about ready to reach through the phone and strangle you. Could you get to the point?"

"Hold on, I'm getting there. My dad's firm was listed as the executor of Dr. Sanborn's estate. It's a bit unusual to have the attorney's firm as executor, but all the paperwork was filled out correctly."

"I don't give a shit about the paperwork. I'm dying here. Hurry it up."

"Okay. It turns out none of Sanborn's fortune was ever distributed."

"What?" Hunter yelled. "How's that possible? Where'd all that money go?"

"It's been held in a blind trust all these years, managed by a Swiss bank. When it was set up by my dad after Sanborn died, it was worth fifty-five million dollars. Over the past twenty-four years, it's grown to two hundred thirty million."

"Holy shit. That's a lot of money. Is there a plan, or is the money supposed to stay in that Swiss bank forever?"

"This is where it gets interesting. The doctor had left detailed instructions about distributing the money. The distribution is to be one year from yesterday."

"Who gets it? Does Naomi get it after all?"

"The money is to be evenly distributed to all his progeny who are alive on the day of distribution. Any of his children who are not alive at that time get nothing, meaning their heirs get nothing. So Naomi gets something if she's still alive. The fewer half-sibs alive a year from now, the more she gets. If she were to manage to kill all of them, she'd get everything."

"This is certifiably crazy, but it does explain Naomi's motive."

"The tickler file had the key to a safety deposit box in a local bank. I took a look in the box earlier today. There's a copy of the will, probably identical to the one I assume was stolen from our office. There's also a list of the names of Sanborn's children, including their birthdates, the names of the parents, and their last known address. It's neatly typed and most likely a duplicate list was in the office file cabinet and was also stolen during the break-in. The birthdates only go through the beginning of the year the doctor died."

"Are you telling me there may be additional kids of his who aren't on the list?"

"I am. I know that because there's another list. It's handwritten and has the names and other information about babies born up until a few days before Sanborn died suddenly. A few of the entries have only the names of the parents—I assume the mothers were still pregnant when the list was last brought up to date. Paperclipped to the list is a note stating it was on Sanborn's person when he died. Seems like the good doctor kept a running account of all his kids. The names on the handwritten list don't appear on the typed list. I imagine my dad updated the main list every six months or so, using the information Sanborn kept, but never bothered to add those last names."

"Well, well, well," Hunter said as the information sank in. "I'll bet Naomi knew about this list. When she stole the computer, she hoped to get these newer names, in addition to the current addresses of many of her half-sibs."

"Yes, she wanted to find every last half-sib. It's a bit like a tontine," Reginald said.

"Tontine? What's that?"

"You're a detective and don't know what a tontine is?" Reginald asked, chuckling. "It's something you might read about in a mystery novel, or see in a movie. They used to set them up in past centuries to raise money. It involves having a large amount of money, often contributed by the members. The money can be invested, and the members receive payments as long as they're alive. The last surviving member gets all that's left. They're illegal in the US now. Of course, this isn't a real tontine, but Sanborn's daughter seems to be treating it like one, a tontine in which she's the only one who knows about it."

"This is insane. Why the hell did Sanborn do this?"

"He left a long description of his reasoning. To summarize, Sanborn thought he was a gift to the human race, given his extraordinary intelligence. His words, not mine. He wanted to make a lot of smart babies, so he donated sperm to women in need of them, who scored high on an intelligence test he developed. He stated he had great expectations from all his progeny except Naomi. He went on about how disappointed in her he was, but took some responsibility for not choosing an intelligent woman to be his wife. A youthful indiscretion, he said. He wanted to leave each of his brilliant children a large sum of money so they could set out to do even more great things than they had already accomplished by the date of distribution, which he had established as twenty-five years after his death. Since Naomi was his child, although a big disappointment, he felt obligated to leave her a share of the money, too, so she wouldn't be a drain on society. He sounds like such a jerk, I'm sure he shared all his thoughts about that with her."

"No wonder she's so fucked up. Not that that's an excuse for what she's been doing."

"I don't know if this information will help you find her, but at least now you know Naomi's goal. Kill as many of her half-sibs as possible by distribution day, so she can reap the benefits."

Chapter 52

HUNTER COULDN'T WAIT TO SHARE his new-found information with Martin. He dialed the professor's number and waited impatiently, counting each of the three rings he heard before the call was answered.

Martin received an earful of information as Hunter relayed what he'd just learned from Beaufort.

"That's quite an amazing explanation," Martin said. "I'd say that unfortunately, Naomi's intelligence is a lot higher than the doctor gave her credit for. He just beat her down so much, she was an underachiever."

"I now have a complete list of everyone at risk. I'd like to compare it with your list ASAP."

Over the phone, the detective read off all the names on the two lists. Martin looked for each on Nick's spreadsheet and told Hunter which ones he had. After forty-five minutes, Hunter had determined that Martin had two hundred and twenty-four of the names found in the safety deposit box, including all of the younger ones on the handwritten list. Sixty-two names were not on his list, and a total of seventy-eight had died to his knowledge, all but three murdered. There were still two hundred and eight people left to save.

"I'm going to have my group contact each and every one of these people we can find to tell them of their inheritance, and warn them of the danger they are in," Hunter said.

"A case of some good news and bad news."

"Right. At her current pace, Naomi could murder every single one of them before the money is distributed."

"Could you set up a place for the people at risk to live until she's captured? Where they can be guarded twenty-four-seven? We know this will be over in a year. "

"I doubt I'll be able to find the money for anything like that. But I could set up a line where people can call to find out definitively if they are on Sanborn's list," Hunter said.

"Yeah, at risk for the mutation and for being murdered. Meanwhile, I'll ask The Rocket about setting up a guarded facility. By the way, do you have any idea how Naomi intends to collect her inheritance? Everyone knows what she's done, and she knows they know. She'll be arrested as soon as she surfaces to get the money."

"Good question. She's a smart woman. She probably has a plan. I wish I knew what it was."

\#   \#   \#

Martin wasted no time connecting with Elmer. In three days a new paid announcement aired nationally, featuring The Rocket and Martin having a conversation, explaining to the public that only people on the list of Sanborn's children, numbering just over two hundred, were at risk. Their staff would be trying to contact everyone, but people could call the number provided if they wanted to know right away. Anyone on the list would be offered free testing for the mutation and asked if they want to stay in an out-of-business hotel The Rocket had purchased in Idaho. He would provide security around the clock.

Over the next week, the tip line was inundated with calls. By the week's end, The Rocket's facility had sixteen half-sibs in residence. Three were accompanied by a spouse, one by two children. Food was brought into the office and pool area. When Cat arrived with Emerald, the number of residents rose to eighteen. Two days later, there were three more.

Although all were encouraged to stay on the premises, some ventured into the surrounding town. One of the half-brothers was murdered after dining at a local restaurant, convincing the other half-sibs to stay on the hotel grounds, although their family members came and went. Four guards were stationed around the facility at all times.

Meanwhile, one half-sib in Idaho, another in Colorado, and two in California were murdered. Naomi was nothing if not persistent.

#   #   #

Martin and Nick had notified everyone they could reach about the option of staying in the safe house, leaving only seven people on Sanborn's lists who hadn't been contacted. Although there had been a flurry of calls to the tip line after the recent public service announcements had aired, a week after Cat and Emerald had moved into the protected facility, there was just a trickle of calls.

Naomi was still out there, but like most of the others on the list, Martin didn't want to take a leave from work to live in the guarded hotel. He felt relatively safe with the knowledge Naomi knew he could identify her. For extra assurance, when he left home, he carried his pistol in a holster he wore around his waist. Initially uncomfortable, he'd gotten used to it quickly. The police canceled Martin's protection, reasoning that if he was worried about Naomi, he should move to the safe haven offered by The Rocket.

Martin's life, and the lives of his family members, were getting back to normal. The professor continued to go to work as usual, spending countless hours on his grant proposal while fending off his chairman's attempts to have him assist the local petroleum company. He still had some catching up to do, having somewhat neglected his university work due to prioritizing his search for half-sibs, not to mention the time he'd spent in prison. A week went by with no murders. Martin wondered if Naomi had seen the futility of it all, and decided to give up on her plan to claim her inheritance. Perhaps she had slunk off to a remote area where she could live out the rest of her sad life in obscurity.

Unsure if Naomi was still a threat, Martin continued to keep his state-of-the-art alarm system activated when he was home. He always kept his gun nearby, storing it in his desk drawer when he worked in the office.

A difficult week at work ended with Martin finally having the discussion with the department chair he'd been putting off. Friday afternoon he told him in no uncertain terms he wouldn't contribute to the joint project with the petroleum company. Being on the hit list of a ruthless murderer had emboldened him to face less serious obstacles. Martin felt no need to remind the chairman he was tenured, although he was pretty sure he'd have been fired without that safeguard. Free to delve into his pet project while the chairman weighed his limited options, the professor was more relaxed than he had been for some time. He'd been sleeping well and had performed with the Potato Heads twice in the past two weeks.

It was Saturday night, and Martin was working in his study with his shades drawn, thinking of promising tweaks he could make in his cactus extraction procedure as he analyzed the data from two of his graduate students. Greg was at a party with his girlfriend, and Georgia and Nick were going to a movie to release some of the stress they'd been feeling. With no half-sib murder in over a week, the police figured Naomi was on the run someplace, but it was only a question of time before she was caught. They imagined she might even turn herself in, knowing she'd never be able to collect the inheritance money and live freely.

Minutes after Georgia and Nick left, Martin checked the alarm and confirmed it had been set properly. Although the threat from Naomi was no longer looming as large as it had been, he didn't want the family to become lax about taking proper precautions. He poured himself a tall glass of water, remembering his physician's admonishment about drinking enough fluids, and brought it to his office, trying to lean less on his cane so he wouldn't spill any liquid.

He took several gulps of water when he reached his desk, then sat and began to work. Time ticked by quickly as he immersed himself in chemical equations, data, and reaction yields. He finished proofing his work and noticed he'd been at it for almost two hours. He realized he'd been in the zone, a state where he was one hundred percent present in his work, not distracted by thoughts of anything else. It had been quite a while since he'd experienced that. He took another sip, and dove back in.

Martin's ears perked up when he heard a slight creaking sound. He looked up and saw nothing. *The front door. Still on my list of things to fix. I doubt it's Greg. He never comes home this early. Must be Georgia and Nick. They probably didn't like the movie and came home early. I need to hurry through jotting down this concept before Georgia interrupts me.*

Dismissing the outside world, he dove back into the realm of molecules and chemical reactions. He reached out to his water glass again, looking up momentarily. There she was standing before him, black hoodie and sunglasses hiding most of her face, a gun aimed at his head. He hadn't heard her when she'd entered the study. Perhaps he'd been too engrossed in his work to perceive any noises, or she'd learned to creep silently. He didn't have time to ponder that.

"What are you doing here?" Martin asked, despite knowing exactly why she was there. *Damn. How'd she get in? Greg must have bypassed his window to let his girlfriend in earlier this week, and somehow Naomi figured it out. If I survive this, he's going to be in serious trouble.*

"I don't think I need to explain it to you," she responded. "I see you've all figured out that I've been eliminating all my dear siblings to get the inheritance I'm due. It was never personal with any of them. But with you, I'm afraid it is personal. You've caused me nothing but trouble, and I've grown to hate you. You and The Rocket. I'll get him soon enough. I'll have to take out some of his bodyguards. No way around it."

"We all know you were treated terribly by your father. If you turn yourself in now, you'll be treated fairly. If you don't, you'll be killed."

"Let me worry about that."

"A few weeks ago a number of us talked about signing an agreement that we would forgo our share of the inheritance. We can have the papers drawn up quickly, or you can hire your own attorney. We'll sign whatever papers you want. You'd have nothing to gain by killing us."

"At this point, I think I'd have a hard time finding an attorney to write up an airtight agreement. Don't even have the money to hire a lawyer. Not yet, anyway. The only way I can be sure you don't get any of my money is to kill you."

"What's your plan? Are you just going to kill me in cold blood?"

"You're so smart, you catch on really quick." Naomi removed her sunglasses and set them on the desk. Without her thick, black glasses, and with her hair now short and auburn, she barely resembled the police sketch of her that had been distributed. "There, that's better," she said. "Now I'll be able to see every detail of your expression."

"How did you get in here without setting off the alarm?" Martin nervously eyed his desktop, knowing his gun was just below it in the center drawer, but he had no way to retrieve it unnoticed.

"Easy. All I had to do was watch as Cat entered the code when I left here after dinner with your son's computer."

For a split second, Martin had a pang of guilt for thinking Greg had been responsible, but he quickly regained focus on the problem at hand. "How do you expect to collect your inheritance? You'll be arrested as soon as you try to claim it."

"Gee, I hadn't thought about that," Naomi said, sarcasm oozing from every word. "I appreciate your concern, but you needn't worry. I've got that covered. I'm not going to answer any more questions before I finish what I came here to do."

"Can I at least call my wife to say goodbye?" Martin reached for the cell phone on the desk as he spoke, hoping to speed dial Hunter so he could hear the conversation.

"Don't touch that," Naomi yelled. "None of the others had that opportunity."

"Please, I'm begging you." Martin used his cane to push himself to a standing position. *I'll try stalling for time.* He slowly reached for the water glass still on his desk.

"Mouth feeling dry? Fear will do that. Go ahead and take a sip. Consider that your last meal." Naomi chuckled.

I've got to think of something. Fast. But what? "Can I at least leave a note?" Martin asked.

"No note. No nothing," Naomi said. Her answer was as clear as it was cold.

Martin raised the glass to his lips, then turned sideways and stumbled, his cane tumbling to the floor. Falling to a crouched position behind the desk, he heard a bullet pass over him, through the space where his head would have been had he not fallen.

Naomi's footsteps were the only sound in the room as she began to slowly walk around the desk. From his hidden position on the floor, Martin used his cane to knock down some of the vials on the ledge behind him and grabbed the bottle of the element he received on his eleventh anniversary. As he rose to his feet, he emptied the contents into his water glass, then threw the now burning and smoking water mixture at his half-sister's face. Naomi screamed and stepped back, almost stumbling, as the burning elemental sodium splashed on her exposed skin.

Momentarily forgetting he'd been unable to stand independently since his stroke, Martin dashed around his desk, held his cane straight out parallel to the floor, and lunged at Naomi, hitting her in the chest with all four prongs. Off-balance already, she fell backward, landing on her back. Her head hit the wall behind her, leaving her neck bent at ninety degrees, her head propped up by the wall. Naomi's gun landed several feet from her right hand, and at least twice that far from Martin.

He had hoped at least one of her prosthetic legs would have fallen off, but both remained in place. Dazed for a few seconds, Naomi tried to reach for the gun, but Martin, now standing over her, rammed his cane into her upper body, pushing her down. Her eyes were bloodshot and almost swollen shut, her face red with blisters forming from the burning sodium, but Martin was unsympathetic.

For several minutes, Naomi kept attempting to reach the gun and Martin repeatedly pushed her down, each time getting closer to the weapon himself. With Georgia and Nick not expected to return for over an hour, he wondered how long he could keep this up. When he was close enough to the gun, he kicked it through the doorway, into the hall where neither could reach it. Then he took off his shirt while continuing to keep Naomi in her place by shoving her with the cane.

Martin got on his knees and wrapped his shirt around Naomi's head so she couldn't see, easily overcoming her attempts to push him away. After he stood back up, he whacked Naomi's right arm with the cane as she reached up to remove the shirt. The aluminum on the shaft bent slightly as Naomi screamed. Undeterred, Martin whacked her left arm, then thrust his cane into her chest again. He ran to the hallway to get her gun, but when he returned seconds later, Naomi was almost on her feet. Although she had removed the shirt from blocking her vision, he noticed her eyes were swollen shut. She couldn't see.

"I have the gun and it's aimed at you," he said. It was only then that Martin appreciated his ability to walk unaided.

Naomi ran towards his voice, screaming, but he easily sidestepped her attack. She stopped before she hit the wall, then stood still.

She's listening for sounds. He tiptoed away, but a creek in the floor revealed his location. Naomi ran towards the sound, but Martin had enough time to extend his cane in front of her path at ankle level, causing her to fall.

"Stay there, or I'm going to shoot you," Martin said.

"You don't have the guts to shoot me," Naomi said, as she struggled to stand. Once erect, she stood, listening for any sounds Martin might make.

Martin watched her for several seconds, then spoke. "You seem to have forgotten that we're related. Like you, I do have the guts to use this gun." That said, he aimed at Naomi's chest and squeezed the trigger. The blast hurt his ears. When he was done, his half-sister was still standing, her right upper chest bleeding, her mouth agape as if surprised. Martin stepped closer and shot her in both thighs. They were related, but unlike her, he wasn't a killer. He felt the weight of the world dissipate from his shoulders as she collapsed to the floor. It was over.

Martin called Hunter and told him what had transpired. Local police arrived in less than ten minutes, followed by an ambulance minutes later. By then, Naomi had already lost a lot of blood, and her breathing was labored. After she had been secured on a gurney, Hunter arrived.

The first thing he did was walk over to Naomi as the paramedics were preparing to load her into the ambulance. She looked pathetic with blisters on her face, bruises on her arm, and a bullet hole in her right chest. Her eyes were swollen shut, and copious amounts of blood were seeping from both legs. She appeared unconscious as paramedics tied tourniquets above her leg wounds, slowing the hemorrhage from those sites. Her chest wound continued to bleed profusely. An officer assigned to accompany her for the ride was already in the ambulance.

"Better take her legs off so she doesn't try to escape," Hunter said to one of the paramedics, a young female. She looked confused until Hunter explained. "This serial murderer here has two prosthetic legs. She's a flight risk, so remove them. She may look helpless now, but believe me, she's not."

The paramedic raised both of Naomi's pants legs and removed the prosthetics.

Hunter looked at Naomi and shook his head. "Looks like you got yourself in a bit of a pickle," he said as he shook the longer of her legs, protecting his hand from getting bloody with a wadded-up sheet between his hand and her lower extremity. "When you get to court, I'm afraid you won't have a leg to stand on." He laughed. "You don't know how long I've been waiting to say that," he said to one of the paramedics.

Naomi was motionless, barely breathing by the time she'd been wheeled into the ambulance. With the siren on, she was on her way to the nearest trauma center.

Chapter 53

HUNTER AND SEVERAL OTHER OFFICERS stayed with Martin, questioning him about the details of Naomi's visit. Fifteen minutes after the ambulance left, crime scene investigators arrived to take pictures and collect specimens.

Thirty minutes later, Hunter received word that Naomi was dead. She had a cardiac arrest in the emergency room, probably due to extreme blood loss and a punctured lung. Despite their best efforts, the hospital staff was unable to resuscitate her. An autopsy would be performed the following day. He shared the news with Martin, who felt nothing but relief. Despite knowing she was a close relative, he felt no empathy. He might have wanted a chance to try to understand her, how her suffering had twisted her mind so deeply, but there would be no escaping justice. Ending it here was probably the best outcome for her. He felt sympathy for her mother but believed it was better for her to know Naomi's fate than spend years wondering where she was and if she were still alive.

An hour after Hunter received word of Naomi's death, Georgia and Nick returned home. Seeing Martin standing in the living room, Georgia asked, "What's with all the police cars outside?" Then she noticed crime scene technicians and pools of blood on the carpet. "Are you okay?" she asked, looking Martin up and down, as Nick stood by appearing to be at a loss for words.

"Peaches, I've never been so okay," Martin said, smiling.

At that moment Greg entered, home earlier than usual from his date. He looked around, a baffled expression on his face as he ran his fingers through his hair. "What the hell, Dad?" Greg said. "You okay? Did you cut yourself?"

"That's not my blood. It belongs to Naomi Sanford. Now deceased."

Georgia and the boys were speechless for a few seconds, then cheered. Looking around, they noticed Hunter and two crime technicians talking in a corner.

"Did you kill her, Dad?" Greg asked.

"I think so. I shot her with her own gun. Couldn't avoid it."

"Aren't they going to put down that yellow crime scene tape?" Greg asked.

"They don't need to do it in this case. But we have a helluva mess to deal with here." Martin's eyes filled with tears. He looked from Georgia to Nick to Greg, wanting to tell each how much he appreciated them, but the words didn't come.

"Your dad's been through a lot," Georgia said turning to her sons. "Why don't you let him sit down? We can learn what happened later. But I must say, I'm very, very relieved."

Martin felt like he was in a dream the next few days. The intense emotional relief he felt from Naomi's death was counteracted by the incessant intrusions of members of the press wanting an interview.

When police went through Naomi's possessions, they found an Oregon driver's license and other identifying documents under the name of Wynona Speck. With Naomi's image on the license, it was assumed Wynona was going to be Naomi's next identity. The name hadn't been chosen randomly. It didn't take long for Martin to remember that Wynona Speck was on his list of half-sibs. She was one of the few they hadn't located.

An immediate investigation revealed that Wynona Speck was a reclusive fantasy writer who lived in a remote area of Oregon, not far from Roseburg. Nobody had seen her for months, although that wasn't unusual as she rarely appeared in public, getting most of her food and other supplies delivered. A search of her five-acre property produced a partially decomposed female body. DNA retrieved from the remains matched the DNA found in a hairbrush in Wynona's house and proved she was one of Dr. Sanborn's progeny. It was clear that Naomi planned to collect her inheritance under Wynona's name.

Satisfied that his case of a lifetime had been solved, Hunter began to reflect on the last months of his career. He'd made a grave mistake when he began working on this investigation. Once confident, he now realized that given the right set of circumstances, he could lead himself astray. He'd learned his lesson and would be a better detective for it. Nevertheless, he wanted to hang up his badge and start a new chapter in his life. He turned in his retirement papers, but refused to attend a retirement party—some would have called it a celebration—knowing that although his service would be missed, he himself wouldn't be. As soon as his condominium sold, he moved to Kentucky to be near his mom and volunteered to help investigate cases for the local police department, which was seriously short-staffed.

\#   \#   \#

Oliver Feinberg, one of the first half-sibs Martin had spoken to so many months earlier, hosted a large party for all the siblings to get to know each other. It was held in the space where his expanded shoe store was going to open shortly. The building was finished, but the chairs for customers to try on shoes and the merchandise hadn't been delivered yet. Ninety-six half-sibs attended. Spouses weren't included, so the brothers and sisters could get to know each other without worrying about entertaining their better halves.

Martin arrived with Elmer shortly after the appointed time. Although he was often mobbed by fans when in public, the ex-fighter received no extra attention from his half-siblings. The mood was festive, and champagne flowed. Dr. Sanford's heirs had been recently notified they would be receiving approximately ten million dollars each in ten months. As the sibs eyed each other, looking for family resemblances, Martin noticed an unusually high number of puns being thrown around, many of which he'd used himself. The most often repeated was "I sure can relate to you." He made a note to tell Georgia he was not to blame for being an insufferable punster—it was in his DNA. Martin exchanged puns with many of his siblings, including Brandon Bradberry and Andy Miller, who he'd met on Zoom early on.

Groups formed where siblings compared nose bumps, curved

pinkies, cleft chins, toe lengths, the ability to curl one's tongue, and other characteristics.

Originally skeptical of Oliver, Martin observed that the shoe store looked top-notch, with areas of low and high-end footwear for children, men, and women. Treadmills were in the athletic shoe section so customers could try the goods out. He learned that Brandon Bradberry, an accountant as well as a punster, had analyzed Oliver's business plan, and invested in the shoe store.

Martin enjoyed meeting the other half-sibs who seemed intelligent, mostly accomplished. Many had advanced degrees. Not one asked Martin for financial assistance. He met a half-brother and half-sister who had been engaged to each other in the past but were now married to others.

"Our parents told us to love one another," the man said.

"But fortunately we decided to interchange the last two words," the woman added, then laughed. Martin overheard them telling the same joke repeatedly as the evening progressed.

By the end of the night, Martin was glad he'd gotten to know these family members and looked forward to more get-togethers with his brothers and sisters. Some were already starting to organize a platform aimed at helping members of their group benefit from the expertise of others.

Networking had already started that evening. He had overheard Cat talk to a half-sister who was a publisher, and who had offered to look at the children's book she'd been working on. Two of his half-brothers besides Oliver Feinberg had played minor league baseball but had switched careers when injuries cut their careers short. Both had started successful businesses, making Martin guardedly optimistic about Greg's future.

Martin spoke to four half-sibs who indicated they would be willing to partner with him after he inherited his money, quit his job at the university, and started a company specializing in renewable energy. He planned to do this after he finished his grant proposal for the university and the important research was established under the capable direction of Dr. Stephen Bowditch. He wouldn't give up teaching, something he loved, but would lecture part-time at the local community college.

Georgia had bottle number eleven of her husband's periodic table re-filled with sodium. Martin had always wondered what Georgia would do if they were lucky enough to be married seventy-nine years. That would require a vial filled with gold. Once he received his inheritance, that would be no problem. Maybe the universe was watching over him.

Acknowledgements

I AM GRATEFUL TO EVERYONE who has helped me shape this book into what it is today. First and foremost, I am indebted to my Amazing Husband, Glen Petersen, who was, as usual, the first person to read this work. As always, he offered critical feedback.

A big shout-out goes to my brother, Seth Greenberg, who had many thoughtful suggestions. Thanks to Suzanne Spradley for reading the manuscript, sharing her genealogy knowledge, and offering her support.

Tim Janzen, MD, kindly offered his genealogy expertise. Any errors that may exist in this book are mine, not his.

My editor, Violet Moore, again worked her magic, paying careful attention to detail.

The Family Tree Guide to DNA Testing and Genetic Genealogy, by Blaine T. Bettinger, was an invaluable aid in researching genealogy. I also relied on Google and YouTube for countless details.

The publisher, Castle Bridge Media, was great to work with as the manuscript was transformed into a published book.

CASTLE BRIDGE MEDIA RECOMMENDS...

If you liked this book, you might also enjoy reading the following titles from Castle Bridge Media available on Amazon or by order at your favorite book store:

Animal Charmer
By Rain Nox

Austinites
By In Churl Yo

Bloodsucker City
By Jim Towns

THE CASTLE OF HORROR ANTHOLOGY SERIES
Volume 1
Volume 2: *Holiday Horrors*
Volume 3: *Scary Summer Stories*
Volume 4: *Women Running From Houses*
Volume 5: *Thinly Veiled: The 70s*
Volume 6: *Femme Fatales**
Volume 7: *Love Gone Wrong*
Volume 8: *Thinly Veiled: The 80s*
Volume 9: *Young Adult*
Volume 10: *Thinly Veiled: Saturday Mournings*
Edited By Jason Henderson and In Churl Yo
*Edited By P.J. Hoover

Castle of Horror Podcast Book of Great Horror: Our Favorites, Top Tens and Bizarre Pleasures
Edited By Jason Henderson

Dream State
By Martin Ott

Dominic
By Lee Guzman

FRENCH DECEPTION
A Forgery in Paris
By Janice Nagourney
A Forgery in Lyon
By Janice Nagourney

FuturePast Sci-Fi Anthology
Edited by In Churl Yo

GLAZIER'S GAP
Ghosts of the Forbidden
By Leanna Renee Hieber

Isonation
By In Churl Yo

JAYU CITY CHRONICLES
The Hermes Protocol
By Chris M. Arnone
Necropolis Alpha
By Chris M. Arnone

Junk Film: Why Bad Movies Matter
By Katharine Coldiron

MID-LIFE CRISIS THRILLERS
18 Miles From Town
By Jason Henderson
Lost Angel
By Sam Knight
Ties That Kill
By Deven Greene

Nightwalkers: Gothic Horror Movies
By Bruce Lanier Wright

THE PATH
The Blue-Spangled Blue
By David Bowles
The Deepest Green
By David Bowles

SURF MYSTIC
Night of the Book Man
By Peyton Douglas
Dark of the Curl
By Peyton Douglas

Yesterday's Tomorrows: The Golden Age of Science Fiction Movies
By Bruce Lanier Wright

Please remember to leave us your reviews on Amazon and Goodreads!

THANK YOU FOR SUPPORTING INDEPENDENT PUBLISHERS AND AUTHORS!
castlebridgemedia.com